CHRISTMAS AT THE WARTIME BOOKSHOP

Lesley Eames

PENGUIN BOOKS

TRANSWORLD PUBLISHERS
Penguin Random House, One Embassy Gardens,
8 Viaduct Gardens, London SW11 7BW
www.penguin.co.uk

Transworld is part of the Penguin Random House group of companies
whose addresses can be found at global.penguinrandomhouse.com

Penguin
Random House
UK

First published in Great Britain in 2023 by Bantam
an imprint of Transworld Publishers
Penguin paperback edition published 2023

A CIP catalogue record for this book
is available from the British Library.

ISBN 9781529177374

Typeset in Baskerville by Falcon Oast Graphic Art Ltd.
Printed and bound by Clays Ltd, Elcograf S.p.A.

The authorized representative in the EEA is Penguin Random House Ireland,
Morrison Chambers, 32 Nassau Street, Dublin D02 YH68.

Penguin Random House is committed to a sustainable
future for our business, our readers and our planet. This book is
made from Forest Stewardship Council® certified paper.

To my precious daughters, Olivia and Isobel,
who fill my world with sparkle.

CHAPTER ONE

Naomi

September 1941

Churchwood, Hertfordshire, England

There was a thief in Churchwood.

'He's struck again, madam,' Suki announced.

'What has he taken this time?'

'The same as before. A full pint of milk. He left this behind.' Naomi's little maid held up a posy of greenery bound together with ivy. Since Naomi recognized the greenery as having been taken from the trees, bushes and ivy in her own garden, the posy was hardly fair compensation for the theft, but perhaps the thief had nothing else to give.

'I'll be walking into the village later so can buy more milk then,' Naomi said. 'Can Cook manage without it this morning?'

'She says so, madam.'

'Very well. Thank you, Suki.'

The maid nodded and left the room.

Suki was a sweet girl, and Naomi would miss her if they had to part. Of course, the parting might arise from happy circumstances. Suki wasn't courting yet, as far as Naomi knew, but one day she might leave to get married. Or she might go off to help the war effort through factory work or by joining one of the services, in which case Naomi would admire her pluck and wish her well. But there was a more depressing reason they might have to part, one that was weighing heavily on Naomi's mind. Soon, Naomi might simply be unable to afford to keep paying her staff – Suki, Cook, Sykes the gardener and Beryl the cleaning lady. It grieved Naomi to think that losing their jobs could cause them real hardship.

Naomi might have to give up her home, too. Foxfield, the house she loved.

Restlessness brought her to her feet, and she paced the sitting room, a space she'd always preferred to the grander drawing room when she was alone or entertaining close friends. Pacing wasn't enough to settle her, though, so she called to Basil, her faithful old bulldog. 'Let's go for walkies.'

Basil heaved himself up willingly. He always seemed to sense her mood and offer sympathy. They'd been companions for many years, and Naomi often thought that they were alike in appearance as well as temperament, both having heavy jowls, wide hips and short legs. Catching sight of herself in the mirror above the mantelpiece now, Naomi winced. She was forty-six but, with furrows of worry creasing her face, she was sure she looked much older.

They left by the front door but walked around to the back of the house where the gardens spread into the distance, testimony to Sykes's skill and care. There were two acres of them in total, comprising green lawns, herbaceous borders, a walkway where roses grew in beds throughout the summer, and a pergola that was festooned in wisteria in May and June. As well, there were trees. Magnificent trees – tall, noble oaks; sycamores; horse chestnuts; copper beeches; cedars; laurels . . . The approach of autumn was beginning to turn some of the leaves from green to yellow and soon the trees would be ablaze with oranges, reds and russets too.

How beautiful it all was.

Of course, Sykes had also created a Dig for Victory vegetable patch at the far end. It was doing well, providing fresh vegetables for the house and often a surplus which Naomi gave away to Churchwood's needier families.

Turning, she looked up at the house itself. Foxfield had been built in Victorian times with some later additions. It wasn't the most classically graceful house, perhaps, but the red bricks had grown venerable with age and there was an air of comfort about it. Whatever its architectural merits, it was home. For more than a quarter of a century it had been home.

The letter she'd received last week from Messrs Goodison & Bright (Solicitors of Lincoln's Inn Fields, London) came into Naomi's mind.

Dear Mrs Harrington,
  I write to confirm your appointment with Sir Ambrose Goodison on Thursday, 11 September at two o'clock . . .

Nervousness crumpled Naomi's stomach like a sheet of old newspaper. 'Don't imagine I'll be generous if we have to divide our assets,' Alexander had warned. 'Divorce me, and you may lose Foxfield.'

He'd *want* her to lose it because he knew how much she loved it, and he was a vindictive man. A dishonest man, too, who might well hide away some of those assets where she could neither identify nor access them. Naomi could trust Alexander to play fair no more than she could trust

3

a cobra but, even so, she'd answered him boldly. 'If losing it is the price I have to pay for breaking free from you, I'll pay it gladly,' she'd told him.

Fighting talk, but oh dear, she hoped it wouldn't come to that. She'd miss Foxfield dreadfully, and where on earth would she go?

But perhaps she was getting ahead of herself. She shouldn't expect the worst prematurely. She might emerge from the battle more comfortably off than she feared, especially with Sir Ambrose fighting in her corner.

Enough brooding. The appointment was only three days away, so she'd soon have a clearer picture of what might happen.

A squirrel darted across the lawn and leaped up the trunk of the splendid oak tree that stood in the middle and stretched its branches far and wide. The squirrel had the tree to itself today, but last month, when all of Churchwood had gathered here for the wedding reception of Naomi's dear friend Alice Lovell, children had chased each other around that tree, laughing merrily.

What a joyful occasion the wedding had been. Who would have guessed when she first moved to Churchwood that Alice – a small, fair-haired and slightly built young girl less than half Naomi's age – would shake up the village and make it so much better? Certainly not Naomi, who'd resented Alice at first. After all, many years of being the Queen Bee of Churchwood – well off, influential and owning its largest, loveliest house – had given Naomi a sense of identity and purpose. For Alice to uproot the old ways and certainties had unnerved Naomi and made her realize that, despite what she liked to regard as her good works in the village, she wasn't actually much liked.

Over time, a new Naomi had emerged – less bossy and

more democratic, less snobbish and more approachable, less critical and more tolerant. One of the gang, in fact. This new Naomi had found friends. Real friends, who valued her for herself rather than her status as the richest woman in the village.

Kate Fletcher was one of them, similar to Alice in age but tall and striking with a mass of gorgeous chestnut hair, bold eyes and a fierce temper. For years Naomi had treated Kate with disdain because she was a member of the notoriously rough Fletcher family that lived at Brimbles Farm, a mile or two outside the village. Alice had helped Naomi to see that Kate was actually a wonderful person and now they were close.

Bert Makepiece was another. A middle-aged, plain-speaking market gardener, he'd lived in Churchwood for even longer than Naomi, but, as a labouring sort of man with no taste for finery – a scruff, in fact – they'd moved in different circles. Once again, Naomi had come to look beyond her snobbery and see that he was shrewd and kind and stood for no nonsense. It was Bert who kept Naomi in check if she started getting what he called 'uppity' again.

Naomi, Alice, Kate and Bert organized the Churchwood Bookshop alongside two other friends. More than just a bookshop, this was a venture dreamed up by Alice to bring the community together. As well as selling and lending books, newspapers and children's comics, they also held story times, talks, activities and social events. Naomi loved being part of it but, with her divorce looming, this new life was under threat too.

Oh, heavens. Her thoughts had circled back to her appointment with Sir Ambrose and her stomach crumpled again.

Casting around her mind for a change of subject, she returned to the Churchwood thief. More than a month had passed since Suki had first reported that milk was missing from the Foxfield doorstep. Naomi would have assumed that the milkman had made an error had it not been for the little posy left behind in the milk bottle's place. Even so, she'd had far too much on her mind to dwell on the incident until it happened again a week later.

Then, Alice had mentioned that bottles had gone from her doorstep too, and the next day an argument had broken out in the grocer's when Mrs Hutchings had accused a neighbour's child of taking the milk. 'Don't talk soft,' his mother had retorted. 'My Jack is being brought up properly, and can you seriously imagine him making a posy?'

It was a good point. If Jack Finton had an artistic side, it had yet to be discovered.

Intervening, Naomi had explained that her milk had gone missing too, and it transpired that several residents had lost milk in recent weeks. 'Maybe the thief will take fright and stop stealing now we've all noticed,' Naomi had said but, clearly, milk was still disappearing.

Would something have to be done about the thefts? Naomi hoped no one would look to her to take a lead. Her mind was too full of her other problems – which brought her back yet again to her appointment with Sir Ambrose. A mere three days away, but she suspected those three days were going to feel very long indeed. Even then the appointment would only be the first step in what could be a long and arduous battle to free herself from the man who'd treated her with such contempt.

That battle stretched before her in her mind and wilted her spirits. She'd have to cope somehow, and maybe it would help to have a goal of some sort – to look to a time in the future when at least some progress would have been made.

Christmas, she decided. She'd focus on Christmas. It would be too much to expect complete freedom by then – all sorts of legal hoops would need to be jumped through first – but progress . . . Yes. By Christmas she hoped to have at least reached an understanding on her financial affairs, so she could begin the new year feeling she was stepping into a future that was all hers, untainted by Alexander and the heartache of the past.

There. Did she feel better? A little. There was every chance that her future might take an unwanted shape – a shape of financial insecurity and worry – but any certainty was surely better than the anxiety and dread she was feeling now.

'Christmas,' she told Basil. 'Let's look ahead to Christmas.'

He looked at her mournfully. She hoped he wasn't thinking that she was a fool.

CHAPTER TWO

Kate

The courgettes and marrows were reaching the end of their season, but Kate was pleased with the crop she'd grown. She picked some courgettes and an early cauliflower to serve with dinner. Both would be tasty.

Farming had its challenges, not least bad weather, blights and too much back-breaking work, but it was satisfying to see the crops thrive and know that they were putting food on Britain's tables. Not that Kate wanted to stay on Brimbles Farm for ever. Her father – Ernie to all his children, probably because it suited him to be the household tyrant rather than a father – might expect her to be the spinster daughter who stayed at home to skivvy for her family, but Kate had other ideas. Quite what form those ideas might take remained to be seen, but once the war was over, she was sure an adventure of some sort would beckon.

In fact, she hoped adventure was already beckoning in the form of Flight Lieutenant Leo Kinsella, who—

'Kate!'

Looking up, she saw Timmy Turner running towards her.

'Ruby says she's made a pot of tea and cut some bread,' Timmy reported. Then, to Kate's delight, he added, 'Oh, and there's a letter from you-know-who.' He tapped the side of his nose.

'If that's the case, what are we waiting for?' Kate teased, and Timmy grinned.

'Ruby said the letter would make you come quickly, even if the tea didn't.'

They walked up to the farmhouse together, Kate striding out eagerly and Timmy half walking, half jogging beside her, obviously enjoying her excitement. Kate hadn't known Leo for long before he'd been posted to North Africa, but it had been long enough for her to fall in love with him, and vice versa.

He'd seen her looking her worst the first time they'd met. Kate was tall and slender but that day she'd been wearing ancient breeches with a sweater and boots that had once belonged to her brothers. Her hair had been tied back in its usual braid with escaped wisps fluttering around her face, and her hands had been filthy with soil. It was heartening to know that Leo had seen past all that to the person she was underneath.

She missed him badly and dreaded the thought that he might not come through the war unscathed. After all, Leo was an RAF Spitfire pilot and that was horribly dangerous work. But like everyone who had loved ones away in the forces – her best friend, Alice, especially – Kate was staying positive, getting on with life while hoping that the war would end soon. Over by spring, they'd said in the beginning. Then over by summer, by autumn, by winter . . . each milestone being succeeded by another and then another.

'Hopefully, it'll be over by Christmas,' Mrs Larkin had said in the baker's only the other day. Wouldn't that be wonderful?

Stepping into the kitchen, they were welcomed with a smile from Ruby. A warm, natural smile, which Kate returned in kind. What a change from when Ruby had first arrived at Brimbles Farm.

Ruby Turner was one of two land girls who'd come to help after the youngest of Kate's four brothers – twins Fred 'n' Frank – had enlisted in the army as a foolish lark, despite being needed on the farm. It had been a mystery to Kate why Ruby, a short and curvy platinum blonde from the East End of London, had volunteered for farm work when she so obviously disliked it. Gradually, it had emerged that her goal was to carve out a home for Timmy, the boy she'd described as her brother, who was then an evacuee living with a couple who treated him badly. Striking up a romance with Kate's eldest brother, Kenny, Ruby had coaxed him into allowing Timmy to come and live at Brimbles Farm instead.

Only when Kate had guessed at the relationship had Ruby admitted that Timmy was in fact the son she'd had at the age of just sixteen, after a man had taken advantage of her at work.

The girls had become friends after that, agreeing that, while land girls weren't supposed to undertake domestic work, everyone would benefit if Ruby – a good cook – helped in the house and freed Kate to spend more time on farm work.

'Keep a lookout, Tim,' Ruby urged now, and taking a letter from her pocket, she passed it to Kate.

The boy went to the window, a keeper of secrets at seven years old. He didn't need to be told that he was to watch out for Kate's father, who'd be furious if he learned that a handsome pilot might one day whisk his daughter away to a better life. Kate had defied Ernie to make friends in the village, and she'd defy him again to keep seeing Leo, but, while Leo was away, nothing was to be gained from Ernie knowing about him. It would only cause unpleasantness on the farm for everyone else.

Kate sat at the table to read her letter.

My darling Kate,

I hope this finds you well and happy. It was such a pleasure to receive your last letter, and you made me laugh out loud with your story of the stray dog tugging on the string and opening the lavatory door when Ernie was inside.

Thank you also for the pressed leaf. It's a lovely idea to send one with each of your letters so I can see how the seasons are progressing over there. Don't fear that the leaves will only remind me that I'm far from England and from you, my angel. They'll help me to picture you observing the changing colours on behalf of both of us. They'll also remind me that one day this war will be over, and I'll be home again to watch the seasons changing with you . . .

Kate's romance with Leo was her first venture into love, but the signs were promising and she had only to think of him – his laughing blue eyes, his smile, his kisses – to yearn for him desperately.

'Leo is well, I hope?' Ruby asked.

'He's fine.' So far, anyway.

'Kenny's coming,' Timmy announced, and a moment later Kate's eldest brother stepped into the kitchen.

'Hands,' Ruby instructed, pointing him towards the sink so he could wash the soil from them.

The Fletcher men had never bothered much with hygiene, but Ruby was reforming Kenny's habits in a way Kate had never been able to manage. Of course, Kenny was romantically involved with Ruby and realized that, if he wanted the relationship to continue, he needed to smarten up his ways.

He was a good-looking man – tall and well built with hair the same shade of chestnut as Kate's – but in temperament he'd always been morose, until Ruby's arrival. As far as Kate was concerned, Ruby was a force for good with Kenny. He was still miserable at times, but at other times he was positively cheerful. He was also good with Timmy and even knew the truth about the boy's birth. As well, he'd been trusted with the secret of Kate's romance.

'Pearl's coming now,' Timmy reported.

A moment later, Pearl – real name Gertie Grimes – appeared. She was another land girl and well suited to the role as, far from being a dainty fairy, she was a wiry six feet tall with a plain face, short brown hair, and enormous hands and feet. She was hard-working and good-natured, too, though Kate could never get her to believe that she was both useful and liked.

Gloom settled on Pearl's face as Ruby passed her a letter as well. 'It's from home,' Pearl said, staring down at the envelope, which bore her mother's handwriting. 'Best get it over with, I suppose.' She tore into the envelope and drew out a sheet of notepaper.

'Usual thing,' she reported, scanning it. 'My mother says I need to wear dresses sometimes and practise walking elegantly for when I've got this farming nonsense out of my system. My sister says she was much admired at a cocktail party last week. And my father says . . .' She paused and turned the paper over to see if anything was written on the back. 'My father doesn't say anything this time. Thank goodness.'

She shoved it into her pocket and noticed that Kate was holding Leo's letter.

'Leo all right?'

'Yes, thanks.'

'Vinnie!' Timmy called, and Kate's second eldest brother walked in.

In appearance Vinnie took after their father, being on the small side with a narrow, fox-like face and thin hair that was more ginger than chestnut. In character he had a sly, mean side to him, though he too was improving thanks to Ruby and Pearl, who stamped hard on his tendency to find glee in other people's misfortunes.

For a while he'd shown an interest in Pearl, but that might have been because Kenny was showing an interest in Ruby and Vinnie didn't want to be left out of the fun. Nothing of a romantic nature had developed, though, and they'd settled down as loose friends – much to Kate's relief. She couldn't help but feel that Vinnie was a long way from being ready for a responsible relationship, and she hadn't wanted to see Pearl get hurt.

Vinnie hadn't yet been trusted with the knowledge of Timmy's parentage, but he knew about Leo and, so far, he hadn't blabbed about it to anyone, probably fearing the girls' fury if he let out even a hint. He headed for the table but saw the look on Ruby's face and joined Kenny at the sink to wash his hands.

Timmy sounded the alert again. 'Ernie!' he called, and everyone scrambled to look casual, especially Kate, who tucked Leo's letter into the pocket of her breeches.

They gathered round the table for mid-morning tea and bread. Ernie sat in his usual surly silence, only asking Kenny about the tractor, which played up periodically. Having answered Ernie, Kenny winked at Timmy to signal that the boy could have a second slice of bread, as long as he kept it hidden from skinflint Ernie. Kenny the Misery winking! Who'd have thought it possible only a few months ago?

Afterwards, everyone returned to work and the day proceeded as normal. Until later, when Kenny, happening to be in the farmyard as the second post arrived, carried a new letter into the kitchen, where everyone was gathered for the mid-afternoon cup of tea. He was frowning.

'It's from the War Office,' he said. Kate's thoughts flew to the twins. 'It's addressed to you,' Kenny told Ernie.

'You read it,' Ernie said. He had to be the least loving man in Churchwood – outwardly, anyway – but even he looked as though a frisson of fear was passing through him.

Kenny tore the letter open.

'What does it say?' Vinnie wanted to know.

Kenny looked up and his eyes appeared to have sunk into dark hollows. 'Fred's been injured.'

'How badly?' Kate asked.

'It doesn't give any details. But he's being sent back to England.'

Which must surely mean that his injuries were severe.

CHAPTER THREE

Alice

Alice had a secret. At least she thought – and hoped – she had a secret, brought back from her recent honeymoon in Brighton. Sitting on the bed in her small cottage bedroom, she ran feather-light fingers over her middle, though there wouldn't be anything to feel for another two months or so, even if she was right about the cause of the interruption to her body's usual pattern.

Until she was sure, she planned to mention her suspicion to no one, not even Daniel. Especially not Daniel, in fact, as she didn't want to build his hopes only to dash them to the ground if time proved her wrong. Stationed hundreds of miles away in North Africa as he was, she wanted him focused on staying alive and not distracted by disappointment.

Already, Daniel had been exposed to extreme danger since being called up to the army in the early part of the war. He'd been rescued from the beaches of Dunkirk while enemy aircraft rained bullets and bombs down from on high. Then he'd been taken as a prisoner of war and, having escaped from the enemy, had undertaken a hazardous journey home with the assistance of brave resistance fighters. Lady Luck had been with him so far, and Alice was keen for that to continue.

She looked over at the three framed photographs on the small cupboard next to her bed and picked up the earliest of them. It showed Daniel glancing over his shoulder to smile at the camera, which Alice had been holding. She liked this photograph because, even though it had been taken shortly after his terrifying ordeal on the beaches of Dunkirk, it had captured much of what she loved about him. Not just his appearance, though there was plenty to gladden her heart in that, as Daniel was tall and trim with glossy dark hair that had flopped over his smooth forehead before the army had shorn it. He had well-cut features, expressive brown eyes, straight white teeth, and a mouth like soft velvet that lit fires inside Alice the moment it touched hers.

But it was the glimpse into the essence of Daniel that pleased her most about this photograph – the humour playing in his grin, and the kindness, courage and sensitivity in his eyes.

Returning the photo to its original position, she picked up the second frame. This photograph showed Daniel and Alice arm in arm on their wedding day only three weeks earlier. How radiant with happiness they looked!

The third photograph had been taken on their honeymoon. They'd been walking along Brighton seafront when Alice had begged a passing stranger to take their photo. It showed them arm in arm again but this time in casual clothes, their hair dishevelled by the breeze. Alice was looking up at Daniel and he was smiling down at her. She remembered how humour had danced in his eyes along with something more intimate – the knowledge that she'd be lying in his arms again that night. What a blissful experience that had been!

'It's a pity we didn't rent a cottage where no one would disturb us,' Daniel had said, on the morning after the wedding.

Their nights together had been wonderful but so had their days, even if only convention had forced them into getting up and going out. They'd strolled around The Lanes, the narrow streets in which small shops sold antique furniture and ornaments, dusty old books and jewellery for those who could afford it. They'd walked to the pavilion – a former royal residence that looked like a building from a fairy story with its domes and stone pineapples – and gone Dome Dancing, as it was called, rubbing shoulders with countless other servicemen and local girls. They'd taken the train to Hove, where they'd had tea overlooking the sea, and, of course, they'd walked beside Brighton's beach, though it had been closed off with barbed wire as mines lay beneath its stony surface to repel enemy invasion.

'I'm having a lovely time,' Alice had told Daniel, even if it had been impossible to break free of the war. Servicemen from Britain, Canada and elsewhere crowded the town. There were signs of bomb damage here and there, and they couldn't look out over the English Channel without thinking that just beyond the horizon Germany occupied France and doubtless also planned to invade Britain.

All too soon the honeymoon had ended. Fit again, Daniel had returned to active service overseas and Alice had returned to her cottage, and her retired doctor father, to take up the reins of her life in Churchwood.

Replacing the third photograph, she got to her feet and went downstairs, where she paused in front of the hall mirror. It was her habit to check she looked neat before she went out. Usually, she gave her appearance the merest glance, but today she wondered if her secret hope showed in a certain glow and softness in her face.

'Off to the bookshop?' her father asked, appearing in the doorway to his study.

'I am indeed.'

Should she bother with a coat? With only small leaded windows to let in daylight, the cottage could be chilly – even damp – and often it was warmer outside. Suspecting that today was one of those days, Alice decided to leave her coat behind but keep her serviceable grey cardigan on.

'I'll be late back,' she warned, and her father nodded.

'You're going to be talking about this thief?'

'Trying to get to the bottom of the mystery, yes.'

'He or she might need help.'

'Exactly.'

It was typical of Archibald Lovell to take the view that the thief might be desperate rather than bad. Alice's father was a kind man. She reached up to kiss his cheek. Not that he was tall – he was a round little cherub of a man with a halo of white hair floating around his head like dandelion clocks – but Alice was short, too. 'See you later.'

She let herself out and walked down the short path to Churchwood Way. There she paused to wave at her father as he stood at the old oak door. The Linnets was a picturesque cottage with a pretty garden that still had some colour in the form of late yellow roses growing around the door, the dangling heads of scarlet fuchsia in the borders and, coming through, the first of the lilac Michaelmas daisies.

Alice had moved here with her father almost two years after he'd retired from his medical practice. Their house in London's Highbury had been much larger, but the garden had comprised only a small patch of lawn and a few bushes. Here Alice had room for a vegetable patch and chickens – lifesavers given the current rationing.

They'd given her an interest, too, at a time when her spirits had been low.

From an early age she'd been a skilful typist and organizer of her father's medical practice, but an accident to her hand had left it scarred and weak. For a while she'd feared she might never again have the satisfaction and financial independence of working for her own living. Fighting back against despondency, she'd volunteered at the local military hospital, set up the Churchwood Bookshop, made new friends and – best of all – married Daniel. Now she even had a part-time job, too, and—

'Afternoon, Mrs Irvine.'

Alice turned to see one of her friends, bear-like Bert Makepiece, smiling through the open window of his ancient truck.

Mrs Irvine. How strange it still sounded to be called by her married name, but how wonderful too! Alice couldn't resist a glance at her left hand where, amongst the scars, a gold wedding band sat beneath an engagement ring of aquamarine and diamonds.

Bert swung his large frame out of the truck, and they walked side by side towards the Sunday School Hall, which housed the bookshop several times each week. Adam Potts, soon to be vicar of St Luke's, had just put up the bookshop banner over the entrance. Not yet thirty and still a bachelor, he was a slightly built young man with an abundance of untidy brown hair and untidy clothes to match, but also with the sweetest of natures.

'That's a sight for sore eyes,' Bert told him, nodding at the banner.

'It certainly is.'

Not long ago, Churchwood had lost its vicar of thirty years and the man who'd first replaced him – Julian Forsyth – had almost brought the bookshop to an end with his stuffy attitude and haughty wife. Luckily,

Reverend Forsyth and his lady had soon realized that they and Churchwood weren't a good fit and had moved on, leaving the job available to Adam – much to the delight of Churchwood. Not only was he thoughtful and gentle-hearted, he was also an enthusiastic supporter of the bookshop.

It would be a while before he could take up the position full-time, as he was still serving out his notice as curate at St John's Church, five miles away in Barton. But the vicar of St John's was allowing Adam to visit Churchwood often.

'Will you be able to stay for our team meeting later?' Alice asked.

'Reverend Blake has given his permission, so yes,' Adam said, smiling.

'He's a good man.'

'He is. I'll miss him when I come to Churchwood permanently. Not that I'm having second thoughts about coming here. I can't wait. Roll on November.'

'The village can't wait either,' Alice assured him.

Inside, Naomi was setting out tables and chairs with the other two members of the bookshop organizing team, homely Janet Collins and glamorous May Janicki. Janet had lived in Churchwood all her life, so she and Naomi had known each other for many years. Not as friends, though. Naomi would be the first to admit that she'd lorded it over Janet in the past, treating her as a follower who knew her place rather than an equal. But Naomi had changed since then and now they were friends.

Like Alice, May was a newcomer. After a wretched start in an orphanage, she'd forged a career as a designer and manufacturer of women's clothing – until the war had forced her to leave London to make a safe home for three refugee children, the two nieces and nephew of her Polish husband. In her early days in Churchwood, May had struggled. She'd loved her career and had never wanted children. But she'd gradually settled into her changed circumstances and now she was a wonderful mother figure to Rosa, Samuel and Zofia. She was also the village dressmaker and a source of inspiration for all things clothing-related.

'Let me carry that table, young May,' Bert said, bustling towards the tall, slender Londoner. 'It's heavy.'

Alice went to help Naomi, concerned that, while her friend was putting on a brave face to the world, she also looked strained. It was no wonder, given what she'd recently discovered about her marriage. Alice was one of only three people who'd been trusted with the whole sorry story, the others being Kate and Bert. The rest of the village knew no more than that Naomi and Alexander were separating. Even that must make Naomi feel uncomfortable, so Alice wanted to be especially kind to her just now.

Once the furniture was in place, toys, books, newspapers and magazines were brought out. Comics too, including the *Beano* to which the Forsyths had taken great exception. Alice caught Adam reading the 'Lord Snooty' story. 'Don't let the archdeacon catch you reading that vulgar nonsense,' Alice teased, and Adam laughed.

Soon, the sound of merry chatter outside heralded the arrival of those villagers who were coming to today's session. 'Come in!' Alice invited, opening the door.

'Don't mind if I do,' Mrs Hayes said. She headed inside then paused, looking around in satisfaction. 'It's good to see things back to normal.'

'Just like old times,' her friend Mrs Hutchings agreed.

They bustled away and Alice greeted more arrivals before moving to the table on which books stood ready to be bought or borrowed. 'I'm returning *The Earl's Embrace* and I'd like the book Edna Hall loved so much, if it's available,' Mrs Hayes said.

'*Midsummer Kisses*?'

'That's the one. Unless Wilf would like it?'

Wilf Phipps had come up beside her. 'A book about kisses?' he scoffed. 'Give over – you'll be giving my Winnie ideas. I'd like one of those Agatha Christie books.'

'A book about murder? It'll give your Winnie ideas of a different sort if you don't get your front fence mended.'

Edna walked away, chuckling, and Wilf chose *Murder in the Mews*.

Alice noted more book returns and loans in the register. She was busy for a while, but the pressure eased off as people found seats near their friends and caught up on the latest news and gossip. Her gaze strayed back to her rings, and she wondered how much time would pass before she saw Daniel again.

She wasn't alone in Churchwood in having a loved one away fighting. May's husband, Marek, and Janet's youngest son, Charlie, were both serving in the army, while Kate's sweetheart, Leo, was a pilot in the RAF.

Would Kate manage to come to the bookshop today? Even with the land girls, there was far too much work needing to be done on the farm, so getting away could be tricky for Kate, especially during daylight hours and even more especially during the harvest season. With luck, Kate would at least make it to the meeting after today's session.

Alice's thoughts were interrupted by Jonah Kerrigan wanting, 'Summat that'll make me laugh.'

Alice suggested a P. G. Wodehouse book about the pigs at Blandings Castle and Jonah accepted the recommendation. 'Let me know what you think of it,' Alice said.

'I'll do that. Must be time for a cup of tea and a biscuit soon.'

Alice hid a smile. Jonah was always eager for a cup of tea and a biscuit or two. Or even three, if he could get away with it. 'Soon,' she confirmed.

Jonah shuffled away and Alice left her post to walk around the room. May had asked people to bring in their worn-out or damaged old clothes and now she was demonstrating how they could be adjusted or cut up to make fresh garments. 'With clothing being rationed, we need to use our imaginations if we're to avoid looking dowdy. This dress here could be lengthened using a band of this blue fabric . . . This coat has torn pockets, but they could be replaced with new ones cut from this jacket. The fabric isn't the same but it'll look as though it was designed to be different . . . A cigarette burn like this could be darned and hidden behind a larger button . . .'

In another corner of the room Bert was giving tips for planting vegetables in autumn, while elsewhere Janet was busy collecting clean jars for jam-making now that an extra sugar ration was to be given for that purpose.

Rationing and food shortages were making Churchwood – like so many other villages and towns – turn creative and husband resources carefully. But was there one person in the village who was struggling more than anyone else? Struggling to buy or grow enough food to keep body and soul together? Had that person resorted to stealing milk from doorsteps? Alice had smiled at Jonah Kerrigan's eagerness for biscuits, but had his usual greed given way to desperate need?

Alice was thankful that she hadn't been driven to such despair. Her father wasn't rich, but the money he'd put by for his retirement meant he could keep a roof over their heads and buy food. Alice had a modest income of her own, too. For the moment. Her job helping Hubert Parkinson with his family memoir would soon come to a natural end, but Alice hoped to find other work.

Now she was married to Daniel she was also being allocated a one-third share of his service pay. 'It won't be a fortune,' he'd told her. 'In fact, many of the chaps and their families complain that it's grossly inadequate, but I'll be glad to know that it'll provide you with a bit of security.'

Alice was pleased to have it, though she planned to save it, for who knew what would happen when the war was over. Daniel had been an engineer who designed racing cars before the outbreak. He hoped to go back to that line of work, but whether that would be possible remained to be seen. Many servicemen had struggled to find work after the 1914 war, and Alice didn't want Daniel to worry that they had no money to fall back on if he had the same experience. As well as a job for Daniel they'd need a home, furniture, pots and pans . . .

Tea was announced and Jonah Kerrigan was at the front of the queue. Pam Cooper took a cup but had a baby to juggle too. 'Let me take the little one,' Alice suggested, and she rocked the baby as Pam drank her tea in peace.

Marjorie was talking to Naomi about the thief. 'It's got me in a tizzy, I can tell you. I scarcely dare go to bed in case the thief breaks into the house and ransacks it, as well as . . . Well, who knows what the man might do to me?'

Naomi sighed. 'Marjorie, we don't know that the thief is a man but, even if he is, he hasn't hurt anybody. Not physically. Probably, the thefts are either childish pranks or – more likely, in view of the posies that are left – the acts of someone in dire straits.'

'Until we know for sure, I'm taking no chances,' Marjorie said, clearly put out by Naomi's way of reducing the dramatic to the commonplace.

In time the session finished. As usual, those who were able to help clear up did so, then everyone filed out with calls of 'Cheerio!' and 'Thanks!' and smiles of satisfaction in a couple of hours well spent.

Soon only the organizing team remained, including the newest member, vicar-to-be Adam Potts. He gestured to a table. 'Shall we?'

They sat around it. Alice was just regretting that Kate hadn't managed to come when the door opened and in she walked, her long legs taking her swiftly to the chair next to Alice. 'Sorry I'm late,' she said.

She looked sombre, and Alice felt alarmed. 'Leo?' she whispered.

'Leo is fine.'

Thank goodness for that. But something else was wrong.

'I'll tell you later,' Kate said, obviously not wanting to hold up the meeting.

Poor Kate. She'd never had an easy life, but after meeting Leo and making friends with the land girls, Alice had hoped that things had begun to look up for her. Perhaps whatever was troubling her could soon be mended. On that thought, Alice turned her attention to the meeting.

'About our thief,' Adam began.

'He struck again this morning,' Naomi told them. 'My milk went missing off the doorstep again.'

'Did he leave a posy?' Alice asked.

'The usual greenery tied together with ivy.'

'I'm inclined to think the posies are meant as gestures of thanks and apology,' Alice said.

'Me too,' agreed Adam.

'Our milk was taken yesterday,' Alice reported. 'And Wilf Phipps's the morning before.'

'Milk has gone missing every day for the last few weeks,' Adam said. 'I don't know if anyone else has noticed but, as far as I know, the thief has never taken anything from the houses where our frailest parishioners or children live.'

Alice nodded. 'That suggests he's trying to cause as little harm as possible, so either he knows the village or he's been watching to see who lives where and who might suffer least from a missing pint of milk. Or *she* has. We mustn't rule out the possibility that the thief might be female.'

'That's true,' Adam agreed. 'So who might our thief be? Have any of you seen a stranger about?'

No one had.

'The only newcomers to the village are the Gregsons, and they didn't arrive until at least two weeks after the stealing started,' Naomi pointed out.

'We can assume they're nothing to do with the thefts, though I think we should have a chat about how they're settling in,' Adam agreed.

'Or not settling in,' Alice said.

'Quite. But back to our thief. Could he be a child?'

'Pam Cooper's younger brother delivers newspapers, so he's out and about soon after the milk has been delivered,' Janet said. 'He doesn't strike me as the sort of boy who'd steal, though.'

'Nor me,' Kate said forcefully, and Alice wondered if she was remembering how it felt to be condemned

26

unfairly as a bad lot. Those days were gone now but the memory must still sting.

'I don't think any of us want to point fingers,' Alice said. 'We just want to get to the truth in case someone in our village isn't coping.'

'I'm sure we're already keeping our eyes and ears open, but it wouldn't hurt for us to encourage people to talk if we suspect they might be struggling,' Adam said. 'We'll need to be tactful, though. The last thing we want is to insult people or injure their pride.'

'You could put up a notice on the church door, too,' Alice suggested. 'A notice appealing for anyone in difficulties to speak to you privately.'

'Good idea,' Adam said. 'I'll put one on the vicarage door and in this hall as well.'

There was nothing more to be said about the thief for the time being. 'On to the Gregsons,' Adam proposed.

Mrs Gregson had recently moved to Churchwood with her children, two young boys of about eight and ten, but so far she'd repelled all efforts to befriend her. She'd never shown her face in church or at the bookshop, and while she shopped in Churchwood, that was probably only due to necessity.

'I've said hello several times but never had more than a nod in return,' Janet reported.

'Neither have I,' May told her. 'It's the boys I feel sorry for. They don't meet other kids at school because she's educating them at home, and they don't meet other kids elsewhere because it seems they're not allowed to go out without their mother keeping watch. Samuel invited them both to join in when he was kicking a ball around on the village green, but their mother just tugged them on their way. They looked ever so disappointed.'

'At least the boys have each other,' Alice pointed out. She'd once drawn a begrudged 'Afternoon' from Mrs Gregson but it hadn't been repeated.

'I've had no more luck than the rest of you in trying to draw her into a conversation,' Naomi said. 'I only know what her voice is like because I heard her ask the grocer if she could take her fat ration as half lard and half margarine. In fact, the only reason we know she's called Gregson is because Marjorie looked over her shoulder and glimpsed her ration book.'

'And the only reason we know the boys are called Roger and Alan is because my kids heard them calling to each other in their back garden,' May said.

'If I thought Mrs Gregson simply preferred her own company, I wouldn't be concerned,' Alice said. 'But I've never seen her without a frown, and she always looks so harassed. You're right, though, Adam. We need to respect her wishes.'

'She might be shy,' May suggested. 'Or have some other trouble that's stopping her from making friends. I kept myself to myself when I moved to Churchwood.'

May had been ashamed of the resentment she'd felt at having to give up her career in vibrant London to throw herself into domestic life in a country village instead.

'It's thanks to all of you that I managed to settle in.' May's gaze landed on Alice, and she smiled. Alice had been the first person to reach out to her.

Kate stirred too, though she didn't speak. They all knew she'd been shunned in Churchwood until Alice had befriended her and shown the village that there was another side to the tall, striking girl with the bold eyes and the cutting tongue.

'Mrs Gregson's first name is Evelyn,' Janet said. 'The

28

postman told me he'd seen it on an envelope.' She paused for a moment and then added, 'Goodness. That makes me sound like the village gossip.'

'We all know the name of the village gossip and it isn't Janet Collins,' Bert said. 'I hope you won't think it's Bert Makepiece either when I tell you I was walking behind Mrs Gregson and her boys one day and I heard her mention their father's regiment. Mr Gregson must be away fighting.'

'Then she has something in common with many of us,' Alice said.

'It can't have helped that virtually the first person from the village to pounce on her was Marjorie,' Bert added, glancing at Naomi because Marjorie was her oldest friend.

Not that Naomi was under any illusions about her. Tall and lanky, Marjorie wasn't a bad person, but she often let her love of gossip get the better of her. It was the reason Naomi hadn't trusted her with details of the forthcoming divorce, telling her only that they'd decided on a formal parting because they rarely saw each other anyway.

'But you must be upset,' Marjorie had said. 'I hope you know you can talk to me about your feelings. It isn't as though I'm the sort of indiscreet person who'd mention your private business all over the village.'

So had said Churchwood's biggest gossip.

Naomi had insisted that she was fine.

Marjorie wasn't the best advertisement for the village and Naomi acknowledged it now with a wry, 'Oh dear.'

'Maybe Mrs Gregson thinks we're all gossips after Marjorie cross-examined her,' May suggested. 'I'll try to have another chat with her when I see her next. My kids are a friendly little lot, so maybe they can break the ice with the Gregson boys.'

'I'll call round with flowers,' Alice said. 'I won't expect her to invite me in, but I hope it'll show that Churchwood really is a welcoming sort of place.'

'In the meantime, I suggest the rest of us simply encourage her with smiles and greetings when we happen to see her,' Adam proposed. He paused and then said, 'If I may keep you for a moment longer, there's something else I'd like to discuss.'

They looked at him expectantly.

'Christmas,' he said, and he gave them a sweet smile tinged with embarrassment. 'I'm probably going to sound like a child but I'm ever so excited about my first Christmas as vicar of St Luke's. I want to make it special. Has anyone else thought about it yet?'

'Christmas Day falls on a Thursday this year. We're thinking of holding a bookshop party on the previous Saturday, though we haven't made any actual plans so far,' Alice told him.

'It's early, I know,' Adam said, with another embarrassed grin. 'The party would be for everyone in the village, I assume?'

'For hospital staff and patients, too.'

'That sounds wonderful. What about church services? A nativity play?'

'Reverend Barnes liked a nativity play on Christmas Eve, but it's been a fairly low-key affair,' Naomi said.

'Have the children worn costumes?'

'A few of them, though the costumes we have aren't much to look at.'

'They're in a sorry state,' Janet expanded. 'Ancient, faded, falling apart . . .'

Adam nodded as though he'd expected that. 'I know Christmas is still three months away, but the reason I'm mentioning it now is because I'd like every child in the village to have a chance to dress up and take part in a special service on Christmas Eve – a nativity play, with carols being sung after every scene. I can't organize that on my own, though, and as you run the bookshop . . .'

'We'll be glad to help,' Alice said, and the others agreed. 'We can take a look at the old costumes, keep any that are worth saving and make new ones too.'

'I know it won't be easy, given the shortages,' Adam said. 'That's why I'm mentioning it early. Not that you need to get started straight away.'

'It'll be in our thoughts,' Alice said.

'Thank you. Well, I won't detain you any longer.'

Alice looked at Kate, who dipped her head towards the door to signal that she wanted to talk outside. They bade goodbye to the others then left the Hall and walked along Churchwood Way towards home, Kate pushing her bicycle at her side.

'It's Fred,' Kate said. 'He's been injured.'

'Oh no! Badly injured?'

'Badly enough to be sent back to England, but we don't have any details yet. Kenny is trying to find out more.'

'It was good of you to come to the meeting when you must be worried sick.'

Kate shrugged. They both knew that moping at home wasn't the answer to wartime woes. 'You won't mind if I rush away? Kenny may have more news.'

'Of course I don't mind. But let me know when you've heard more. Only when it's convenient, though.'

Kate mounted the bicycle and rode away at speed. Alice felt for her. For Fred, too. Hopefully, he'd recover from his injuries, even if it took time.

Alice knew that some men even welcomed wounds if

they set them free from the fighting. Her father had taken his medical skills into the 1914 war, serving in France, and he'd told her how some soldiers had been glad to be hurt if it meant they could return home for long recovery periods or, better still, for ever. Some had even harmed themselves, considering relatively minor incapacities preferable to what might await them in the form of more grievous damage or even death if they continued to fight. Alice couldn't imagine Fred being separated from his twin, Frank, voluntarily, though.

Thoughts of the war quickened Alice's pace. There might be a letter from Daniel at home.

CHAPTER FOUR

Naomi

Evelyn Gregson was scuttling along the pavement, eyes
cast down as though she couldn't get home fast enough,
and probably hadn't seen Naomi walking towards her.
Evelyn was a good-looking woman in her thirties, attract-
ively dressed in a well-cut green coat that flattered her
dark wavy hair, but the deep frown cutting into the space
between her arching eyebrows gave her a harassed appearance. Eventually, she must have heard Naomi's footsteps
because she finally looked up, only for her gaze to dart to
the pavement on the opposite side of the street. Was she
wondering if she'd left it too late to avoid a conversation
by crossing the road?

'Fine day, isn't it?' Naomi called, closing the distance
between them.

Evelyn glanced up at the sky with a bewildered air that
suggested she had more important things on her mind
than the weather. 'A fine day,' she agreed, and scuttled
onwards.

Naomi made no attempt to detain her. Hopefully, she'd
done some good simply by showing that Churchwood
people could be friendly without being pushy. Naomi continued onwards too – to the bus stop.

'Good for you, woman,' Bert had said when she'd told
him about her appointment with Sir Ambrose.

'I hope I'm doing the right thing.'

'What's the alternative?'

Trust Bert to lay it out plainly. The alternative was . . . intolerable.

'It'll be good to have this Sir Whatsit on your side,' he'd added.

In other words, there was no need for her to feel nervous. Naomi couldn't help it, though. Her life was being turned upside down.

'If you need company, I could dust off the funeral suit and come along for the trip,' Bert had offered.

'Thank you, but I won't take you away from your work.' Besides, Naomi was supposed to be a woman of mature years. She shouldn't need a babysitter. Not liking to appear weak, she'd changed the subject. 'How old is your funeral suit?'

Bert had grinned. 'I've had it for thirty years, give or take a year or two. Funerals, the occasional wedding and christening . . . It's done me proud, and it'll keep doing me proud for a good while yet.'

No one could accuse Bert Makepiece of being a dandy. His usual outfits were comfortable but ancient, the fabrics limp and the colours leeched by age. In Bert's world, holes meant clothes needed patching instead of discarding, and if a belt wasn't to hand, a length of twine would do just as well. He was unimpressed by vanity and pomposity. He had other priorities, not least kindness.

They'd been talking over a cup of tea in Bert's kitchen, which was as old and comfortable as his clothes. He'd become Naomi's confidant over the past months.

Getting up to leave, she'd thanked him for listening.

'I'll listen anytime you like.' He'd seen her to the door. 'Don't forget what I said. You're paying this Sir Whatsit to look out for *your* interests and, like all good people in trade, he should do right by his customer. He'll have heard many a sordid tale over the years, too, so don't worry that anything you say will shock him.'

Wise words. Naomi remembered them now and repeated them to herself often as she rode the bus to St Albans and then the train to London.

Arriving at St Pancras station, she took a taxi to Lincoln's Inn Fields and stood looking up at the tall, elegant town house in which Sir Ambrose had his office. She mounted the steps to the door and rang a bell.

'I'm Naomi Harrington. I have an appointment,' she said, when the door was opened by a woman who looked professional from her coiffed hair to her polished shoes.

'Of course.'

Naomi was shown to a spacious reception room where this woman appeared to work alongside a man who was probably some sort of clerk. There were several chairs for visitors. Naomi was invited to sit but didn't have long to wait before the woman approached and said, 'Sir Ambrose will see you now.'

Her tone suggested it was an honour to be granted an audience with the Great Man of Law. It didn't help Naomi, whose stomach was crumpling again.

Sir Ambrose was a large man with a broad smile and an air that suggested he too considered it an honour for Naomi to meet such a Great Man as he. 'Come in, Mrs Harrington.'

Rising from behind an enormous desk, he offered a well-manicured hand, which he used to squeeze her fingers briefly before waving it in the direction of a much younger and thinner man who looked almost as nervous as Naomi, his Adam's apple bobbing up and down like a living thing that was trapped in his throat. 'My articled clerk, Mr Hughes.'

Mr Hughes attempted a smile and pushed his glasses along his nose. They were black and too heavy for his narrow face.

'Sit down, Mrs Harrington. Tell me how I can help.' The Great Man waved her to a visitor's chair then sat back down behind the desk, one leg crossed over the other and his hands behind his head, the picture of ease.

Naomi sat on the edge of the visitor's chair and tried to soothe her jiggling nerves with a couple of deep breaths. An image of her friends came into her mind.

If Alice were sitting here, she'd be a small, neat, upright personage with a calm manner but a light of determination in her clever eyes. Kate's long legs would be sprawled in front of her as she waited suspiciously for the least sign of contempt or patronage from the Great Man, to which she'd react with glares and bold words of her own. Bert would be sitting with his arms crossed over his substantial middle, unimpressed by the plush carpet, polished furniture, leather-tooled books or the Great Man's manicure, and expecting solid, down-to-earth advice delivered with neither floweriness nor pomposity.

The images gave Naomi the courage to begin, even if nervousness still squeezed her stomach. 'I'm here about my marriage.'

He gestured for her to continue. Obviously, she was here about her marriage, because the Great Man's area of speciality was marriages that had soured or exploded.

'My husband . . . He's . . .' Goodness, it was hard to share private details with a stranger, even one who was on her side.

'He's what? Committed adultery? Beaten you? Failed to support you financially?'

'Yes,' Naomi said, then felt foolish because not all of those possibilities applied. She narrowed them down. 'He's . . . He's involved with another woman.'

There. She'd said it. Humiliation scalded her cheeks, though it wasn't the worst thing she had to tell Sir Ambrose. That had yet to come.

'Then you'll be pleased to hear that, since Parliament passed the Matrimonial Causes Act in 1923, it's possible for a woman to divorce her husband on the grounds of his adultery alone.' He made it sound as though Parliament had been gracious in conferring a favour on women rather than simply righting the wrong that had allowed only men to divorce on the grounds of infidelity without the need to prove additional faults such as cruelty.

'Yes,' Naomi said, not knowing what else to say.

'Since then, further law has allowed divorce for cruelty, desertion or incurable insanity even without infidelity.' He raised an eyebrow, presumably to question whether any of those grounds applied as well.

'My husband isn't insane. He hasn't exactly deserted me, either. But he's certainly cruel.'

'He beats you?'

'Not that kind of cruelty. He has . . . He has . . .' How excruciating this was! Naomi took another deep breath. 'Alexander had a secret family. A woman and two children.'

The knowledge had crushed her.

'He's the father of the children? Beyond a doubt?' Sir Ambrose asked.

'He admitted it.' And no one who'd seen those children – as Naomi had – could doubt it.

'I see.'

Naomi had spent years trying to kid both herself and the world that her marriage was happy before she'd finally faced the truth, which was that Alexander had married her for her money. It had grieved her, but she'd come to terms with it, reasoning that, as long as there was trust and respect in the marriage, they could continue as before – Alexander throwing himself into his career and golf while Naomi found pleasure and purpose in the village life of Churchwood.

But a few months ago, she'd begun to suspect Alexander of an affair. The day Naomi had followed Alexander into Marcroft's Hotel and discovered that not only did he have a lover, but two children too, had been the worst day of her life. She'd felt betrayed, degraded and cheated of the life that might have been hers had she married a better man, a life that might have included the children for whom she'd yearned all her adult life.

Even now, weeks later, the merest nudge at her memory was enough to undo her self-control and reduce her to tears. She could feel the prickle of tears now but blinked them away with as much determination as she could muster. It was mortifying enough to share the intimate details of her life without adding to the embarrassment by weeping.

'So what is it you want, Mrs Harrington? Is it for your husband to break off this relationship? An agreement to separate? Or a divorce?'

A separation had been the first option Naomi had considered in her eagerness to wash her hands of Alexander's treachery as privately and as quickly as possible. But she'd decided to opt for a divorce instead. It would make the break complete and final.

'Of course, divorce can shock one's friends and, in

some cases, lead to a scandal,' the Great Man said. 'But it's becoming increasingly common and the newspapers tend to be interested only in the affairs of people in the public eye – politicians, actresses . . . those sorts of people.'

He was suggesting that Naomi's divorce would barely merit a mention in the newspapers. As for shocking her friends . . . Well, perhaps there'd be talk amongst some of the people she used to know – rich or at least comfortably-off women with whom she'd served on charity committees before petrol rationing meant she no longer had the use of the car. But even though she'd once thought of them as friends, the truth was that they were little more than acquaintances. Naomi wouldn't miss them any more than they'd miss her if she moved out of their social circle.

Her real friends were in Churchwood – ordinary people, by some standards, hard-working and watching every penny. But they were also kind, generous and big-hearted. It was these friends who mattered to Naomi now. None of them would look down on her if she were divorced. They'd rally round her instead.

There was another consideration. Naomi owed Alexander and his lover nothing, but the children were innocent and deserved parents who were married. They shouldn't have to carry the stigma of illegitimacy into their adult lives.

'I'd like a divorce,' she said. A divorce would give Naomi the clean break she wanted and leave Alexander free to marry his Amelia Ashmore.

'Very well.' The Great Man looked pleased and, though he didn't move, Naomi pictured him rubbing his hands in glee because this was the bread and butter of his professional life.

He began to ask questions and the articled clerk wrote down her answers – the date of the marriage, Naomi's date of birth, Alexander's date of birth, addresses, the names of Alexander's lover and children . . . Then he moved on to the financial aspects of the marriage.

'Alexander is a stockbroker,' Naomi said. 'A partner in a firm which has offices in Clark Street in the City.'

The articled clerk wrote down the details in so far as Naomi was aware of them, but she didn't know how much Alexander earned, the value of his partnership, nor even the likely values of Foxfield and the London flat if they were to be sold.

'Much of our money came from my father,' she continued and explained about her father's business – Tuggs Tonics – which had sold medicines. Quack medicines, she suspected, but left that out of the history. 'He sold the business when I was sixteen or so and on his death he left the proceeds to me. I believe it was about fifty thousand pounds, and he left it in such a way that Alexander couldn't simply dispose of investments without my consent.'

'The money was placed in a trust fund?'

'It was.' She hesitated, hating to appear an even bigger fool but seeing no way around it. 'But I should tell you that sometimes I signed papers my husband put in front of me without reading them fully.' Without reading them at all in many cases. 'I trusted him.'

Had it been trust or a wish to please him? Or even the fear of his anger if she asked questions? Tall and trim with hard blue eyes and the sort of crisp voice that could slice through steel, Alexander could be cutting and intimidating. Perhaps all three reasons had made Naomi more compliant than was wise.

The Great Man looked as though he thought nothing

good could have come from involving a woman in business anyway. 'I'll write to your husband to ask him to confirm his consent to the divorce – simpler and more discreet for both of you than a disputed petition – and request disclosure of financial information. With luck, it will be possible to agree a settlement instead of airing the sorry business in a court hearing. You're entitled to a fair division of the assets and your husband will be obliged to maintain you in the future.'

'No,' Naomi said, then, seeing the Great Man's surprise, explained, 'I'd prefer a divorce to be final in every way. I don't want to depend on Alexander for money. I'd rather have my father's fortune back so I can maintain myself.'

'There's no need to make hasty decisions. We'll see what's possible once I have full information.' He paused, then said smoothly, 'Naturally, I'll need a retainer against my fees.' He stroked his lips as though trying not to smile at the thought of the largesse that would be coming his way.

'What – er – level of retainer?' Naomi asked, hoping she didn't sound as worried as she felt.

'One hundred guineas to begin with. Just to get the process started, you understand.'

'And after that?'

He opened a drawer in his desk and took out a sheet of paper, which he passed to her.

Glancing down at it, Naomi felt the colour drain from her face as she saw the Great Man's charges. A fee for each hour of his time, a fee for each telephone call, a fee for each letter, a lesser fee for the services of the other mortals in his office, like Mr Hughes . . . And then something called disbursements – more charges for incidental expenses incurred on her behalf.

41

It had given her a sense of power to tell Alexander that she was consulting Sir Ambrose. It had had the desired effect, too, as he'd blanched a little. But at that stage she'd only spoken to the Great Man's office to be sure he could see her should she wish it. Now she regretted not finding out his fees in advance, as a Not-so-Great Man might have been more economical. Should she tell the Great Man that she'd changed her mind and start all over again by consulting a solicitor with more modest charges? Or was it already too late for that? Guessing that Alexander would take it as a sign of weakness if she went for cheaper advice now, Naomi decided to stick with the Great Man for the present and see how matters developed.

'Are you able to give me any idea of how long it will take for a settlement to be reached?' she asked. 'And how much it's likely to cost? Just so I can arrange my finances to accommodate it.'

'How long is a piece of string, Mrs Harrington?'

She smiled thinly.

'I think we've taken matters as far as we can today,' the Great Man pronounced, and Naomi scrambled to her feet, aware that every minute she spent in his company would cost her dear.

'Thank you for seeing me.' She gave the Great Soft Hand a final shake and nodded at bespectacled Mr Hughes with the frantic Adam's apple.

The Great Man showed her to the door. 'I'll be in touch when I have news, though that's unlikely to be for several weeks. In the meantime, rest assured that your affairs are in safe hands now.'

Hmm. With Alexander draining her money on one side and the Great Man now draining it on the other side, Naomi didn't feel safe at all.

CHAPTER FIVE

Kate

A week had passed since Kate had received Leo's last letter. She'd written back the same evening and posted her letter the following morning, but it was still too soon to expect a reply.

Writing back, she'd thought long and hard about whether to mention that Fred had been injured. Leo knew all too well that injury or worse had befallen many a serviceman since the war began and would befall many more before it was over. But would it help him to hear of another such victim? Surely not. Besides, Kate knew nothing of the nature and extent of Fred's injuries. Once she was in possession of all the facts . . . That would be the time to decide what, if anything, to tell Leo.

Meanwhile, she was trying to stay cheerful by thinking of other things she might say in her next letter. Deciding on an early night now, she retreated to her room to lie back against the pillows and compose the letter in her mind.

Darling Leo,
It was lovely to receive your letter and to know that you're well.

Was she tempting fate by anticipating that Leo would be well? Kate refused to believe in superstitious nonsense but even so she moved quickly to the rest of her letter, deciding she'd write about life in Churchwood as he always said he liked to hear about it.

The thief continues to strike and leave posies behind as some sort of compensation for his pilfering, but we're no closer to knowing who he is. We all call him he but the thief might be a she, of course.

We've been lucky here on the farm in that nothing has been taken from us, as far as we know, though we wouldn't notice if a few apples and pears went missing. I'm keeping a close eye on the vegetables I grow for the house, so I'll be better able to judge if any suddenly disappear. As for our eggs, we're collecting around the same number as usual, though, again, we wouldn't be able to tell if the odd one had been stolen.

People in the village sometimes grumble when their milk is taken, as it's a nuisance as well as a cost, but no one has lost milk more than once a week so far. The thief seems to be spreading the burden of his pilfering around.

I went to the bookshop on Saturday – always fun! – and brought home Agatha Christie's Death on the Nile. I can't wait to read about Hercule Poirot investigating what will doubtless be dastardly deeds. It'll make me feel closer to you as it's set in Egypt, not so far from where you must be.

Here, autumn is working a tapestry of colours across the trees. The daylight hours are shortening and there's a chill in the air. There's no chill in the deserts of Africa, I suppose. I hope you're not too uncomfortable over there. At least you won't have frozen fingers and iced-up windows when winter creeps in.

Kate paused, wondering if what she planned to write might bore him or – worse – be too poignant a reminder of all he was missing. She could always change her mind about what to write, as it might be days or another week before his reply to her last letter reached her.

She shifted her thoughts to the next day and the developments it might bring. Kenny had announced that he planned to go into the village to make some phone calls and try to track down more information about Fred.

'Maybe we should think about having a telephone installed here,' he'd said over supper.

'Telephones cost money,' skinflint Ernie had growled.

'So does *not* having a phone when it means stopping work to go into the village to make calls from the post office,' Kenny had pointed out.

'That doesn't happen often.'

'Perhaps not – in the past. But times are changing and we need to change with them. Think how much quicker and easier it would be if we could ring customers and suppliers instead of having to write to them. Not that I suppose we could get a telephone installed quickly with the war on. A truck would help, too, as we could load it with much bigger and heavier stuff than Pete can pull in the cart. Pete's getting on a bit, anyway. Another year or two and we'll have to put him out to grass.' Kenny rubbed his jaw, looking tired. Worried, too.

They were all worried about Fred. Even Ernie's grumbling seemed like an echo of his usual grumpiness, put on because he didn't know how else to be rather than because he was unconcerned about his son. Perhaps he too lay awake at night, anxiety keeping him from sleep.

Ernie wasn't in the best of moods when morning came. Pearl ate her breakfast in wary silence, slinking down in her chair as though trying to hide from him, though there was no hiding her six-feet frame from anyone. Timmy left for school early, doubtless hoping to escape the atmosphere, while the rest of them tiptoed about their business as quietly as possible.

They'd all worked in the fields before breakfast, lifting cabbages and carrots, but there was plenty more to be done. 'If you're too busy, I can go into the village and make the phone calls,' Kate told Kenny, but Ernie put a swift end to that idea.

'You just want to gossip the day away with those people you call friends,' he sneered. 'Not a chance.'

'I'll come straight back,' Kate promised, but Ernie didn't bother to answer.

'I can go instead,' Vinnie offered, but even Kenny baulked at that idea. Vinnie would almost certainly take advantage of the errand to shirk his work.

'*I'm* going,' Kenny told him. 'You lift those beets like I asked.'

Vinnie looked sulky but no one had sympathy to spare for him.

They settled back into the day's work when Kenny left, though it was a struggle to concentrate – for Kate at least.

More than an hour passed. Kate worked hard but her mind was on Fred and every few minutes she glanced at the watch Naomi had kindly given her. 'It's an old one but it keeps perfect time,' she'd said.

'It's wonderful!' Kate had told her, gratefully.

The watch hadn't escaped Ernie's notice. 'Where did that come from? Don't give me a pack of lies.'

'It was a gift from Naomi Harrington.'

'Why should *she* give you a gift? Who did you really get it from? Some man? You'd better not be misbehaving, girl, because—'

'You can see it's an old watch, for goodness' sake. Ask Naomi about it if you don't believe me.'

46

'Humph. I don't know why you hobnob with snobs like her.'

'She isn't a snob – as you'd know if you took the trouble to get to know her.'

'Ideas above your station, that's what you've got. Your place is on the farm and don't you forget it.'

As ever, Kate bit back the retort that she had no intention of staying on the farm for ever.

When she finally saw Kenny returning, Kate threw down her spade and went to meet him in the farmyard. Vinnie, Ernie and Pearl came over from the fields and Ruby approached from the chicken run she'd been cleaning. All looked at Kenny expectantly.

His expression was flustered. Annoyed. 'It took me an age to speak to someone who could tell me something about Fred, but I still got hardly any information. All I know is that he's reached a hospital in London. I'm supposed to ring back tomorrow to find out more.'

Ernie made a disgusted sound, as though the authorities had conspired to deprive him of Kenny's labour at such a busy time on the farm. 'Back to work!' he barked, but Kate didn't feel as irritated with her father as usual because she could see that his temper was fuelled by concern.

She too hated the fact that they were still waiting for news. It gnawed at her peace of mind but, as with most things connected to the war, she could only endure it and hope that things would improve on the morrow.

'This had better not be another wild goose chase,' Ernie said, scowling at Kenny as he prepared to walk down to the village again the following morning.

As if Kenny had any influence over the authorities!

'I need money for the phone,' he said, and with his

47

usual show of reluctance, Ernie parted with some coins before looking round the kitchen at everyone else. 'Why are you all standing here gaping like stranded fish? There's work to be done.'

Once again, there was a long wait for Kenny's return. And once again, they all congregated in the farmyard to hear his news. 'They expect Fred to live,' he announced, and there was a general slump of relief.

'He'll make a full recovery?' Kate asked.

'I'm not so sure about that. He was hurt in his legs but I don't know more than that. They suggested someone should visit.' He looked at Ernie, as it would be natural for a father to rush to visit his son.

Ernie was no ordinary father, though. His expression was as sour as ever but, just for a second or two, Kate had seen alarm ripple over his features at the mention of Fred's injured legs. Ernie would be all at sea talking to doctors in a London hospital and doubtless his feelings would emerge as bad temper. That would help no one.

'*You* need to go,' Ernie told Kenny, and Kate was glad because her brother would make a far better job of the visit.

Not that he was the perfect person to speak to a doctor, something that Kenny appeared to realize himself. 'I need someone to come with me.'

'I'll come,' Vinnie offered. 'I've never been to London.'

'It isn't a sightseeing tour!' Ernie snapped. 'You can stay here and work.'

'I'll take Kate,' Kenny announced.

'What use will she be?' Ernie sneered. 'She can stay here and work as well.'

Ruby gave Kenny the sort of look that said, 'Don't give in.'

48

'We don't know what we're facing yet,' Kenny said. 'Kate might be useful.' He drew himself up taller and stood his ground. 'I'm taking her.'

'Bah!' Ernie waved a dismissive hand and gave up the fight.

'When will you go?' Ruby asked.

'They said next week will be better as it'll give Fred a few days to settle in. Monday, I think. We'll go on Monday.' Kenny suddenly slapped his forehead as though a thought had struck him. 'I'm seeing the chap from Walkers about bulk-buying fertilizer on Monday. I wonder if . . .' His gaze took in Ernie and Vinnie, and Kate guessed he was considering asking one of them to see the Walkers man. 'No,' he said, obviously thinking better of the idea. 'Tuesday, then. We'll visit Fred on Tuesday.'

Kate nodded, wondering what they'd find when they got there.

CHAPTER SIX

Alice

Spotting Evelyn and her boys ahead of her, Alice broke into a run and caught them up. 'I'm glad I've seen you,' she said, smiling. 'I have flowers for you.' This was her second attempt to bring flowers to Evelyn, who'd been out the first time Alice had tried.

'Flowers?' Evelyn took a step back from Alice's yellow roses, looking annoyed at having been accosted on her way back from the shops and even more annoyed at having a gift foisted upon her.

'They're only from my garden but I thought they'd make a nice way of saying welcome to Churchwood.'

'There's really no need for flowers.'

'Don't worry. I'm not expecting anything in return.'

Short of thrusting them away – and Evelyn appeared to be reluctant to do anything quite so rude – she had no option but to take them, though she did so grudgingly. 'Thank you. But please don't bother—'

Alice cut Evelyn off before she could say anything that might make it embarrassing for them to meet in public another time. 'Lovely day, isn't it? The autumn colours are beautiful, don't you think?'

'I do. Now, if you don't mind, we need—'

'I hope you're settling into Churchwood well? Your boys too? It's lovely to have you in our little community.

This may be a small place, but we make it a lively one. Have you heard about our bookshop?'

'Yes, but—'

'It's more than a bookshop in the traditional sense. It's a place that brings people together as well. We have talks, social events, and there's plenty for children, too. One thing we're planning is a big nativity play at Christmas. Every child in the village is welcome to take part and there'll be costumes for everyone.'

The boys looked at their mother but she ignored the entreaties in their eyes. 'I don't think so,' she said, obviously disappointing them.

'Perhaps they might join the church choir, then? Or is there anything else which interests them? Adam, our new vicar, isn't with us full-time yet, but I know he's keen to listen to ideas. It might be good for your Roger and Alan to meet other children, especially as I've heard they don't go to school.'

'You've heard that, have you?' Evelyn snapped, temper rising, as though Alice were as big a gossip as Marjorie Plym.

'I have a friend whose children attend the school,' Alice explained. 'You may have seen them – Rosa, Samuel and Zofia Kozak. They came from Poland to flee the persecution there and, luckily, they're thriving in Churchwood. It's a friendly sort of place, Mrs Gregson. Or may I call you Evelyn?'

'I'd prefer to keep to Mrs Gregson, though I don't see why you have to call me anything at all. How do you know my first name, anyway?'

Alice didn't want to admit that the postman had passed it on.

'We came here for peace, quiet and clean air,' Evelyn

continued, pushing open the gate of their small house. 'That's all we require of this village. This *friendly* village, as you put it. But the people here seem determined to stick their noses into our private business. Perhaps you'd like to come in and inspect our possessions and report back on them?'

Alice felt as though she'd been slapped across the face. 'Friendly doesn't mean intrusive, Mrs Gregson.'

The older woman glared at her for a moment but then her anger faltered. 'I'm sorry. I shouldn't have spoken to you like that. But I'll be obliged if you'll leave me to make my own decisions about how we live in this village.'

'Of course.'

'Then I'll wish you good day.' Evelyn steered her boys to the door, opened it, and closed it firmly the moment they were all inside.

Message received, loud and clear. Alice wasn't welcome here.

She turned to retrace her steps, feeling rather stunned. Evelyn might have apologized for her shortness, but the encounter had still been shocking in its vehemence. Even so, Alice wasn't without sympathy for a woman who might be coping with something tragic – a bereavement, perhaps – the only way she knew how. Maybe she'd come to a rural village in search of solitude and healing only to find nosy Marjorie Plym making it seem as though all the residents wanted to pry into Evelyn's personal concerns.

Alice decided that the best thing she could do now was to leave Evelyn alone. For a while at least. Not that Alice would hold a grudge over the way her friendliness had been thrown back in her face. Her path was bound to cross with Evelyn's often in a village the size of Churchwood, and when it happened . . . well, Alice would be as smilingly polite as ever. Not gushingly so, as clearly that would be no help at all. But with enough warmth to make it easy for Evelyn to strike up a conversation without embarrassment if she began to feel the need for company.

Hoping to make more progress with the problem of the thief, Alice called on Jonah Kerrigan on her way home. Jonah lived in a small, terraced house that opened straight on to the pavement – two rooms upstairs and two rooms downstairs, if it followed the standard pattern. Approaching, Alice noted that the brown paint on the window frames and door was beginning to flake. Probably, it hadn't been renewed in years.

Jonah had to be at least seventy. Possibly, he'd reached eighty, so it wasn't surprising if house maintenance had dwindled along with his energy. He might even be thinking that the current paint would last long enough to see him exit this world. On the other hand, it might be a sign that he was struggling financially.

She knocked on the door, and Jonah answered. 'Alice! What brings you here today?'

'I came to remind you that Bert's woodworking group is meeting at the bookshop this afternoon, and to ask how you are?'

'I'm fine and dandy, thanks.'

'That's good to hear.'

He wasn't looking fine and dandy. From his cream shirt and knitted sweater down to his trousers and slippers, everything about his appearance looked faded and limp with age. He reached up to scratch his head and Alice saw that there was a hole in the elbow of his sweater.

'Come in,' he said, as though suddenly remembering his manners. 'I've got the kettle on for tea.'

'That sounds lovely.'

She stepped directly into a little sitting room which was as faded and worn as its owner. 'No fire today?' she asked.

'At this time of year? I'm not so old and soft that I need a fire before October, and not always then.'

Was that true or was he simply no longer able to afford coal? Alice and her father weren't lighting fires in The Linnets at this time of year either, but they weren't as old as Jonah. Some of Churchwood's more elderly residents needed fires to keep them warm on all but the hottest days.

'Sit yourself down,' Jonah invited, then stepped into the connecting kitchen, returning shortly after with a tray on which stood two cups of tea and a plate holding two biscuits.

The same biscuits he'd taken from the bookshop? They certainly looked the same.

'Tuck in,' he suggested.

'Thanks, but I'll be having an early lunch. I'm due at the hospital this afternoon.'

Jonah nodded. He didn't take a biscuit either. Was he saving them for later because he needed them to bulk out his meagre meals?

'Did you read about Mr Churchill's latest statement to Parliament in the paper?' Alice asked.

'I don't take a paper any more. They're all doom and gloom these days.'

Again, Alice wondered if this was a decision forced on him by financial necessity. A few pennies saved on newspapers each week might make it possible to buy a loaf of bread or a tin of soup. It would be tactless to ask him directly if he was struggling, though. Working up to it gradually, she said, 'Apparently, Britain has sent fighter planes to help the Russians. The more fronts Germany has to fight on, the better, I believe. Bert showed me the puppet you're making in the woodworking sessions, by the way. It's wonderful.'

'Don't know about wonderful, but I'm pretty pleased on account of I'd never turned my hand to woodwork before Bert started teaching us. It's handy, being able to make stuff. To mend stuff, too, and give things a new lease of life. They should teach that sort of thing in schools. Equip people for the world better, that would. Help them to get by when money is tight.'

It was the perfect opening for what Alice had come here to say. 'You're absolutely right, Jonah. We can all learn how to make and mend things, from socks to kitchen cupboards. And we're lucky in Churchwood as we all want to help each other. I hope you'll ask for help if you need it, Jonah, whether it's help with meals or money for coal.'

'Me? I don't need help.'

'There's nothing to be ashamed of if you do. We shouldn't let pride get in the way of friends and neighbours lending a hand.'

He stared at her, frowning. 'Is that why you're here? Because you think I'm struggling?'

'I just want to be sure you're coping, because if you're not, there's no need to suffer in silence.'

'Suffer in silence?' Jonah's voice had risen in outrage. 'I'll have you know I'm coping just fine. Always have and always will. I've got my pension coming in and, while that doesn't amount to much, I've saved a little nest egg too. Suffer in silence indeed!'

'I didn't mean to offend you, Jonah.'

'Perhaps you didn't *mean* to.'

But she'd offended him all the same.

He shook his head as though puzzled. 'What brought this on, anyway? This visit, I mean?'

'I'm just concerned for people's welfare. I want to be sure that everyone is managing through these difficult times and not being driven to . . . to . . .'

'What?' he demanded when she broke off, fearing she was only making matters worse.

She saw the exact moment he understood. 'Driven to desperate measures. Is that what you mean? Like stealing milk off folks' doorsteps.'

'I'm not accusing you, Jonah.'

'You just suspect me.' Clearly, that was bad enough. 'I'll have you know I've never stolen a thing in my life. Apart from the time I took a marble from Jimmy Metcalf when I was a lad, and that was only to even the score because he'd taken one of mine.'

'Jonah, I'm sorry.'

'Humph.' He picked up his cup but half turned away from her, a movement that Alice guessed was a hint that she should leave, even if she'd barely touched her tea.

'I've blundered badly, and I apologize,' she said, getting up. 'I hope you'll forgive me.'

Jonah didn't answer, so Alice simply left.

Oh dear. She walked home, berating herself for upsetting two people in the space of half an hour. It wasn't like her. Alice prided herself on being the sort of person who was a calming influence rather than a stirrer of tempers and troubles.

Had she alienated Evelyn and Jonah permanently instead of bringing them into Churchwood's neighbourly fold? She fervently hoped not.

Another thought struck her: she was no closer to identifying – and helping – the thief, so she'd upset Jonah for nothing.

Alice wasn't feeling quite crushed, though. Nothing

56

could crush her while the signs continued to point to the strong possibility that she was carrying Daniel's baby.

The prospect buoyed her up against gloom all evening and into the following days, each one adding to the likelihood of her pregnancy. Walking into the village on Monday morning, she braced herself to greet Evelyn and Jonah with quiet good manners if she happened to see them. But as she approached the shops, she realized someone was shouting up ahead of her. *What on earth . . .?*

CHAPTER SEVEN

Naomi

'I've seen him!' Marjorie yelled, dashing across the road to where Naomi stood talking to a few of Churchwood's other women.

'Seen who?'

'The thief! He was in my garden last night. Or should I say this morning? After midnight, anyway.'

'What were you doing up at that time?'

'What was I . . . ?' Marjorie blushed.

'Using the chamber pot,' Mrs Hutchings whispered, knowingly. 'You can't last through the night at her age. It's even worse when you get to my age.'

Marjorie's blush deepened. 'After I'd gone about my . . . business, I looked out of my bedroom window – just to be sure no one was lurking outside – and there he was!'

'What was he like?' Mrs Hayes asked, and Naomi realized the commotion had drawn customers from all of the shops along the row. Alice had joined them too.

'Big. Huge,' Marjorie said, clearly delighting in being the messenger of shocking news.

'Six feet tall?' Mrs Hayes prompted.

'Bigger. A monster with the broadest shoulders you can imagine. So strong-looking!'

Naomi glanced towards Alice and saw that she appeared to be equally sceptical.

'What about his face?' Naomi asked.

Marjorie hesitated. 'He had a beard, I think. A black beard.'

'You only *think* he had a beard?' Edna Hall said, exchanging looks with Mrs Hayes and Mrs Hutchings. They were those *here we go again* kinds of looks that people often exchanged when Marjorie was having a flight of fancy.

'Did you actually see his face?' Mrs Johnson questioned.

'Perhaps I didn't see it clearly,' Marjorie admitted.

'Are you even sure you saw a man?'

'Rather than a bush or a tree?' Mrs Hutchings added.

'Or even a shadow,' Mrs Hayes contributed. 'It was very dark last night, after all.'

'Of course I saw a man!' Marjorie had turned puce and a look of desperation had entered her eyes.

'It's nothing more than one of Marjorie's stories,' someone muttered.

'Typical,' said someone else.

'Really, I saw a man!' Marjorie cried, but her audience was already shuffling away.

Mrs Hutchings had turned to the butcher, who'd come out from his shop to see what the commotion was all about. 'No beef today, I suppose?' she said. 'I'll take a lamb's heart instead, then. Not my Albert's favourite, but I'll roast it with onions and that'll help disguise the taste.'

'I did see a man,' Marjorie called to their departing backs, but no one was listening apart from Alice and Naomi.

Then Alice walked away too, patting both Naomi and Marjorie on their arms. Naomi heaved a sigh, knowing that it was going to fall to her to pacify her upset friend.

'You believe me, don't you?' Marjorie appealed.

'I don't doubt that you believe you saw a man,' Naomi

conceded, knowing that Marjorie was far from being a clever woman and often saw things she wanted to see. It was one of the things that made her tiresome, but she was fiercely loyal to Naomi.

'I don't know why no one else believed me. It isn't as though I'm prone to exaggeration, is it?'

Her lack of self-awareness never failed to stun Naomi, but at heart Marjorie was a decent person who simply needed to find ways of being noticed.

'Come back to Foxfield for a cup of tea,' Naomi invited, knowing it was the best way to cheer Marjorie up, though hoping to send her on her way again before too long.

'You're such a wonderful friend!' Marjorie said, with the sort of pitiful gratitude that stirred Naomi's conscience over all the times she'd felt irritated with the woman.

Abandoning her shopping expedition, Naomi gestured for Marjorie to lead the way. After a couple of half-hearted observations about the autumnal weather, Naomi was glad to let quietness fall between them, though her thoughts were sober. Marjorie's family had once lived in luxury, with a country house, horses in the paddocks, and paintings, fine china and silverware indoors . . . But those days were long gone, eaten up by death duties, the stock market crash of the 1920s and perhaps financial mismanagement, too. Now Marjorie lived in a small, terraced house, eking out an existence on a tiny income – all that remained of her family's glory days – and always glad to be saved the cost of a meal by coming to Naomi's.

Would Naomi be reduced to living like Marjorie after the divorce? Would she too be counting the pennies and be scared to put coal on the fire? It was a ridiculous thought for someone who'd been left fifty thousand pounds by her father, but Cedric Tuggs hadn't reckoned on her marrying a man who'd fleece her. Naomi couldn't wait to hear from the Great Man, and to start working towards some certainty for the future.

'Tea, madam?' Suki asked, taking their coats when they arrived at the house.

'Yes, please. Perhaps a biscuit or two as well, if we have any.'

'I'm sure we do, madam.'

Suki left to set a tray and Naomi invited Marjorie to settle in the small sitting room. Alexander had rarely even stepped in here. The study had been his territory and this comfortable room had been hers.

It wasn't hard to tune out Marjorie's prattle, and Naomi's heart beat faster when she noticed the post-man walking up the drive to make the second delivery of the day. It was past noon according to the clock on the mantelpiece, but Marjorie showed no sign of leaving. Suki brought the post in, and Naomi saw a letter she assumed to be from Sir Ambrose, given that the envelope was the same luxurious cream as before and postmarked from London.

'I won't think you rude if you want to open your post,' Marjorie said, with what she doubtless thought was graciousness.

'It can wait,' Naomi said, vexed because she couldn't open such a sensitive letter in front of the worst gossip in Churchwood.

Another fifteen minutes passed. Fifteen became thirty and then forty-five. Suki returned, wanting instructions about lunch. Marjorie looked so hopeful that Naomi's resolve against inviting her to stay weakened.

'Will Cook be able to stretch the lunch to two?' Naomi asked, and from the corner of her eye she saw Marjorie perk up in pleasure. How easy it was to be kind. But how difficult, too, when the Great Man's letter sat unopened by Naomi's side.

'It's soup and salad so I'm sure she can,' Suki reported.

Probably Cook had assumed Marjorie would wangle an invitation and had prepared lunch accordingly.

'Well, it's been lovely of you to give me your company,' Naomi said, when, meal over, they'd dabbed their mouths with starched white napkins. 'I won't take up any more of your time.'

'I've no need to rush off,' Marjorie answered, oblivious to hints as always.

'I'm afraid I've an afternoon of administrative tasks ahead of me and I wouldn't like to bore you.'

'But I could—'

Naomi rang the bell for Suki before Marjorie could offer to help.

'Miss Plym's coat?' Suki guessed, no fool despite her tender years.

'Yes, please, Suki.'

'I'll fetch it right this minute.'

Between the efforts of both Suki and Naomi, Marjorie was soon ushered off the premises.

'Thank you,' Naomi told her maid with heartfelt sincerity.

Returning to the sitting room, she tore open the letter from the Great Man, though doubtless such fine stationery deserved a silver letter-opener rather than a thumb.

Dear Mrs Harrington,

It was a pleasure to meet with you, though, naturally, I regret the circumstances that brought you to Lincoln's Inn Fields.

I can inform you that Mr Harrington now has legal representation, having instructed Messrs Macauley Grey to act on his behalf. I am sure it will come as a relief to you to know that he will not contest the divorce.

Contest it? When he had two children as evidence of his infidelity? Of course he couldn't contest the divorce. But he'd show his teeth in fighting for his money.

Mr Harrington wishes the divorce to proceed as smoothly and discreetly as possible.

Of course he did. Divorce might be more common these days, but he might still have clients who frowned upon it.

I have agreed with Messrs Macauley Grey that we will exchange statements of our clients' financial positions as a first step towards what we all hope will be an amicable – or at least a trouble-free – settlement. I already have a note of the chief assets of the marriage – Foxfield, the London flat and the Daimler – but should be grateful for information about other assets, such as jewellery, paintings, furniture and money held in private bank accounts. I look forward to receiving it. Should you have any questions in the meantime, please do not hesitate to get in touch.
Yours sincerely . . .

So the ball was rolling towards divorce officially now. Naomi would start on her statement of assets without delay, and it would be an honest statement, though she feared the same could not be said for whatever Alexander would produce.

CHAPTER EIGHT

Kate

On the day they were to visit Fred, Kate and Kenny were up even earlier than usual so they could put in an hour or so of work on the farm. Afterwards they ate a quick breakfast, and Kate packed a bag with food and water for their journey.

'We need money for our fares,' Kenny said, approaching Ernie with his hand held out.

'What do you call your wages?' Ernie snarled.

'I call them *our* money. We're going to London on family business.'

Ernie cursed under his breath but gestured Kenny towards the cash box. Kenny brought it over, and Ernie counted out some coins.

'More,' Kenny insisted, and, begrudgingly, Ernie added a ten-shilling note.

'I want the change,' he grumbled.

Kate was in no doubt that Ernie wanted to know about Fred. It was just that the old skinflint wanted the visit to cost as little as possible.

They headed into the village to catch the bus to St Albans, and from there they caught the train to London. Kenny fidgeted the entire journey, shuffling his feet, rubbing his jaw and sighing. He was worried about Fred, of course, and also ill at ease about the prospect of entering the unfamiliar territory of a hospital full of sick people and starchy nurses.

Kenny could drive a hard bargain when it came to sales and supplies. He was also confident and assured with other farmers. But away from that environment he was all at sea – tongue-tied, uncertain and barely able to speak above an awkward grunt. Having grown used to mixing with all sorts of people in the village, Kate thought she stood a better chance of getting the information they needed to understand Fred's prognosis. It made her glad she was there.

'Have you been to London before?' she asked as they got off the train and made their way through the station.

She considered it highly unlikely, as surely she'd have heard about an earlier visit. 'Never,' he confirmed, looking disconcerted by the noise and bustle that surrounded them.

Whistles blew and steam billowed from train engines. Newsvendors called out, 'War latest!' and a porter yelled at two young boys who were fighting. Meanwhile, people raced this way and that way in a jumble of humanity. ''Scuse me,' one soldier said as he pushed past them, his kit bag sending Kenny into a spin.

'This is hell on earth,' Kenny muttered.

Kate had often longed to come to London, but she'd pictured a different side of the city from this. Her imagination had been full of beautiful buildings like Buckingham Palace and St Paul's Cathedral; of carefully tended parks laid out with flowers; of theatres and picture houses; of shops selling soaps, fragrances and exquisite dresses; of tall, elegant houses like the white-painted one Alice had described as her home before she came to Churchwood.

Leo had once spoken of bringing Kate to London.

'We could see the sights from the upper deck of a bus,' he'd said, 'and stroll arm in arm along the avenues of St James's Park and Kensington Gardens. We could take in a show, too, and I could buy you chocolates in a pretty box tied up with ribbons – if you still had room for chocolates after we'd dined at the Savoy or the Ritz.'

It had sounded wonderful, but May had spoken of the city in less romantic terms. 'It's dirty and smoky, and in places the river smells terrible, particularly in the East End where I come from.'

'But you miss it?' Kate had asked.

'Dirt, smoke, smell . . . They never bothered me because I love London.'

'You'll go back one day,' Kate said. 'When the war is finally over.'

'Perhaps. I hated Churchwood when I first moved here. It seemed so dull! But now I love village life too.'

Alice had been kindness itself in providing a map and directions to the hospital. 'We need to go on the underground railway,' Kate told Kenny now.

'Underground?' The idea clearly troubled him, used as he was to wide fields and open skies.

'It shouldn't take long.' She looked around for a sign. 'Come on. It's this way.'

Kenny shuddered as they headed down the steps into the station. 'You'd be glad of the Underground if you were caught in an air raid,' Kate said, having read about large numbers of people taking shelter in stations.

Kenny made no answer, but his head retreated into his shoulders and his eyes moved from side to side with obvious unease. 'Do you want to carry your own gas mask?' she asked, wondering if it might make him feel more secure. She'd brought both masks just in case of an

66

attack, though she'd never seen Kenny, Vinnie or Ernie even try their masks to check how they fitted.

He shook his head, no.

They hadn't long to wait for a train. Kenny cringed as it rattled into the station and passengers surged forward to be first to reach the seats. Kate was happy to stand, and Kenny stood beside her, swaying as the train made its way through curving tunnels.

It was a relief to both of them to get outdoors again.

The hospital was on the east side of London, a Victorian building with higgledy-piggledy additions here and there. Inside they found white-tiled walls and the smell of anti-septic. 'We're here to see Frederick Fletcher,' Kate told a portly man who was on duty behind a desk. 'Private Frederick Fletcher.'

A telephone call was made – to whom, Kate didn't learn – but it ended with the man saying, 'I'll do that.'

'Second floor,' he told Kate. 'E wing. Stairs that way. Lift over there.'

'Stairs,' Kenny said fervently, clearly having had enough of small, cramped places.

Two flights of stairs were no problem for young farm-workers. A nurse was waiting for them in the corridor and led them into what appeared to be a waiting room. 'Can we see our brother?' Kate asked.

'Soon. Best to speak to the doctor first.'

She left them to wait and they both sat down, but it wasn't long before Kenny was up and pacing. 'Where's that water?' he asked, and Kate passed him the bottle she'd brought.

He was drinking when the door opened and a white-coated doctor entered. Whipping the bottle from his lips, Kenny spluttered and coughed, then put the lid back on the bottle and thrust it towards Kate, who returned it to her bag.

'I'm Dr Mitchelmore.' He was young but looked weary. No wonder. Helping men who were injured in wartime must drain a person. 'You're Private Fletcher's siblings?'

'Eh?' Kenny said.

'His brother and sister,' Kate confirmed.

The doctor gestured them to sit then sat down opposite them. 'The good news is that Private Fletcher's life isn't in danger. Not as things stand at present.'

'We heard something about his legs,' Kate said.

'I'm afraid he lost one above the knee and the other below the knee.'

Oh no. Kate swallowed hard to keep a rush of emotions contained.

'He's a farmer,' Kenny said, as though it wasn't possible for farmers to lose their legs.

'Heavy physical work may be beyond your brother's capabilities in future,' the doctor explained. 'Though perhaps he might work on a farm in an administrative capacity. Correspondence, accounts . . . that sort of thing.'

Kenny stared at him incredulously. Brimbles Farm didn't need an administrator. Paperwork and accounts got done – badly – around the serious work.

Kate put a hand on Kenny's arm to stop him from exploding. 'Will he be able to have artificial legs?' she asked the doctor.

'Hopefully, in time. It depends how well he heals, amongst other factors. But a wheelchair will help him to get about – once he starts to put his mind to it. He's a strong young man. Good upper-body muscle for moving himself along, though, so far, he's resisting the very idea of a wheelchair.'

Fred in a wheelchair. The thought of it was bleak. Fred 'n' Frank had been full of energy all their lives – running, climbing, play-wrestling and tramping for miles with ease. But that was in the past. Kate had to deal with the present. 'Do you know what's behind Fred's resistance?'

'I'm afraid your brother hasn't taken his injuries very well.'

Kenny looked even more incredulous at that reply. As if any man would take well to losing his legs!

'Injuries of this nature are hard to accept,' the doctor acknowledged. 'Coming to terms with them can take a while. But Private Fletcher seems . . . exceptionally bitter.'

Happy-go-lucky Fred? How he must be suffering.

'I hope you'll be able to help him to understand that, while his life may be different from what he expected, it can still be fulfilling and useful.'

'May we see him?' Kate asked.

'Certainly.'

He got up and Kate and Kenny did the same. Kenny rubbed his palms down the front of his trousers and ran his tongue around his lips. Kate settled for taking a deep breath and blowing it out slowly. Poor Fred. Would she and Kenny be able to help?

The doctor led them into a ward, a long room with beds on both sides. Fred was halfway down on the window side. 'You have visitors, Private Fletcher,' the doctor said, then left Kate and Kenny with the sort of rueful glance that wished them luck while fearing there wasn't enough luck in the world to help them make progress with this patient.

A nurse appeared. 'Chairs are over there, if you'd like to sit,' she told them, pointing.

Neither Kate nor Kenny moved. They were watching

Fred, who was scowling at them. He looked pale and thin as well as full of scorn. 'Took your time getting here, didn't you?' he said. 'Too busy having fun, were you?'

'We were advised to let you settle in before we came,' Kate explained.

Fred only sneered, as though she was making excuses, then said, 'I suppose you've only come at all because you want to gloat.'

'Gloat?' Kenny looked mystified.

'Well, you told me I was a fool to join up, didn't you?' Fred said. 'You told me I could be hurt. Aren't you glad you were right, you smug—'

'Fred!' Kate protested.

'What?' he demanded. 'You don't like my tone of voice? If you've only come to feel good about yourselves by dispensing tea and sympathy to a cripple, you can go home now. I don't want you here.'

'We just want to see how you are,' Kate said.

'How am I?' Fred laughed but it was a bark of bitterness. 'I'm all washed up, that's how I am. A crippled wreck. And just in case you're thinking of it, don't say that at least I'm alive. I'd rather be dead than . . . than . . . this!' He gestured down the bed towards what remained of his legs, his lips curling in disgust.

'You think that way now but you'll think differently eventually. You need time to adjust,' Kate told him.

'You'd know that, would you? Funny, I don't see anything wrong with your legs.' He turned away as though the conversation was over.

Kenny looked as though he didn't know what to do. Kate didn't know what to do either, but she had to try to help Fred somehow. She nodded towards the chairs and Kenny went to fetch some, obviously relieved to have something to do. He brought two chairs over and they sat down, Kenny looking to Kate to take the lead.

'Why are you still here?' Fred asked, without turning around.

'We're here because we care,' Kate said.

'Or because you feel guilty since you're still whole while I'm . . . broken.'

Kate decided not to rise to that. 'Does Frank know about your injuries yet?' she asked instead.

'Frank!' Fred made it sound as though the only thing Frank deserved was contempt, which was strange. The twins had fought all their lives, but rivalry had simply been a game they played. A lark. It was never serious and soon forgotten.

'He'll be worried and he'll want to help,' Kate said. 'He's your twin.'

'Not any more.'

Kate was confused. She glanced at Kenny, who pulled a face to show he didn't understand either. 'Have you fallen out with Frank?' she asked Fred.

'I didn't need to fall out with him for things to change.'

'You'll have to explain.'

Fred turned to her, his expression sour. 'We used to be the same. Now we're not. We used to be . . .' He gave up trying to express his feelings. 'You're the one who reads books. You should have a better way with words than me.'

Kate worked it out. 'You mean you're no longer equals?'

He shrugged, but yes, that was what he meant. Fred was now the lesser twin. The old closeness was no more.

'I don't think Frank will feel that way,' Kate said.

'It doesn't matter what he thinks. It won't change the way things are.'

71

'I wish you'd give it more time before you let your feelings settle into bitterness,' Kate said.

'You wish it, do you? *I* have a lot of wishes that'll never come true either. I wish I'd never joined up. I wish I had two legs. I wish I was dead.'

'Please, Fred. Be patient.'

'Patient?' Anger fizzed in him like electric sparks. He struggled to sit up only to fail and slump back against the pillows. 'Patience won't bring my legs back. My life is over. Why can't you understand that?'

'It isn't over. It's just different,' Kate insisted.

'You're wrong. How can I be a farmer again, like this? It's not as though I'm fit for anything else. I haven't the brains for book learning. A labouring sort of man, that's me. At least I used to be. Now I'm just a sad idiot in a wheelchair, fit for nothing.'

'But—'

'Just go. Both of you. You shouldn't have come.'

Kate waited for Fred to calm down a little then said, 'We brought you some things.'

She unpacked a bag on to his bed. 'Cigarettes, soap, a slice of home-made apple pie, some sweets . . .'

He picked up the small paper bag of pear drops only to toss it aside. 'Is that the best you could do? A handful only?' He made it sound as though Kate was as big a skinflint as Ernie.

'Sweets may not be rationed yet, but they're hard to get hold of these days,' Kate explained. 'The grocer hadn't had any in the shop for months until these pear drops came in. He was keeping them for children but let me have some especially for you. I wasn't allowed more than two ounces, though. No one was.'

'Just go,' Fred repeated.

'All right,' Kate finally agreed. 'But we'll come back another day. And I hope we'll be able to convince you then that your life is still worth living.'

'Go! I'm tired.' He shifted position and winced.

'Are you in pain?' Kate asked.

'Of course I'm in pain!'

'I'll send a nurse over. Goodbye, Fred. We're not giving up on you.'

He'd turned away again.

Kate wanted to reach down and kiss his cheek but there was nothing wrong with Fred's arms and she guessed they'd push her away. Deciding that the best thing she could do for him just now was to get help for his pain, she beckoned Kenny to come away, and, as he returned their chairs to a stack in a corner, she went in search of a nurse.

'Private Fletcher was difficult, was he?' the nurse guessed, looking sympathetic. 'Injury takes some men like that. Most come to terms with it eventually.'

Most. But not all. Would Fred be one of those who let bitterness swamp the rest of his life? Kate could only hope not.

Kenny was silent as they made their way outside. Then he shook his head in shocked bewilderment. 'He isn't Fred any more.'

'Yes, he is. Underneath it all.' They just had to find him.

They journeyed home again, eating the picnic Kate had packed, though she imagined Kenny was tasting it as little as she was.

Ernie said nothing when Kenny explained Fred's injuries and how badly he'd taken them. But Ernie's mood was foul all evening, and everyone crept around him. Kate wondered if she should suggest that Ernie visit Fred, but she suspected it would only end with them both shouting on the hospital ward.

'I'd like to visit Fred again in a week or so,' she said instead, and for once received only a grudging nod instead of a complaint. It showed that, for all his inadequacies as a father, Ernie did care.

CHAPTER NINE

Alice

'I can't thank you enough for all the help you've given me,' Mr Parkinson told Alice as they fastened up the last box of papers and photographs that had formed the raw material for his family memoir.

It had been Alice's job to put them all in order and list them, so Mr Parkinson could see the resources that were available and access them easily. It had also been her job to copy out his scrawling handwriting into more legible versions so they could be typed out by a secretarial agency before going to print. It *should* have been her job to manage the typing herself, but Mr Parkinson had kindly decided that the other skills Alice had to offer outweighed the limitations of her injured hand.

Actually improving the words he'd used shouldn't have been her job, but gradually he'd left more and more of it to her. 'You'll know the best way of explaining this information, my dear,' he'd often said, along with, 'You have a better way with words than I, so if you wouldn't mind . . .'

Alice hadn't minded at all. She'd enjoyed it, in fact.

'You should be proud of what you've achieved,' she told him now. 'Your memoir will be a family heirloom, passed down from generation to generation.'

'I'll be content if it's simply of *some* interest. It wouldn't have been completed so quickly – in fact, it might not have been completed at all – without your assistance, Alice. I was all of a muddle until you came.'

'It was a pleasure.' Alice had found satisfaction in bringing order to chaos.

Unfortunately, it meant that she'd worked her way out of a job, as Mr Parkinson no longer needed her services. 'I hope my next job will be as interesting, though perhaps that's too much to hope for,' she said.

'Your next job?' Mr Parkinson looked surprised. 'I thought with you being married now . . .'

'I like to work,' Alice told him. She wanted the satisfaction. She also wanted Daniel to feel proud of her achievements. And she wanted a wage to save for their future. But would she ever find another employer who could see beyond her disability to her other skills?

'Admirable, my dear. I'll keep an ear open for any opportunities.'

'That would be wonderful. Thank you.'

'I can't promise to hear of anything, of course.'

'I understand.' Even so, Alice pinned some of her hopes on him being able to help.

There were plenty of jobs around with so many men away in the services. There was in fact talk of making some sort of war work compulsory for single women. But those jobs were for women with two fully functioning hands, whether for assembling aircraft parts or typing letters. Alice had struggled to find work before Mr Parkinson took her on and she feared she might struggle again. Only yesterday she'd received a rejection from a hat-making factory in Hatfield because typing was considered an essential part of their office work.

'A reference might be helpful,' she said, hoping it would prove that she could be useful despite her injury.

'I'll be delighted to provide one, and a glowing reference it shall be.'

Hubert Parkinson was a kind man. Alice was going to miss seeing him regularly, though he'd formed a friendship with her father so they wouldn't lose touch completely.

'You'll come to celebrate the memoir when it returns from the printer?' he asked. 'Your father too?'

'We'd love to come. In fact, we can't wait to see the finished version.'

'You're very sweet, my dear.'

There was nothing more to be done except to say goodbye. Mr Parkinson offered a hand, which Alice took, but then he folded her into his arms. 'Your father is a lucky man having you as a daughter, Alice.' Mr Parkinson had never married.

'I'm lucky having him as a father. And I've been lucky in having the opportunity to work with you.'

'The pleasure has been mostly mine, I'm sure. Do call in whenever you're in St Albans.'

'I will. And you must come to Churchwood. You know my father will be pleased to see you.' Alice realized tears had come into her eyes. She'd developed real affection for this polite and gallant gentleman. She blinked them away, smiled and finally left the house to catch the bus back to Churchwood.

Once there, she got off the bus to the sound of her name being called. Jonah Kerrigan was hastening towards her. Had his anger festered even more?

'I'm glad I caught you,' he said, wheezing from the effort he'd put into catching her up.

'What can I do for you, Jonah?'

'You can accept my apology, if you've a mind to,' he said, surprising her. 'I spoke out of turn the other day. I should have been grateful that you wanted to help instead of snapping at you.'

'I was insensitive,' Alice said, but he waved away the excuse for his behaviour.

'I let my pride get in the way of seeing a kindness. I'm sorry and I hope you won't think badly of me?'

'Of course I won't.'

'I'm not struggling with money, though I'm careful with it, and I'm not the one who's been taking milk from door-steps, but you're right to think there might be someone in our village who needs our help. I'll keep my eyes and ears open for clues as to who it might be, and I'll let you know if I've any ideas. Discreetly, like. We don't want someone else's pride firing up and getting in the way of things.'

'Thank you, Jonah.' She touched his arm to show she appreciated his change of heart and then walked on thinking that it had been one of those see-saw kind of days – the loss of her job had tipped her downwards, but making up with Jonah had tipped her up again. Not that she was riding high, exactly. She still had to find paid work and she still had to find answers.

Who was the thief? Why were they stealing? And did they need help?

CHAPTER TEN

Naomi

Children's laughter, bright with sparkle, made for a lovely sound as Naomi walked through the woods behind Foxfield towards the side entrance to Bert's market garden. She could have walked along Churchwood Way to the main entrance, but she'd got into the habit of approaching by this more private route and besides, the walk was beautiful, especially now autumn was turning the trees to a tapestry of gorgeous colours. Naomi was hoping to draw calmness from it.

'Catch me if you can!' a voice called, and more laughter followed, accompanied by the crashing sounds of small people racing through bushes.

Two boys burst on to the path in front of her and came to an abrupt halt before edging backwards, looking worried. 'It's all right,' Naomi told them. 'Alan and Roger Gregson, isn't it? I'm Naomi. I live—'

'Boys!' Evelyn followed them on to the path, her expression fierce. 'I'm sorry if they disturbed you, Mrs Harrington,' she said as the boys ran to her. 'We'll leave you in peace now.'

'There's no need,' Naomi countered. 'It was nice to hear them—'

But she was talking to the air, as Evelyn and her boys had already walked off at speed. Naomi pitied those boys.

It was good that they had each other, but surely they'd thrive better in other company too?

Naomi walked on, reflecting that her encounter with Evelyn had at least been less bruising than the one poor Alice had reported. Not that Alice would hold a grudge. She might be young, but she had none of the flouncing melodrama of some young women. She was wise and compassionate beyond her years.

Reaching the hedge that bordered the narrow lane between the woods and Bert's property, Naomi peered over, hoping to spot Bert at work. 'Come on in whenever you like,' he'd told her, but she wouldn't feel comfortable barging in on him.

Luckily, he was over by his house. Spotting her, he beckoned her to come through the gate in the hedge.

'Good timing,' he said as she reached him. 'I was about to put the kettle on.'

They went into the kitchen, a room Naomi loved because, despite its old and faded appearance, it always wrapped her in warmth and welcome. He shrugged away her offer of help – he'd been a widower for many years and was at ease fending for himself – so she sat in one of the armchairs beside the fire.

Bert's cat, Elizabeth, was lying on the rug. She raised her head and looked at Naomi sleepily as though to say, 'Isn't this just the cosiest place on earth?' before settling back contentedly. How uncomplicated Elizabeth's life seemed to be.

'Get this down you.' Bert placed a cup of tea beside Naomi.

He carried his own cup to the opposite armchair and sat down like a big bear lowering its hindquarters to a fallen log. 'News?' he asked.

Naomi told him about the Great Man's letter.

The mention of Alexander's name drew a sneer of contempt from Bert. 'Your statement of finances will be as honest as the day and his will be the opposite,' he predicted.

Naomi feared he was right. 'The trouble is that I've played right into his hands all these years by letting him control the finances and signing everything he put before me. You don't need to tell me that was idiotic, Bert. I know it.'

'I *could* call you an idiot,' he agreed, 'but I won't because I know you acted in a way you thought might help your marriage.'

'True, but I suspect that it only allowed Alexander to fleece me. Year after year after year.'

'Don't languish away feeling sorry for yourself, woman. The past is the past and it can't be changed. What matters now is the future. Is there any way of getting hold of any figures independently of that iceberg you married? Just so you know what to expect?'

'I could ask the trustee of my trust fund, though he must be very old now and Alexander might have run rings around him. I told him to take his instructions from Alexander, you see.'

'Is there any reason you can't tell this trustee that there's been a change of plan and he's to take his instructions from you from now on?'

'I can't think of one.'

'Then getting in touch with him sounds like a good first step.'

Bert was right. 'I'll feel better if I'm actually doing something rather than just waiting,' Naomi said.

'That's my girl.' Bert raised his glass to her and already

Naomi started to feel a little better. She was still worried, though. Desperately worried.

At home again, she telephoned the firm of solicitors where her trustee worked. 'Mr Carraway is mostly retired now,' she was told by someone she took to be a secretary. 'He isn't taking any new clients, I'm afraid, though we have other solicitors in the practice who—'

'I'm not a new client. My name is Naomi Harrington. My late father, Cedric Tuggs, set up a trust for me with Mr Carraway as the trustee.'

'I'm familiar with it. It's your husband who's been liaising with Mr Carraway, I believe.'

'Yes, but I'd like to see Mr Carraway personally, if I may?'

'Certainly. He doesn't come in often these days and he's unwell with a chill at present, but I can make an appointment for you.'

They fixed on a date a frustrating thirteen days hence.

'One more thing,' Naomi said. 'I'd like to instruct that no withdrawals or changes are made to the trust fund until I've met with Mr Carraway.'

'I'll make a note of it, Mrs Harrington.'

Should Naomi ask how much money remained in the trust? She hesitated but knew she'd regret it if she didn't ask. 'Are you able to tell me the present value of the fund?' she asked.

'I'm afraid I'm not privy to that sort of information.'

'Never mind. I'll look forward to seeing Mr Carraway soon.'

Sadly, it wouldn't be soon enough for her liking, but she had other tasks to occupy her in the meantime, not least her own financial statement.

All the records relating to the purchase of Foxfield and

the London flat had been kept in files in Alexander's study alongside more files of paperwork relating to the car and some of the better furniture. After she'd told Alexander to leave, she'd packed up his things and sent them to him, but she'd hung on to these files so he couldn't fudge the figures they contained. She was learning to look after herself at last but had the depressing feeling that anything she did now would be closing the proverbial stable door after the horse had already bolted. Naomi would simply have to salvage what she could.

CHAPTER ELEVEN

Kate

What's going on with our Fred? Frank had written. *All I've heard is that he was injured somehow. Write back with news as soon as you can. I'm going out of my mind with worry.*

Kate read the letter out over supper and looked from her father to Kenny and then, in desperation, even to Vinnie. 'What shall I tell him?' she asked, but none of the Fletcher men had any suggestions.

It was Kate who'd have to find words to explain to Frank that his brother – the twin brother with whom he'd shared a cradle, a bedroom and a life full of larks – had lost his legs. Frank was going to be devastated. Stuck out in North Africa with his regiment, he'd also be raging in frustration at being unable even to see his stricken twin.

'Maybe we should . . . you know. Hide the truth,' Kenny finally said, after Ruby had jolted him out of his silence via a kick to his ankle.

It was to Kenny's credit that he wanted to protect Frank, but Kate couldn't agree. 'If we don't tell him the truth, he'll think Fred's life is in danger. He'll find out the truth eventually anyway, and when he realizes we kept it from him deliberately, he'll stop trusting us. Besides, even if Frank can't do much from Africa, he might be able to get through to Fred in letters. They've always had a special bond, and if anyone can help Fred to come to terms with what's happened, it's Frank.'

Kenny shrugged helplessly. 'Maybe you're right.'

Kate noticed Ruby put a hand on his leg and squeeze it with approval. He gave her a smile, though it was a sickly ghost of one.

'Ernie?' Kate asked.

Their father shrugged too and reached for a cigarette. He was hopeless in situations like this.

'I'll write to Frank today,' Kate said. 'Any messages for him?'

'Tell him we've got a good crop of fruit this year,' Kenny said.

Ernie merely drew on his cigarette, but Kate noticed a slight tremble in his fingers.

The meal over, Kate dried the dishes as Ruby washed them and Pearl put them away, banging them into cupboards in a way that made Kate wince but managing not to break any. Afterwards, Kate sat back down to write to Frank, though she was dreading it.

I hope this finds you well, she wrote. She considered beginning with farm news before working her way gradually to Fred's situation but abandoned the idea, picturing Frank cursing with impatience as he raced through the letter for the information that really mattered.

The good news about Fred is that he's alive and his life isn't in danger. He's in hospital in London where he's receiving the best possible care for his injuries. Kenny and I went to see him and found him sitting up and talking. He can see, hear and talk just as always and has the full use of his arms.

Unfortunately, he's lost both of his legs, one above the knee and one below. In time, he'll be out and about in a wheelchair and after that he may be fitted with artificial legs. Many men who lose their legs cope well with these sorts of injuries.

Naturally, it's come as a blow to Fred and he's down in the dumps to say the least. Kenny and I didn't have much luck with cheering him up when we visited him, but it's early days yet and we're hoping to do better next time. You've always been close to Fred, so a letter from you might be just the tonic he needs. I'm including the hospital address below.

Do let us know if and how Fred replies. In the meantime, we'll keep you posted about our next visit to him.

I'll write a longer letter soon and try to get a parcel off to you. Ernie, Kenny and Vinnie send their love. Of course, they didn't use that word – Kenny said to tell you the fruit crop has been good this year – but you know what they're like, hiding their true feelings behind commonplaces. I'm not afraid to admit to my feelings so I'll say here that I love you, Frank.

Look after yourself,

Kate x

She read it through but could think of no way of improving it.

A glance out of the window showed that night was falling but she still decided to cycle into the village to post the letter so it could be collected early in the morning. The sooner Frank received it, the sooner he might write a helpful letter to Fred. Not that letter-writing came naturally to him, but Fred's plight would move him to put heart and soul into helping his twin – or so Kate hoped.

Careful to let the minimum light escape due to the blackout, she slipped outside, fetched her bike from the barn and set off for the village. The sky was clear, and stars were appearing like pinpricks of silver on a background of inky velvet. Kate was unafraid of darkness and was familiar enough with Brimbles Lane to know where the worst potholes, rocks and tree roots presented hazards.

All was quiet in the village. The residents were tucked behind curtains and no footfall disturbed the peace. Only the swish of the bicycle tyres made a sound, though doubtless there'd be more noises later as owls, foxes and badgers ventured into the night.

She posted the letter then cycled back the way she'd come, only to stop off at The Linnets, where Alice lived.

Welcomed in as always, Kate sat in Alice's cosy kitchen and told her about the letter she'd written to Frank. 'I only hope he can do some good.'

'Be patient, Kate. Fred's injuries are life-changing. Adjusting to them will take time, especially for a man who was always so active.'

'It isn't his physical injuries that bother me,' Kate began, then corrected herself. 'No, that's nonsense. Of course they bother me. A lot. But I'm more worried about his state of mind.'

It occurred to Kate that she wasn't being fair to Alice. 'Sorry. I shouldn't be talking to you about Fred's injuries.'

'Because they'll remind me of what might happen to Daniel?' Alice asked. 'Kate, I visit the hospital several times a week and see men who are disabled, disfigured and damaged in all sorts of ways. I'm already aware of what might happen.'

Yet Alice visited the patients because she wanted to help them. She was brave.

Kate wasn't used to witnessing that level of suffering. Some of the hospital patients came to bookshop socials, but they were the fitter servicemen who were on the mend.

'You're new to it and the person suffering is your brother,' Alice said. 'Seeing a beloved family member in such torment must be terrible. It must make the danger to Leo seem closer, too. Being in love with a serviceman in wartime . . . It's a form of torture, isn't it?'

It certainly was.

'Fred needs time to adjust and so do you,' Alice continued. 'As for Leo – Daniel, too – we can only keep hoping they come through this awful war unscathed.'

Alice was right. No matter how churned up inside they might be feeling, they had to find a way to cope. Fred needed Kate to be strong, and so did Leo.

CHAPTER TWELVE

Alice

It felt strange no longer to be getting up early to catch the bus to Mr Parkinson's house. Being unemployed meant Alice had more free time, of course, and that time was going to be easy to fill. The bookshop . . . Hospital visits . . . She needed to look through the old nativity play costumes, too, to assess what new costumes they'd need and whether they could get their hands on sufficient fabric for them.

Then there was her vegetable patch, her chickens and general housekeeping. Alice still craved more, though – mental stimulation and a wage that she suspected would be much needed in the future.

She was thinking about her job hunting as she walked along Brimbles Lane to the hospital. She'd seen no suitable jobs advertised in the newspapers yet. It was early days, but if nothing came her way soon, perhaps she'd return to St Albans simply to knock on the doors of businesses there and try to persuade them that she had something to offer, even with an injured hand.

A loud crack like a rifle being fired sounded suddenly in the wood to Alice's right that ran from behind The Linnets to Stratton House. There were woods on the other side, too, now she was past Brimbles Farm. Startled, she stopped in her tracks and scanned the trees and bushes, seeing no one but aware that someone could still be hidden amongst them, watching her. The thought sent a ripple of cold tension along her spine.

Then a squirrel leaped from one tree to another. A bird took flight, causing a branch to dip and bounce, loosening the tenuous grip of several bronze-coloured leaves, which fluttered to the pulpy ground. And then a small creature – possibly a rabbit – stirred the grass near a hornbeam tree. Was that what she'd heard? A squirrel? A bird? A rabbit? Or perhaps something larger, such as a deer? Just nature going about its daily business? The crack had certainly been loud, but perhaps Alice was simply jumpy from the knowledge that there was a thief at work in the village. She might not have been thinking about the thief at that precise moment, but maybe her nerves had simply been lying in wait.

She walked on, more briskly now, her senses on full alert.

There it came again. A loud crack like rifle fire. She whirled around to face the trees again. Surely, the sound had been caused by a heavier footfall than the wood's small creatures possessed, even deer? Once again, Alice looked hard, but she saw nothing suspicious.

Somewhere in the woods a crow cawed, a call that was usually merely mournful but sounded sinister today. Quickening her pace, she continued walking, reminding herself that, even if the thief were watching her, he might be doing so only to be sure that she hadn't seen him. Stealing milk from doorsteps was a long way from attacking a person, and those little posies of greenery suggested that whoever it was wanted to make up for his theft, if only in a small way.

Or did they? She was only assuming that the posies were well intended. What if they meant something very different? Mockery, perhaps, or even calling cards to signal, 'I'll be coming to get you'?

Prickles of unease wrapped themselves around her, but Alice fought them off. Where was her usual level-headedness? She still arrived at Stratton House feeling hugely relieved to be in a place of safety.

Throwing herself into the business of her visit, she pushed the scare from her mind, glad to be distracted by her nursing friend Babs Carter, who presented her with a parcel. 'Books from my cousin,' she said, looking pleased. 'They're old but still good reads for the chaps in here, I should think.'

Alice opened the parcel and took out John Buchan's *The Thirty-Nine Steps*, which was an exciting story set just before the 1914 war, together with Edgar Rice Burroughs's *The Return of Tarzan* and Hugh Lofting's *The Story of Doctor Dolittle*. 'These are wonderful,' she said.

Babs grinned. 'He offered to send *Lady Chatterley's Lover*, but I thought Matron would have a fit.'

Alice smiled back. 'I imagine some of the men would have liked it, but yes, Matron would have had a fit.'

'Good morning, Alice.'

The girls jumped as Matron emerged from a side room. Had she heard them talking? She gave no sign of it, but Matron could be subtle.

'You're looking well, Alice,' Matron said.

Was that a reference to her blush or was Alice being fanciful? 'I'm feeling well, thank you.' It was true. If Alice was pregnant – and every passing day deepened the suspicion that she was indeed carrying Daniel's child – then she was having an easy time of it.

Matron nodded then turned to Babs. 'Are you in need of occupation, Nurse Carter?'

91

'No, Matron. I'm just . . .' Babs's words trailed off as she went on her way.

Matron sent Alice one of her inscrutable smiles then she too went on her way.

Alice added the three new titles to her records and wasted no time in lending them out to patients who were delighted to receive them. Two patients wanted help with writing letters to their families and afterwards Alice read out loud a story about a man suspected of being the thief of a gold bracelet until it was discovered that a jackdaw had taken the jewellery along with a gold button and a silver sixpence.

It was an entertaining story but perhaps not the best one to read today, as the thief it featured turned Alice's thoughts back to the person who might − or might not − have been spying on her from the trees, the person who might − or might not − be the Churchwood thief. The prospect of her isolated walk home began to nudge at her nerves. And when she stood on the hospital steps ready to set out, she had to straighten her shoulders and breathe deeply to get a grip on herself.

Had she ever walked home so fast? Probably not, but she reached The Linnets safely, chiding herself for allowing fear to drive away her common sense. If she wasn't careful, Alice would turn into another Marjorie Plym. The thought made her smile. There, that was better!

Even so, she knew she was going to feel nervous walking to and from the hospital until the Churchwood thief was caught or moved on elsewhere.

CHAPTER THIRTEEN

Naomi

'Have you heard about Joe Simpson?' Marjorie asked, as Naomi walked into the post office.

'What about him?'

Marjorie looked thrilled to have news to share. 'He's moved to Barton so his sister can look after him.'

'Poor man.'

Joe had been ill for a long time with a persistent cough that had been diagnosed as cancer some months earlier. Naomi had called on him with a bowl of soup a few days ago and found him smoking.

'I know,' he'd said. 'The ciggies can't be doing me much good, but there's no point in giving up on them now. It might have made a difference if I'd eased off 'em twenty, thirty or, better still, forty years ago, but I didn't and there it is. I'm done for, but I'm not complaining. I've had seventy-three years, which is more than many have, especially the poor souls fighting in this war and the last one. The way I see it, I might as well enjoy my ciggies while I can.'

'You're a philosopher, Joe.'

'Dunno about that, but we all come to an end and my end will be soon. Makes way for the next lot of folk. England's green and pleasant land would be horribly crowded if we all lived for ever.'

Naomi was far from being the only person to rally

round Joe in his final months. He'd been a regular face at the bookshop and, as always, everyone there had done what they could to ease his exit from life with meals, shopping, washing, cleaning . . . It was natural for him to want to spend his last weeks with his sister, though.

Walking back from the shops after escaping from Marjorie, Naomi paused outside Joe's house. Her first thought was that it looked abandoned and sad now that Joe would never return to it. But then a second thought came unbidden into her mind: Joe had neither wife nor children, so the house would presumably pass to his sister, Ellen, who might be glad to sell it when the time was right. Churchwood properties fell vacant only occasionally, and maybe Joe's house would become available just when Naomi was looking for a new home – if her fears about losing Foxfield came to pass. One door might literally open when another closed in this case. But could she picture herself living there?

It was a much smaller property than Foxfield. Unlike most Churchwood cottages, which had a kitchen behind the front sitting room, this house had them side by side, making one large room downstairs with a front door opening into the middle. Naomi couldn't recall going upstairs but there had to be two, possibly even three bedrooms. Probably no bathroom, of course.

The answer was no, she couldn't picture herself living there, though that might be because the very thought of having to move filled her with panic. In any case, she didn't want to think about buying Joe's house when he was on his deathbed over in Barton. It felt distasteful.

Reaching home, she returned to the statement she was making of her financial affairs – basically a list of what she owned, though most items on her list were jointly owned with Alexander. There was a question mark over the value of Foxfield itself. Naomi had telephoned the house agents who'd sold them the house all those years ago and they were to revisit their old records and let her know an approximate figure. 'We can give a more precise valuation if we come out and see it,' they'd told her, but Naomi was content with an approximate figure for now. Alexander could challenge it if he thought it inaccurate. She'd undertaken the same exercise in relation to the London flat.

There were figures for some of the finer pieces of furniture and figures for her jewellery collection. Her father had bought her several expensive pieces in her youth but most of them had been sold, as they were too garish for her taste. Naomi remembered having hopes of those pieces being replaced with tasteful items chosen by Alexander but, apart from a single string of pearls, no replacements had ever materialized and the money had gone into their bank account – or so she'd assumed. Now she wasn't so sure.

One gold watch, she read, consulting her list now. *One string of pearls, one sapphire and diamond brooch, one gold bangle, one gold bracelet, one gold chain with oval locket, one gold wedding band, one gold engagement ring set with sapphires and diamonds . . .*

Doubtless, many people would consider this jewellery to be treasure beyond their dreams, but Naomi's father would have been appalled by what he'd consider a paltry collection, especially compared to the flamboyant – and expensive – jewels he'd gifted her.

As for actual money, the amount standing to her credit in the bank wouldn't last for long, especially with the Great Man clocking up frighteningly high fees. Naomi simply couldn't afford a long, drawn-out battle with Alexander.

*

In bed that night, too churned up in her mind to fall asleep, she heard rain rattling against her window. Heaving herself out of bed, she eased back the curtain. The wind had got up and she could see the silhouettes of trees swaying in the wet, inky night. Whatever happened with Alexander, Naomi was certain to be left with at least a modest roof over her head and enough money to keep body and soul together. If the Churchwood thief was a stranger to the village, he might have neither of those things.

Tomorrow, October would begin and, if he was truly without a home, the advancing autumn weather would make life even more uncomfortable for him. Was he out there now, shivering and trying to take shelter beneath the trees? If so, Naomi pitied him. Or her. It was important to remember that the thief might be female.

CHAPTER FOURTEEN

Kate

Well, I've written to our Fred and I'm waiting for his reply, Frank had announced in his latest letter. *When are you going to see him again? Write and tell me if he's any better. It's hard being over here when Fred is over there.*

Kate hadn't heard from Fred either but would learn more when she and Kenny made their second visit today. Two weeks had passed since their first journey to London and Kate hoped the intervening fortnight had begun to knock the rougher edges off Fred's bitterness as well as heal him physically.

'Money for the train,' Kenny said, holding his hand out to Ernie, who scowled as always when asked for money.

He took some cash from his box but slammed it down on the table as though he didn't want anyone to get the idea that he was a soft touch.

Kenny scooped up the coins without comment, doubtless too familiar with his father's skinflint ways to bother with a response. He looked questioningly at Kate instead.

'Let's go,' she said, picking up the bag she'd packed with some lunch and a few more things for Fred – cigarettes, apples from the orchard and a book. Not that Fred had ever been any sort of reader, but being confined to a bed for weeks might make any kind of distraction welcome. 'Any messages to pass on?' she asked.

Neither Ernie nor Vinnie spoke. 'Tell him everyone here wishes him well,' Ruby suggested, and Pearl nodded agreement, though neither land girl had met Fred yet.

As before, Kenny fidgeted throughout the journey . . . and when he emerged from the underground railway, he was like a caged animal newly released from captivity, filling his lungs with air and striding out with vigour. His steps slowed as they neared the hospital, though. His nerves must be taking hold again – just as they'd taken hold of Kate.

Fred greeted them with a scowl that splintered Kate's hopes and made her heart feel as though it were sinking through deep water. 'You took your time before coming back,' he grumbled.

'It's a busy time of year on the farm,' Kenny said. 'You know that.'

'I know what it's like to be stuck in here, seeing other people with visitors when I've had none.'

Kate doubted that all the other patients received regular visitors, as they must have to come from all over the country. Not a single patient on the ward had visitors right now. Fred simply wanted to moan. 'I've brought you some more things,' she said.

Kenny fetched chairs for them, and Kate handed over her gifts. Fred took the cigarettes as though he had a right to them and more besides, but he ignored the apples and turned his nose up at the book. It was Richmal Crompton's *Just William*, a book Alice had given her, saying, 'I had it as a child but it might be just the thing for getting a poor reader like Fred started on enjoying books.'

'Just try it,' Kate urged Fred now. 'You might be pleasantly surprised.'

'And pigs might fly,' he said, with surly contempt.

Kate left the book with him anyway. 'Don't worry if it gets lost,' Alice had said, generous as ever.

'What have the doctors been saying?' Kate asked Fred, as Kenny simply sat in his chair looking awkward.

'What do you think they've been saying? That they've found my legs hidden in a cupboard?'

Kate drew on her reserves of patience. 'Are you healing well?'

'Humph. They tell me I'll heal faster if I calm down a bit, but that's easy for them to say when they're walking up and down on legs that are fine and dandy.'

Fred's rage was a living, sizzling thing. It wasn't hard to imagine how it might interfere with the healing process.

'Have you heard from Frank?' Kate asked next.

Fred made another scoffing sound. Yes, he'd heard from Frank, but it obviously hadn't helped.

'Do you still have the letter?' Kate wanted to see what Frank had written.

'I threw it away.'

'Whatever he wrote, I'm sure he was only trying to help.'

'By reminding me of the times we had when I was whole? Working on the farm, seeing who could pick the most apples and lift the heaviest crate, running to the Wheatsheaf for a pint, wrestling with the chaps . . .'

Oh dear. 'You'll still be able to do some things, like having a pint in the Wheatsheaf,' Kate reminded him. 'You're not completely incapacitated.'

'Not completely *what*? You and your big words! You think you're some kind of fine lady, but you're just a girl. An ordinary girl.'

'All I'm saying is that, while you won't be able to do some things as well as before, there'll be other things that you *can* do. The sooner you heal, the sooner you'll find out.'

'An ordinary girl who thinks too much of herself,' Fred continued, as though she hadn't spoken. 'Anyway, I'm sick of this place. I've asked to go home, seeing as I'm no good as a soldier any more. They say I'm not ready, but they may think about moving me to that hospital near home.'

'Stratton House?'

'That's the one. You'll have no excuse for not visiting me then, and you'll have to put your hands in your pockets to buy me ciggies more often than once a month or so.'

Within half an hour of their arrival Fred had lapsed into moody silence and there seemed to be little point in staying longer. 'Oh, that's right,' he complained as they got to their feet. 'Off you go on your healthy legs while I'm stuck here.'

'Do you want us to stay?' Kate asked. 'We can stay longer if that's what you want.'

But Fred was intent on being a martyr. 'Don't bother. I'm sure you've got more important things to be doing than sitting here with me. You're no help to me anyway.'

He brushed aside Kate's attempt to kiss him, and she walked out with Kenny feeling as depressed as she had on their first visit. Worse, in some ways, as Fred's bitterness was clearly becoming entrenched.

Would a move to Stratton House be good for him? It would certainly bring him closer to his family. But – and the thought felt appallingly selfish – unless his attitude changed, the move might make life difficult for the rest of them. It wasn't hard to picture Fred insisting that he should be visited every day no matter how much work needed doing on the farm. Insisting, too, on gifts that would bleed Kate's meagre wages dry, since she couldn't see Ernie coughing up often.

Already she could feel Fred throwing tentacles out

100

to ensnare her and take her back to the old days when getting time off to see her friends and visit the bookshop had been a major battle. Even now, time off wasn't easy with the sheer quantity of work she had to shoulder. Daily visits to Fred would eat up more time, leaving precious little to spare for herself. Kate's friends and the bookshop had become her lifeline. If she were to be cut off from them . . .

She pushed the guilty thought aside to make space for considering what she'd write to Frank. She wouldn't chastise him for reminding Fred of happy times — those reminders had been well intentioned — but she might suggest he write about things they could do together in the future, things Fred could manage from a wheelchair.

The journey home was sombre and quiet. 'How was it?' Ruby asked, when they arrived at Brimbles Farm.

'Bad,' Kenny reported.

'What's that supposed to mean?' Ernie demanded.

'It means—' Kenny broke off, flicking a hand in Kate's direction. He wasn't good with words. 'Tell 'im, Kate.'

'He's still angry about what happened.'

'Well, of course he is!' Ernie barked.

'He's angry to the point where it's affecting his recovery, and he isn't learning to adjust,' Kate explained. 'He wants to come home or at least be transferred to Stratton House.'

Ernie looked alarmed. He wouldn't know where to start if expected to visit a sick and angry son.

'Of course, that may not be possible,' Kate finished, though she was disappointed in Ernie. Annoyed with him, too. He should be a better father than this.

Vinnie appeared to be equally unsure what to say. Rolling her eyes, Kate changed into work boots and, though the light was fading, went out to tend her vegetable patch, hoping it might soothe her a little. Following, Ruby handed over an envelope. 'From Leo,' she whispered.

Kate thanked her and pushed the envelope into her pocket. She set aside some onions and runner beans for supper then hurried down to the orchard to read the letter in privacy, sitting on the fallen log that was used as a seat.

Darling Kate,

It was such a joy to receive your last letter. I love hearing about life on the farm with all the changing seasons. Your descriptions bring England to life for me and remind me of what I'm fighting for. They make it easy to picture you too – your fresh, clear skin, your lovely brown eyes and, of course, your glorious hair. I can't wait to see you again!

Much as I enjoy reading about you and the farm, I hope the work isn't wearing you out. You have wonderful friends, but I wish I could be there to give you a break from the work by taking you out for some fun – a dance, a tea, a dinner . . .

Kate realized she was blinking back tears. Home had long been a battleground and she'd never felt appreciated there, but just now she felt particularly weighed down with worry. To have Leo caring for her . . . It was lovely, like finding soft, cosy shelter in a storm.

She finished the letter with tears streaming down her cheeks. Then she wiped her face and read it again. What a wonderful man Leo was. Kate missed him dreadfully.

Returning the letter to its envelope and her pocket, she got up and was pushing her hair from her eyes when something caught her attention. She walked over for a better look. In front of the hedge that separated the orchard from Brimbles Lane there was a patch of mud and in it was a footprint. There was a second footprint beneath the hedge, as though someone had pushed through it. Looking around, Kate saw two discarded apple cores and a cigarette butt. Someone had been here in the orchard, helping themselves to apples and smoking a cigarette. The Churchwood thief?

Stepping into the nearest footprint, Kate saw that it was much bigger than her own boot. Bigger even than Pearl's boot. The thief wasn't a child, then. He was a fully grown man and probably a stranger, because why would a village resident walk all the way up Brimbles Lane for a few apples when there were easier pickings to be had in village gardens? Kate looked through the branches of the hedgerow into the lane. There was no sign of the thief now, but she shivered and hastened back indoors.

CHAPTER FIFTEEN

Alice

'Thank you all for staying behind,' Alice said to the bookshop team as they sat around a table after the session had finished. 'I thought it might be useful to have another chat. The first thing to mention is that May and I looked through the old nativity costumes.'

'We can use hardly any of them,' May said. 'Most have been ruined by mice, moths or simply old age.'

'Which means we need to make new costumes,' Alice said. 'It isn't going to be easy because we can't expect anyone to use their clothing coupons. But I suggest we appeal for donations of any fabric that people might already have hanging around their houses. Also things like old clothes, sheets, pillowcases, bedspreads and tablecloths that we may be able to cut up or adapt. We'll need to ask for help with sewing, too.'

'We can have some sewing sessions at the bookshop,' May added.

'Does everyone agree?' Alice asked.

Everyone did, and Adam looked delighted.

'On to the Gregsons,' Alice said next. 'They've been here for almost six weeks now and, as you all know, neither May nor I have made any progress with Evelyn. Has anyone else fared better?'

'Not me,' Janet said.

'Me neither,' said Naomi.

'I offered her and the boys a ride home from the shops in my truck one day when I thought her shopping basket looked particularly heavy, and it was raining too,' Bert said. 'The boys seemed keen but all I got from their mother was a stiff, "No, thank you."'

'I don't think she's exchanged more than an essential word or two with anyone in the village,' Alice said. 'I heard Edna Hall telling Ivy Hutchings that Evelyn must think Churchwood folk aren't good enough for her because she turns her nose up at them.'

'I hope we'll all discourage that sort of talk,' Adam said.

'I did discourage it,' Alice confirmed. 'I pointed out that some people take time to settle into new places and that Evelyn might have a lot on her mind.'

'Both of those things may be true,' Adam said, smiling at her, 'though I wonder if we might actually be alienating her by trying too hard to get her to join in with village life.'

'I've been wondering the same thing,' Alice said. 'Maybe we should leave her to choose her own moment to join in, if she decides that's what she wants.'

'Take the pressure off her,' Bert said, nodding. 'Sounds a good idea to me.'

Everyone else nodded too.

'Obviously, we all need to keep smiling and saying hello to her,' Alice said. 'That way we make it possible for her to open up to us without awkwardness.'

She paused and then moved the conversation along. 'On to the thief. He's still hanging around the village.'

'Or *she's* still hanging around the village,' May pointed out.

'Actually, I'm pretty sure now that the thief is both male and a stranger.' Alice told them what Kate had reported about the footprints, apple cores and cigarette butt.

'A grown man, then,' Bert said thoughtfully.

'It's hard to say if he's read the notices I put up,' Adam said. 'He probably doesn't venture into the village until it's dark and then he won't be able to see them well enough to read them. Even lighting a match to see by would draw attention to him since the rest of the village is in blackout, and he might not be willing to risk it. I've been leaving flasks of soup by the vicarage door when I've been here in Churchwood, but they've never been taken.'

'Maybe he thinks they're some sort of trap,' Bert suggested.

'Maybe he does,' Adam agreed.

'The man can't live on cold milk, apples and a few carrots,' Bert said then. 'For one thing, there's talk of fresh milk being rationed, and people are a lot less likely to tolerate pints disappearing from their doorsteps if they can't buy replacements. And for another thing, it's getting colder and wetter. I wonder if he might soon feel desperate for more substantial meals.'

'What are you suggesting, Bert?'

'I'm saying there's only one way of getting more substantial meals, to my way of thinking.'

Alice worked it out. 'You think he might start going into people's houses to find food?'

'I don't know the man so I can't know what he's thinking. I'm simply raising a possibility and wondering what we should do about it.'

'Such as warn people to keep their doors locked?' she asked.

'It's something to think about.'

'I wouldn't want to send the village into a panic when we've no evidence to suggest our thief will go further than pilfering from doorsteps,' Alice said.

'Think how Marjorie would react to such a warning,' Naomi said, and there were murmurs of 'Goodness, yes' and 'She'd be hysterical'.

'I imagine none of us wants to set Marjorie off,' Adam said. 'Why don't we think on the pros and cons of giving a warning and talk about it another time?'

'Sounds fair to me,' Bert said.

'Maybe the thief will move on soon anyway,' Alice said. 'I should think he'd be more likely to find shelter in a city or town than a village.'

She had no wish to pass on their problems to a nearby city or town, but it would be a relief to walk to and from the hospital without the feeling that someone might be watching her. She'd seen only birds and squirrels in the woods since the day she'd first felt spooked in the lane, and she'd heard only birdsong and the rustles of small creatures. Even so, the feeling that someone was watching her persisted, acting on her like icy fingers running up and down her spine.

Yes, it would be a relief if the thief moved on soon.

CHAPTER SIXTEEN

Naomi

Mr Carraway, Naomi's trustee, was an old man now, with white hair like thistledown and milkiness in his once-sharp blue eyes. Age had shrunk him, too, and rounded his shoulders so that his head hung forward from his neck, giving him the look of a tortoise peering tentatively from its shell.

'It's been a long time since we last met, Mrs Harrington,' he said, gesturing her to a chair in his office, which couldn't have changed much since Queen Victoria's reign.

It was furnished – desk, chairs, bookcases – in dark mahogany with faded green carpet underfoot. The paintings that hung from the walls hailed from yesteryear and the books on the shelves looked ancient enough to crumble to dust if they were to be picked up and perused.

'Mostly, I'm retired,' he continued. 'I just keep my hand in with a few of my long-established clients and trusts such as yours. I had dealings with your father for many years before his untimely death. An interesting man.'

Mr Carraway spoke beautifully, but Cedric Tuggs had been cut from a different cloth. Starting out poor in London's East End, he'd never lost his Cockney accent, but he'd worked incredibly hard to build up a business of his own. Naomi had been adored by him and had loved him in return, feeling hurt every time she'd heard him described as a 'common little man' by the snootier people in the society he wanted to join.

He'd been bowled over by Alexander's debonair good looks and breeding, but perhaps he'd have seen through him in the end. As it was, Cedric had died unexpectedly, leaving Naomi with no family at all since her mother had passed away years before. Lonely and fearful of trying to cope by herself, she'd been only too willing to fall into what she'd expected to be the protective arms of a man who loved her. Ah, well. There was no point in dwelling on if-onlys.

'It's good of you to make time to see me,' she told Mr Carraway.

They sat down, Naomi in front of the desk and her trustee behind it. 'What errand has brought you to me today?' he asked.

'I'm here about my trust. I recall it was worth fifty thousand pounds when my father set it up, but I wonder if you might tell me how much it's worth now.'

Mr Carraway shook his head despondently. 'Only five thousand pounds, I'm afraid.'

Naomi reeled inside, feeling as though her bones were dissolving in dread.

'When your father established the trust, he intended it to provide security for the rest of your life,' Mr Carraway said. 'But he also knew there might be times when you needed more than the investment income the trust provided, so he allowed for up to five per cent of the capital to be withdrawn in any twelve-month period. It was thanks to such withdrawals that Foxfield and the London flat were bought. He envisaged only occasional dips into capital after large purchases like those, but I'm afraid your husband withdrew close to the maximum allowed almost every year. I hope you don't feel I mismanaged the trust, Mrs Harrington?'

'By no means,' Naomi assured him, though she was feeling sick.

'I did my best to persuade your husband to take a more cautious approach. I warned him the funds were being run down too quickly and wouldn't last. Unfortunately, I failed to get my point across, and as Mr Harrington had your support . . .'

Naomi could picture the scene. Alexander would have been haughty and arrogant, claiming to be an expert in finance acting in his wife's best interests and with her full cooperation.

'If you remember, you told me in person that I should follow your husband's instructions, and he always produced paperwork bearing your signature.'

How could she forget trying so hard to placate him, cowering if Alexander turned impatient and assuring him that of course she trusted him. Not that he'd been frank with her about what he was doing. He'd talked of switching out of some investments to make better ones, and perhaps he had done that to some extent. But clearly not often.

Had he spent all the money he'd withdrawn? He was a man who liked fine clothes, food and luxurious living. He had his secret family to support too, which doubtless involved providing a home for them and paying expensive school fees for the children's education. Even so, Naomi suspected he'd squirrelled away large sums into investments and accounts that he'd hidden from her.

If she'd had an ounce of sense, she'd have insisted on being kept informed about how her money was managed. She'd also have challenged the decisions that had left her financially vulnerable. But, as Bert had said, there was nothing she could do about the past. She could only try to conserve what remained of her father's fortune for the future.

'My husband and I are separating,' she told Mr Carraway now. 'He no longer has authority to make decisions on my behalf.'

'I understand.' Despite his age and apparent frailty, his milky eyes looked determined and Naomi suspected that Alexander would have no luck trying to bamboozle this old man in future.

Mr Carraway didn't like Alexander. Naomi could see that now. She wished she'd seen it long ago.

'I have to say I was surprised when you sold your shares in the Naomi Beauty Company,' Mr Carraway said. His voice was carefully neutral, but his words shocked Naomi.

Her father had bought those shares for his daughter because the name had tickled his fancy. 'It's as though the business was named especially for my beautiful daughter,' he'd said. His love for her had always blinded him to the fact that, even as a girl, she'd been dumpy and plain.

Naomi would never have sold those shares willingly, and Alexander knew it.

Mr Carraway opened a folder on his desk and drew out a letter of instruction for the shares to be sold. Naomi's signature was on the bottom. At least, it looked like her signature.

Heavens, was it possible that Alexander had sometimes forged it? She inspected the letter closely. The signature certainly looked convincing in the size and shape of the letters but, while she couldn't swear it was a forgery, something about it sent prickles of suspicion over her scalp.

She looked at Mr Carraway. He made no accusations,

but from his steady regard it was clear that he too wondered if Alexander had felt complacent enough to sign her name on occasion, confident that she'd have no way of proving it given the way she often signed papers with barely a glance. She guessed that Mr Carraway was warning her that Alexander wasn't a man to be trusted in financial matters or anything else.

'I'm sorry the trust won't provide you with the secure income your father craved for you,' Mr Carraway said. 'But I hope what remains will provide you with at least a modest few pounds a year on top of the financial settlement you should receive from Mr Harrington.'

There was nothing to be gained by telling him that she wasn't seeking a settlement from Alexander. Mr Carraway already looked worried about her.

'I'll keep a tight hold on your trust monies from now on,' he assured her, and, after thanking him, Naomi left, as there was nothing more to be said.

CHAPTER SEVENTEEN

Kate

It was happening. Fred was being moved to Stratton House. 'They think it might aid his recovery,' Kenny reported, having returned from the village after telephoning the London hospital.

Perhaps they were right. With thousands of patients in their care, the hospitals would surely have neither the time nor the resources to transfer a patient without sound clinical reasons. Unless they simply wanted rid of Fred because he was dragging down the other patients' spirits, not to mention the staff's.

'Did they say when he'll be transferred?' Kate asked.

'As soon as possible. That's all I was told.'

'I suppose it'll depend on when an ambulance and driver can be spared.'

Ruby took a cheerful view, telling the Fletcher men, 'You'll all be able to pop in and see him in between work. You won't need to take time off to trek up to London any more.'

The men only looked at Kate, clearly considering hospital visits to be her role. Not that they'd make time for her to visit by relieving her of some other work. Hypocrisy ran through the Fletcher men like lettering through sticks of seaside rock. When it suited them, Kate was a female, so should take on what they considered to be all the womanly tasks of the household – cooking, cleaning, sewing, and hospital visiting too. But when it came to labouring in the fields, they treated her no differently from a man.

At least Kate now had Ruby's help indoors and Pearl's help outside. She'd squeeze visits to Fred into her days somehow, though it was hard to see how she could also keep up her already rushed visits to friends and the bookshop.

The thought of seeing even less of her friends cost Kate a pang, but she'd do what she could for Fred, even if it meant some loss to her own happiness. She loved him and wanted the best for him. She only hoped he wouldn't expect visits from the Fletcher men. Kenny would show his face at Stratton House now and then, but Ernie and Vinnie wouldn't know where to start when it came to cheering up a moody invalid. If they managed to talk to Fred at all, their conversations would be about the farm – sad reminders of the vigour that Fred had lost.

There was a bookshop session that morning. Kate rarely attended in the daytime because she needed to work but, determined to make the most of her time before Fred's arrival, she headed for the shops, intending to show her face at the bookshop afterwards, if only for a few minutes.

She was in the baker's talking to Naomi when Marjorie burst in. 'I've seen the thief!' she cried.

Mrs Hutchings rolled her eyes. 'Here we go again!'

Everyone else looked equally cynical at the prospect of another of Marjorie's fairy tales.

'I know you didn't believe me the first time, but now I really have seen him,' Marjorie insisted.

'All right, then,' Mrs Hayes indulged her. '*Where* did you see him?'

'In Mrs Gregson's front garden last night.'

Evelyn Gregson and her boys had been standing apart from everyone else, but now her eyes widened and she stepped forward. 'You saw a man in my garden?'

'I can see your house from mine,' Marjorie told her. 'I was taking a final peep outside, just to be sure I was safe, and I saw him.'

'It was probably a shadow,' Mrs Hutchings murmured.

'Or nothing at all, knowing Marjorie,' Mrs Hayes muttered back, but their cynicism did nothing to dampen Evelyn's alarm.

'What did he do? This man you say you saw?' she demanded.

'I only saw him for a moment. A cloud moved over the moon and I couldn't see him any more.'

'Probably, she didn't see him at all,' Mrs Hutchings said.

'Marjorie, you're frightening Mrs Gregson and her children,' Kate pointed out.

Evelyn had her arms around her boys, holding them close because they both looked wide-eyed with fear.

'You've got to stop this nonsense or who knows what damage you'll cause to people's peace of mind,' Naomi said.

But Evelyn's alarm wasn't eased. 'I need to know what you saw,' she urged Marjorie.

'Just a man.'

'But what was he doing?'

'I don't know. I only . . .' Marjorie was becoming upset now.

'Did you see his face?'

'Well, I—'

'Mrs Gregson, let me apologize on Marjorie's behalf,' Naomi intervened. 'It sounds as though Marjorie's imagination rather got the better of her.'

'Humph!' Evelyn glared at Marjorie. 'It's irresponsible to tell lies. You're a menace. That's what you are. A menace.' With that, Evelyn turned and hastened her boys from the shop without buying whatever she'd called in for.

Marjorie had flushed puce. 'I didn't mean to upset her, Naomi.'

'I'm sure you didn't.'

With no family, little money and a weak brain, melodrama was Marjorie's way of making herself feel important in the village, but heaven knew what damage she'd now caused to their chances of making Evelyn Gregson feel comfortable in Churchwood. Probably, Evelyn would isolate herself and her boys even more.

Naomi shared a frustrated look with Kate then turned back to Marjorie. 'You need to think before you speak. Those poor little children looked terrified, and I doubt they'll be getting much sleep tonight if they think someone might be trying to break into their house. Neither will their mother.'

'I'm sorry.'

'Are you absolutely certain you saw a figure?'

'I thought I did.'

'But you couldn't swear to it?'

'Maybe not in a court of law.'

Naomi sighed and exchanged another look with Kate.

'Are you cross with me, Naomi?' Tears had begun to shimmer in Marjorie's eyes.

'I'd be lying if I said I was pleased with you.'

'Do you think I should go and see Mrs Gregson?'

'I'm not sure she'd be in a mood to listen. I'll drop a note through her door later, explaining that, on reflection, you can't be confident that what you saw was a man or, indeed, any person.'

'I'm going to be ever so embarrassed next time I see her.' A tear dripped down Marjorie's cheeks.

'That can't be helped. But learn from it.'

'I will.'

Naomi looked as though she doubted that Marjorie would ever learn from her mistakes, but compassion won out over her annoyance. 'Why don't you come across to the bookshop with me, Marjorie? You could help to make the Hall ready.'

Marjorie cheered up instantly. 'Thank you, Naomi. You're always so kind.'

Kate gave Naomi's arm a sympathetic pat as the older women passed by on the way to the door. 'I'll be over in a moment,' she said, before re-joining the queue for bread.

By the time Kate reached the bookshop, Naomi was having a quiet chat with the other members of the organizing team as Marjorie laid out cups and saucers in the kitchen. Kate was beckoned over. 'I was just telling the others about Marjorie's latest fantasy,' Naomi said.

Kate nodded. 'Evelyn didn't take it well.'

'It's a shame about Mrs Gregson,' Adam said. 'We'll just have to hope she doesn't let Marjorie's histrionics sour her against the rest of us. But we can't know for sure what Marjorie did or didn't see. If she *did* see a man in Mrs Gregson's garden last night, he couldn't have been taking milk because it wouldn't have been delivered by then.'

'You think he might have been breaking in to find food?' Kate asked.

'The thief has never taken anything from families with children,' May reminded them. 'Or from frailer residents. That suggests he's trying to avoid causing hardship where it can least be afforded.'

'That's certainly how it looks,' Alice agreed, 'but

117

that could be down to coincidence. We're only making assumptions about what the thief does and doesn't know about the people in this village.'

'Besides, desperation might be driving him to overlook the scruples he began with,' Adam said. 'Personally, I suspect there was no one in Evelyn Gregson's garden last night, but we can't be certain of that, so I wonder if you think the time has come to keep their doors locked until the thief moves on?'

'Churchwood is a trusting sort of place. Locked doors are rare,' Naomi ventured. 'It would be a shame to change that.'

Adam's look invited more views.

'A warning would give credence to Marjorie's fantasies,' Janet suggested.

'We'd have the whole village in hysterics,' May said.

Bert nodded. 'Some in hysterics and some spooked into becoming hopping mad. I'd be worried that folk might keep their pokers and cricket bats by their doors and bop innocent visitors on the head.'

'Goodness, yes,' Naomi agreed. 'Old Humphrey Guscott gets deafer by the day. Imagine what he'd do if he caught sight of someone in his garden. He wouldn't hear anyone calling out, "Cooee!" He'd just rush out with a makeshift weapon.'

'So we all think it would be unwise to risk putting our residents on edge?' Adam concluded.

'For the moment,' Alice agreed. 'But let's keep it under review.'

'Very well,' Adam said. Then he turned to Kate. 'It's good to have you with us.'

'It's only a brief visit,' Kate explained. 'And you may see even less of me in the foreseeable future.'

'Oh no,' Alice said, doubtless thinking that there was always something getting in the way of Kate seeing her friends and coming to the bookshop. 'Is it . . . ?'

'Fred, yes,' Kate confirmed. 'He's being moved to Stratton House.'

The news met with a mixed reception, for these were good friends who understood how the move might impact on Kate as well as Fred. 'I hope this means that Fred is on the mend,' Alice said. 'He'll be given excellent care at Stratton House. The staff are lovely, and they're used to helping patients with missing limbs to become as mobile as possible. To adjust to their new situations, too.'

'I just hope Fred allows them to help.'

'You need to look after yourself as well,' Alice said, and the others nodded agreement. 'You must insist on some time of your own, even if you only manage a few minutes here and there.'

Kate's smile emerged lopsided and doubtful. 'We'll see,' she said. 'But just now . . .'

'You need to leave,' Alice finished for her.

'The more I can get on top of the work before Fred arrives, the better.'

Hard work was the story of Kate's life.

CHAPTER EIGHTEEN

Alice

'It looks wonderful,' Alice said, leafing through a copy of Mr Parkinson's memoir.

'Professional *and* fascinating,' her father declared.

'Mostly thanks to your dear daughter,' Mr Parkinson insisted. 'Not only is she extremely organized, she also has a good eye for photographs and an excellent way with words. A real talent for words, actually. She could write professionally for a newspaper or perhaps even as a writer of speeches. She'd be very persuasive.'

'Speech-writer to Winston Churchill?' her father suggested with a smile.

'Our esteemed leader could do considerably worse,' Mr Parkinson replied, and he smiled too.

It was sweet of him to compliment her, but Alice's ambitions were more modest. She simply wanted work for a few months that would enable her to build up a little nest egg. Interesting work would be ideal, of course, but she'd sooner take dull work than none. Unfortunately, the 'Situations Vacant' columns in the newspapers she'd perused had so far yielded nothing.

For a moment she was tempted to remind Mr Parkinson that he'd offered to keep an ear open for any likely opportunities, but this was his day to shine in the glory of his memoir. She wouldn't cast a shadow by mentioning her own needs, especially if it might make him feel guilty.

Instead, she simply smiled when, beaming with satisfaction, he continued with, 'It was Alice who found the printer, and I couldn't be more pleased with the finished product. I've only had twenty copies printed so far, due to the paper shortage, but that's enough to be going on with. I can order more copies later, if there's an appetite for them. Talking of appetites, please come through and partake of the luncheon my housekeeper has provided.'

They were in the drawing room of his home in St Albans. The house was far from being a mansion, and the furnishings were old-fashioned, but it was a sizeable, solid Edwardian property with stained glass in the front door and elegantly proportioned rooms. It suited its owner and Alice was fond of it.

Afterwards, they returned to the drawing room for tea before heading into the study so Alice's father could inspect his host's book collection. An hour or so later it was time to leave. Again, Alice was tempted to remind Mr Parkinson of her need for work but, again, she let the moment pass, not wanting him to feel under pressure to help. They parted with promises to stay in touch.

On the way to the bus stop Alice bought an evening edition of the *Hertfordshire Reporter*. 'Keeping up with the war news?' her father asked, and she smiled to avoid having to tell him that she'd bought it for the jobs pages.

When the bus came he took out his book – *The Mayan Civilization: a Study* – and Alice was able to work her way through the newspaper, arriving at the jobs pages only to find that there was nothing that would suit her. A solicitor wanted a secretary, but that would surely involve typing at a faster speed than she could manage now – frustrating, as she'd been fast and accurate on her typewriter before her accident. A house agent wanted a secretary too, but her slow typing would doubtless be a barrier to that post as well.

Should she at least apply for those jobs and explain that she had other skills to offer? As Mr Parkinson had said, she was an excellent organizer and good with words. Managing a diary, telephone calls, supplies, financial records and clients . . . she liked to think she was skilful there too. Certainly, her father had never had cause for complaint when she had managed his medical practice.

But no, she'd be wasting time and postage. Rejection was inevitable and rejection came hard. Not that it would throw her into despair, because there were other things to appreciate. The bookshop party on the Saturday before Christmas had been announced and there was much excitement about it in the village and at the hospital, too. As well, Churchwood was proving generous with donations towards the nativity costumes. There were sheets and tablecloths for angel dresses, silver tinsel for halos and wings, old clothes to be cut up for shepherds' outfits, a lovely blue dress that May could make suitable for the girl who played Mary, and Naomi had come up trumps with a couple of old cocktail dresses adorned with beads, which could be cut up to make grand costumes for the three wise men. Bert had made a lovely wooden manger to hold baby Jesus and toy sheep were being knitted for the shepherds to carry.

Best of all, Alice was almost certain she was pregnant now. Soon she'd ask Dr Lambert in Barton to confirm it. The thought of Daniel's baby had her floating above her cares on soft clouds of joy.

CHAPTER NINETEEN

Naomi

I have pleasure in enclosing your husband's statement of his financial position, the Great Man had written.

Sending the statement might have given the Great Man pleasure, but receiving it only confirmed Naomi's worst fears. The statement made for sorry reading. Like Naomi, Alexander had included estimates of the value of Foxfield, the London flat and the Daimler. They weren't dissimilar to hers, though he'd stressed that they could be over-optimistic bearing in mind that sales might be tricky in wartime, when so many men were away serving their country and belts had been tightened.

It was in relation to the money that the statement was shocking. Alexander's income from his stockbroking profession was decent enough but the figures for his savings, investments and even his pension were pitiful. Had he really put such small amounts aside or had he hidden money where he intended Naomi never to find it? Naomi was inclined to believe in the latter possibility. After all, Alexander was greedy and calculating, and she couldn't believe he'd have left himself facing financial embarrassment in the not-too-distant future. No, he'd have squirrelled the money away somewhere.

Sensing that she was troubled, Basil heaved himself out of his basket and waddled over to nudge her fingers with his nose.

Grateful for his sensitivity, Naomi stroked his neck then said, 'Come on. Let's get some air.'

They moved into the garden. The October day was chilly, so Naomi wore her coat and Basil wore a little tartan dog's blanket buckled around his middle. She could challenge Alexander's statement, but she was at a loss over how to prove that he'd hidden money from her.

Even with dwindled finances Naomi was unlikely to be poor by many people's standards, but the loss of Foxfield was increasingly likely. She looked up at the house that had been her home for more than twenty-five years and felt a pang of regret deep inside her.

She'd been a young woman when she'd arrived here, though, for a while after their marriage, she and Alexander had lived in a rented flat in London. It hadn't taken her long to realize that not only was Alexander away at his office during working hours, but he was also absent during many an evening and weekend, entertaining his clients or playing golf. Even when he was at home he wasn't as attentive as she'd hoped, but she'd still felt a starry-eyed optimism for the future, especially if it might include the children for whom she yearned. She'd pictured Alexander spending less time away from her once he was settled in a lovely home and had become a father.

The children she craved had never materialized – how could they when Alexander barely touched her? – but despite that heartache she'd carved out a life for herself in Churchwood as a sort of lady of the manor who 'organized' the village and also involved herself in charity committees further afield when she had the use of the car. Despite this, Alice's arrival had brought Naomi face to face with the realization that she wasn't actually much liked in Churchwood, and that had hurt her deeply. For a while she'd withdrawn into herself, but Alice's kindness and Bert's teasing had gradually forced her out again and she'd found a wonderful group of friends.

She hadn't thought to leave Churchwood after her divorce, but how was she really going to feel seeing someone else in these gardens and in this house, settling down and entertaining people in the rooms that had once been dear to her? Would that person pity her or smirk over her misfortune? Naomi had no way of knowing.

The village would pity her, though. Could Naomi bear that sort of humiliation? She might tell herself that pride shouldn't matter, but it *did* matter. Would she be making a terrible mistake if she remained in Churchwood? Would she be better off making a fresh start somewhere else?

CHAPTER TWENTY

Kate

Stratton House had once been the home of landed gentry but had stood abandoned for several years before being pressed into service as a military hospital. Kate had often seen it before but never had she climbed the stone steps to the magnificent pillared entrance doors and stepped through them into an equally splendid hall – until today.

The porter, Tom, was familiar because he often visited the bookshop when he wasn't on duty. He smiled in recognition as Kate walked to his desk, but it seemed to her that it was the sort of sympathetic smile that boded ill for what lay ahead.

It was the same when Kate walked down the corridor towards Fred's ward. Alice's nursing friend Babs Carter was coming the opposite way. She smiled too but, again, there was sympathy in it. 'Fred isn't settling in well?' Kate guessed.

'Early days,' Babs said tactfully.

Dread settled over Kate as she stepped into the ward, and it didn't lift when she saw her brother halfway along. It was as though a thundercloud were hovering above his head, the slump of his body and his jutting lip speaking of festering anger.

He must have heard her approach because he looked round and speared her with a glower. 'Good of you to bother showing up,' he said.

'We were told not to come yesterday because they wanted to get you settled,' Kate explained. 'I came as soon as I could today.'

'It's afternoon.'

'Only just. I wanted to give the doctors time to make their rounds this morning and then I didn't want to interrupt your lunch. Besides, visitors can't just wander in and out at will, getting in the way of the staff. We need to fit around the hospital routine.'

'Humph,' he said, as though he didn't believe a word of it. 'I don't see the others queuing up to see me.'

This was going to be difficult. 'We thought it best not to crowd you when you must be tired after the journey from London.'

'So they sent the family skivvy to look me over?'

'I *wanted* to come. I told the others I'd report back on how you are.' She hardly dared to ask but forced herself. 'How *are* you feeling? Any better?'

'My legs haven't grown back, so what do you think?'

'This is a nice hospital.' She looked around in a feeble attempt to distract him from his woes. 'I know some of the staff from the bookshop and they're lovely.'

'It's easy to be lovely when you're not lying here with a broken body. Anyway, that Matron isn't lovely. She's sharp.'

'Perhaps she's being cruel to be kind.' Trying to jolt Fred's thoughts away from self-pity and turn them towards the future, Kate suspected.

'I suppose you got that sort of nonsense thinking from that stuck-up doctor's daughter.'

'Alice isn't stuck up.'

'She looks down her nose at me. Not that anyone will ever look *up* at me now I've got no legs to stand on.'

'You might get false legs in time. Won't you at least try to get well, Fred?'

'What do you know about getting well?'

'I know it might help if you stop fighting the situation.'

'Accept that I'm a cripple? Easy for you to say.'

Kate sighed, long and hard. 'Have you heard any more from Frank?' she asked.

'He wrote.'

'And? What did he have to say?'

'A load of maudlin rubbish about how we'll still be twins and have fun together. Fat chance of that.'

'You can still go with him to the Wheatsheaf,' Kate pointed out.

'I can just picture that!' Fred scoffed in disgust. 'Frank pushing me into the bar in my wheelchair. Faces turning to stare at me in pity and relief that I've been maimed and they haven't. No one knowing what to say to this pathetic shambles of a man. Maybe they'll put their hands in their pockets to buy me a pint or offer me a ciggie to get them through the awkwardness and make themselves feel better. No thanks!'

It was hopeless. Kate stayed at Fred's bedside for more than half an hour but nothing she said seemed to help. She could only hope that her presence made him feel at least a little bit valued, despite his bleak view of life.

'I should go,' she said eventually.

'That's right. Rub my nose in the fact that you can work on the farm while I'm stuck in here.'

'I'll see you again soon.'

'Who's coming tomorrow?'

'I'm not sure.' Kate hoped Fred wouldn't pick up on the reluctance of the rest of his family to visit. 'Perhaps Kenny?'

'The least he can do,' Fred said, as though his

confinement in hospital was Kenny's fault, despite having joined the army against the family's wishes when he could have been exempt as a farmer.

'Look after yourself,' Kate said by way of farewell, but she earned only a sneer for her trouble.

She arrived back at Brimbles Farm to the news that Frank was coming home on leave. Frank's letters hadn't done Fred any good, but face-to-face visits might make all the difference.

'Any more letters?' Kate whispered to Ruby, but she shook her head.

Kate was disappointed. She'd estimated that a letter from Leo might arrive any day now. In fact, she was surprised one hadn't arrived already. Ah well. Perhaps tomorrow's post would smile on her more kindly.

CHAPTER TWENTY-ONE

Alice

PERSON WANTED, the card in the window announced. Since she had come to St Albans in search of work, the bold capital letters had caught Alice's attention as she walked past. Underneath were more words in smaller writing: *Person wanted to assist with general office duties. Apply within.*

What sort of office was it? A muslin curtain prohibited a clear view of the inside but a brass plate by the door indicated that the premises belonged to a dentist. She knocked on the door and a woman opened it. A harassed-looking woman. 'Miss Galloway?' she asked.

'I'm not a patient,' Alice said. 'I'm here about the job advertised in the window. Is it still available?'

'It certainly is.' The woman's tone made it clear that she wouldn't be here for love nor money if the vacancy had been filled. 'Please come in.'

Alice stepped into a reception area and was gestured to a chair beside a desk.

'You'll forgive me if I have to—' The woman broke off as someone else knocked on the door.

This was the expected Miss Galloway. The woman led her to a consulting room and then returned. 'Sorry about that. I'm Ruth Arnold, wife of Mr Arnold whose practice this is. His last receptionist went off to build aircraft parts and gave us no notice at all, which is the reason I'm working here, though with two boys at home it's far from convenient. Have you done this sort of work before, Miss . . . ?'

'Mrs Irvine, actually.'

'Oh, I'm sorry. You look so young, and you're wearing gloves so I didn't see your ring.'

Alice smiled. 'I'm only recently married. And to answer your question, my father was a doctor and I looked after the office side of his practice before he retired, so I might have some idea of the job here.'

'Do tell me more.'

Alice began to do just that, though they were interrupted again by two telephone calls and a gentleman who came in person to check his appointment time for the following week. Alice had just finished explaining her experience when Mr Arnold showed Miss Galloway out of the consulting room. 'Just a check-up today,' he told his wife.

'What do I owe?' Miss Galloway asked.

'My wife will see to you.'

'I'll be pleased to,' Mrs Arnold confirmed, then she looked at her husband. 'Don't rush off. This is Mrs Irvine. She's here about the job.'

'Oh, excellent.'

'She has just the sort of experience you're looking for.'

'There's something I should mention,' Alice said, following the dentist into his consulting room and feeling the familiar tension as she prepared to disclose her injury. 'I have a damaged hand. I can still type but not as fast as in the past. If you can tolerate that, you'll have a very hard worker in me.'

She unbuttoned her glove and was removing it just as

Mrs Arnold came to join them. Both of the Arnolds' faces fell. 'Typing is important,' Mrs Arnold said with obvious regret. 'It isn't just a case of invoices and letters. My husband carries out research and writes papers for medical publications. They need to be typed out, too. There's also a need to handle heavy boxes of supplies.'

Which Alice would struggle to manage. She sighed, feeling rejected all over again. 'I'm sorry I wasted your time.'

Outside, she walked briskly from the dental surgery then came to a halt as disappointment washed over her. Surely, there was some sort of work out there that she could do?

Crossing the road, she bought a lunchtime edition of a different newspaper. Someone was advertising for a companion to an elderly lady, but the work involved lifting the old lady and Alice knew she wasn't up to that, not just because of her hand but also because she didn't want to put her baby at risk. She was going to consult Dr Lambert in Barton next week, but all the signs were that her pregnancy was now well established.

The thought reminded her that she had many other blessings in her life so she shouldn't feel too downhearted at her failure to find work. Not that her failure was a trivial matter exactly, as a nest egg would help to tide them over if Daniel struggled to find a job when the war was over and there were also the expenses of a new baby to consider. But, even so . . .

She spent a little more time studying cards in shop windows and asking a number of businesses if they had any openings, but there was nothing. 'I'm sure you could get work at de Havilland's over in Hatfield,' someone suggested kindly. 'That's where they're making aircraft.'

But Alice's injured hand would never cope with fiddly tasks involving nails, screws, welding or stitching. Not at any speed, anyway. All factory work was out of the question. She thanked the man with a smile, glanced at her watch and headed for Avenue Road, where Mr Parkinson lived. She'd telephoned in advance to tell him that her father had charged her with delivering a book in which his friend had expressed an interest.

A young maid opened the door and invited Alice inside. 'How are you, Ivy?' Alice asked.

'Can't complain, miss. You're keeping well too, I hope?'

'Very well, thank you.'

'Mr P. is expecting you.' Ivy lowered her voice. 'I think he's missing you, so he's looking forward to seeing you today.'

'I'm looking forward to seeing him.'

He got up from behind his desk as Alice entered the room he used as a study. 'My dear, what a pleasure this is.'

Alice kissed his cheek. 'I couldn't come to St Albans without looking you up.'

Ivy went to make tea and Alice handed over the book she'd brought. It was a dull-looking tome about the gods of ancient Egypt, but Mr Parkinson gave it a satisfied pat. 'Please assure your father that I'll take good care of it.'

They chatted about her father for a few minutes then Ivy brought the tea, which Alice served. 'Thank you,' Mr Parkinson said, when she passed him a cup. 'What other business brings you to St Albans today?'

'I bought a couple of books for the bookshop. We don't have a big budget for new books, but we do our best to offer variety.'

She made no mention of her job search, but he brought the subject up himself. 'I haven't forgotten what I said about keeping an eye open for job opportunities for you. Sadly, I'm unaware of any openings at present, though I took my memoir to my history society meeting a few days ago and made sure that everyone knew you'd helped with the writing as well as organizing the research papers. The other members were very complimentary, and it may be that some will welcome your help with their own projects in the future.'

'You're very kind, but please don't worry about me. Hopefully, I'll find something soon and, even if I don't, it won't be the end of the world.'

'Of course it won't, especially now you're married. You young brides wanting jobs . . . It's all rather different from in my day.'

The modern world was a puzzling place for traditionalists like Hubert Parkinson, bless him.

Eventually, Alice got up to leave, and he walked her to the door. 'Given your talent for writing, I wonder if the local newspaper might have a position for you,' he said.

It was a good idea and Alice wasted no time in going along to the office to explore the possibilities. But, once again, she had no luck because typing fast was an essential skill and there were no openings anyway.

Out of ideas, she took the bus back to Churchwood. She was heading home from the bus stop when she saw Evelyn Gregson and her boys walking in her direction. Bracing herself for the likelihood of being ignored or – worse – glared at, Alice uttered a polite, 'Good afternoon,' but kept on walking.

'Yes. Good afternoon,' Evelyn said. She kept on walking too, but at least she'd been polite, so Alice was pleased by the encounter.

As well, she was reminded that other people had far

greater problems than a failed interview, and Evelyn might be one of them.

Noticing Naomi up ahead, Alice ran to catch her up. Naomi always wore a brave face in public, but now she was alone and probably believed herself to be unobserved, the true state of her feelings showed in her bowed shoulders and laboured tread.

'Oh,' Naomi said, rousing herself to smile as Alice reached her. 'How are you, Alice?'

'Fine, thanks, though I imagine you can't say the same. Is it the divorce going badly?'

Sighing, Naomi came to a halt. 'I always suspected Alexander would be difficult.'

'Don't you mean sneaky and dishonest?'

Naomi let out a small laugh. 'Yes, I suppose I do.'

'Is he hiding money from you?'

'I think so.'

'Your solicitor will find it, though? He's a big man in London, isn't he?'

'With big bills to match,' Naomi answered ruefully.

'Hopefully, his fees will be worth the investment.' Alice paused and then put a comforting hand on Naomi's shoulder. 'A divorce is bound to be horrible, but please don't suffer in silence. I want to help, if only by providing a sympathetic ear. I'm sure all our other friends want to help too.'

'Thank you, dear. I know I'm lucky to have such good people around me.'

'You'll still have us even if you lose every penny to Alexander. Not that it'll come to that.' Alice looked closely at Naomi and added doubtfully, 'Will it?'

'I'm sure it won't, but without some sort of miracle, I think I'll lose Foxfield. I won't be able to afford the upkeep.'

'I'm sorry.'

'It was always a possibility. A price I decided I was willing to pay to cut Alexander from my life.'

It was, in fact, to give Foxfield a swansong that she'd offered to host Alice's wedding in the summer. The possibility of losing a much-loved house was one thing in theory, though, and quite another in practice.

'Hopefully, Foxfield will be yours to keep, but if it isn't . . . you won't leave Churchwood, will you? You'll need your friends more than ever.'

'I've decided I won't make any plans for the future until I have a clearer picture of what is going to be possible financially,' Naomi told her.

'Please don't rush into any drastic decisions even when you know where you stand. We want you here, Naomi. Churchwood wouldn't be the same without you.'

Naomi smiled but it was a sad smile.

Poor Naomi. She too made Alice's troubles seem light in comparison.

Fred Fletcher was another person burdened by far worse problems than Alice. He'd been away from the ward having therapy on her last visit to the hospital but now he was back. 'Good luck!' Babs Carter murmured, passing by as Alice entered the ward.

Alice didn't single him out but worked her way along the room, giving books out here, taking books back there, and having a friendly word with the patients who wanted to chat.

'Good morning, Private Fletcher,' she said, when her route took her to Fred's bedside. 'I'm Alice Irvine. Kate's friend.'

Anger came off him like steam from a boiling pot.

'You're the interfering busybody who never knows when she isn't welcome,' he said. 'A bad influence on our Kate, too, giving her ideas above her station.'

'Your sister is an amazing person who deserves to be appreciated,' Alice told him, 'but I'm not here to argue.'

'Then I suggest you move on.' He made a dismissive gesture. 'Go on. Get out of my sight.'

'Don't worry, I'm going. I just want you to know that I'm the person to ask if you ever want any books to read.' Kate had been mortified to report that Fred had lost or otherwise got rid of Alice's copy of *Just William*, but Alice wasn't going to hold that against him. 'I also read out stories to the men who are interested,' she said.

'I'm not one of 'em.'

'As you wish – as long as you don't stop others from enjoying the stories.'

'I'll speak as I find,' he warned.

Alice let it pass, suspecting that he'd soon be shouted down by his fellow patients if he tried to heckle when she was reading out the stories they so enjoyed. 'I'm sorry for what's happened to you,' she said by way of a parting. 'I hope you'll let the staff here help you to become as healthy and capable as possible.'

Fred only sneered as Alice stepped away. What a bitter young man he was, but she could understand his devastation. The loss of a person's legs would be a terrible blow to anyone, but to Fred Fletcher – once tall, powerful and full of vigour – the blow must have fallen particularly hard. He didn't yet know how else to be.

Kate rushed over from the farm when Alice walked home along Brimbles Lane, still nervous because she couldn't rid herself of the feeling that she was being watched. 'Did you see Fred?' Kate asked.

'I did.'

Kate must have read something in Alice's expression because she slumped and said, 'He was awful, wasn't he?'

'He wasn't nice, but I didn't mind that for my sake,' Alice assured her. 'I'm more concerned about *him*.'

'I don't know what to do,' Kate admitted. 'When I see him, I'm torn between wanting to slap him and wanting to burst into tears because everything I say is wrong.'

'It isn't wrong. He's just so overwhelmed and frightened that he'd bite back at you whatever you said. I've seen Stratton House work wonders on angry patients before. Hopefully, they'll help Fred too. Has anyone else been to see him yet?'

'Kenny visited but I suspect he spent most of the visit in silence. He feels out of his depth.'

'Your father?'

'I'm working on getting him to visit. I think he's afraid of seeing Fred like that and is even more out of his depth than Kenny. But Fred needs to know his father cares enough to see him, even if they only argue.'

'And Vinnie?'

'Same thing. He's bound to say the wrong thing, but I'm encouraging him to visit just so Fred feels wanted.'

Alice nodded. Fred needed his family around him, even one as hopeless as the Fletchers.

'The good thing is that Frank is coming home on leave,' Kate said then. 'He didn't make much headway with Fred through letters, but neither of them is good at writing. I'm hoping that, once they're together, they'll draw close again and Frank will persuade Fred that he still has a future, even if it's not the one he always expected.'

'Frank could make all the difference,' Alice agreed, and then changed the subject. 'Have you heard from Leo?'

Kate looked woebegone. 'Not for a while.'

'It's awful when post from the front is held up, isn't it? I'm sure you'll hear from him soon.'

Kate managed a smile and the girls parted.

Walking home, Alice reflected that her list of people who were struggling just now was growing. Evelyn, Naomi, Kate, Fred and the other Fletchers . . .

Her problems were minor in comparison, a thought that was reinforced when she arrived at the cottage to find a letter from Daniel awaiting her.

My darling girl, he'd begun. She read about how much he missed and loved her and smiled at his funny story of a misunderstanding between two fellow officers. A golden glow stole over her. Yes, she had her disappointments, but she had a husband she loved and who loved her in return. Soon she'd have their baby, too.

CHAPTER TWENTY-TWO

Naomi

'Mrs Harrington!' The Great Man greeted her with all the bonhomie of an old friend who'd invited her to come and sit by his hearth and drink his port as they reminisced over happy days gone by.

Naomi tried to appreciate the welcome, but this was far from a happy occasion for her. It would be an exaggeration to describe the status of her financial affairs as a life-or-death situation, but it was a huge weight on her shoulders and was giving her sleepless nights.

'About my husband's statement of his finances,' she began.

'Yes, we'll come to that. First things first, though. Let me ring through to my secretary and ask her to bring us tea.'

'None for me, thank you.' Mindful of the Great Man's exorbitant rates, Naomi was keen to keep this meeting short.

'Perhaps later, then.' He gestured for her to sit in one of the visitors' chairs while he settled back behind his enormous desk. 'Good journey down?' he asked.

'Fine, thank you.' The train had been crowded with servicemen and women, and Naomi had struggled to get a taxi at the station. She'd half wished she could save the fare by walking but had known that her dumpy little legs would struggle with the distance. Probably, she could have taken a bus, but she was unfamiliar with the routes. The next time she came to London, she'd allow time to investigate them. 'I'm keen to talk about Mr Harrington's statement of his financial position.'

'Of course. Please don't worry, dear lady. You're in good hands.' He picked up a sheet of paper and studied it.

Naomi wanted to scream at him. *Get on with it!*

'Now, then,' he finally said, holding the paper towards her and pointing. 'Mr Harrington has given details of several accounts and investments here. Do you believe the amounts he indicates are accurate?'

'I'm sure they're accurate.'

'Naturally, I'll request documentary proof of that.'

And naturally, it would be a waste of time and money. Alexander wouldn't make crass mistakes that could easily be exposed if his bank were asked for confirmation.

'You still appear to be troubled, Mrs Harrington.'

'I suspect there are other accounts and investments that he hasn't disclosed,' Naomi explained.

'You have grounds for your suspicions?'

'Instinct – and knowledge of the man I married.'

The Great Man's expression told her that instinct didn't count for much in the legal world but Naomi already knew that. It was the very thing that bothered her. 'He might have accounts with other banks,' she added. 'He might have money held in the name of his . . . of his lover. Or in the names of his children. He might have bought the house in which they live.'

'He makes no mention of such a house in his statement. They might be renting a property, of course.'

'And they might not.'

'I'll make enquiries about it. I'll also give further thought to the possibility of other accounts.'

'Do you have any ideas for finding out if they exist?'

'My dear lady, your husband won't be the first man to try to hide the state of his finances – if that's what he's actually doing – and I'm sure he won't be the last. You've come to me because I am a specialist in the area of divorce and marital separation, and I have teams of clever people on hand to carry out investigations in accordance with my instructions.'

Teams of clever people who'd add to her bill with no guarantee of finding anything untoward. Launching them off on what might be a wild goose chase could leave her with even less money. How upset her father would be if he could see what was happening. *You're my precious girl and I'm going to look after you for the rest of your life*, he'd said when he'd told her about the trust. *There'll be no scratching around for pennies to buy bread for my girl! You'll live like a proper lady and I'll be as proud as a peacock!*

It grieved Naomi to think that she'd let Alexander fleece the trust that represented her father's lifetime's work. She was stupid, stupid, stupid!

'I need to think about the best way forward but, firstly, I'd like to know why so much money was withdrawn from my trust fund and how it's been spent,' she said.

'For sure, Mrs Harrington. I'll be making enquiries about that too.'

His benign smile conveyed the message that she should leave things in his capable – and horribly expensive – hands.

'Well?' Bert asked. He'd seen her getting off the bus in Churchwood and had offered her a lift home in his truck. Weary from travelling and chastising herself for her years of foolishness, she'd accepted the offer gratefully.

She told him what the Great Man had said.

Bert nodded thoughtfully. 'Let's hope he's as good as he seems to think he is.'

'Indeed,' Naomi agreed, but her imagination supplied a picture of Alexander looking cunning and smug. He'd had a long time to squirrel her money away and, doubtless, he was confident that it would never be found.

If the Great Man could puncture Alexander's complacency and find the missing money, he'd be worth every penny of his fee. But if he failed, Alexander would be sitting pretty on Naomi's fortune and laughing at her behind her back.

'Let's get you home,' Bert said.

CHAPTER TWENTY-THREE

Kate

'Frank!' Kate called from the cart, when she saw him getting off the bus.

Jumping down, she ran across the road and threw her arms around him, glad to see him, not only for his own sake but also for Fred's. When she'd hugged the twins on the day they'd set out for the war, they'd been equal in size and strength – strapping lads, both. Frank's brawn now brought home to her how shrunken Fred had become.

She expected Frank to step away with a gruff 'Don't go all soppy on me', but he submitted to the hug for a surprisingly long time before he drew back to say, 'How is he?' There was no need to explain that he meant Fred.

'Not good,' Kate said. More than a week at Stratton House had made no visible difference to Fred's mood. 'But it's wonderful that you're here now. Come on. Throw your kitbag into the cart and we'll get off.'

Frank did as she suggested and climbed up beside her. Kate nudged Pete, the old pony, and the cart lurched forward.

'How are you?' Kate asked, thinking that, despite his size, he looked anxious. Gone were the laughing, joking twins of old.

Frank shrugged as though he didn't know how to

answer. 'What shall I do?' he asked instead, and again there was no need to explain that he was referring to Fred.

This was the reason Kate had been keen to be the one to meet Frank. She wanted to talk to him about Fred without Ernie, Kenny or Vinnie pouring scorn on her point of view. 'Fred's life has changed out of all recognition,' she said. 'It's natural for him to grieve for his old life but he also needs to start thinking about a new one. It'll be different, but it can still be worthwhile.'

'Maybe you're right, but how the heck am *I* supposed to make him see it?' Frank looked all at sea.

'I'm not saying it'll be easy. Do you know of any other soldiers who have lost their legs but are still finding a sense of purpose? Any who are getting by on false legs or in wheelchairs? Have you any ideas about how Fred might earn a living? How he might have some fun?'

'Steady on, Kate, give me a chance to think.' Frank went quiet for a moment. 'There was a chap from Barton who lost a foot,' he finally said, 'but I don't know how he's getting on. And all Fred 'n' me know is farming. I suppose Fred could be taken down to the Wheatsheaf for a pint or two if they'd let him out of hospital for an evening, but I can't think of anything else.' Frank looked glum.

'Please keep thinking,' Kate urged. 'Meanwhile, do whatever you can to cheer him up. Tell him some stories. Tell him some jokes. Do anything to stop him from brooding about his situation.'

'I'll try,' Frank said, uncertainly.

How had it come to this? Less than two years ago the twins had been like inseparable wild bear cubs. They'd launched themselves at each other with carefree abandon to wrestle in play fights. They'd challenged each other to beer-drinking sessions and whooped as they'd downed their pints. They'd played jokes on people and got up to all sorts of high jinks that had made them the terror of Churchwood.

Laughing at life, they'd effervesced with spirit – two halves of a whole. Now war had torn them apart and broken them, and Kate could only hope that they'd find their way back to each other.

They reached the farm and headed into the kitchen. After a push from Ruby, Kenny greeted his brother with a slap on the shoulder and a 'Welcome home.'

Tactless as ever, Vinnie simply asked, 'Are there any pretty girls in the forces, Frank? Those WAAFs or Wrens or whatever they call them?'

Frank didn't bother answering but looked at Ernie, who nodded by way of a greeting. It was an ordinary sort of nod with no sarcasm or bite behind it. Coming from Ernie, it was almost a gush.

Kate introduced him to Timmy and the land girls, and Frank managed to say he was pleased to meet them. 'Likewise,' Ruby told him, but Pearl only grinned nervously.

'The soup's ready,' Ruby announced, and they all sat at the table.

Gone were the food fights of old. This was a quiet, sombre meal. Afterwards, Frank went off to Stratton House, but it wasn't long before he was back, his dejected expression telling them all they needed to know about his visit. 'I can't recognize our Fred,' he said in appalled wonder. 'It's like the shell that took his legs took the real Fred with them and left a stranger behind.'

As Frank told Kate more about what he'd tried to say and how Fred had reacted, it became clear that Fred had been savage towards his twin. 'He told me not to bother going back,' Frank said.

'But you *will* go back?' Kate pleaded, thinking that there'd never be a breakthrough in Fred's attitude if Frank stayed away.

To Kate's relief, Frank replied, 'It'll be like offering my head to a lion, but yes, I'll go back tomorrow.'

The next day, Kate made the most of Frank's presence to look in on the bookshop. She needed to talk to someone and, as always, that person was Alice. The session was going with a swing and the girls seized the moment for a private chat in a corner.

'I wish I could offer some advice,' Alice said, when she heard about Frank's failure to work some magic on Fred. 'I can only suggest that you all keep trying, but he will need time to rid himself of his anger and bitterness.'

'Do people in his situation always get over those feelings in the end?'

'I spoke to Matron about that. I won't lie and pretend that she said *all* people learn to adjust, but most manage to come to some sort of terms with their situation.'

Would Fred be one of those who *never* came to terms with his?

'Fred has a family who loves him, even if not every member of that family is capable of showing it,' Alice continued. 'It's early days yet, but once Fred has regained some level of fitness, I'm sure you'll all rally round to help him see that he still has a good life ahead of him. Perhaps he could learn to drive the tractor with artificial legs or some other adjustments. If not, he could keep the farm records and accounts, or train to do work of a completely different nature. He may not have used his brain much in the past, but that could change.'

Alice was right. Kate needed to be patient, though she

still couldn't suppress the fear that Fred would forever let his life be ruined by resentment and fury. She didn't want to be selfish and talk only of her own problems, though.

'You're looking well,' she told Alice, realizing it was true. 'You've had a letter from Daniel?'

'I have, and it was a lovely letter. I'd rather he was here in person, but letters are some compensation for his absence. Have you heard from Leo yet?'

'No.' The delay was niggling at Kate.

'When you consider the thousands of letters that must be heading to and from the war, it's surprising that more don't get lost or delayed,' Alice soothed. 'Knowing that doesn't make it easier when we're expecting letters, though.'

It certainly didn't. In fact, Kate had begun to fear that something bad had happened, though she was trying to keep a grip on her imaginings.

But she was talking about her own problems again. 'How is Naomi?' she asked, changing the subject. 'She looks tired.'

'The divorce is getting her down, understandably.'

'I wouldn't trust that snake of a man she married further than I could throw him,' Kate said. 'I don't think I ever spoke to him, but he made no attempt to hide the fact that he looked down on people like me. There was an air of something else I didn't like about him, too.'

'Arrogance, selfishness and slyness?' Alice suggested.

'All of those things.' Kate looked around at the book-shop. 'What's going on today?'

'We've got the books and newspapers out as usual, and we'll be having story time later. Some of us are working on new costumes for the nativity play.'

'It sounds lovely,' Kate said. She'd never been a

churchgoer but was tempted to go along and watch the play – if she could make the time. Christmas was still two months away, so maybe it would be possible.

'Hey, Kate!' someone called.

Turning, Kate saw Edna Hall holding up some knitting in brown wool. 'Do you like the sheep I'm making for the shepherds?'

'It looks terrific,' Kate told her, though it didn't look like any sheep she'd ever seen.

'I know it's the wrong colour, but I've only got brown wool from an old cardigan I unravelled,' Edna explained. 'I'm pretending it's a sheep that rolled in mud.'

'Good idea,' Kate approved.

'How do I look?' Mrs Lloyd asked, trying on a half-finished crown. 'Do you think I'd make a good wise man? Wise woman, rather?'

'You make a great woman, Molly. But are you wise?' Kate teased.

Molly Lloyd cackled at that. 'My Tom doesn't think so, but I know enough to give him his favourite dinners when I want some shelves putting up or a bit more money in my housekeeping. I can't be that much of a dunce.'

It felt lovely to slip back into the Churchwood community, but, as ever, Kate was needed back on the farm.

She returned to Alice to say goodbye. Nodding at the costume-making around her, she asked, 'Does all this mean you've already given out the parts in the play?'

'Not at all. These costumes are intended to last for several years, so they're not being made with particular children in mind. We're going for loose fits to suit all shapes and sizes. We can roll up sleeves and tuck fabric into belts if needed.'

'It's just that Timmy hopes to take part.'

'We're welcoming all village children who want to be involved. We'll be giving out the parts and starting rehearsals at the beginning of December.'

'I'll tell him that. He'll be very excited.'

Alice smiled. 'A lot of children are getting excited about the play.'

Kate headed for the door only to be pulled back by Edna Hall clutching her hand. 'You're a good girl, Kate,' Edna said. 'It's a pity we don't see more of you.'

'I'll come back as soon as I can,' Kate assured her, though she had no idea when that might be.

Naomi came over to hug her. Janet and May both waved, and Bert walked her to the door, saying, 'Keep your chin up, young Kate. Nothing lasts for ever, so hold on to that thought and come back to us when you can.'

She cycled home to find Frank already returned from the hospital. 'I did my best with Fred, but he called a nurse over and got her to tell me to leave. She said she was sorry to have to do it, but she couldn't let Fred cause a commotion and upset the other patients.' Frank paused then added, 'He said you'd abandoned him, Kate.'

'Abandoned him? Just because I haven't visited for two days?'

'I told him I was visiting instead but it made no difference.'

Fred was being unfair. Horribly unfair.

'Could you go back tomorrow?' Frank asked.

She hadn't helped Fred on her previous visits and couldn't see that she'd be any help tomorrow. But Frank was looking downtrodden, and he deserved a break on his few days of leave. He must have friends from the Wheatsheaf to see, or simply want to rest up at home.

'All right, I'll go tomorrow,' Kate told him, still hoping

that at least her presence might reassure Fred that he was loved.

'One more thing,' Frank said. 'Fred talked of coming home.'

'I'm sure he'll come home eventually.' Where else could he go when he was finally discharged from hospital?

'He wants to come home *now*. He says he hates the hospital and he'll be better off here.'

'The doctors won't allow it. Fred needs medical care.'

'He thinks you can give him all the help he needs.'

'I'm not qualified. It's a ridiculous idea.'

Frank shrugged. 'Just passing on what he said.'

Surely, it wouldn't be possible? Guilt struck Kate's conscience as she realized that the very thought of it filled her with dread. If Fred came home, she'd be run ragged with his demands. It would be terrible.

Hoping a letter might have come from Leo to cheer her up, she looked questioningly at Ruby. But the blonde girl only shook her head.

CHAPTER TWENTY-FOUR

Alice

The look on Adam's face warmed Alice's heart. 'They're coming along wonderfully!' he declared, staring round at the first of the completed nativity costumes. He'd come to the Sunday School Hall specially to see them.

There were pretty little angel dresses trimmed with silver tinsel, special wings for the Angel Gabriel, and shepherds' outfits in brown and green.

'They're well made so should last us for years,' Alice said.

'I can't thank you all enough.' Adam kissed Alice's cheek and then moved on to kiss Naomi, May and Janet before shaking Bert's hand. 'My first Christmas at St Luke's really is going to be joyful.'

'So many people in the village helped with fabrics and sewing or both,' Alice said.

'I'll be happy to thank them all,' Adam assured her.

They stored the costumes in the Hall cupboard for safekeeping and Adam locked the door. 'We don't want grubby-fingered children getting curious and smearing them with dirt, do we?' he explained.

'All of the village children are keen to take part,' Janet said. 'Apart from the Gregson boys, of course.'

They all exchanged regretful looks at the mention of the Gregson boys, but no one had any ideas for how to persuade their mother to let them be involved.

It was time to leave. 'Are you walking home?' Naomi asked Alice, obviously hoping they could walk together.

'Not just now,' Alice told her. She didn't give a reason and, luckily, Naomi didn't ask for one.

They smiled their farewells then Alice saw a bus approaching and hastened to the bus stop to catch it, eventually getting off in Barton.

Less than an hour later, Dr Lambert finished examining her. 'Congratulations,' he said. 'I'd say you're just over two months along, so the little one should make his or her appearance in May.'

Alice had already worked out the dates, though it was wonderful to have confirmation that she was indeed expecting Daniel's child. May was a lovely time to have a baby. Alice pictured herself taking it on long walks in the summer sunshine and sitting outside in the garden as clouds floated in a blue sky above them.

'How have you been feeling?' the doctor asked.

'Very well. I've been lucky to avoid morning sickness.'

'Lucky indeed, and long may it continue.'

He outlined the care she'd receive then said, 'A home birth is a possibility, of course, but I suggest the maternity home here in Barton. You'll be in the best possible hands.'

'Can I decide closer to the time?'

'Of course. Your father may have ideas about what's best. Is he aware of your situation?'

'Not yet.'

'I imagine he'll be delighted.'

'He will, though I'm not going to tell him yet. The first person who should know is my husband, but he's away serving in the war. I won't tell him until I'm at least three months along. I'll feel . . . safer then.'

'You don't want him to be disappointed if the pregnancy doesn't hold?'

'Exactly.'

'That's understandable. A chap shouldn't hear that sort of news when he isn't in a position to comfort his wife.'

And especially not when a moment of distraction could cost him his life.

'Well, you haven't long to wait before you reach three months, and so far there's every reason to hope for a positive outcome.'

'That's good to hear. Now, how much do I owe you?'

'Nothing at all, my dear. Your father was a great help to me in caring for patients during the measles epidemic not so long ago, and he wouldn't take a penny for his trouble. I owe him a lot and waiving my fee is my way of paying him back. Don't let that stop you from returning, though. I want to look after you.'

'You're very kind.'

Alice said goodbye then left his surgery to catch the bus back to Churchwood. A baby! Daniel's baby! The injury to her hand and her unemployment faded into the background of her mind, driven out by sheer joy. Daniel was going to be thrilled!

She'd be three months along in the second half of November. A few more weeks on and it would be Christmas. The more she thought about it, the more she warmed to the idea of waiting until then to tell him the news. Yes, she decided. News of this baby was going to be the best Christmas gift of all.

'Well?' her father asked when she returned to the cottage.

'Well, what?'

'Am I going to be a grandfather?'

So much for secrecy. 'You guessed?'

'My dear, I was a doctor for forty years, though I didn't need my qualification to interpret your secret smiles and your newfound radiance. Don't worry. I understand why you've kept your suspicions to yourself. Daniel should have been the first to hear the news, and I'm sorry I've stolen a march on him. I couldn't bear the suspense, I'm afraid. All's well, I hope?'

'Very well. The baby is due in May, but I'm not going to announce it to anyone yet. Not even Daniel. I want the news to be part of my Christmas gift to him.'

'I understand, and you can trust me not to breathe a word to anyone in the meantime.' Her father circled his arms around her, and drew her close. 'You're making me a very happy man, my dear.'

Alice was glad to hear it. She wished she could help to make Kate and Naomi half as happy, but all she could do was stand as a good friend to them in their troubles.

She'd bought a newspaper in Barton and after making a cup of tea she sat at the kitchen table and scanned the 'Situations Vacant' pages. She knew she wouldn't be able to work for long – a few months only – but the money she earned would help towards a pram and all the other things the baby would need.

Nothing remotely suitable was being advertised today, though. Ah well. She'd keep looking, though she might find it even harder to persuade an employer to take her on once her pregnancy started to show.

She took a sip of tea and allowed her mind to wander back to the baby. Boy? Girl? She'd be happy with either. Would it be fair-haired like her or dark-haired like Daniel? It was easy to visualize herself as a mother, rocking a baby in her arms, scooping water gently over its little body in the bath, powdering its soft, apricot-like bottom and reading stories as it listened, wide-eyed and rapt . . .

With that thought, something Mr Parkinson had said came into her mind.

CHAPTER TWENTY-FIVE

Naomi

The only good thing to be said about Alexander's reply to the Great Man's enquiries into her trust fund was that it had arrived after only a week. Naomi had braced herself for lies and evasions, but the unfairness of what Alexander had to say was breathtaking. According to him, the disappointing state of their finances was *her* fault.

The letter had come through their solicitors, of course, and Alexander had probably dashed it off in a hurry. Why not? He'd had years to plan how he would cover up his plundering of her money.

He'd begun his reply by complaining that, having married Naomi in good faith – ha! – he couldn't be expected to produce records and receipts going back a quarter of a century or more because he'd never thought he'd need them. However, to the best of his ability – another ha! – he'd provide as much information as possible.

In the first year of their marriage, money had been needed for their wedding – rather a plush affair, as Naomi's father, Cedric Tuggs, had expected his only child to be married in style, and Naomi herself had appeared to expect no less even after her father's death. What nonsense. The ceremony and reception in London had indeed been plush, but few guests had attended. Naomi had been surprised by the small number, in fact. Not that she'd had many people to invite, but she'd expected Alexander to invite plenty. With hindsight, she wondered if even then he'd been preparing to keep her in the background of his life.

The honeymoon in Scotland had followed – another expense. When Alexander had proposed Scotland as their destination he'd described it to her as a tour, which had sounded lovely, but the reality had turned out to be mostly a circuit of some of the more exclusive golf clubs in Scotland. Gleneagles, St Andrews . . .

As well, they'd needed to furnish the flat they'd rented at the beginning of their marriage. It had been a flat in Mayfair. 'Can we really afford this?' she recalled asking, and Alexander had assured her that they could.

They'd employed both a maid and a cook, and bought costly china, glassware and silverware, though Alexander usually preferred to dine out. Again, he implied now that it was Naomi who'd wanted those things, though the truth was that she'd have been content with more modest collections.

After that had come the purchase of Foxfield, which also required kitting out with furniture, carpets, curtains and the like. Staff had been needed to look after it, too. A year or two later had come renovations of the house itself – new bathrooms being added – and some landscaping of the garden. Both of these projects had been undertaken at Naomi's request, she read. True, but the extravagant scale of the work had been Alexander's choice.

They'd kept the Mayfair flat for a while but then bought the apartment in St John's Wood where Alexander lived now – when he wasn't living with his lover, though he didn't mention that. That apartment, too, had required redecoration, carpets, curtains and more furniture.

It was Alexander who'd wanted a permanent place in London, arguing that he needed it because he often worked late and spent evenings and weekends entertaining clients. But he argued now that Naomi had wanted it so she could visit the theatre, dine out and participate in the sort of society she'd favoured.

A stranger reading this account would assume that Alexander was the one to be pitied – the poor husband who'd worked himself to the bone to provide for a greedy wife who liked to show off her wealth. Naomi's blood boiled at the injustice of it. Yes, she'd visited the theatre and dined out on occasion, but not often. She'd have been satisfied with a much more modest style of life.

It was the same with the motor cars that Alexander had bought over the years. He claimed now that, while they'd been useful when he saw clients away from his office, Naomi had enjoyed the use of them for her social life and charity work. Not – the tone suggested – because she'd particularly wanted to do good in the world, but because she'd liked to be seen rubbing shoulders with the rich and being taken for one of them.

Of Alexander's handmade suits, shirts and shoes no mention was made, and when he touched upon his golfing interest it was done in another attempt to pretend that it had been Naomi who'd insisted on keeping up the appearance of wealth.

Then came the final stab of the knife. Alexander had never withdrawn money from her trust without Naomi's consent and he had her signature on all the paperwork to prove it. She really had played into his hands and allowed him to cheat her.

She looked again at some of the figures he'd included.

He'd fudged them with words like *approximately* but they were shockingly high – too high to be true? Naomi suspected so. Even if she'd been half as extravagant as he was trying to suggest, there was no way they'd have run her trust fund down by forty-five thousand pounds, especially not when taking into account Alexander's income from his stockbroking work.

Naomi was more convinced than ever that he'd hidden money away. Not that he'd have taken thousands of pounds all at once. He was too clever for that. No, he'd have taken a hundred here and a hundred there, pretending their bills and expenses were higher than they really were. And he'd have done it over decades to hide his plundering in the impenetrable mists of the past.

As for his lover, Alexander claimed that Amelia Ashmore's house was hers alone, funded by inheritances she'd received from two uncles who'd been killed in the 1914 war. Perhaps she had received inheritances, but had they really covered the full cost of purchase or had Alexander supplemented them? He admitted that he was supporting Amelia and their children but considered it his duty to continue to do so. Duty? What about his duty to Naomi? He made no mention of that but instead implied that he'd been driven into his lover's arms by finding no welcome from his greedy, snobbish wife at home.

A wave of helplessness washed over Naomi. The Great Man might uncover evidence that a few of the figures had been exaggerated, but Alexander would plead that any miscalculations were errors of memory rather than attempts to mislead. Doubtless, he'd also argue that, whether they'd spent more or less on particular expenses, it made no difference because all that was left was the money he'd disclosed in his statement.

Should she cut her losses and tell the Great Man not to bother investigating because the costs would likely outweigh any small gains? It felt feeble to give in to Alexander's scheming, but Naomi had to be practical about it. The more she spent on fees, the less money she'd have to live on after the divorce.

CHAPTER TWENTY-SIX

Kate

There was no point in asking Frank if he'd enjoyed his leave. How could he have enjoyed it when he'd made no headway with Fred and the mood on the farm had been so glum? Kate took him to the bus stop in the cart, put the reins down and simply wrapped her arms around him, saying, 'It's been wonderful to see you, Frank, and I'm sorry the circumstances weren't happier. You'll take care of yourself, won't you?'

'You can bet on it.' He shuddered and Kate guessed he was thinking of Fred's injuries, dreading that he might suffer the same.

'Fred has been unlucky,' she said, but Frank only gave her a sceptical look. Neither of them could know what the future held for him.

'Are you sure you remembered to pack everything?' she asked.

'I'm sure. Thanks for the lunch, by the way.'

She'd packed him a picnic for the journey. 'My pleasure.'

He got down from the cart and stood in the street, shuffling his feet awkwardly. 'I'm sorry I couldn't help Fred.'

'You tried. That counts for something.'

'Nothing I said or did was right for him.'

'Nothing any of us say or do is right for him at the moment. Hopefully, that will change.'

'Do you think they really will let him go home?'

'He'll receive better care in hospital amongst professionals than we could give him.'

'That's as may be, but Fred's made his mind up so they might let him have his way.' Frank paused, then said, 'Fred's my twin and I hate what's happened to him, but I hope they keep him in hospital for your sake. I've seen how much you have to do around the house and farm. Fitting looking after our Fred into all that . . .'

Frank shook his head at the impossibility of the workload then continued. 'Those land girls aren't doing a bad job and the little lad helps as best he can, but they can't match what Fred 'n' me used to do in a day. There's too much work even without our Fred needing to be looked after. We were stupid to join up and leave you all in the lurch. It wasn't as though we weren't already helping with the war effort, because we were putting food in the bellies of British servicemen and the people at home. Doing the right thing had nothing to do with it, though. We just wanted . . . oh, I don't know. Adventure, I suppose. What an adventure, with Fred's legs gone!'

Kate felt a wave of love for this brother who'd grown up at last but come face to face with tragedy along the way. 'Let's hope Fred's anger burns itself out and he starts to feel more optimistic,' she said. 'He might come on in leaps and bounds then.'

'You're trying to make me feel better. You're a good sister, Kate.'

The bus approached. 'I'd best say goodbye,' Frank said. 'You look after yourself too.' He jogged to the bus and got on, leaning towards a window to sketch a final salute.

Kate realized she was crying. Sending up a silent prayer for Frank's safety, she dashed the tears away, turned the cart and headed for home, feeling bleak and tired. So very tired. Was it disloyal to hope that the doctors would keep Fred in hospital for longer? Surely, it would be better for him as well as everyone at Brimbles Farm?

If Fred behaved at home with even half of the aggression he showed at the hospital, he'd make their lives a misery. Kenny and Vinnie would argue with him, and Ernie would shout at them all. Ruby would go around with her lips tightly sealed but ready to spring to her son's defence if he came into the firing line, while Timmy himself would tread warily around the house, terrified of this man with the frightening rage, and absenting himself as often as possible. As for Pearl, she'd tread warily, too, but be as awkward as a clumsy giant in her movements and intimidated into silence at mealtimes.

Of course, Kate was also low because she still hadn't heard from Leo. There could be all sorts of explanations. His letter might have been lost or delayed. Or Leo might be on a mission which gave him no chance to write or post a letter. But other possibilities crept into her mind and wouldn't budge. He might have lost interest in her. He might be ill. He might be injured . . .

So far, they'd always taken turns to write letters, but by now Kate was desperate. She decided to write again even though she hadn't yet received a reply to her last letter. Her pride might suffer if it turned out his silence was an indication that his feelings had changed, but surely that was preferable to not knowing what was going on with him?

CHAPTER TWENTY-SEVEN

Alice

'Your daughter could be a professional writer,' Mr Parkinson had said, but Alice had dismissed it from her mind after being rejected by the newspaper office in St Albans.

That rejection had been based on her inability to type quickly, though, rather than on anything she'd actually written. Thinking about it again, it had occurred to her that not all published writers worked in offices. Some beavered away at home and sent their articles and stories in by post. Maybe Alice could try to become one of those people and earn a few shillings by writing a short story for a magazine. Several stories, even. She could start by scribbling a story in a notebook using her uninjured hand and then type it up if it were any good. Typing would be slow and laborious, but she'd get there in the end.

The more she'd thought about the idea, the more she'd warmed to it. After all, she loved reading stories for her own benefit and also enjoyed reading them out loud at the bookshop and hospital. She knew what sorts of stories her listeners most enjoyed – or hoped she did.

After a lot more thought, she'd sat down at the kitchen table and written a story about a stray cat that, after a tough start in life, was adopted by a lonely elderly woman, bringing happiness to them both. She'd been full of enthusiasm as she wrote, but afterwards, when she'd read through what she'd written, Alice had felt disappointed.

She'd set the story aside in her bedroom for a couple of days in the hope that she might like it more when she returned to it with fresher eyes. But now she was reading it again, she decided the break had made no difference. Her writing read smoothly enough, and she didn't think she was being conceited in believing she had a nice way with description. But the story lacked something. It felt flat. Lifeless.

Sighing, she set it aside again. Perhaps she hadn't the talent to be a writer, after all. It was disheartening, but Alice tried not to dwell on it, because who knew what could happen next? She might look at a 'Situations Vacant' page and find the very job that would suit her.

Just now it was time to leave for the bookshop. Alice put on her coat and hat – it was getting colder by the day – said goodbye to her father and set out for the Sunday School Hall.

She helped Naomi, Bert, Janet and May to set up. Then the visitors streamed in, calling, 'Hello!' and, 'It's chilly out there,' and, 'I hope you've got that Agatha Christie book I wanted . . .'

'Don't let Marjorie near this,' Mrs Larkin said, over by the book table. She was holding *The Hound of the Baskervilles*, a scary Sherlock Holmes story by Sir Arthur Conan Doyle.

'Goodness, yes,' Miss Gibb agreed. 'She'll be seeing the thief again, only this time he'll have a huge dog beside him. A huge, savage dog with glowing eyes.'

The people around her laughed. Alice could see the funny side too, though she pitied poor Marjorie, the butt of so many jokes. Fortunately, Marjorie had claimed no more sightings of the thief, though milk was still going missing, as were vegetables from Brimbles Farm and village gardens. However, the thief still appeared to take food and milk only when there was plenty to leave behind, which was to his credit.

'I'm still putting flasks of soup outside the vicarage when I'm over here in Churchwood,' Adam told her. 'I make sure the notices are still in place, too, urging the thief to ask for help. He's never taken the food and, as far as I know, he hasn't knocked on the vicarage door either. He might have knocked when I've been staying over in Barton, of course, but I suspect he hasn't. He really must wonder if we're setting a trap, which is a pity. The poor chap must be hungry much of the time. Uncooked vegetables fresh from the chilly ground can hardly satisfy a man's appetite. It must be horribly uncomfortable sleeping in the woods or wherever he camps, too, especially now it's getting colder.'

'Rainy nights and frosty mornings,' Alice agreed. 'He's still showing no sign of moving on.'

'I just wish he'd make contact.'

'Too afraid or too ashamed, I suppose.'

'Or too troubled in his mind,' Adam added, and Alice nodded because the thief might well have been unbalanced by a bereavement, an injury or a traumatic experience.

'I wonder why he hasn't moved on,' she said.

'Maybe it's because Churchwood is a kind sort of place. We haven't involved the police or hunted him down. He might have seen the food and notices I've left out even if he hasn't worked up the resolve to respond. And people are still having milk delivered to their doorsteps in the full knowledge that it might be their turn to have it stolen.'

'So far that's true,' Alice said, 'but I've heard grumblings now milk rationing is imminent.'

She'd overheard Miss Gibb talking in the grocer's. 'I shan't be happy if I can't buy fresh milk to replace what's taken,' Miss Gibb had said.

Others had nodded agreement and nodded again when Mrs Hutchings had gone on to say, 'I can't abide the dried stuff that comes in tins.'

'Of course, the thief might know nothing of milk rationing,' Adam said now. 'If he's living in the woods somewhere, he won't have access to the wireless or newspapers. It's possible that he's an uneducated man who couldn't read the notices I've been putting up anyway.'

'Or he might just be unable to read them in the dark.'

'The blackout is unfortunate from that point of view, though it must help him to move around the village unseen.'

'It's sad to think he might have knocked on the vicarage door when no one was home to answer it. Still, it won't be long before you're in Churchwood full-time.'

Adam smiled. 'Just another week or so. I'll be living in a fairly spartan way to begin with, as there's little furniture in the house and I haven't any of my own, but I shan't mind that. I can't wait to be here and making plans, especially for Christmas.'

'We're all looking forward to the Christmas Eve service. Carols and a nativity play are just what we need.'

Adam frowned suddenly. 'It's draughty in here. Has someone left the door open?'

The draught made Alice shiver too. 'Let's hope a toddler hasn't seized the chance to go adventuring.'

They hastened into the foyer, but the outer door was

closed. Alice opened it anyway and took a good look up and down the street. 'I can't see anyone.'

They went back inside, and she counted the children. 'All present and correct,' she concluded.

Perhaps the door had indeed been left open, but a gust of autumnal wind had closed it again.

'Time for tea,' Janet announced, getting up from her chair. 'Betty, you're on duty with me.'

The two women headed for the kitchen, where kettles were simmering on the stove and cups and saucers had been laid out earlier. A moment later, Janet walked out again, looking stunned. She made discreet eye contact with Alice and Adam, who went over to find out what was wrong. 'Someone has taken the biscuits,' she whispered. 'We'd laid them on a plate as usual, and someone must have come in through the kitchen door and taken them. About half of them, anyway.'

That would explain the draught. So the thief had finally escalated his activities and entered a building.

'Have you any spare biscuits to make up the shortfall?' Adam asked.

'A few.'

'Then put those out but keep quiet for now. Could you tell Betty to keep quiet too?'

'The soul of discretion is Betty,' Janet said.

She returned to the kitchen and Adam turned to Alice. 'We need to think about what we do next,' he said.

CHAPTER TWENTY-EIGHT

Naomi

'We have to tell people,' Bert said.

Bert, Naomi, Alice, Adam, Janet and May had stayed behind after the bookshop session to talk about the thief again.

'Taking milk from doorsteps was one thing,' Bert continued. 'But our thief crossed a line in entering a building. He may only have taken a few biscuits from a public hall, but he still crossed a line, and we can't be sure he won't cross another one by entering people's houses. Folk should be warned to keep their doors and windows locked. Maybe to hide their valuables, too.'

'I agree,' Naomi ventured. 'People will be terrified if he gets into their homes and someone could be hurt if there's a scuffle.'

Adam nodded. 'Any different views?' he asked.

Janet and May shook their heads.

'I agree that people should be warned,' Alice said, 'but I think we need to be careful in what we say. I'm not just thinking of the more hysterical members of our community . . .'

Marjorie, Naomi guessed.

'. . . but also of the people who might feel genuinely vulnerable, particularly our elderly residents and those living alone.'

'Very true,' Adam said. 'We should stress that we've no reason to suspect the thief will actually enter anyone's house, but it won't hurt to lock doors and windows as a precaution.'

'We'll still upset some people, but I don't see how that can be helped,' Bert said.

'Let's talk to people individually,' Naomi suggested, and they drew up a list of who would speak to whom.

Naturally, it fell to Naomi's happy lot to speak to Marjorie. 'I'll go and see her straight away,' she promised, because the last thing Churchwood needed was Marjorie hearing a rumour and launching her hysterics into the stratosphere.

Meeting over, they all made their way outside, agreeing to talk again if there was any trouble.

'Good luck with Marjorie,' Bert told Naomi.

'I suspect I'll need it.'

He studied her. 'Want to chat?'

'Yes, please.'

'Meet me by the truck when you've finished with Marjorie.' His eyes twinkled. 'I've only got four chaps to warn, so I'll probably be there before you.'

Naomi appreciated the humour, though she struggled to force a smile.

Marjorie looked pleased to see her, even if she was also surprised as they'd been together at the bookshop less than half an hour ago. 'I'll make some tea,' Marjorie said. 'I don't have cake or anything like that, though.'

'I don't need cake anyway,' Naomi said. 'I mustn't spoil my appetite for dinner.'

Marjorie put the kettle on and organized a tray while repeating again and again how delighted she was by the visit. The words struck at Naomi's conscience. Marjorie

171

was as loyal a friend as could be and deserved more of Naomi's time. Unfortunately, she was also exhausting.

Naomi waited until they were sitting down and drinking tea before mentioning her mission. 'We had a few biscuits taken from the bookshop today.'

'Taken?'

'Someone took them from a plate in the kitchen.'

'A child? Some of those young mothers let their children wander everywhere.'

'We think it might have been the same person who's been taking milk.'

'The thief?' Marjorie sat up straighter, blotches beginning to appear on her cheeks.

'It was hardly the crime of the century,' Naomi pointed out quickly.

'But the thief broke into the Hall!'

'He didn't *break* in. He just *stepped* in. And then he stepped out again without doing any harm.'

'But he's gone from theft to burglary! We're not safe in our homes!'

'I'm sure you're perfectly safe, but it won't hurt to keep your door and windows locked. Not that it's the time of year for open windows anyway. It's chilly, isn't it?'

Naomi was trying to keep things calm – to change the subject, too – but Marjorie's imagination was racing in wild directions.

'We could be murdered in our beds! Or held at gunpoint until we hand over all our worldly goods. We could be taken as hostages! We could—'

'Stop it this minute, Marjorie.' Naomi's voice was firmer now. 'I don't want to speak severely to you, but remember what happened when you frightened Mrs Gregson and her boys?'

'That was different. I might have been mistaken about what I saw then, but this time something has been *taken*. There's evidence!'

'Only a few biscuits, Marjorie. Don't make more of it than it justifies.'

'How can you be so calm? The thief came into the Hall kitchen!'

'Where he did no harm to anyone.'

'He might have done harm if there hadn't been so many people there to overpower him.'

It took a long time to bring Marjorie down from the rafters and secure her promise that she wouldn't stir up feelings in the village. Not that Naomi had much confidence in the promise.

Feeling even more exhausted, Naomi left to meet Bert. Unsurprisingly, he was sitting in the truck waiting for her. 'You managed not to throttle Marjorie?' he asked.

'Just about, though she thinks she's in danger of being throttled by the thief.'

'Unlikely, in my opinion.'

'In mine, too.' But the truth was that none of them knew how desperate the thief might become, nor what he might do if challenged.

'I hope you'll keep *your* doors locked,' Bert said.

'I'll talk to my staff about it as soon as I get home.'

'Do you want to go home now or come back to my house?'

'May we go straight to your house?' There was less chance of their chat being interrupted at Bert's, and his warm, homely kitchen eased her soul.

Fifteen minutes later, he sat down opposite her. 'This is about that long streak of ice you married,' he guessed.

Naomi told him about the latest letter from the Great

Man. 'I know I'll be luckier than most people even if I accept Alexander's figures,' she said. 'I'll still be able to afford somewhere to live and have some money to live on.'

'That you will,' Bert agreed.

'So you think I should stop fighting and accept the situation?'

He gave her a sceptical look. 'Not on your life, woman. That man is fleecing you and he shouldn't get away with it.'

'But if I fight, I'll spend huge amounts on fees and may not be any better off. I may be worse off, in fact. Alexander will have hidden the missing money well. I'm sure of it.'

'At the moment, the icicle holds all the cards. At least he thinks he does. What you need is to find a chink in his armour, and I don't mean spending a fortune on lawyers' bills. I mean finding one yourself.'

'How, though?'

Bert told her his idea.

But it was too fantastical for serious consideration. 'No,' Naomi said. 'I appreciate the suggestion, but Alexander wouldn't. He couldn't.'

'Couldn't he?' Bert gave her a long, challenging look then turned away and sipped his tea.

CHAPTER TWENTY-NINE

Kate

Fred greeted Kate with a smile for once, but it wasn't a pleasant one. On the contrary, it looked triumphant – and mean.

'I'm being allowed home,' he crowed, and it was obvious to Kate that not only was he unconcerned about how inconvenient this would be to his family of busy farmers, but he was also relishing it.

'Have they actually said you can come home? Or are they simply considering it?'

'I'm coming home,' he repeated. 'What do you think of that?'

'I'm glad, if it means you're getting better.'

Fred laughed. 'Liar. They just want rid of me, and you don't blame them because you don't want me either.'

'I want the best for you, Fred.'

'No, you don't. You're dreading the thought of looking after me, but that's tough. I was hurt fighting for my country – your country – so you owe me. Ernie, Kenny, Vinnie, even those land girls . . . they owe me too.'

'You sound as though you *want* to be difficult.'

'That's because I *do* want to be difficult.' He sounded proud of it. 'Off you go, then.' He made a twirling gesture with his fingers. 'There's no point in hanging around here, so turn around and go home to get things ready for me.'

'When will you be coming?'

'I don't know yet. Soon, though. Very soon.'

Kate tried to fight off the feeling that the walls were drawing ever nearer and would soon box her in. 'I brought you some cake that Ruby made. We saved our sugar rations especially.'

'Put it on the cupboard.'

'You'll eat it later?'

'Maybe I will. Maybe I'll just throw it away.'

Kate bit back the criticism that throwing it away would be wasteful. Fred knew it and was simply trying to provoke her.

'I'll say goodbye, then,' she said instead.

Fred waved his hand dismissively. 'Cheerio!' he mocked.

Matron caught Kate in the corridor. She looked solemn.

'It's true?' Kate asked. 'You're sending Fred home?'

'It's sooner than we'd like, but your brother isn't cooperating with us and it's thought that he might be one of those patients who fare better at home. At least for a while. He may be able to work through his anger there, and perhaps he'll realize that he's better off accepting the care here. It isn't as though your home is far away. He can come back for regular checks and therapy so we can keep a general eye on him, and he can be here in a jiffy if there's a serious problem.'

'Going home might work for some patients, but Fred seems to hate us.'

'The person he most hates is himself,' Matron said. 'Not that he understands that yet. He's confused about this new body and its restrictions, and he needs to hit out because he's scared. No one is suggesting that he'll definitely be better off at home, only that it's a possibility that's worth exploring. It won't be easy for the family, though. Especially you.'

'If I could believe that it'd be best for Fred, I wouldn't be quite so worried.'

'If Fred's health suffers, or if it becomes intolerable for the family to have him at home, we'll have him back straight away. But give it a try, hmm?'

With that Kate had to be content. She went home to share the glad tidings and saw her own apprehension mirrored in everyone else. 'Perhaps Fred will change his mind,' Kenny said, but no one answered. The gloom pressed down on them and kept them silent.

Ruby caught Kate's eyes and gave a tiny movement of her head that meant Kate should follow her. Was there a letter from Leo?

They went upstairs to Kate's bedroom and Ruby handed over a letter. 'It doesn't look like a letter from Leo, but I thought it best to give it to you in private, just in case it's something personal.'

Kate smiled her gratitude, waited until Ruby had gone and then studied the envelope, which bore her name and address in handwriting she didn't recognize. It was post-marked Dover. She ripped it open and drew out a single sheet of paper.

Dear Kate,
I hope you remember me from the time Leo brought you to a dance near our air force base at Hollerton.

Her gaze flew to the bottom of the letter. It was signed by Max Evershed. Kate did remember him, but why should he be writing? Feeling a chill of foreboding, she read on.

177

I'm sorry to report that Leo's plane was shot down. He man-
aged to steer it out of enemy airspace and land it on Allied
territory without damaging either people or buildings – which
was heroic of him – and let me hasten to assure you that he
was pulled out alive. Unfortunately, he was injured and by now
I imagine he's back in Britain being treated for his wounds. I
don't have any more information, I'm afraid – including where
he's been sent – but I'll let you know if I hear more. In the
meantime, I'm sure you want to hold him in your thoughts . . .

Kate's legs suddenly weakened. She sat down on her
bed and leaned forward with a groan of dismay.

CHAPTER THIRTY

Alice

'Let me walk with you,' Alice's father said as she prepared to leave for the hospital. He was taking the escalation in the thief's activities seriously.

'I've been walking to and from the hospital ever since the thief arrived in Churchwood, and that was more than two months ago now,' Alice pointed out. 'He's had every chance to attack me if he wanted, but I've never even seen him. Just because he's taken a few biscuits – driven by desperation, probably – it doesn't follow that he means anyone any harm.'

'But—'

'It's food he wants. He won't find any on me, but he may find some here, so be sure to lock up after I've gone.' Alice didn't begrudge the thief some food but feared he might panic and hit out if her father discovered him in the kitchen.

'It's no bother for me to walk with you,' her father persisted.

But it *would* be a bother. Adding together the two trips he'd need to make – one to deliver her and one to collect her – he'd have to walk several miles in total and it would eat up his day. 'I'll be fine,' she insisted.

She fastened her coat and kissed his cheek. 'Don't forget to lock up,' she said and set out.

She'd spoken bravely but couldn't suppress a frisson of apprehension as she left Churchwood behind. She scanned the trees that bordered the lane and several times had to obey an overwhelming compulsion to look behind her. But she saw and heard only woodland wildlife and the familiar rustle of trees.

She reached Brimbles Farm and turned her thoughts to Kate. The poor girl had barely taken on board Alice's warning about the thief because far heavier troubles were pressing down on her slender shoulders – Fred's return, which would set the farmhouse into a tizzy of bustle and bad temper, and Leo's situation.

'You may be worrying about Leo more than his condition warrants,' Alice had advised when they'd last met. 'He may make a complete recovery.'

'I don't *know* that's the case, though,' Kate had argued. 'I don't *know* if his life is in danger. I don't really *know* anything.'

It seemed cruel of the Fates to place her in such torturous uncertainty for a second time. She'd been through it with Fred and now she was going through it with Leo.

'Hopefully, you'll hear more news soon,' Alice had said. And hopefully, it would reassure Kate that Leo was faring far better than Fred.

Kate had shrugged, her frustration and worry evident in her restless movements and the frown that cut between her brows.

'When does Fred arrive?' Alice had asked.

'Tomorrow. Am I being a terrible sister when I say I'm dreading it?'

'Not at all.' Alice had seen Fred at the hospital several times and not once had he even approached civility. The ward was going to be a happier place without him, and the staff would be relieved to see the back of him too, if only temporarily. As Babs Carter had confided, 'The other patients need a rest from him, though I feel sorry for your friend.'

Kate had sighed then. 'I'm trying to hold on to what Matron said about Fred being frightened beneath his awful behaviour.'

'She's probably right. Matron has seen men react to their injuries in all sorts of ways during her career. She's very wise.'

Kate had nodded. 'Fred will still need to go to the hospital several times a week to have his wounds checked over and for therapies. We'll have to take him in the cart unless Kenny manages to persuade Ernie to buy the old truck from the people over at Meadows Farm. They're willing to sell it, but you know what a skinflint Ernie is.'

'He'll come round if you tell him how many working hours you'll all lose if he doesn't buy it.'

'I've already started doing that. So has Kenny. Vinnie too, though he just wants the truck to show off down at the Wheatsheaf. Not that Ernie or Kenny would allow Vinnie anywhere near a truck once he had a few pints inside him. The truck would end up in the lake – if he didn't run down a blameless pedestrian first.'

'Good luck with it all,' Alice had finally said, and she'd walked away wishing she could do more to help.

There was no sign of Kate in the nearby fields as Alice passed now, though she caught sight of Vinnie in the distance, leaning against a tree and sneaking a cigarette. Was Kate stuck indoors, doing Fred's bidding? Alice hoped not.

Walking on, her thoughts turned to Evelyn Gregson, whom she'd also visited on Saturday. She'd been braced for a rebuff when she'd knocked on her door.

Evelyn had opened it the merest crack and her eye had appeared in the narrow space. 'Yes? What is it?' she'd asked, before appearing to recognize Alice and opening the door just a fraction wider.

'I'm sorry to impose, but might I have a word with you? In private? I promise I'll be brief.'

'In private?' Evelyn had looked alarmed.

'It may be best if your boys don't hear,' Alice had explained.

Indecision had rippled over Evelyn's face, but then she'd sighed. 'All right. If it really is important.'

'Thank you.'

Evelyn had stepped back to allow Alice entry but closed the door behind her after a swift glance up and down the street that suggested she didn't want anyone else to know she was receiving a visitor. 'Come through to the kitchen.'

She'd led the way and then excused herself momentarily. Alice had heard her say, 'It's just a visitor for Mummy. Be good and play in here. She won't keep me long.'

She'd returned to Alice then. 'If you want tea, I could—'

'Thank you, but I really only need a minute of your time.' Evelyn had remained standing, so Alice had done likewise. 'It's about the thief who's been taking milk and raiding vegetable patches.'

'Oh?' Alarm had flared in Evelyn's eyes. 'That woman hasn't seen him again, has she? Or pretended to see him?'

'No more sightings,' Alice had assured her, then hesitated.

'Well?' Evelyn had prompted.

'Look. I don't want to make you anxious, but I feel you should know that the thief came into the Hall kitchen. He only took a few biscuits, but, even so, it's the first time we've heard of him actually entering a property. He may

182

never do it again – and there's still no reason to think he intends anyone any harm – but it's just possible that desperation and the worsening weather might drive him to take more chances. We're warning people to keep their doors locked as a precaution.'

Evelyn's hand had gone to her mouth.

'I didn't want to mention it in front of your boys in case it frightened them.' Clearly, it had frightened Evelyn.

'I appreciate your discretion,' she'd said.

She'd gone quiet for a moment, frowning and chewing her lip, then she'd crossed briskly to the kitchen door and turned the key. Even that hadn't satisfied her, because after another moment she'd pulled the key from the lock and placed it on a shelf. 'It would be the work of a moment to break the glass and reach through to open the door from the outside,' she'd explained, for the door had a window set into its upper half.

The shelf would hide the key from the boys too, Alice had supposed.

'I'm sorry I had to be the bearer of worrying tidings,' she'd said, 'but I thought you should know.'

'I . . . I appreciate it,' Evelyn had told her, though it obviously cost her an effort to show the visit had proved useful.

'If you ever need help—' Alice had begun, but Evelyn had cut her off with a nod.

It had been the signal for Alice to leave.

What a puzzling person Evelyn Gregson was. Alice wished she could understand her better, but even though Evelyn was a mystery, it was hard not to pity her. Whatever her circumstances, they were making her a sharp, nervy woman and probably a lonely one, too.

A loud crack had Alice's thoughts snapping back to the present. She turned towards the woods but saw only a

183

squirrel racing across the ground and launching itself up a tree. She breathed in deeply and willed her heartbeat to return to normal but was glad to see Stratton House in the distance.

Ward One was noticeably more relaxed now Fred wasn't souring the atmosphere. Alice threw herself into her usual routine of collecting and redistributing books, reading stories to patients and writing letters for those who couldn't manage to write themselves. In between she chatted with patients and also managed a few minutes with her two nursing friends, Babs and Pauline.

'Any more thefts in the village?' Pauline asked, and Alice told them about the stolen biscuits, adding, 'Nothing has been taken from here?'

'It would take a brave man to steal from a hospital that has military men on the premises,' Pauline said.

'Or a very stupid one,' Babs agreed.

Talk of the thief put Alice in mind of her isolated walk home. The advance of autumn meant the days were growing short and, wanting to reach home before twilight fell, she left the hospital in good time.

She occupied the long walk with thoughts of the letter she planned to write to Daniel later. She'd received one from him that morning and was eager to reply as soon as possible. His letter had been as loving as ever and he'd done his best to report cheerily on life with his fellow servicemen, but towards the end she'd picked up a sense that his spirits were lower than usual.

I wish I could be there with you, my darling. You feel even further away than usual tonight and it saddens me to think that we'll be spending Christmas apart, he'd written. After that, he'd rallied and urged her not to worry about him because he was perfectly fine and healthy.

Yet the wistful – even despondent – tone of those few words had already registered in her mind. It was unlike Daniel to be depressed, but he was only human and no one's morale could hold out against the cruel effects of the war all the time. She cast around in her thoughts for new and cheery things to tell him but came up blank. She could think only of the sort of news she'd included in her letters many times – developments in the garden, life with the chickens, sessions at the bookshop . . . Even Adam's plans for a more exciting village Christmas had been mentioned before.

Of course, there was one subject she hadn't mentioned yet: the baby. She'd planned to tell Daniel about it closer to Christmas, but perhaps he needed to hear the joyful news now. It would lift his spirits in an instant, especially as she'd be able to assure him that she felt incredibly well and that Dr Lambert was pleased with her.

After dinner that night she sat down with pen and paper, glowing with anticipation. Daniel was going to be thrilled!

Darling Daniel,
  As ever, it was wonderful to receive your last letter and I'm so glad to hear that you're well. I'm delighted to be able to bring you some good cheer with my news . . .

CHAPTER THIRTY-ONE

Naomi

Walking into the post office, Naomi saw that her fellow customers looked sombre.

'Joe Simpson passed away early this morning,' Mrs Lloyd explained.

The news had been expected for days, but even so . . . 'I'm sorry to hear that,' Naomi said. 'Joe was a lovely man. I'll send his sister a letter of condolence. It's much too early for information about the funeral, I suppose?'

'Adam has gone to see about it. Joe always said he wanted to be buried here in Churchwood.'

Naomi nodded, glad to hear that Adam had lost no time in visiting Joe's sister even though it was his day for moving into the vicarage. 'I don't have many possessions, so I don't need any help,' he'd said. 'Mrs Harris will sort me out anyway.'

Mrs Harris was to be his housekeeper.

Naomi was also glad to hear that Joe would be buried here. Having lived in the village all his life, it felt right that he be returned to his community and given a headstone in the churchyard of St Luke's, where people could visit and remember him.

Walking home a little later, her thoughts passed from Joe to the frailty of life in general. At forty-six, Naomi was still in her prime, according to Bert, but who knew how much longer anyone had left on earth?

How did she wish to spend her remaining time? Keeping strictly to budget because Alexander had taken her money? Or fighting him now in the hope that she could stop that from happening? Hoping to wipe the smugness from his face, too?

She reached Joe's house and paused to look up at it. Was it fanciful to imagine it was bowing its head in sorrow for the man who'd made it his home for his whole life? It would seem fitting, if so.

But what of the future? Once again, Naomi tried to picture herself living here while someone else took over Foxfield, perhaps ripping out the furnishings and gardens to mould them to a different taste. Could she bear seeing it daily when it would surely remind her of the starry-eyed optimism she'd felt coming to Churchwood as a young bride with hopes of a happy marriage and children? When it would also remind her of her folly in leaving herself vulnerable to Alexander's infidelity and financial chicanery?

Days had passed since she'd read Alexander's letter blaming her for the squandering of her trust fund. The Great Man was awaiting her reply, but she needed to decide whether to cave in now or risk more of her money in a fight. There was Bert's idea, of course, but Naomi still thought it too unlikely for words. And yet . . .

She reached the Foxfield gateposts, but instead of walking between them she turned and made her way down Brimbles Lane and into the woods, emerging in the narrow lane beside Bert's market garden.

He was nowhere to be seen, but the truck parked on the drive suggested he was at home. She passed through the small side gate and approached his kitchen door. His muddy boots had been left outside and when he opened the door he was in his stockinged feet. There was a toe peeping through a hole in his sock, and patches over both knees of his ancient trousers. Bert never cared for sartorial elegance.

'Come in,' he said. 'I was just checking on my scones.'

Naomi entered and Bert left her to take the scones from his oven. They smelled delicious, even though Naomi's stomach was tight with anxiety. 'You'll have a scone,' he said, and it was a statement rather than an invitation.

Bert's all-seeing eyes would have noticed that her skirts were growing looser around her middle. Not that she was slender. She was built on lines too solid ever to be svelte.

He glanced up at her. 'Taking root over there, are you?'

Naomi was still standing by the door.

'Or are you waiting for permission to sit down?'

Used to his sarcasm, she went to sit in one of the armchairs by the hearth and held her hands out to the fire. Winter was approaching fast.

'So,' he said, when he'd given out teacups and plates and sat down opposite her. 'You've been thinking about what I said?'

'I have.'

'Now you're going to argue that I'm wrong. Not because you want to convince me, but because you want to convince yourself.'

Bert always seemed to know what she was thinking. It could be infuriating.

'Let's eat our scones before we clash swords,' he said. 'If I say so myself, they're rather tasty.'

They were. Still warm from the oven, they were dripping with melted butter.

'You must have used up all your butter ration,' Naomi said.

'I've been saving it for scone day.'

They drank their tea too, then Bert sat back and said, 'Go on, then, woman. Tell me I'm wrong.'

'Alexander couldn't have married his lover,' Naomi argued. 'Committing a crime like bigamy would be the ruin of him, professionally and financially. It would damage his social standing, too.'

'Which he wouldn't like because he thinks highly of himself and believes he occupies an important place in the world?'

'Precisely.'

'It would only damage him if he got caught,' Bert pointed out.

Naomi still shook her head. 'I actually asked him if he'd married her. That was before I thought through the havoc it would have wrought in his life. He told me no, because how could he marry her when he was married to me?'

'And the icicle is such an honest man,' Bert said.

'He wouldn't have done it. He'd have been risking everything.'

'You know the long stick of ice better than me, but wasn't he risking everything by having a secret family anyway? You could have found out anytime and kicked off a public scandal that would have been the ruin of him. Colleagues, clients, friends . . . would they all have stood by him? I doubt it. The man is a risk-taker, Naomi, and while bigamy *may* have been a step too far for him, there's a chance that it wasn't.'

Could Bert be right? Clearly, there was a side to Alexander that Naomi didn't know at all, but one thing she knew for certain – he was a greedy man who took whatever he wanted. He'd wanted Amelia Ashmore and he'd taken her, regardless of his marriage vows. And instead of being honest about it, he'd strung Naomi along too, doubtless for her money and perhaps also for an appearance of respectability.

'If I could prove that he's a bigamist, I'd be in a much better position for negotiating a financial settlement, wouldn't I?' she asked.

'Indeed you would, woman.'

'Some people would call that sort of thing blackmail.'

'Others would call it levelling the balance of power. That man has spent years swindling you out of money. If you can swing some power back in your favour, I'd say that's only fair.' He paused, before pointing out, 'Of course, you need to find out if he really is a bigamist first.'

CHAPTER THIRTY-TWO

Kate

'Where do you think you're going?' Fred demanded.

'Into the village to buy bread.'

'Into the village to visit that stupid bookshop, more likely.'

'The bookshop isn't running today.' Her real errand was to try to buy a little treat to send to Leo once she knew where he was.

'If we need bread, someone else can fetch it. Ruby or Pearl. Your loyalty should be to me. Don't you think so, Ernie?'

Their father was looking through a newspaper, his shoulders hunched over. Kate suspected he was pretending not to have heard.

'Ernie!' Fred shouted.

Their father finally looked up and glowered at Kate. 'Do your duty and stay with your brother.'

Fred gloated maliciously and Kate turned away to walk to the kitchen window, her fists clenched at her sides. She pitied Fred and his situation from the bottom of her heart, but this spite was hard to bear no matter how often she reminded herself that he was a frightened man.

It didn't help that Kate lacked the sort of personal qualities that made for a good nurse, patience especially. Alice would be perfect in the role as her well of patience ran deep, but Kate was the opposite. Her temper was quick to rise, and her tongue jumped all too rapidly to retorts. She dreaded losing her temper with Fred, but it was a struggle to rein it in.

He'd only been home for two days but her worst fears had been realized. While Kate was the particular object of his grievances and complaints, he was horrible to everyone. Unless he was put on the spot and forced to acknowledge him, Ernie went around as though Fred were invisible. Vinnie was sulking because Fred had lashed out at him for making a stupid joke about missing legs, and Kenny coped by staying out of the house as much as possible.

Ruby, Pearl and Timmy avoided Fred, too. Ruby spoke quietly in his presence. Timmy whispered if he had to speak at all. And other than a forced, 'Pleased to meet you,' Pearl had said nothing to him since he'd arrived. She didn't look at him either – not in the eye – but sent sideways glances in his direction now and then as though terrified he might actually speak to her.

'I want . . .'

'I need . . .'

'Fetch me this, fetch me that . . .'

Fred's demands rang out all day long. Occasionally, Kenny, Vinnie or Ruby did Fred's bidding. Once, Pearl had fetched Fred a glass of water, but in her haste to place it beside him and leap away again, the water had spilled over his newspaper, meaning Kate had needed to rush in with a cloth to mop it up and try to calm Fred down. With everyone else unwilling to go near him, nine times out of ten it was Kate who helped Fred.

His demands rang out during the night, too. Fred was

sleeping downstairs in the little-used front room. Frank had slept in there on a mattress stuffed with hay on his leave, but Stratton House had loaned a bed for Fred, together with a wheelchair. Kate had provided him with a bell so he could ring for help during the daytime, and Fred had also insisted on being given a broom so he could bang on the ceiling during the night. The night-time interruptions had left them all tired and irritable.

For Kate, the timing of Fred's arrival couldn't have been worse. She was already frantic with worry over Leo and finding it hard to sleep. She'd written back to Max and asked to be kept informed, but so far she'd heard nothing at all.

'Time I was off for my therapy,' Fred announced now, clearly delighted that Kate would have to down tools to take him there. Having lost power over his body, Fred appeared to be trying to compensate by exercising his power over everyone else.

Kate helped him into his coat, biting down her annoyance when he barked, 'Careful, there! You're hurting me!' because she knew she'd been extremely careful. Then she steered the wheelchair outside, where Kenny had the newly acquired truck waiting with an old barn door ready to act as a ramp to get him on the back. It was more comfortable for Fred to ride in his chair instead of being lifted out and hoisted into the cab.

Kate had been shocked when Kenny had told her that she was to drive Fred to the hospital. 'I haven't passed a driving test,' she'd pointed out.

'Testing has been stopped for the duration of the war,' he'd told her. 'A provisional licence will be good enough, and I'll get Ernie to pay for that. He'll argue about it, but if it means I can stay working . . .'

'Aren't you forgetting I don't know how to drive?'

'I'll show you.'

He'd talked her through the basic controls and movements then let her have a practice drive around the farm. 'Is that all I'm getting?' she'd said afterwards. 'One practice and I'm being let loose on the roads?'

'You're only going up and down Brimbles Lane, for pity's sake.'

Yes, but that lane was a hazard of potholes, stones and tree roots.

She didn't argue further, though. The farm simply couldn't afford for Kenny to be away from it several times a week. He was the strongest worker by far.

Kate set off slowly and carefully, trying to make the ride as smooth as possible for Fred. Not that he appreciated it. 'I was beginning to think we wouldn't get here before nightfall,' he mocked when they arrived.

She ran up the steps and into the hall to see Tom, the porter, who arranged for a proper ramp to be brought out. Fred was taken inside and Kate sat in the truck to wait for him. It would have taken only a few minutes to return home, but it was impossible to know how long Fred's therapy was likely to take. It depended on his mood and whether he was willing to cooperate.

At yesterday's session, he'd refused to cooperate at all and complained savagely about having to wait more than an hour to be collected because Kate had gone home to put in some work before coming back. It wasn't as though the hospital could ring the farm to let them know when he was ready.

Sitting in the truck now, her thoughts turned back to Leo. Would today be the day more news came? She could only hope so.

Fred looked haggard when he emerged from the hospital. Kate felt for him, though he was as surly and rude as always. She drove the truck home carefully and Kenny came to meet them as they reached the farmyard. 'How was your therapy, Fred?' he asked.

'How do you think it was? Awful!'

Sighing, Kenny turned to Kate. 'You waited at the hospital?'

'No, I decided to drive into the village to see my friends and take them on a jaunt to the teashop in Barton.'

For a moment Kenny looked outraged – until he realized she was being sarcastic. Tutting, he walked away, leaving her to wheel Fred inside. As if Kate didn't know that petrol supplies were limited, even for businesses like the farm! There was no chance of her being allowed to use the truck for personal reasons. Nothing was to be gained by annoying Kenny, but Kate's nerves felt ragged.

She opened the kitchen door and saw from Timmy's bright face and Ruby's small nod that a letter had finally come for her. 'Let me help you off with your coat, Fred,' Ruby offered, stepping forward.

'Kate can do it. You'll hurt me.'

'No, I won't, and Kate's got something caught in her eye. She needs to get it out.'

Winking, Ruby handed the letter over behind Fred's back and, seeing that the envelope was addressed in Leo's own handwriting, Kate raced upstairs to open it.

Dearest Kate,

I'm sorry you haven't heard from me for a while, but I hope Max managed to let you know the reason why. As you can see from the address at the top of this letter, I'm now in hospital.

Not Stratton House, unfortunately, but near Manchester, which is many miles away from you.

Well, I've never believed in hiding from the truth, so I'll be blunt and say I'm not a pretty sight. Not that I was Prince Charming before, but now . . . definitely not. A broken left arm is the least of it. That will mend soon enough. But I'm also burned on my left-hand side – face, ear, neck and hand. They're doing their best to heal me and minimize my scars, but I'll never be quite the same again.

Which brings me to an important point. We've never had much luck in our short relationship, have we?

Oh no. Was he going to break up with her? He'd split up with her once before because he hadn't wanted to burden her with grief if he should be killed. Was he now thinking that he didn't want to burden her with an injured and scarred man as her sweetheart? Did he think she'd be repulsed by him?

If you feel that this changes things between us, I'll understand. I don't want you to stay with me because you pity me or feel obliged to stick by a man who was injured in the service of his country. That wouldn't make either of us happy, and, if we're to part, the sooner the better for both of us. Dragging out the uncertainty will only pile pain upon pain.

A letter will do the job if you'd rather remember me as I was. Please don't feel obliged to visit to end things face to face. I know it may be difficult for you to get away from the farm anyway.

I'll always be glad to have known you, Kate. You're an incredible girl and it's been a privilege to be your sweetheart, if only for a short time.

Please write back to let me know your decision. I don't

wish to pressure you but time hangs heavily when a chap is
stuck in a hospital bed, so I hope you won't keep me waiting
too long.
 Fondest love,
 Leo x

Kate paced the room, her feelings in turmoil. Poor Leo! The thought of his physical and emotional suffering dug savage claws into her heart.

After a while she stopped pacing and read the letter again. And again. He was trying to do the noble, selfless thing in opening the way for her to break up with him. But that wasn't what she wanted at all.

She needed to convince him that she didn't care a jot that he was disfigured because what she cared about was *him*. Leo Kinsella, the man who loved her and made her laugh even as he also made her feel cherished and safe in his warm regard. She could write to tell him this, of course, but would he believe it when she hadn't actually seen his injuries? What Leo needed was for Kate to see him face to face and assure him that nothing had changed. How could she get away, though?

There was Fred, the farm, the fact that Ernie still knew nothing of Leo . . . Kate felt the restrictions shackling her like chains. But just now Leo needed her the most. Fred had a house full of people who could help him. He might resent her absence, especially as it would leave him dependent on Kenny for his most intimate needs, but Kenny was his brother.

Both Ruby and Pearl would do what they could to cover Kate's absence, Ruby by working mostly in the house and Pearl by working in the fields. It would be a stretch for them all to cope – probably they'd fall further behind than ever – but this was an emergency and Kate would only be away for a day or two.

Ernie would be furious to learn that she'd been seeing a man behind his back, but what could he actually do? Lock her up? Not with Ruby and Pearl in the house. Doubtless, he'd rain verbal abuse down on her head, but Kate could bear that for Leo's sake.

She headed downstairs to announce that she was going away only to notice that Pearl was sitting in the kitchen reading a letter of her own – a letter that had clearly delivered a shock. 'Pearl?' Kate asked.

The land girl blinked and roused herself. 'My father says I need to go home. My mother is having an operation.'

'Oh, Pearl, I'm sorry to hear that,' Kate said.

She was indeed sorry – for Pearl's mother; for Pearl, who always said she was unhappy at home; and also for Leo, because there was no way Kate could leave the farm if Pearl went too.

'I'm allowed a leave of absence, I suppose?' Pearl asked.

'I'm sure the Land Army won't object in the circumstances,' Kate told her. 'I'll ring them from the village to let them know.'

'What did your letter say?' Ruby asked Kate. 'It looked like Leo's handwriting on the front.'

'It said . . .' Kate paused, took a deep breath and told the land girls about Leo's injuries.

'You need to see him,' Ruby said.

'I do, but . . .'

'She can't go if I'm away too,' Pearl guessed bleakly.

'I'm sure we can manage somehow,' Ruby suggested, but they all knew it wouldn't be possible.

'What rotten luck, Leo being in hospital at the same

time as my mother,' Pearl said. 'Hopefully, I won't be away for long and the moment I get back you can go off to see him.'

'You must stay as long as your mother needs you,' Kate insisted, but secretly she wanted to weep.

Ernie took Pearl's news with his usual lack of grace. 'What can *you* do for a sick woman?' he asked, for the land girl was big, clumsy and often loud.

'Probably nothing,' Pearl admitted, for she was under no illusions about herself. 'I expect I'll break something or make too much noise or just get in the way.'

But her father had ordered her home, so to home she would go.

She left the following morning. 'If you can find the time to write, we'd love to hear how you're getting on,' Kate told her.

'We would,' Ruby seconded. 'Come here, girl.'

She held out her arms and folded Pearl into a hug. Then it was Timmy's turn to wrap his arms around Pearl's middle. 'Come back soon, won't you?'

'I'll try.'

Kenny gave Pearl a nod. 'I hope your mother gets better soon,' he said, which was a testament to Ruby's attempts to turn him into a civilized man.

Vinnie nodded too, accompanying it with an awkward grin.

No one expected much from Ernie. 'Goodbye, Mr Fletcher,' Pearl said. 'I'm sorry I won't be here to help for a while, but at least you can save on my wages.'

They all knew Ernie begrudged every penny he paid in wages, even when they were earned through more hard work than it was reasonable to expect.

Kate insisted on driving Pearl into the village in the cart.

From there she could catch the bus. 'You'll be missed,' Kate said, when they reached the bus stop.

'Don't be daft.'

'It's true. You're wonderfully helpful on the farm and we like having you around in the evenings, too.'

Pearl made the sort of gesture that meant Kate was talking nonsense, but her plain face had blushed bright red with pleasure.

She jumped down from the cart and slung her bag over her broad shoulder.

Kate jumped down too, hugged her and watched as the bus rumbled into the distance. Then she jogged to the pillar box to post the letter she'd written to Leo last night.

Dearest Leo,

It was such a relief to receive your letter and to know that you're alive and being cared for. Max had indeed written to warn me that you'd been injured, but he had little information to share so I've been desperate to hear from you.

But look here, Leo Kinsella. I'm not the sort of shallow girl who likes a man only for his handsome good looks. Are you the sort of shallow man who thought he had handsome good looks anyway? As you said yourself, you were no Prince Charming even before your injuries.

She hoped that would make him smile, because he'd never been vain about his appearance.

I've fallen in love with you, not your face. And I'm going to prove it to you. Unfortunately, I can't visit yet, as I'm tied to the farm looking after Fred. Things are particularly difficult because Pearl has had to go home due to her mother needing an

operation. But trust me, Leo, as soon as I can get away, I'll be
on a train to Manchester to see you . . .

The question was: would he believe that she really couldn't visit? Or would he think she was simply buying time because she didn't want to be the sort of girl who walked out on a man at the first sign of trouble? Would he think she'd stay away until she plucked up the courage to tell him it was over between them?

CHAPTER THIRTY-THREE

Alice

It was too soon to expect Daniel to have received Alice's letter, let alone reply to it, but she still felt a delicious fizz of joy every time she thought of how he'd feel when he read her news about the baby and what he'd write in reply. Naturally, she'd have preferred to break the news to him face to face, but she wasn't going to let that detail interfere with the elation of the moment.

Would he cry out in delight? Punch the air? Shed emotional tears?

He'd be concerned for Alice's health, of course, especially as he wasn't here to see for himself that she was amazingly well. But she'd soon reassure him on that score and let him know that she wasn't taking foolish risks.

Alice was walking as much as ever with the blessing of both her father and Dr Lambert, but she was avoiding lifting, pulling or pushing heavy weights. Even when she hung washing on the line to dry, she made more than one journey with the laundry basket to ensure it was light to carry – if her father didn't insist on carrying it himself. She was eating well and going to bed at a reasonable hour, too.

No one else had guessed about the baby but she could see and feel that her body was beginning to change. Only very slightly as yet, but she was tender in places and her waist was thickening.

It wouldn't be long before she felt the baby's first quickening as a faint flutter. How exciting that would be!

She liked the name Richard for a boy and Eleanor for a girl, but Daniel might have different ideas. Would he be home in time for the birth? Alice certainly hoped that the war would be over by then, though it currently appeared doubtful. If it continued, she'd have to hope that Daniel would be granted leave soon after the birth so he could meet his son or daughter. In the meantime, she'd be sure to take photographs to send him. The thought reminded her of a conversation she'd had with her father towards the end of her wedding reception.

'The next time one of us goes to St Albans we should take the camera in for repair,' he'd said, because it had stopped working.

'You've exhausted it, taking so many photos,' Alice had teased.

'I only have one daughter and she's precious to me,' he'd told her. 'I can never have too many photographs of her and the handsome young man she's married.'

Alice's father might spend hours each day closeted in his study reading about the world's more ancient civilizations, but he was going to make a wonderful grandfather.

Somehow the broken camera had since been forgotten, but as Alice walked to Stratton House now, she made a mental note to take it in for repair soon.

Once again, she saw and heard no sign of the thief, but he was still in Churchwood because Naomi's milk had been taken yesterday and Bert had reported that some of his vegetables had been stolen. 'Not that I begrudge them to the poor chap,' Bert had said. 'They can't make for much of a meal on a frosty night.'

Glowing from her own good fortune, Alice pitied the

thief more than ever, though it didn't stop her feeling nervous and, as always these days, she was relieved to arrive at the hospital unmolested.

Perhaps her own happiness was infecting others, because it was one of those days when the patients appeared particularly to enjoy her visit. Making her rounds with her books, she shared laughter and jokes, listened to the men's news from home and admired the photographs they'd been sent. Private Jed Hicks showed her a photograph of his sweetheart, Valerie.

'She's too good for 'im,' said Roy Talbot, the man in the neighbouring bed. 'Wait till she visits and gets a look at me. Jed'll be history then.'

It was only good-natured teasing. Jed was handsome while Roy was a sturdy gnome of a man, but he knew it and didn't care.

Alice caught another man smiling at the exchange. Private Peter Wilkinson. He'd been brought in around the same time as Fred and had appeared equally traumatized by his injury – the loss of an arm – though, where Fred had torn into people, Peter had merely retreated into quietness. It was good to see him beginning to emerge from it, and when he beckoned her over as she was preparing to leave, she went straight to the chair he was occupying beside his bed. 'Am I too late to hear a story?' he asked.

'Go on, Alice,' Corporal Dodds called. 'I'd like to hear a story too.'

'So would I,' Private Lawrence Mellor said. 'You read them so well.'

'Flatterer,' Alice joked, and Lawrence grinned.

Alice sat down to read a story called *A Mystery for Harold Snow*. It was quite long, but it held her audience rapt.

'. . . *There was a big smile on Harold's face as he walked up to collect the silver cup for biggest marrow, after all*,' Alice said, glad to have reached the end because she'd been sitting on a hard chair for too long and her back was aching.

'That was great, miss,' Peter said, and Alice was delighted to have pleased him.

Corporal Dodds nodded. 'Who'd have thought marrows could be used for smuggling stolen diamonds?'

'Maybe there'll be a stolen diamond or two in our dinner,' Lawrence said. 'I could use a boost to my finances so me and my Maureen can set up home together. When we're wed, of course.'

Alice said her goodbyes to the patients and to the nursing staff too, then made her way along the corridor towards the grand entrance hall, where she said goodbye to her friend Tom the porter. 'It's kept fine for your walk home,' he said.

Rain had threatened earlier.

'Enjoy your evening, Tom.'

She made her way through the tall doors and paused at the top of the steps to stretch her aching back. She was feeling tired now and would be glad to get home. Tiredness was only to be expected when she was pregnant, of course. Pregnant! What a beautiful word. She thought of Daniel's baby tucked up inside her and felt joy bubble up through the fatigue.

She set off down the drive and along Brimbles Lane, wishing it wasn't growing dark already. Her senses were on full alert to the noises of animals and birds moving in the woods beside her, though nothing sounded out of place.

She hoped her backache would ease as she walked, but if anything it worsened. At least the rain was holding off, though perhaps not for long.

She winced as a sudden burning cramp squeezed her lower middle. It hurt enough to make her breath catch in her throat. Then the realization of what might be happening sliced into her brain. *Oh, no . . .*

The cramping faded. Alice walked on, hoping her fears were groundless. But she hadn't gone far before the burning cramp returned, holding her motionless in its grasp as she fought through the pain. *No, no, no!*

A sob tore at her throat. The hospital and Brimbles Farm were behind her. Home was closer. But it still felt distant . . .

She waited for the cramping to ease off once more then walked on. But again, she hadn't taken more than a few steps before it tightened its claws, and she bent over as she braced herself to endure it.

Rainclouds had stolen over the sky, darkening the world around her even more. Was she making the situation worse by trying to walk? Might she save her baby by sitting down on the lane and waiting for someone to come along and help? The trouble was that no one might come along for hours. She'd left her father in his study, deep in a book about the Aztecs of Central Mexico. When he became engrossed, his mind floated above physical awareness. With his lamp on, he wouldn't notice how dark it was growing, and hunger and thirst rarely distracted him.

Alice had to walk on. Somehow. She took a tentative step forward. Another and then another. But a sob burst out of her as she doubled over in pain yet again.

She became aware of movement over in the woods – the rapid approach of something large and dark. Some*one*, rather.

He came up behind her. 'It's all right,' he said, gruffly. 'I'm going to help.'

He scooped her up into his arms and started walking at speed. Alice tried to look at him and caught a glimpse of dark hair and a beard, but another bite of pain overtook her and left her whimpering in the stranger's arms. She was aware of him in other ways, though. His breath came thickly as he laboured forward, carrying her in front of him. She was aware of his smell, too. Sour and musty. An unwashed smell, though that was only to be expected from someone who'd lived rough for weeks, if not months. For this man must surely be the Churchwood thief.

Alice stirred, aiming to tell him where she lived, but he needed no directions from her. He pushed through the small gate of The Linnets and balanced her against the porch so he could bang on the door. Hard.

'Someone's coming,' he said, and he set her down on the narrow shelf inside the small wooden porch, which made a convenient seat for anyone who wished to kick off muddy boots before they entered.

'Good luck,' he said, stepping away.

He retreated to the edge of the shadows and the moment the door opened he blended into them. Alice heard his footsteps moving away speedily.

'Alice!' her father said. 'Are you all right?'

'No!' she wailed.

He lifted her into his arms and carried her inside. She hoped for a miracle, but no miracle occurred. Within minutes, Daniel's baby was gone and Alice wept more tears than she'd thought possible.

CHAPTER THIRTY-FOUR

Naomi

'It's a pity Alice isn't here to see this,' May said, holding up the dress she'd just finished for the child who was to play the Angel Gabriel in the nativity play. 'It's only made from old sheets, but I'm pleased with it.'

The dress was a simple A-line design, reaching to the floor and with long sleeves that widened at the ends, but, as with everything May created, it hung beautifully.

'It's lovely,' Naomi told her, but the smiles they shared were sad and worried rather than triumphant.

Two weeks had passed since Alice's miscarriage and neither of them had seen her. Not even Kate had seen her. Dr Lovell had answered the door to their calls but always responded the same way: Alice was recovering physically but her emotions had been hit hard and she needed time to get on top of them before she faced the world.

Naomi had some idea of what it was to grieve for a child. In her case the child had never even been conceived, but the sense of loss at her failure to have children still cut deep. How much worse it must be for Alice, who'd cradled a child inside her for weeks and weeks, anticipating its birth and picturing the life they'd share.

Yet Alice had always been powerful in spirit, despite being a slip of a girl who looked as though a mere fairy could blow her over. Her blue eyes could be gentle but they could also blaze with courage and conviction. It felt disconcerting for such a natural leader to be brought down so low. Poor Alice really must be suffering.

Naomi wished there was something she could do but Dr Lovell had simply advised, 'Please keep asking after her. Alice may not be able to welcome visitors yet, but I know my daughter and she'll be touched by the concern of her friends.'

As they sat in the bookshop now and worked on the costumes, the atmosphere felt unusually quiet. Clearly, everyone's thoughts were with Alice.

'Here's the dress for the girl playing Mary,' Janet said. 'I've kept most of the original dress but managed to insert a new panel down the front where there was a stain.'

'Beautiful,' May declared.

There was also a leather jerkin for the innkeeper to wear over a brown tunic, and a dark tunic with jacket for Joseph. As well, there were three sumptuous outfits for the wise men, two with golden crowns and one with a jewelled turban. Small, decorated boxes and a bronze-coloured pot held the wise men's gifts of gold, frankincense and myrrh, while a bag held knitted sheep for the shepherds to carry along with wooden crooks made by Bert.

'You've done so well in finishing the costumes early,' Adam said. 'We'll have lots of time for rehearsing the play.'

'For planning the bookshop party, too,' May added.

'Indeed. I've spoken to Matron at the hospital and they'll bring along as many patients as possible,' Adam told them.

'Will Dr Marwood bring his gramophone and records?'

'He will indeed.'

'I think I can fit into my old Santa outfit,' Bert said. 'If we're still planning on giving small gifts to the children?'

'Tangerines might not be possible with the war on, but I imagine we can come up with something nice,' May said.

There were murmurs of enthusiasm, but Naomi guessed that they were all wishing Alice was there to share the planning with them. She'd always been full of ideas and energy.

Naomi passed Joe Simpson's empty house on her walk home. Joe had been buried in St Luke's churchyard the previous week, following a service in the church. Adam had made a wonderful job of it. He might still be new to St Luke's but he'd gone to a great deal of trouble to get to know his parishioners and Joe had been no exception. It was traditional to say, 'Lovely service,' afterwards, but when Adam was presiding it was true.

A funeral tea had been held in the Sunday School Hall following the burial. Naomi had judged it neither the time nor the place to raise the subject of Joe's house with his sister but had overheard Mrs Hutchings ask Ellen 'I suppose you'll be selling your Joe's house?'

'I suppose I will.'

Maybe Mrs Hutchings had asked about it because she had her eye on it for her daughter, who currently lived in a tiny house in Barton with her husband and two young children. Joe's house would give them more room – not least an extra bedroom. Other people might be interested in Joe's house too, and if Naomi didn't act to secure it soon, she might miss out.

She had to reach a decision – either to come to a financial arrangement with Alexander based on the figures he'd provided, or to instruct the Great Man to launch his investigators into a fight.

A letter had come from the Great Man earlier in the week, reminding her that he was awaiting her orders. Doubtless, he'd have charged her for writing the letter and she didn't want him to have to write again, but reaching a decision had so far been impossible and she was dithering about her reply.

Bert's idea about Alexander still felt ridiculous, but every time Naomi made up her mind to dismiss it, a tiny doubt would begin to niggle at her. Alexander might present himself to the world as a successful, professional and highly respectable man, but underneath the superbly cut suits and the crisp accent, he was greedy, dishonest and devious. And perhaps he was also arrogant enough to believe himself untouchable for his misdeeds.

'How would I go about finding evidence of bigamy?' she'd asked Bert the day he'd first mentioned it. There had to be hundreds – no, thousands – of churches and register offices across the country where Alexander and his lover might have married.

'Somerset House,' Bert had said, undaunted.

Somerset . . . Of course!

'The central registry,' he'd confirmed. 'They have records of every marriage in the country. Every birth and death too, come to that.'

'Is it possible to view those records?'

'I believe it is – if you've a mind to.'

Had she a mind to go to London on what might be a wild goose chase? She veered between wanting to go and being afraid to go, because another possibility had occurred to her – Alexander might have married Amelia Ashmore *before* he'd married Naomi. If that were the case, it would be Naomi's own marriage that was bigamous and therefore invalid. Was she prepared to face the humiliation of being an even bigger fool than she already believed herself to be? Of being an adulteress, too?

She reached The Linnets now and looked up at it as she passed. She'd left a note and a potted cyclamen for Alice but wished she could do something more to show how much she cared. She was tempted to knock on the door again in the hope that she'd be allowed to see her friend and hug her. But every knock on the door might be an unwelcome disturbance, especially if it roused Alice from much-needed sleep. Naomi could only hope that she wasn't falling into the sort of deep depression from which it was terribly hard to recover.

Walking on, Naomi passed through the Foxfield gate-posts and headed up the drive towards the house. She needed to come to a decision about the best way forward, starting with whether she should go to Somerset House. The Great Man wasn't the only person who was waiting to know what she planned to do next. Bert, too, was wait-ing, though so far he was being patient.

'Don't worry, woman, I only want to ask if you want more chairs putting out,' he'd said at the bookshop earl-ier when Naomi had clearly looked apprehensive at his approach. 'I'm not going to nag you about that other matter, but think on this. Going to Somerset House might prove nothing, but at least you'd know. One way or another, you'd *know*.'

Naomi needed to stop putting things off. Time was marching on towards Christmas and she really didn't want to spend the festive season worrying. Neither did she want to begin the new year with uncertainty still hanging over her head. Perhaps she should simply toss a coin – heads she'd go, tails she wouldn't.

Hearing the sound of a plane approaching from the

south, Naomi looked up at the sky. But when the plane came into view, she frowned. Surely not . . . ? She screwed up her eyes to try to focus and felt a kick of fear as she saw that instead of the identification roundel used on British planes – an outer blue circle, an inner white circle and a central red circle – this plane bore a black cross outlined in white. The insignia of the German Luftwaffe.

CHAPTER THIRTY-FIVE

Kate

Leo's latest letter had seared itself into Kate's brain, so she knew it by heart. At work in the kitchen garden, she went over it again in her mind.

Dearest Kate,

It was lovely to hear from you and to read your sweet words. Bless you! But while it's kind of you to want to stand by me, the fact is that my scars run deep and their disfigurement is permanent. Therefore, I'm not going to hold you to what you said. You're young and beautiful, and you deserve to walk down the street with a man without feeling embarrassed by him.

Please don't write straight back and assure me that my appearance doesn't matter. I'm not going to tie you down, whatever you say. It wouldn't be fair of me.

Please don't feel you have to write back at all, but, if you do want to write one last time, tell me about the farm and Churchwood and the bookshop. You know how I love to hear about them and picture you there in my mind.

Just one more 'please' before I sign off, and that's to say please don't worry about me. Although my injuries are unsightly, I still have all my limbs and my senses too. Sight, sound, touch, taste . . . I have them all. There's a chance my hearing may be slightly impaired on one side but not profoundly, so in many ways I'm a lucky chap and certainly better off than

*many of the poor souls in here. In short, I'm going to be fine,
so let me repeat that you're not to worry that you'll be leaving
me in the lurch.*

*Go forth and live a wonderful, exciting life, darling Kate.
You deserve it.*

*I'll never regret the day that brought me to Churchwood and
your farmyard. I'll treasure them always.*

With love from Leo x

How could she bear to stay here when Leo needed
her? Letters simply wouldn't persuade him that she was
standing by him, not just to do the right thing but because
it was what she wanted. What she needed. Without Leo,
Kate was bereft.

She wasn't the only person at Brimbles Farm whose
nerves were stretched. Between Pearl's absence and Fred's
demands, the work was suffering badly, and tempers were
raw. Even little Timmy was getting up early to help on the
farm, though the mornings were dark, and he was helping after school too. Yesterday, he'd fallen asleep over his
supper, the poor lad.

Kate hoped daily for Pearl to let them know when she'd
be returning, but all she'd written so far was the briefest
of notes.

Dear Kate, Ruby, Timmy and everyone else,

*Just a quick line to let you know I've arrived here safely and
I've already broken a saucer. Naturally, it had to be from my
mother's favourite tea set. She was furious with me for breaking
it, and my father and sister were furious with me for upsetting
Mother just before her operation.*

*The op is scheduled for tomorrow, by the way. It was
delayed for a few days so she could get over a head cold.*

215

I can't wait to be back with you all,
Pearl (Gertie Grimes) x

By now the operation would have taken place. Hopefully, it had been successful.

Kate forked up some parsnips and shook the worst of the soil off them. She'd put them in a stew with—

The sound of a plane broke into her thoughts. Planes flying overhead always put her in mind of Leo. She looked up, wondering what she'd see. A Spitfire? A Lancaster? A Mosquito?

The plane came into view, a dark dot in the distant sky, but Kate frowned. Was that a thin trail of smoke behind it? The plane drew closer. It looked too small to be a bomber. A fighter plane, then, and yes, there was smoke.

Kate's insides felt as though they were turning to ice when she saw the plane's markings. It was an enemy plane.

Suddenly, the engine emitted a sound like a cough. The smoke went from a faint trail to a burst of roiling grey. And then the sound changed to a whine as the plane began a rapid descent. It was going to crash.

The plane had been travelling in a rough curve, approaching from the south-west. Now it passed in front of Kate and its curving trajectory was sending it roughly to the south-east – where Churchwood stood. *Oh no*. Please God, it would overshoot the village and crash harmlessly in a field. Another speck appeared, falling at speed. Kate identified it as a person and guessed the pilot had bailed out. Sure enough, a parachute opened up above him like an umbrella and slowed a drastic, fatal fall to something survivable.

But what of the plane? Hand to her mouth, Kate watched as it sped through the sky in a death dive.

For a half-second, it was lost from sight behind the trees, but then an explosion rocked the earth and shuddered in the air. There was a flash of orange followed by the flickering light of a conflagration and more smoke rose into the sky, thick and dark with death.

Oh, heavens. Had it harmed any of her friends? Alice? Naomi? Bert? May? Janet? What about little Timmy and the other children in school? No, they'd have left by now, and the bookshop session must have finished too. But people at home . . . in the shops . . . in the street . . . ?

She glanced back at the pilot who was floating to earth. Kate was desperate to get to the village to make sure no one was hurt, but she couldn't leave an enemy airman to wander the countryside. Grabbing her garden fork, she ran to Five Acre Field, where the pilot looked likely to land.

It was enemy airmen like this who'd rained death and destruction on London and other cities during the Blitz, and still flew over in smaller raids. Who'd shot and bombed British servicemen waiting to be rescued from the beaches of Dunkirk last year. Who'd attacked British ships and prevented much-needed supplies from reaching British shores. Who'd shot down Leo, the man Kate loved, who was now suffering in hospital, believing that his burns had placed him beyond the reach of love.

Kate's long, lithe legs had never moved faster. She reached the field out of breath but determined that this enemy airman was going nowhere.

He was releasing himself from his harness, the parachute on the ground behind him billowing as air made its way out from underneath it.

'Stop right there,' Kate ordered.

He turned to her, tugging off his goggles and leather

217

helmet. How young he was! Younger even than Leo. Sweat glistened on his face and a smudge of dirt streaked down his cheek but otherwise he looked fresh and smooth, his eyes the colour of the sky on a summer's day. Kate had never seen a German before. She supposed she must have expected wickedness in his features but this young man looked . . . well, pleasant. But also desperately worried.

He gestured to her fork and shook his head. 'No,' he said, raising his arms. 'I . . . surrender? That is the word, yes?'

He nodded in the direction of the crashed plane and mimed wrestling with the controls. 'The plane . . . I lose it. I hope no one is hurt?'

He asked it as a question. A plea.

'I don't know yet. If you *have* hurt anyone, it's likely to be someone I know and care about.'

'I . . . regret.' He lowered his hand to place it over his heart, but Kate made a stabbing motion with the fork and he raised it again hastily.

She pointed the fork towards the distant farmhouse and called, 'Move! Walk.'

'*Ja*,' he said, beginning to tramp through the plough-rutted field, which was hard with a frost that hadn't cleared all day.

Kate saw figures running towards them – Kenny, Vinnie and Ruby. Kenny was carrying something. To Kate's alarm, she saw it was a shotgun. Fred's injuries had been caused by shelling from land-based troops rather than an air strike, but this airman was a comrade of those troops and Kenny might think him a fitting object on which to vent his fury.

'Halt!' Kate called to the airman as the others drew near.

He stopped in his tracks and raised his arms higher, possibly having spotted Kenny's gun. 'We don't need the shotgun, Kenny,' Kate said. 'This pilot has surrendered.'

'I'm taking no chances with German scum.' Kenny spat at the pilot's feet.

'Fine, but take care or you'll end up being the one who's imprisoned. Let's put him in the barn and you can guard him while I run to the village for help.'

'What sort of help?'

'The police, of course. If they don't want him, I'm sure they'll know who does.'

Kenny scowled at the pilot, who looked nervous. He didn't lower his hands but used his thumb to point at himself. 'Kurt Schultz. Luftwaffe. Home is Dresden. *Mutter* there. *Vater* too. Three sisters. Gretl, Louisa, Ava.'

Was he trying to show that, even if he was their enemy, he was an ordinary mortal with a family whose members would miss him if he were to be killed?

Again, Kate felt the tug of surprise at his simple humanity, though she wasn't sure what she'd expected. It would be stupid to assume he meant them no harm, though. 'I haven't searched him for weapons,' she said.

He listened to her with a frown of concentration. '*Nein*,' he said. 'No weapon.'

'You'd better check, Vinnie.'

Vinnie stepped forward awkwardly and patted the man down.

'Check his legs,' Kate suggested, because she'd read adventure stories in which pistols or blades were secreted in boots or ankle holsters.

Vinnie crouched down and examined the pilot's legs. 'Nothing.'

'Right, then,' Kenny told the pilot. 'Start walking.'

'I want no trouble,' the pilot said, and they set off towards the farmhouse.

'We mustn't let Fred see we've captured a German,' Kate said. 'Ruby, would you mind going inside and distracting him?'

'Heavens, yes.' Ruby's face told Kate that she too could picture Fred's fury if he found out.

She ran off and Kate turned to Vinnie. 'You'd better collect the parachute.'

'Can I keep it?' he asked, his eyes brightening, no doubt at the thought of showing it off down at the Wheatsheaf.

'Just fetch it,' Kate told him.

She, Kenny and the pilot reached the farmyard. There was no sign of Fred at the farmhouse windows, so they hastened across to the barn. Kate unfastened the padlock and chain that kept her bike locked to one of the wooden posts and handed them to Kenny. 'You can use this to keep him secure,' she said, dipping her head towards the pilot.

She took the shotgun and waited long enough to see the pilot sitting on a hay bale with his hands chained behind him and around another post. 'Don't do anything stupid,' she warned Kenny, handing back the shotgun. 'Don't let Vinnie do anything stupid either.'

She steered the bicycle into the farmyard just as Ernie emerged from the lavatory. 'What in God's name is going on?' he demanded.

'A German plane crashed. The pilot bailed out and he's in our barn. I'm going to get help.'

'A German?' Ernie's contempt turned it into a sneer.

'Don't hurt him. He's just . . . Well, he's little more than a boy.' And Kate couldn't help thinking that if they were kind to this unexpected prisoner, someone in enemy territory might be kind to a British prisoner caught on their land. 'I have to go,' she finished.

Kate was physically fit and used to cycling but she rode at a speed that burned her muscles. She'd never been a churchgoer but entreaties trembled on her lips. *Please let the village be safe . . . Please let no one be hurt . . . Please let no one have lost their home or their livelihood . . .*

She reached the end of Brimbles Lane and was relieved to see that Alice's cottage and Naomi's Foxfield were undamaged. But the glow of flames was brighter here, and she feared the plane hadn't overshot the village, after all.

The closer she drew to the village centre, the more convinced she became that disaster had befallen Churchwood. She could hear a commotion ahead, smell the smoke and also something else. Burning fuel?

Kate reached the village green and skidded to a halt. *Oh, heavens . . .*

The plane had come to grief on the far side of the green. The elementary school was missing tiles from the roof and its windows were broken. The vicarage had broken windows, too, and a falling chimney had smashed a hole through the roof. But it was between those buildings that the plane had fallen − right where the Sunday School Hall had once stood. Now it was a mass of burning debris.

CHAPTER THIRTY-SIX

Naomi

'I thought the plane was going to come down on top of me,' Marjorie was wailing to anyone who would listen, but no one was paying her any attention.

Naomi had been relieved to see the plane flying north, only to feel the stabbing knife of dread when she'd realized that not only was it in trouble, but it was changing direction in a wide curve that meant it was heading for the village. She'd watched its death dive with her hand over her heart, hoping against hope that it would pass over the buildings and people to crash in a field, startling a few cows or sheep but causing no serious damage. It wasn't to be. Horrified, she'd watched it dive lower until there was an almighty explosion somewhere in the heart of the village.

Moments later Suki had opened the front door, wide-eyed and white-faced in alarm. 'Did you hear a loud bang, madam?'

'A German plane has come down. I'm going out to investigate and see if I can help.'

'Shall I—'

'Thank you, Suki, but I suggest you stay here with Cook.'

Naomi hadn't been the only person to hasten towards the crash site. It had seemed that the entire village was heading that way, shock apparent in frightened eyes and breathless voices.

There'd been universal horror at the sight that met their eyes – the Sunday School Hall ablaze, with blackened, half-fallen walls between the flames and the outline of what remained of the plane. 'Has anyone called the fire brigade?' Naomi had asked passers-by, but no one knew.

She'd seen Bert keeping people at a safe distance from the conflagration and hastened to ask him the same question.

'First thing I did,' he'd told her grimly. Then he'd looked back at the fire. 'Less than an hour ago the Hall was full.'

Naomi too had shuddered at the thought of what might have happened had the plane crashed earlier. 'Is everyone all right?'

'As far as I know.' But Bert had shrugged his bear-like shoulders. Just because he hadn't *heard* that anyone was missing . . .

He'd put his head to one side suddenly. Listening. 'Here comes the cavalry,' he'd said, and Naomi's ears had picked up the bell of the approaching fire engine.

Bert had walked off to meet it and Naomi had wondered how she could help in this disaster. *Think, Naomi. Think!* The fire brigade would deal with the flames. The best thing she could do was to make sure that everyone in Churchwood was safely accounted for.

Spotting May and Janet, she'd asked them to help organize teams to go door to door, checking on people's welfare. 'Good idea,' they'd agreed, and off they'd gone.

Naomi had looked around for some other likely helpers and sent them on their way, too.

223

Now she heard her name being called and, turning, saw Kate running towards her.

'It was a plane,' Naomi said, when Kate reached her. 'A German plane.'

'I saw it.' Kate stared at the flames and Naomi saw a ripple of emotion pass through her.

Was she thinking of Leo and all he'd suffered – was suffering still – after his plane had crashed and set on fire? Naomi liked the flight lieutenant very much and sincerely regretted what had happened to him. It was especially hard that poor Kate couldn't visit. Might there be a chance of him being transferred to a hospital closer than Manchester? Even a hospital in London would be easier to reach. But perhaps Leo was in the best possible place, given the nature of his injuries.

Kate's focus returned to Naomi. 'Is anyone hurt?'

'Not as far as we know, apart from Jean Harris, and she only has a minor cut. I think she's mostly just shocked.'

Jean was Adam's housekeeper. She'd been inside the vicarage when the force of the explosion next door had blown out some windows. Now she was sitting on a bench by the war memorial, being looked after by Mrs Hayes and Mrs Hutchings.

'Janet? May? Bert?' Kate asked.

'Safe and sound. Janet and May are checking on everyone living near them. Bert's over there with the fire brigade.'

'And Alice?' Kate asked, as though the thought of her friend being hurt was more than she could bear.

'I haven't seen her. But look. Here comes Dr Lovell.'

Naomi waved to him. 'Alice is safe and sound at home,' he told them, and Kate and Naomi breathed out slowly, though it probably occurred to both of them that Alice's spirits must be at the lowest possible ebb if she was staying indoors during a catastrophe like this. In the past, she'd have been one of the first on the scene, doing everything possible to calm nerves, check that everyone was all right and provide practical help to anyone who needed it.

'Is anyone hurt?' Dr Lovell asked. 'Apart from the poor pilot, who must be beyond all earthly help.'

'Actually, he bailed out over the farm,' Kate told him. 'He's fine, but I need to call the police to come and get him. Then I need to get home before Kenny shoots him.'

She left them to run to the post office to use the telephone. Dr Lovell went to tend to Mrs Harris, and Naomi set about recruiting more people to check on their neighbours.

After a while Janet rushed up. 'Edna Hall is missing!'

'No, she isn't,' Naomi assured her. 'She was in the butcher's and now she's gone home with Molly Lloyd.'

'Well, that's a relief.'

Other people began to report in. So far no one was unaccounted for, but Naomi hadn't heard from May yet.

She looked back at the conflagration and saw that the fire hoses were making progress. But the Hall was wrecked, which meant that so too was the bookshop.

CHAPTER THIRTY-SEVEN

Kate

Kate could hear the shouting even before she reached the farmyard.

'Let me get at him!' Fred was yelling. 'Out of my way, Kenny. I want to shoot the German scum.'

Oh no. Clearly, Fred had learned about their prisoner somehow. Kate rode the bike up to the barn and then sprang off and went inside. Fred was in his wheelchair but covered in mud on one side, as though he'd fallen out crossing the yard.

Ruby was trying to hold the wheelchair back while Kenny reasoned with Fred. 'You've lost enough, man. You'll lose even more if you shoot him.'

'I don't care! Give me the gun!'

Ruby gave Kate a helpless look. 'He got out of the kitchen himself,' she explained.

She'd spoken quietly but Fred heard her anyway. 'Yes, I did get out by myself. I had to, because you lot were out here hiding this . . . this . . . German scum from me.'

Kate glanced at the pilot. He was watching Fred warily, which was understandable, but she also saw compassion in his expression. As though sensing her gaze, he looked up at Kate and gave a small shrug that was eloquent with a sense of tragedy – for both sides in the war.

'The police are coming,' Kate told Fred. 'Come inside before you do something you might regret.'

'I won't regret killing him!'

'You say that now, but you might regret it in the future.'

'I don't *have* a future. Can't you understand that? Not a future that's worth having, anyway.'

'You may change your mind.' Kate took the handles of the wheelchair from Ruby.

Fred tried to slap her hands away but couldn't manage it without toppling out of the wheelchair again. Fuming, he finally gave up the fight and Kate steered him back into the farmhouse kitchen, where Ernie was sitting at the table, smoking. As ever, appropriate words were beyond Ernie, but he pushed the packet of Woodbines and a box of matches across the table towards Fred, who helped himself to a cigarette with shaking fingers.

'I'll make tea,' Ruby said, coming in behind them.

Leaving her to it, Kate returned to the barn, anxious that Kenny shouldn't use the chance of being alone with the pilot to hurt him. Why *was* he alone with the pilot? 'Did Vinnie find the parachute?' Kate asked.

'It's over there.' Kenny's head dipped towards a pile of silver-grey silk in a corner.

'Where's Vinnie now?'

'Your guess is as good as mine. One minute he was here. The next minute he'd gone.'

Kate would have liked to think he'd returned to work but, knowing Vinnie, it was more likely that he'd gone into the village to take a look at the burning wreckage. She hadn't passed him on her way home, but it would have been typical of him to have hidden behind a bush if he'd seen her approaching.

'Would you like anything to eat or drink?' she asked the pilot.

'What?' Kenny was outraged. 'He's the enemy, not

a guest. And after what his lot did to our Fred, I don't think—'

'What if Frank were to be captured? Wouldn't you want him to be fed and watered?'

Kenny turned sulky but didn't answer. Kate looked back at the pilot.

'Water,' he said. 'If no trouble.'

She fetched some from the kitchen and held the glass to his lips as his hands were chained behind his back.

'*Danke*,' he said. 'Thank you.'

'The plane,' he said a moment later. 'It bring no hurt?'

'I don't think it hurt any people, but it destroyed an important building.'

'I am sorry. I try . . .' He leaned to one side as though to mime something he lacked the words to explain.

'You tried to steer the plane away from the village?' Kate guessed.

'*Jawohl. Ja*,' he confirmed. 'But the plane . . . It was shot.'

'Was yours the only plane?'

His face creased in puzzlement. He didn't understand.

'Just one plane?' she asked.

'Ah! *Nein*. Five plane. Mine shot. Others . . .' He shrugged.

'Where were you attacking?'

He frowned again, but this time worked it out. 'Place of making plane.'

Kate nodded. Hertfordshire had several factories where aircraft were constructed – Hatfield, Radlett . . .

The sound of an approaching vehicle caught their attention. 'Go and see who it is,' Kenny ordered, tightening his grip on the shotgun, as though he suspected a team of enemy agents might have come to rescue the prisoner.

'It'll be the police,' Kate said, but she went out anyway to greet them.

There were two of them. Kate didn't recognize them, but then the police were rarely called to Churchwood. In fact, she didn't know if they'd ever been called. These policemen might have come from St Albans or another town.

They entered the barn and stared hard at the pilot, who attempted to get to his feet only to be prevented by the chains. He gave his name, rank and number instead.

The two policemen listened impassively, then one of them said, 'Let's be having you, then,' and the other gestured to Kenny's shotgun, saying, 'I don't think there's any more need for that, sir.'

Kenny propped the shotgun against the barn wall – well out of the pilot's reach – then took the padlock key from his pocket and released the pilot's hands. The German got up, holding himself with dignity, though Kate thought she saw vulnerability behind the surface calm.

'Turn around,' one of the policemen instructed, and the pilot's hands were restrained again, this time with proper handcuffs.

'Parachute?' the other policeman asked.

Kate fetched it from the corner and handed it over. Vinnie was going to be disappointed and, for a very different reason, Kate was disappointed too. All that silk would have been useful for making new clothes, especially in May's capable hands.

The pilot was nudged towards the doors and out into the farmyard where a car waited. A rear door was opened for him with an, 'In you get.'

But he paused and made eye contact with Kate. 'Thank you,' he said. 'You are kind.'

Kate smiled and whispered, 'Good luck,' under her breath.

She supposed he'd be interrogated then taken to a prisoner of war camp, where he'd sit out the war, far from his family and with no idea how long his imprisonment would last. She hoped he'd be treated decently.

Ernie came out of the farmhouse as the car drove away. 'The German scum has gone, has he? Good riddance. Now, back to work. We've wasted half the day already.'

Kate returned to the barn to retrieve her fork then headed back to the kitchen garden. She launched the fork into the ground but then halted again, thinking of Leo and his burns. How she longed to visit him and put his mind at rest! She also thought of Alice, missing her and worrying about her too.

A plume of smoke was still rising into the sky from the crash site. What a loss to the village the Hall was going to be. What a loss it was going to be to Kate personally, too. There was no doubt that her life had changed dramatically over the last couple of years. Leo, Alice, her other friends, the land girls and even the improvements in her brothers had all made it much better than before. But the bookshop had still been vitally important to her. The camaraderie of people working together and helping each other, the books, the chatter, the jokes, the laughter, the dancing . . . Kate was going to miss all that dreadfully.

But no one had been hurt today. At least she hoped that continued to be the case.

CHAPTER THIRTY-EIGHT

Naomi

'Careful,' the fireman warned. 'Fires have a way of start-ing up again unexpectedly. That's why we stay for a while after we put them out.'

'We'll keep our distance,' Naomi assured him.

Two hours had passed since the plane had crashed and darkness had fallen. To the relief of all, no one had been reported missing, but there was grief over the bookshop. Not only had it lost its venue, it had also lost all its books – apart from those which were out on loan – together with all its toys, rugs, chairs, tables . . . Even the new costumes for the nativity play had gone up in flames.

'Let's see if the blast threw out anything we can sal-vage,' she'd suggested to Janet and May.

They'd equipped themselves with torches and a lamp bor-rowed from the grocer, and now they were looking over the ground in front of the crash site. They found all sorts of debris, some of which they could identify and some of which they couldn't. There were shattered chips of slate from the Hall roof, bricks or half-bricks from the walls, bits of mortar, glass and metal, a tattered shred of blackout curtain . . .

'Look!' Janet cried. She picked up a book – or what remained of a book. The cover was intact but many of the pages were missing. 'It was *The Three Musketeers*,' she said sadly.

'There are more books,' May said, pointing.

They were scattered over the grass – *Tarka the Otter*, *The Inimitable Jeeves*, *Sorrell and Son*. All were ruined. 'This one is all right, I think,' May said, picking up *Ivanhoe*. But then she grimaced. 'Sorry. I spoke too soon. Half of it isn't here.'

Then Naomi saw the remains of the tea chest in which some of the books had been stored. Only three books remained inside – *Pride and Prejudice* and two more modern romances. 'Three books aren't many to be going on with, but it's a start,' she said, hoping she sounded more cheerful than she felt.

'Do you think we can launch the bookshop again somewhere else?' May asked. 'While the Hall is being rebuilt, I mean.'

'I've no idea,' Naomi admitted, 'but if we have books, we can still lend them out to people in the village as well as at the hospital.'

They found the remains of some toys, including the hobby horse Kate had once mended. It was beyond help now. More tattered bits of fabric looked as though they'd come from the nativity costumes.

They weren't permitted to walk beside the fallen walls, so they circled around the back of the vicarage and approached the site from the rear. Here there was more debris, including two shredded angel costumes blasted into the trees, where they hung like sad, limp ghosts, dripping with water from the hoses. Amidst a dented kettle, mangled cutlery, a chair with two legs missing and more bricks and broken mortar, they found another two books, but they were sodden too.

'It's hopeless,' May declared.

'You're right,' Naomi agreed. 'We're wasting our time.'

Then a voice spoke out of the shadows. 'What are you doing?' Marjorie stepped into the light. Clearly, she'd seen their torches moving and come to investigate.

'Just looking to see if we can find anything that hasn't been ruined,' Naomi told her. 'Sadly, there isn't much.'

Marjorie turned to May. 'Did I tell you I thought the plane was going to come down on top of me?'

'You did, Marjorie.'

'It scared me half to death.'

'It scared everyone.'

'Yes, but I was—'

'Standing a few yards away from me outside the grocer's.'

'I was nearer the edge of the pavement, though.'

Something caught Naomi's eye. She moved closer to investigate.

'Watch out,' Janet called. 'You'll have a fireman complaining you're too close.'

'What is it, Naomi?' Marjorie asked.

'It looks like it could be a boot.'

Marjorie, May and Janet came up for a better look. Naomi glanced around, picked up some sort of metal bar and used it to move the debris aside.

The boot came into view and Marjorie started screaming.

CHAPTER THIRTY-NINE

Naomi

'Poor chap,' Bert said, after the body had been taken away. 'He wasn't one of ours?' Not a Churchwood resident, he meant.

'I don't believe so,' Naomi told him. 'Although I never saw his face.'

'Perhaps he was our thief.'

Naomi was thinking the same thing. 'I don't know if he had any identification on him. If not, the police may never be able to let his family know what happened – if he has a family. They may spend the rest of their lives wondering what became of him.'

Churchwood would probably never know now what circumstances had brought him to the village. They'd meant well by never hunting him down and running him off but, far from helping him, their tolerance might have been the reason he'd stayed. If they'd been less tolerant, he might have moved on and kept himself safe. It was all desperately sad.

Bert gave her one of his understanding looks. 'Go home, woman. Put your feet up and have a cup of tea. Better still, have a sherry. There's nothing more you can do here.'

He gestured towards the crash site.

Naomi supposed he was right. Presumably, people would come and remove the remains of the plane then the crash site would be secured. Children were bound to be interested, but it was bad enough that the thief had come to grief without a child being injured clambering over the derelict remains.

Adam came to join them. 'Bad day,' he said. 'If they can't find that poor chap's family, it'll be a pauper's funeral for him.'

'He'll have mourners at his graveside, though. He'll have us,' Naomi said.

'I'll certainly offer to bury him here,' Adam told her. 'Why don't you go home now?' he added, echoing Bert's words. 'You've done all you can for today.'

She had, and she was weary. Luckily, Janet had kindly taken Marjorie off her hands so Naomi could have a quiet evening by herself.

A thought struck her. 'Was the building insured?' she asked Adam.

'I imagine so, though I don't know if the insurers accept liability for crashes by enemy aircraft. I'll telephone the Diocese for advice, but even if we're insured to the hilt, I fear it could be years.'

Naomi nodded, and so did Bert. Building materials – and builders – were in short supply, thanks to the war.

The bookshop's possessions hadn't been insured. Not that they were of great value, but it would still take time to raise the funds to replace them, especially the books they'd need if the bookshop was to survive even in a small way.

'I'll say goodbye, then,' Naomi began, only to be interrupted by someone saying, 'Excuse me.'

It was Evelyn Gregson, looking more anxious than ever. Was she alone? Glancing around, Naomi saw her boys standing together on the far side of the green, looking equally anxious.

'I've heard . . .' Evelyn swallowed and tried again. 'I've heard that someone was . . . found?'

'Tragically, yes,' Adam told her.

'Do you know who it was?'

'We don't think it was a Churchwood resident.'

'You only *think* not? Didn't you see him? Or was it a her? Or was the body . . . ?' Her breath caught in her throat and she couldn't go on but, clearly, she'd been asking if the body had been injured beyond recognition.

Naomi had the most information. 'It was a man, I believe, but I couldn't see any injuries,' she said. 'I'd guess he was outside the building when the plane hit and was killed by the force of the blast or falling debris.'

'You saw him?' Evelyn's anxious eyes bored into Naomi.

'Briefly. As soon as I saw him, I went for help.' She hadn't inspected the poor man.

'You must have noticed something about him?'

Why was Evelyn so upset? She'd been desperately worried about the Churchwood thief. Would there be an element of relief for her if she knew he was no longer a threat? Naomi attempted a description. 'Medium height, I think. Dark hair. Dark beard . . .'

'Anything else?'

'He had an old scar on his temple. At least, I think he did. It's hard to be sure as I kept a distance. I might have—'

Naomi broke off in concern because Evelyn had bent over suddenly, her hand to her mouth. She looked undone.

'Mrs Gregson!' Naomi cried, and Bert stepped forward to hold her up before she fell.

'You need to sit down,' Bert told her. 'We can see you've had a nasty shock. Let's get you to a bench.'

236

He steered her towards the benches by the war memorial.

Evelyn's boys were watching, and Naomi saw that both of them were crying now, the taller boy holding his brother close. She walked over to them. 'I'm afraid your mother isn't feeling quite well. Let me take you home and sit with you until she recovers. Do you have a key to the house?'

The boys weren't listening. 'Stay here,' the elder one – Alan – told his brother and he ran off to his mother. After a moment of indecision, Roger ran towards her too.

Naomi followed in time to hear Alan demand tearfully, 'Was it him?'

In answer, Evelyn reached out to gather him close then reached out for her younger son too. 'It was him, wasn't it?' Alan sobbed.

Naomi, Bert and Adam exchanged looks. 'We should get them inside,' Adam said. 'Not into the vicarage, though. It may not be safe.'

'Foxfield?' Bert suggested.

Naomi nodded. 'I think that would be best.'

'I'll fetch the truck.'

He brought it as close to the war memorial as possible then said, 'Up you get, Mrs Gregson. We're taking you somewhere warm and comfortable.'

Evelyn was pale and her eyes were still awash with tears. 'I need to go home.'

'You'll be home soon enough,' Bert assured her. 'First, we're taking you to Naomi's for hot tea and a warm-up.'

'No, I . . .' But Evelyn hadn't the strength to continue.

Bert and Adam helped her into the truck's cab, and Naomi climbed up too. 'We can ride on the back,' Adam told the boys.

Suki looked at them all wide-eyed when they arrived at Foxfield. 'Tea, madam?'

'Yes, please, Suki. Perhaps some warm milk for the boys, if we've got it?'

The Gregsons cried some more when they were installed on a sofa in the sitting room, Mrs Gregson between her boys with her arms around them. They were coaxed to drink the tea and milk when it arrived, and eventually the sobs subsided. 'I expect you've guessed that I knew the man,' Evelyn said, wiping her eyes on a handkerchief Naomi provided. 'He was my husband.'

Naomi had begun to suspect something of the kind. Had he been the sort of man who treated his wife cruelly? His children too, perhaps? Had they come to Churchwood to escape from him? It would explain Evelyn's alarm at the thought of a man being seen in her garden.

But the thefts had started weeks before the Gregsons came to the village. Could there have been two men living secretly in Churchwood or not far from it – the thief for one and Mr Gregson for the other? It felt unlikely. Perhaps Mr Gregson had somehow learned of his wife's plan to move here and come before her. If she'd thrown him out of their previous home, it would explain why he'd been living rough.

'He can't hurt you any more,' Naomi said soothingly, but Evelyn only frowned.

'John never hurt me. He was the gentlest of men.'

'I'm sorry, I thought . . .' Naomi was puzzled. Bert and Adam looked equally confused.

'He was in the army,' Evelyn explained. 'But he . . . he couldn't bear it.'

'He was a deserter?' Bert guessed, and Evelyn burst into tears again.

CHAPTER FORTY

Kate

For once Vinnie wasn't trying to hide the fact that he'd been shirking his work. Probably, the tongue-lashing he'd receive from Ernie had been forgotten in the thrilling moment of being the bearer of news.

'They've found a body!' he announced, bursting into the kitchen where Kate and Ruby were serving tea to everyone, including Timmy, who'd returned safely from school.

Kate felt a ripple of shock, quickly followed by dread. 'Whose body?' she demanded.

'Dunno yet. That posh woman found it. You know the one. Friend of yours.'

'Naomi?' What a horrible experience for her.

'I heard someone say they reckon it might be the Churchwood thief, caught out while hiding round the back of the Hall. Much good hiding did him.'

'Someone has died, Vinnie,' Kate pointed out. 'A human being. Where's your compassion?'

Vinnie looked surprised, as though he hadn't considered that aspect of the matter. 'I was only saying what I saw and heard.'

'Humph,' Ernie snarled. 'The only thing you should have seen was the fence around Five Acre Field and the only thing you should have heard was the banging of your hammer as you repaired it.'

'I wasn't away for long.'

'Long enough. You can forget having a cup of tea. Get out there now and finish the job before it gets dark.' Ernie jerked his head towards the door.

'I saw them taking the pilot away in that big black car. I hope they left my parachute?'

His parachute? 'They took it with them,' Kate told him.

'Door!' Ernie barked, threateningly, and Vinnie moved towards it, grumbling about the unfairness of life and its treatment of him in particular.

There was no doubt that he was improving as a person – growing up at last – but he hadn't managed to shed his spiteful tendencies quite yet. 'You won't be going to your precious bookshop any more,' he shot at Kate. 'It's just a pile of rubble.'

'Which means you won't be going to any more book-shop socials,' Ruby hit back on Kate's behalf.

He'd enjoyed the only one he'd attended. Unsure how to behave, he'd looked on in wonder for much of the time, but he'd had fun dancing with Ruby and Pearl and, with a few more socials under his belt, he might have plucked up the courage to ask another girl to dance.

'All you've got now is the Wheatsheaf,' Ruby continued. 'How dull is that?'

Defeated, Vinnie slunk out.

Kate gave Ruby a smile, grateful for the land girl's support but wishing she hadn't fought with Vinnie. Arguing on a day someone had died felt . . . inappropriate, even if that person had been the Churchwood thief.

Kate felt drained when she went to bed that night but worry kept her from sleep. If no one had claimed the fire victim as their own, it seemed likely that he was indeed the Churchwood thief. How sad to have spent the last period of his life with nowhere to call home, eking out his existence by stealing cold raw vegetables, milk and – only once as far as Kate knew – some biscuits off a plate. Even then, he hadn't taken all the biscuits but had left some behind, the same way he'd left posies of greenery on people's doorsteps. An unloved and unwanted man, it would appear.

Kate's own life on Brimbles Farm left a great deal to be desired. Brought up to skivvy for her father and brothers, no one had given a thought to her hopes, dreams and happiness. Not once in her entire childhood had any of them told her they loved her or tried to comfort her when she'd been sick or desperately lonely. Only in adulthood had she received awkward embraces from Frank and – before he'd lost his legs – from Fred too. Even then, she'd had to hug them first.

But Kate wasn't homeless or starving, and her family might miss her more than they expected if she were no longer here.

She thought of the pilot too, cut off from his loved ones, possibly for many years. Then Kate thought of Alice, grieving for her lost baby, and of Naomi, struggling through her divorce.

And, of course, she thought of Leo, wincing as she remembered the flames she'd seen and imagined what he'd encountered. He hadn't written back to her yet. Perhaps he never would, thinking to spare her the guilt of breaking it off with him by letting the relationship simply dwindle out of existence.

She had to see him soon, not only because he might think she'd abandoned him if she didn't visit, but also because she might never find him if he moved hospitals or was discharged back home. His parents lived in

Cheltenham but she didn't have their address, and Leo might tell his friend Max to ignore any letters she sent to him. Work on the farm was even more behind after today's dramas, though. Keeping up was just impossible.

Kate had several hours of work to her credit when she headed into the village for some shopping the next morning, but she took the time to call in on Naomi, feeling she'd be a poor friend if she didn't bother after the shock Naomi had received yesterday.

'I can't stay more than a few minutes,' she told Naomi, wondering how many times she'd said that before. It had to be dozens – possibly hundreds. 'I didn't want to pass by without asking how you are after yesterday?'

'I feel for that poor man,' Naomi told her.

'Vinnie said no one knows who he was.'

'Actually, that isn't right.'

Kate heard the story of Evelyn Gregson and her husband, John. 'A deserter? Goodness. I suppose it all makes sense, now you've explained it.'

'I don't know why he deserted. Evelyn only insisted that her husband was a good man who'd had his reasons. The only people who actually know he was a deserter are Bert, Adam, me and now you.'

'I won't breathe a word to anyone,' Kate promised.

'You can imagine the unpleasantness if it got out.'

'I certainly can.'

'My view is that I shouldn't judge without knowing all the facts.'

'But others might not be so forbearing.'

'Quite.'

Marjorie was Churchwood's most enthusiastic gossip but she was far from being the only one. It wouldn't help that Evelyn had already made herself disliked in the village. Kate had heard her called snooty and stand-offish.

She parted from Naomi with a hug and moved on to the shops. Calling at the baker's first, she walked in to find a conversation between customers in full flow. 'If Bert Makepiece hadn't caught her, she'd have fallen to the ground, I swear,' Mrs Hutchings was saying.

Her? Doubtless, Evelyn Gregson.

'It was the shock of hearing about the chap who died,' Mrs Hayes said. 'There's a rumour going round that he was her husband.'

'It's no rumour,' Mrs Lloyd told her. 'It's true. And listen to this. He was a deserter.'

'A deserter?' The whole shop was electrified.

'That's what I heard.'

Mrs Hutchings shook her head in harsh disapproval. 'No wonder his wife kept herself to herself.'

'Hiding him, she was.'

'I told you I saw a man in Mrs Gregson's garden!' Marjorie crowed, triumphant in her vindication.

'That woman should be hanging her head in shame for harbouring a man who shirked his duty while other men fought for their country,' Mrs Lloyd said. 'Some might say he got his just deserts in that plane crash.'

'And others might not!' Kate's temper had risen rapidly.

'Kate!' Mrs Hayes said. 'We didn't see you there.'

'Well, now you do see me.'

'Surely, you're not defending the Gregsons? Not with you having a sweetheart in the Royal Air Force?'

'I'm not defending Evelyn Gregson, but I'm not con-demning her either, because I don't know enough about what went on.'

243

'A man deserted his duty and his country, that's what went on,' Mrs Lloyd said staunchly.

'The thing speaks for itself,' Mrs Hayes agreed.

'None of you know the first thing about the Gregsons,' Kate told them. 'I'm disappointed in you all for being so . . . so judgemental.'

Mrs Hayes tilted her chin defiantly and her cronies did likewise.

'Anyway,' Kate added, 'who told you Mr Gregson was a deserter?'

The women exchanged looks. 'I don't remember,' Mrs Hayes admitted. 'We just heard it.'

'And lost no time in gossiping about something that could have been a falsehood, for all you knew.'

'Now, now, Kate. You're speaking out of turn, but we'll let it go because we like you and we know you have a temper on you.'

Kate rolled her eyes, bought her bread and moved on to the butcher's, where a similar conversation was taking place.

Churchwood and its community were wonderful – most of the time. But this wasn't one of those times. This was like the old days when Kate had been the one who was treated as an outsider and judged for circumstances beyond her control – her men's cast-off clothes, her dirty fingernails, the fact that she was a member of the rough and rude Fletcher family . . . It had been horrible, and now it was happening again, not only to Evelyn but to her children, too.

Something needed to be done.

CHAPTER FORTY-ONE

Naomi

'Kate!' Naomi said, surprised to see her friend back at the door. 'Come in,' she invited, only to realize that Kate was upset. 'What's happened?'

'You were wrong when you said that only a few people know about John Gregson being a deserter. The whole village knows.'

'How?' Naomi was bewildered.

Kate raised her arms then let them fall to her sides in a shrug. 'I couldn't find that out.'

'I haven't told anyone. Bert and Adam wouldn't have told anyone either.'

'What about Suki? Might she have overheard you talking and mentioned it to her mother or someone else?'

'I doubt it. She knows better than to repeat anything she hears in my house. She's very loyal. I wonder ... .'

'What?' Kate asked.

'John Gregson was taken away in an ambulance. I saw one of the men talking to Elsie Fuller.'

'How would the ambulance men know John Gregson was a deserter?'

'Perhaps there was identification on the body, papers that showed he was supposed to be a serving soldier. The ambulance men might have put two and two together, seeing as Mr Gregson was away from his regiment and obviously living rough.'

'I suppose it doesn't really matter *how* people know,' Kate said then. 'It's what they're going to do with the information that matters. I suspect Evelyn won't be very welcome in Churchwood any more. Not that she made herself popular before.'

'She shouldn't be driven out of the village by gossips when no one knows John Gregson's story.'

'I pity the boys,' Kate said.

'Me too. Thank you for telling me, Kate. I'll do my best to quash any unpleasantness. I'll ask Bert and Adam to do the same.'

'It's a shame Alice isn't up and about.'

Alice had a way of bringing Churchwood together. 'It is,' Naomi agreed. 'I'm not going to tell her what's happened, though. Alice needs to take care of herself for once instead of worrying about other people.'

Kate nodded in agreement and touched Naomi's arm by way of farewell.

Oh, heavens. What was Naomi to do? She decided the first thing was to speak to her staff – Suki, Cook, Beryl the cleaning lady and Sykes the gardener. 'Please don't think I'm suggesting that any of you have been gossiping,' she began, 'but rumours are flying around the village about the Gregsons. I hope you won't join in spreading them. We don't know enough about the family to judge their situation and, whatever the circumstances, the boys are innocents.'

Afterwards, she put on her coat and hat, added gloves and a scarf to her ensemble, and went to see Bert. Even without the gossip, she'd wanted to speak to him because she'd finally come to a decision about her own way forward.

They talked in his homely kitchen, which felt deliciously warm after her walk through the raw afternoon.

'We can only do our best,' Bert said. 'You said the right thing to your staff and now we have to say the same thing to everyone else we meet. I'll start tomorrow when I go to the shops.'

'I'll do the same. It might help if we knew more about *why* John Gregson deserted.'

'True. I only tiptoed around the subject when I took Mrs Gregson home from your house, but she made it pretty clear that she didn't want to talk about it. Her boys were there too, of course, but I don't think that made a difference.'

'She doesn't help herself.'

'No, but she isn't the only difficult woman Churchwood's ever had, and we've had happy endings before.'

'You're thinking of Kate,' Naomi said, because Kate had once been extremely difficult – glaring at anyone who crossed her path and lacerating them with her tongue if they provoked her.

'Churchwood was to blame there for looking down on the poor girl when it wasn't her fault she'd been born the daughter of Ernie Fletcher,' Bert said.

Naomi winced in shame because no one had looked down on Kate more than she had. It was only thanks to Alice's kindness that Churchwood had been persuaded to give Kate a chance and vice versa. Now everyone knew that Kate had a tender heart, even if her temper could still fire up quickly.

'I'm not *just* thinking of Kate,' Bert added, eyes twinkling, and Naomi cringed again, realizing that he had her in mind.

'Ancient history,' he said, comfortingly. 'The point is

that we had happy endings with you and Kate, and we must hope it'll be the same with Evelyn Gregson.'

'We must,' Naomi agreed. Bert had raised the subject of Naomi's past life, so it felt the right time to say, 'I've decided to take your advice and go to Somerset House. I may find nothing, but I want to try.'

'What's brought on this decision?'

'The present tragedy, I suppose. If I have more money, I can help the village.'

'Help it how?'

'I'm thinking of the bookshop.'

'It may be years before we have a new hall.'

'I'm thinking of an alternative to the Hall. Temporary or permanent, I don't know yet.'

'Not Foxfield?' Bert's frown suggested he considered Naomi's home to be unsuitable, and he was right.

'Not Foxfield, no. I can't imagine young mothers feeling relaxed with their children running around putting the furnishings in danger with paint, biscuits and the like.'

'Or folk sawing wood to make toys.'

'Exactly. But if I can stay in Foxfield myself and have some money to spare, I can—'

'Buy Joe Simpson's old place for the bookshop?' Bert guessed. 'By heck, you've had an injection of ambition, woman.'

'It's taken me a while to get there, but yes.' Naomi still wilted at the thought of the shame she might suffer if she discovered that Alexander's marriage to her was the bigamous one, but she'd square her shoulders and hold her head high anyway. After all, the shame should fall on Alexander's head, not hers.

'When shall we go?' Bert asked. 'To London, I mean?'

'*We?*'

'Two people can do the searching quicker than one, and wouldn't you welcome a bit of moral support?'

She would indeed. 'What about your work?'

'It isn't my busiest time of year. I'll get ahead with the work and ask young Luke Carpenter to keep an eye on the place while I'm gone. He's asked me for a job so it'll give him a chance to show what he can do.'

'You're very kind.'

'I haven't been to London in years. Maybe I just want an adventure.'

And maybe he was just being kind.

Bert promised to let her know when he'd be free, and she left his home feeling purposeful. She was going to do what she could to calm the village down over the Gregsons, and she was going to do what she could to fight back against Alexander. Maybe her future would become clear by Christmas, after all.

CHAPTER FORTY-TWO

Kate

Brimbles Farm always felt a little cut off from the village, but it felt particularly distant now Kate was desperate for news of what was happening there and her usual source of information – Alice – was no longer walking past on her way to and from the hospital. A day went by, and Kate heard nothing from anyone.

By the next morning, she could bear it no longer. She worked hard until the afternoon so no one could accuse her of shirking then announced, 'I'm going into the village. The grocer is expecting a delivery of tinned corned beef and I don't want us to miss out.'

She didn't linger long enough to hear any protests but set off on her bicycle. Nearing the end of Brimbles Lane, she looked up at The Linnets, wondering how Alice was faring. Having never experienced such a thing, Kate had no idea about how much time was likely to pass before a person picked up the threads of their life after a miscarriage. She supposed it must vary.

Alice had always been such a strong person, even when Daniel had been stranded in Dunkirk and again when he'd been taken as a prisoner of war not so long ago. But having held up well through those troubled times, perhaps she had no reserves left for withstanding this latest misfortune. It must have been especially hard for her to lose a much-wanted baby when Daniel was far from home and might not be granted leave for many months.

Kate also looked at Foxfield in passing, hoping that Naomi was coping with the challenges life was throwing at her. Hoping, too, that she wouldn't lose her home. It would surely wound Naomi on a personal level. Not to mention that, in Naomi's hands, Foxfield was an asset to the village because she was generous in opening it up for village events. A new buyer might not be half as welcoming.

Moving on, Kate headed for the grocer's, pausing to stare across the green where the plane had fallen. The school was open, but Kate guessed that the children had been packed into one side of the building, as workmen on ladders were doing something to the other side. A tarpaulin was covering the section of the vicarage roof that was missing its chimney, and boards had been nailed over a couple of the windows.

As for the Sunday School Hall, more boards had been erected around the site, probably to keep it secure from curious children and scavengers.

The loss of the bookshop squeezed Kate's heart. Short of a miracle, she couldn't see how it could possibly be revived for a long time to come. It wasn't as though Churchwood had any other suitable buildings into which the bookshop might transfer. She was going to miss it dreadfully. Churchwood would suffer too. It had been the bookshop that had drawn the community together. Companionship, fun, interesting activities . . . The bookshop had offered them all, as well as practical help whenever it was needed.

With a sigh of regret, Kate stepped into the grocer's. She hadn't been lying about the corned beef. A delivery had indeed been expected. But her primary goal in coming out today was to place a finger on the pulse of the village's mood. She hoped Naomi, Bert and Adam would by now have been able to calm that mood down enough for the Gregsons at least to go about their daily business without fearing they'd come face to face with contemptuous looks and accusations.

Walking into the shop, Kate was aware of the conversation breaking off hurriedly and of guilty faces trying to look innocent. 'What is it?' Kate said.

Glances were exchanged, then Mrs Lloyd said, 'I don't know what you mean.'

'I think you do,' Kate told her. 'I think you all do. You were talking about the Gregsons.'

'We're allowed to have a conversation, aren't we?'

'Of course. But you might want to look into your hearts and ask yourselves if it's a *kind* conversation.'

'We don't want to fall out with you, Kate. You're entitled to your opinion, and we're entitled to ours.'

Kate found there wasn't a sympathetic word to be had in the butcher's or the baker's either. Fuming with disappointment, she called at Naomi's on her way home.

'I'm doing my best to dampen the hostility but I don't seem to be making any difference,' Naomi told her. 'Do you have time for a cup of tea?'

'Unfortunately not.' Kate had already got up to leave.

They said their goodbyes at the door and Kate climbed back on to the bike. She cycled down the Foxfield drive and through the gateposts but then came to a halt, looking up at The Linnets again.

Alice would be the perfect person to pour soothing oil on the troubled waters of Churchwood, but she was still keeping to her home. Was she any better at all? Kate crossed the lane and knocked on the cottage door, softly as she didn't want to disturb Alice if she were sleeping. Dr Lovell answered and gave her a smile, though she thought it rather a sad one. 'I'm here to ask about Alice,' Kate said. 'Is she doing any better?'

'I wish I could invite you in to see for yourself, but I'm afraid she still doesn't feel ready for visitors. To answer your question, I've no cause for concern about her physical recovery, but she needs longer to come to terms with what happened on an emotional level.'

Kate nodded. 'You'll give her my love?'

'I'll be sure to.'

With that Kate had to be content, though she longed to hold her grieving friend in her arms.

Lost in thought, Kate didn't notice the tall figure striding towards Brimbles Farm until she was almost upon her. 'Pearl!' she cried.

The land girl turned to her with a grin. 'I'm back!'

'It's wonderful to see you.' Kate jumped off the bike and folded Pearl into a hug. 'We've missed you so much! But why didn't you let us know you were coming?'

'I left in a hurry,' Pearl explained as they walked up the track to the farmhouse, Kate wheeling the bike and Pearl holding on to the bag she'd slung over her shoulder. 'My mother said I was tearing her nerves to shreds with my big feet clomping around the house. Then my father got mad because I poured him a drink and dropped the decanter. Cut crystal, it was. A wedding present from years ago. Ugly thing, but my father was livid anyway. I'm glad to get away, to be honest. My mother insisted I wore skirts and I'm a trousers sort of girl, as you know.'

'Your mother is well, I hope?'

'Recovering nicely, the doc says. She'll recover even faster now I'm not there.' Pearl laughed, mocking herself.

'Your family may not appreciate you, but we do,' Kate insisted.

Pearl gave her a sideways look.

'It's true. Just wait and see what sort of welcome you get from the others.'

They reached the farmhouse and soon everyone came in for tea. 'Look who's here,' Kate said.

Ruby let out a shriek and ran to hug her friend. Timmy followed, wrapping his arms around Pearl too. 'Welcome back,' Kenny said, which was remarkably civil coming from him, while Vinnie grinned and told her, 'I won the darts match at the Wheatsheaf last night,' as though he valued her approval.

Even Ernie let out a surly, 'P'raps we can get some work done around here now,' which was a compliment of a sort.

'I really do fit in here, don't I?' Pearl said to Kate, sounding amazed.

They all sat down to tea and Ruby asked Pearl about her stay in Croydon. 'It reminded me of why I couldn't wait to get away,' Pearl said. 'It's funny, if you think about it. My father's house is nice by most people's standards. It's got an indoor bathroom, plush carpets that swallow your feet, and it's always warm because my father can afford to keep the fires going. At least, he could keep it toasty before coal was rationed. This place, on the other hand . . .'

She broke off to grin then continued. 'This place can be perishing and the only lav is outside. If we want to wash our hair, we have to dunk our heads under the cold tap at the sink or the pump outside. And if we want a proper wash, we have to boil kettles to fill the old tin bath. Despite all that, I much prefer being here.'

Kate was touched, and so was Ruby.

'I tell you what I didn't miss when I was away, though.' Pearl looked at Fred, who sneered.

'We're all ears,' he drawled.

'I didn't miss your moaning.'

Everyone else froze mid-chew or while raising a cup to their lips.

Fred was startled and then outraged. He looked round at them as though rallying their support. 'Did you hear that? I've lost my legs, for pity's sake!'

'I know you have,' Pearl scoffed. 'I'm sure it must be miserable. But I don't see that it gives you the right to make everyone else miserable too.'

'You can't say that!' Fred roared.

'I said it because it's true.' Unperturbed, Pearl reached for a second slice of bread and bit a chunk out of it.

'Tell her she can't speak to me like that, Ernie!' Fred protested, but Ernie only took a sip of tea.

'Kenny?' Fred appealed.

Kenny opened his mouth to speak only to be silenced by a glare from Ruby.

'Kate?' Fred said then, but Kate wasn't inclined to censure Pearl either. Being nice to Fred hadn't brought him round to a positive attitude. Perhaps some truth-telling was what he actually needed. 'Anyone for another cup of tea?' she asked instead.

'Don't mind if I do,' Pearl told her, and Fred was left to fume in silence.

'Right,' Pearl said, when the tea was drunk and the last bit of bread and jam had been eaten. 'Time to get to work.'

'You don't have to work today,' Kate told her. 'You must be tired after your journey.'

'Tired? Me? I'll be glad to get out there in the air. Being

cooped up indoors and mincing about in a silly frock feeling scared to death in case I broke something or got in the way drove me nuts.'

It must have been music to Ernie's ears, though he didn't have it in him to offer praise or gratitude.

Kate and Ruby washed and dried the dishes. 'You know,' Ruby said, 'with Pearl back, you can go and see Leo.'

The same thought had been leaping and dancing in Kate's mind. 'Will you be able to manage Fred?'

'We'll manage him,' Ruby assured her. 'Kenny can drive Fred to his hospital appointments, or Pearl and I can take him in the cart. Preferably Pearl, as she's better with the pony than me. Whatever happens, it'll be fine.'

'But—'

'As for Fred's more personal needs – washing, dressing, using the lav – he's got two brothers and a father.'

'Thank you, Ruby. I'll let Pearl settle back in tomorrow then I'll go to see Leo the day after.'

'You'll have to tell Ernie where you're going.'

'Isn't that something to look forward to?' Kate quipped, and the girls smiled at each other ruefully.

CHAPTER FORTY-THREE

Alice

Darling Alice,

As you can probably imagine, I was overjoyed to hear that we're expecting a baby. How absolutely wonderful! I whooped out loud when I read your letter and took great delight in telling my friends and comrades that I'm to be a father. I quite understand that you didn't tell me before because you didn't want to disappoint me in case the pregnancy didn't stick, but now we can celebrate as though Christmas, birthdays and other such occasions have come together in a festival of bliss.

I'm so pleased that you're feeling well, though I wish I could be there to look after you. Do take care, dearest girl. You're going to be an amazing mother and I'll certainly do my best to be a good father. It's such a privilege having a child, and I want our child to know all his life (or her life?) how much he (she?) is loved . . .

It had been agony to receive the letter the week after losing the baby. Why, oh why hadn't she kept to her original plan of waiting until Christmas, or at the very least until she was three months along, before telling Daniel that she was pregnant? She'd have spared him the grief she was certain to inflict when she told him about the miscarriage, and it wasn't as though she could comfort him by holding him in her arms.

She'd been trying to write to him ever since the miscarriage, knowing that the longer she put it off, the harder it would be for him to hear the sad news. But she'd abandoned her first efforts because, despite needing his sympathy as much as he would doubtless need hers, she still wanted to present herself as managing to cope. Unfortunately, all of those early attempts at writing had deteriorated into outpourings of sorrow that would only upset Daniel all the more.

Days had gone by with no progress being made, until the arrival of his letter had sent her into a panic and made it all the more urgent that she should tell him the sad news. But once again, she'd been unable to find the right words. Knowing he was awaiting a reply, she'd taken the coward's way out and merely asked her father to post a book she'd bought for him along with a short note that promised him a letter soon and sent her love in the meantime.

'Would you like me to write to Daniel?' Alice's father had asked, but she hadn't wanted Daniel to think she was laid so low that she couldn't write at all.

'Thanks, but I'll manage,' she'd told her father.

More days had ticked by, and more notepaper had been wasted on letters that had turned into false starts and been set aside. But, sitting in her bedroom now, she took up pen and paper and tried again, determined that this time she wouldn't fail.

Darling Daniel,

I'm afraid I have disappointing news and there's no easy way to break it to you. I lost the baby. I was told that miscarriage is a common occurrence — something I already knew — and, luckily, there were no complications that might have made it

difficult to conceive or carry a child in the future. Even so, it
was a blow to me, as I'm sure it must be a blow to you . . .

Oh no. A tear had fallen on to the notepaper and blurred the word *blow*. A second tear fell and blurred the word *complications*. Daniel would realize she'd been crying and she didn't want that. She wanted to be strong so he wouldn't add worry about her to his awful sense of loss.

She scrapped the letter and started again, managing to finish this one and place it in an envelope for her father to post. She wished she could be with Daniel when he read it, holding him in her arms and comforting him. Blast this war.

Exhaustion washed over her, and she lay back against her pillows. Alice had never known tiredness like this. It had seeped into her muscles, bones and every cell of her brain. Breathing required effort. Conversation was almost impossible.

One day she'd feel better. Alice knew that. But she couldn't imagine that day dawning soon. As for Christmas, it was meant to have been such a joyful time, but now she was dreading it, knowing it would be filled with painful memories of what might have been. She couldn't cancel Christmas, exactly, but she could certainly do her best to steer clear of the festivities.

CHAPTER FORTY-FOUR

Naomi

Despite her nervousness, Bert's appearance tugged a smile from Naomi when he arrived to collect her for their visit to London. He looked like a relic from yesteryear in the funeral suit, but she was fond of him and more than a little proud of him, too, because there was something upright, honest and determined in his air. He was a good man to have on her side.

It wasn't far from Foxfield to the bus stop, but Bert proposed driving her in the truck anyway. She guessed he was thinking that it would be helpful to leave the truck nearby, ready for the return journey when her feet might be tired. The bus took them to St Albans and from there they caught the train to London.

They didn't talk about their mission as they travelled and Naomi was glad, as it would only have cranked up the tension that was already cramping her stomach. After all, what they did – or didn't – find today could affect the rest of her life. They talked about the Gregsons instead. Separately, Naomi and Bert had both visited Evelyn, but all they'd seen of her was a hint of her face, given that she'd opened the door the merest crack. Neither had been allowed inside and neither had managed to utter more than a few words before Evelyn had closed the door again, saying, 'Please leave us alone.'

They'd both tried to change village opinion, too, but Churchwood was still turning a cold shoulder to the Gregsons.

'And to think that the milk I needed was taken by a deserter . . .' Naomi had heard Mrs Lloyd say.

'Deserters got rough justice in the 1914 war,' Wilf Phipps had told Bert. 'Taken out and shot, they were, and quite right too. Leaving other men to fight and risk death or injury while they slunk off to keep their own hides safe . . . Disgraceful.'

From St Pancras they took the underground railway then walked the rest of the way to Somerset House, where the central registry occupied part of the building.

The records were kept in big, heavy volumes going back years. 'I suggest we start from the date the icicle married you and work forwards,' Bert said. 'If we find nothing, we can always work backwards instead.'

Working backwards would mean that Alexander had married his lover first. 'Agreed,' Naomi said, reminding herself that the shame would be Alexander's, not hers, but still hoping it wouldn't come to that.

'I'll start with Harrington, and I'll check Harington with one "r" too, in case he's played about with the spelling of his name in the hope of avoiding detection,' Bert proposed.

'I'll start with Amelia Ashmore, though it might be spelt Ashmoor or Ashmoore,' Naomi told him, thinking that they were less likely to miss something important if they attacked on two fronts.

'Amelia might be a middle name or a nickname, so best to look at every possibility,' Bert advised. 'We don't want to have to work through the same records more than once.' The task was already daunting.

They worked for two hours, heaving each volume from its shelf and studying it carefully before replacing it and taking another. They were silent apart from Bert offering to carry the heavy books and Naomi thanking him.

She felt a burst of excitement – or was it dread? – when she came upon an Ashmoor wedding, but it related to a woman called Ruth who'd married a joiner called Edwin Jones in Lancaster. Another, a jolt of something – she wasn't sure what – stirred her when she saw the name Ashmoor again, but it too related to someone else – a Harold Ashmoor who'd married an Elizabeth Jenkins in Ipswich.

'Let's take a break before we lose concentration,' Bert said. They walked back into the chilly air and found a tearoom near Covent Garden flower market where they lunched on soup and salmon paste sandwiches, washing them down with tea.

They didn't discuss their morning's search but talked more about London instead. 'My first trip in more than twenty years,' Bert told her. 'It's a sorry sight in many ways, with those bombed buildings looking like teeth knocked out of a mouth and all those posters and signs reminding us that we live in wartime. *Careless talk costs lives*, *this way to the air raid shelter*, *that way to the soup kitchen* . . . All those folk in uniforms, too. But in other ways it's a tribute to efficiency and resilience. Plenty of people can still summon a smile, and they haven't all forgotten their manners.'

They didn't linger long over their meal but walked back to Somerset House with renewed determination. Another hour passed as they worked through the volumes. Naomi was about to ask Bert how much longer he was willing to stay when she saw that he'd gone still. 'What is it?' she asked.

He looked up and there was triumph in his eyes as he smiled at her, one conspirator to another. 'Got 'im.'

Naomi hastened over and there it was: Alexander had married again after he'd already married Naomi. Bert had been right: Alexander was a bigamist.

'You can see he's given his name as Harington with one "r" instead of two and described himself as a financier instead of a stockbroker – doubtless to try to cover his tracks – but it's the same man, all right. Everything else fits, including the name of the so-called bride, Amelia Ashmore of Virginia Water in Surrey.'

Naomi was stunned. While she'd hoped to find evidence that would be to her advantage, she'd never quite believed that Alexander would be foolhardy enough to risk breaking the law. But here was the evidence. 'Goodness,' she said, because she felt she had to say something.

'Goodness, and a lot more besides,' Bert answered.

She paid for a copy of the marriage certificate, and they headed home. 'You're going to show it to your solicitor?' Bert asked as they settled on the train.

'I'm not sure what I'm going to do yet,' Naomi told him. 'Obviously, I'm going to use it to my advantage, but I want to think about how I do it.'

'Fair enough, as long as that calculating stick of ice gets his comeuppance.'

Naomi was more convinced than ever that Alexander had been siphoning off her money and hiding it. 'All I want is to get back what was mine before I ever met the man.'

'Your trust fund.'

'Less the purchase price of Foxfield and my own living expenses over the years. I'm desperately keen to keep the house.'

263

'That's your priority, is it? To stay living in that big old house? By yourself?'

'I know it's a large house for one person, but I like to entertain there and throw the garden open for village events, like Alice's wedding. Besides, it's home and I love it. I can't really imagine living anywhere else.'

Bert nodded slowly. 'Then it's lucky we found that marriage certificate, isn't it?'

Thoughts of her next steps occupied Naomi's mind for most of the journey home. 'I've been terribly poor company, haven't I?' she said as they reached Churchwood. 'Forgive me, Bert, but I'm all of a daze.'

'There's nothing to forgive.'

'Come in for tea,' she invited. 'Or perhaps sherry would be more in order?'

'Thank you, but I'll be off home. You've got to make plans for your future, and I've got a market garden that needs attention.'

He drove off the moment she stepped from the truck and Naomi felt a gust of guilt for having dragged him away from his work for the day. A gust of gratitude, too. What a fine friend he was.

She glanced at her watch and judged that it was too late to make the phone call she'd planned on the journey. Tomorrow would be soon enough. She went inside with a renewed sense of hope.

CHAPTER FORTY-FIVE

Kate

'You're *what*?' Ernie demanded, after Kate had made her announcement.

'I said I'm going away for a couple of days. To Manchester.'

'No, you're not, girl. This isn't the time for jaunts with those village friends of yours. There's work to be done.'

'I'll do as much work as I can before I leave, and I'll work hard when I get back.'

'The answer's still no.'

'I wasn't asking for permission. I was merely informing you that I'm going away. As a courtesy.'

'You're forgetting your place, girl. This is my house and you're my daughter. You'll do as you're told.'

'I'm afraid I won't do as I'm told. Not by you. I'm being more than fair by staying here and working ridiculous hours to help keep the farm going. I've had hardly any time off recently, but now I need two days.'

'You don't need anything! It's just those fancy friends giving you ideas above your station. That doctor's daughter for one of 'em. And that woman in the big house for another.'

'This has nothing to do with Alice or Naomi.'

'Then who has it—' He broke off suddenly, anger swelling his ferret-like face. 'You'd better not be seeing some man.'

On the edge of her vision Kate could see Ruby and Pearl encouraging her to speak out and assert herself. Kate had every intention of doing just that. She'd spent months keeping Leo a secret from her father for fear of the misery he would inflict, not just on herself, but on everyone else too. But enough was enough. 'I *am* seeing a man, actually. A flight lieutenant in the RAF. He's been injured and I'm going to visit him in hospital.'

Ernie's face turned puce. 'How dare you get up to mischief behind my back! I'll tan your hide for this!' He came around the table.

Kate took one step backwards and then stood her ground. 'Lay as much as a single finger on me and I won't be away for just *two* days. I'll never come back.'

'Kenny!' Ernie commanded, as though expecting his older son to bring Kate to heel.

Kenny glanced at Ruby, who gave him a *don't you dare side with Ernie* look. 'It's only two days,' Kenny said.

'There's no *only* about two days of work! Well, if she goes away, she doesn't get paid.'

'Oh yes she does!' Pearl said, leaping to her feet. 'Kate works harder than anyone I know. She deserves twice the pittance you pay her.'

'Quite right, Pearl,' Ruby said, then addressed Ernie. 'If you're going to be picky about who does what around here, how about I don't do any cooking, cleaning or washing while Kate is away? I'm sure you'll enjoy getting by on cold veg for a couple of days, especially now we're nearly in winter.'

'I need a hot dinner,' Vinnie protested. 'I need breakfast too, and—'

'Oh, shut up,' Ernie told him, then glared at Kate, Kenny, Ruby and Pearl. 'You're a disgrace,' he said. 'The whole lot of you. A disgrace.'

266

'I'm making corned beef hash for dinner,' Kate announced brightly.

Ruby sent her a wink and Pearl made a thumbs-up gesture.

'Wait a minute,' Fred said then. 'Who's going to look after me?'

'No one if you keep grumbling,' Pearl told him.

'Did you hear that?' Fred spluttered, but Kenny cut him off.

'Stop whining, Fred. We'll manage.'

'How dare you call a man who's lost his legs a whiner? You should try being in my shoes. Except that I haven't got any shoes, have I?' He jolted suddenly. 'What the . . . ?'

Pearl was steering the wheelchair into the front sitting room that had become Fred's bedroom. 'You can come out when we know your whines aren't going to give us earache,' she told him, closing the door and shutting him in.

'Any more tea in the pot?' she asked then.

Kate and Ruby exchanged smiles. Pearl's return to Brimbles Farm really had given her confidence a boost, and who knew? Perhaps her blunt approach to Fred was the very thing he needed to shock him out of his slough of self-pity.

Kate set out early in the morning, wanting to allow plenty of time for her journey. Well, she told herself, she'd always craved adventure, and even if she'd imagined Paris or New York, going to Manchester alone was an adventure of sorts. The thought helped her to dredge up a smile, but it lasted no more than a fleeting moment. Giving up on any attempt to take her mind off her nerves, Kate allowed her concerns to take centre stage in her mind.

What if Leo was depressed like Fred? Would Kate be

able to help him face the future with enthusiasm? Could she convince him that life could still be good? And what of his appearance? She was bracing herself to hide any shock she might feel, but what if it showed despite her efforts? Would she ever be able to persuade him that her reaction meant only that she regretted his suffering?

She breathed out slowly, preferring to imagine a different – better – reunion in which Leo's injuries were barely mentioned because they were so happy to be together again.

Leo wasn't alone in having scars. Alice had some too and wasn't entirely able-bodied either, as her injury limited her strength and dexterity to some extent. But look what she'd achieved – a happy marriage, a job, and a bookshop that had straddled both the village and the local military hospital, making such a difference to people's lives.

Leo was clever and educated, unlike Fred, who'd never envisaged a life beyond hard physical work. Leo could surely do all sorts of things to earn a living. There was no need for despondency.

The journey took her into London, where she changed to a different train that would carry her north. The train was busy with soldiers, sailors and airmen, presumably home on leave or travelling on war business. Some women also wore uniforms – women who were WAAFs, Wrens or members of the Women's Voluntary Service. Kate was glad she'd worn the sort of clothes that indicated she worked on the land, even if she wasn't formally a land girl – breeches, cream shirt and an old green sweater that had belonged to Vinnie and was now patched at the elbows. It made her feel that she too was contributing to the war effort.

Not that she intended to visit the hospital looking like this. She had better clothes in her bag but was saving them to keep them fresh.

There were civilian passengers too, and Kate settled in a third-class carriage with a young woman who had a boy of around five years; an older woman, who was sucking a sweet; an elderly gentleman, who opened his newspaper as soon as he got on, as though to hide behind its pages; and one of the more mature soldiers. No one seemed inclined to talk beyond, 'Is this seat taken?' and, 'Sit down, Robbie. Remember what I said about behaving yourself.'

Kate had a seat beside the window and was looking forward to gazing out at the towns and countryside they passed, but she gave it up so the boy could find entertainment in the outside world instead. Taking the boy's old seat between the woman with the pear drops and the man with the newspaper, Kate hoped that the man would offer to exchange positions so she could sit next to the window, since his newspaper was clearly of more interest to him than the view. Sadly, it didn't appear to cross his mind.

Kate would have welcomed the view as a distraction from her churning stomach. She'd brought a book with her – *Mapp and Lucia* by E. F. Benson, which had survived the destruction of the bookshop by being out on loan when the plane crashed. But it was in her bag on the luggage rack above her head and she didn't want to disturb the other passengers by standing up to take it out.

The train chugged onwards. The man with the newspaper appeared to be reading every word because he turned the pages only slowly, sniffing occasionally and once muttering, 'Humph!'

The older woman ate her pear drops, sucking on

them contentedly and staring into space. It would have been kind of her to offer one to the boy, but the thought appeared not to occur to her.

The soldier studied notes he'd written in a black notebook, adding to them now and then. And the mother spoke in hushed tones to her son as he pointed out sheep, a tractor, some birds and a plane going over.

When the train slowed and halted, Kate stood up to reach for her bag.

The soldier jumped to his feet gallantly. 'Allow me,' he said, retrieving the bag for her and presenting it with the smallest hint of a bow.

Kate read a few pages of her book, but the words blurred as her thoughts strayed time and again to Leo. She couldn't help suspecting that their future turned on how she managed the first few minutes of their reunion, and the pressure of it squeezed her stomach mercilessly.

Her appetite failed as a result but she knew it would do her no good to skip meals. She needed the fuel for her brain as well as her body. She'd packed a lunch for the journey, not wanting to spend money unnecessarily, but wasn't sure her fellow passengers would take kindly to a picnic in the carriage.

Fortunately, she wasn't the first to bring out food. The mother of the boy produced a package of sandwiches from her bag. 'Time for lunch, Robbie,' she announced.

Kate ate her meal of pie and apples quickly and quietly as the woman with the pear drops continued to suck on them and the soldier with the notebook continued to write in it.

In time, the train reached Manchester. Kate got off, walked along the platform to the station concourse, then asked a woman in the uniform of the Women's Voluntary

Service if she knew where a night's lodgings might be obtained by someone on a limited budget.

'Bless you, love, you've come to the right woman, because my sister-in-law takes paying guests. She's called Bessie. Bessie Bruff.'

'It'll only be for one night.'

'That'll be fine, I'm sure. Run along to Ankerman Street – number seven.'

'Thank you, I will. Ankerman Street is . . . ?'

'Turn right as you leave the station, then right again by Allsop's Newsagents. Tell her Bessie sent you. That's right, dear. I'm called Bessie too.'

Number seven Ankerman Street was a red-brick terraced house. A sign in the window proclaimed that it was a guest house offering bed and breakfast with a discount for longer stays.

'I'm looking for a bed for the night. Bessie sent me,' Kate said when a homely-looking woman answered her knock on the brown door.

'On duty at the station, is she? A good soul is Bessie. Well, come along in, love. I'll show you a room and you tell me if it suits.'

The room was on the first floor – small but very clean with a linoleum floor, floral wallpaper and faded curtains at the window. There was a single bed, a chest of drawers, a chair, and hooks on the back of the door for hanging clothes.

'I have a bigger room but that's a shilling extra.'

'This room will be fine,' Kate said.

'Just for the one night, is it?'

'That's right.'

She paid the money Mrs Bruff requested then said, 'Would you mind if I changed my clothes here now?'

'The room is yours, dear. Will you be wanting dinner?'

'I haven't thought.'

'I'm making a stew. More vegetables than meat, but that's rationing. You go about your business and if you find you need a meal when you get back, I can warm some up for you. Can't say fairer than that, can I, dear?'

'You're very kind.'

Alone, Kate walked to the window. It overlooked the rear of the property, so her view comprised the backs of other houses and the paved yards that occupied the area between them. Turning, she looked around the room's interior again. She was used to a small space and a small bed so would manage very well. It was strange to think she'd sleep in this bed tonight. It would be the first time in her entire life that she hadn't slept at Brimbles Farm, save for one night spent at Alice's.

She changed into the dress and lisle stockings May had once given her, shaking them out first to rid them of creases. She wore a cardigan and a light jacket on top, borrowed from May, though she suspected they would offer inadequate protection from the late-November air. Not that Kate cared about that. The important thing was to see Leo.

She made her way downstairs and stood in the narrow hall. 'Hello?'

Mrs Bruff appeared from what Kate guessed to be the kitchen. She'd put on an apron over her dress and was drying her hands on a tea towel.

'I'm on my way out,' Kate said. 'Do you know the best way to get here?' She showed her the hospital details and Mrs Bruff's expression turned sympathetic.

'Visiting a patient, are you?'

Kate swallowed. 'That's right.'

'Walk to Piccadilly Gardens and pick up the bus from there. I'm not sure of the bus number but I'm sure you can ask someone when you get there. Good luck, dear.'

Would Kate need good luck? Time would tell.

She walked to Piccadilly Gardens and caught a bus. It was a short journey and soon she was walking into a hospital that had the same antiseptic smell and disciplined bustle of Fred's hospital in London.

Five minutes later she made her way along a corridor to Leo's ward. The shoes she'd borrowed from May made hollow taps as she walked. She felt as though a hollow had opened up inside her too, filled only with fear − fear of what she might see, what she might hear and what she might do.

CHAPTER FORTY-SIX

Kate

'May I help?' A nurse barred the corridor.

'I'm here to see Flight Lieutenant Kinsella. Is this a convenient time? I've come a long way.'

'You're in luck,' the nurse confirmed and pointed. 'Through the double doors and you'll find him in the last bed on the right.'

'Thanks.'

Kate approached the doors, paused to take a deep breath, then pushed through and set off down the ward. She was aware of patients turning their heads towards her, hoping, perhaps, that the visitor might be here to relieve the boredom of their afternoons. Other visitors turned towards her too, and Kate imagined they were hoping she was a nurse come to tend to their beloved or give them information – apart from one female visitor, who moved towards her patient defensively as though to declare, 'He's mine!'

Kate registered them only vaguely. With her nerves coiling around each other like serpents, she kept her gaze on the last bed on the right-hand side. From a distance, Leo appeared only as a hump. The closer she drew to him, the more she could make out details – the bandages and sling that supported his left arm, more bandages around his neck and on the left side of his face. Not that they covered him completely. He was left uncovered enough for her to see the familiar bronze hair and glimpse a hint of pink skin. He had a book open on his lap but appeared to be staring into space.

The tippy-tap of her shoes must have reached him because he turned to look at her, froze momentarily, then made an effort to haul himself higher against the pillows.

Kate smiled. An unforced smile, because in that first moment of recognition she'd seen the sheer joy in his eyes. Both eyes, for both had escaped the flames. It didn't matter that the joy was followed by wariness and doubt. She knew he loved her still, just as she loved him, and she also knew now that she could be strong.

'You came,' he said, and his voice sounded husky from the smoke he'd inhaled and perhaps also with emotion.

'As soon as I could,' Kate confirmed.

He shook his head in apparent wonder. 'You look beautiful.'

'Whereas those hospital pyjamas you're wearing aren't half as fetching as your uniform, and you look like an Egyptian mummy in all those bandages.'

Her answer made him smile, just as she'd hoped, but she could read the anxiety in his expression. 'Sit,' he suggested, patting the bed.

'Isn't sitting on beds against the rules?'

'Without a doubt, but I don't care about rules just now. I want to see you up close.'

He wanted her to see him up close, too.

Kate glanced over her shoulder to check that no nurses were on the prowl then sat on the very edge of the bed and leaned forward to kiss his forehead. Leo closed his eyes and breathed in the scent of her.

'I'm a mess,' he said then, clearly wanting to get to the heart of the issue straight away.

'You've got the sight of both eyes still,' Kate answered. 'That's something to celebrate.'

'It is.'

Yet Kate could sense that there was a big *but* in his thoughts. She took rapid stock of him. Leo's entire face looked pink and sore, but the deeper damage was covered by the dressings on his left cheek and jaw and down over his neck. The bandages on his left hand suggested more serious burns there too. 'Are you in a lot of pain?' she asked.

'I can cope with the pain.' He reached across to the dressing that covered his cheek. 'You need to see,' he said.

'Flight Lieutenant Kinsella!' A nurse bustled up. 'You wouldn't be picking at your dressings like a small boy picking at a scab, now, would you?'

She was Irish. Forceful, but kind-looking.

'Sister, you can scold me all you like once I've given this lovely girl a peep.'

'A peep is all it takes for infection to set in.'

Kate got up from the bed. 'I don't want to be the cause of an infection, Leo.'

He looked at her, and she wondered if he thought her reluctance came from her dread of seeing the horrors beneath the dressings. He turned to the nurse. 'It's important.'

The sister stared at him. Long and hard. Finally, she must have decided that allowing Kate a peep at her patient's injuries was the best way to bring him peace of mind. 'Lord love us! Very well. Wait there. If Doctor sees me, he'll have my guts for garters, so you'd better tell him the dressing came away on its own.'

'I'll defend you with my life,' Leo assured her.

'No need to get carried away.' The nurse bustled off, and Leo reached for Kate's hand.

'You really mustn't feel bad if what you see is more than you can bear, darling girl. I shan't blame you if you need to walk away from me.'

'I shan't be walking anywhere,' Kate said, but she saw that Leo wouldn't believe her until the dressing was off.

The nurse hurried back carrying a tray furtively through the room. 'Now then, you just sit still while I do this, and I'll not be having a sound from you,' she told Leo.

'Understood.'

'And just a peep is all you'll be getting,' she told Kate. She'd brought something to ease the dressing away – something antiseptic, judging from the smell – and fresh sticking plaster to hold it back in place. 'There,' she said a moment later.

Kate braced herself to keep any dismay in check and leaned forward to look. It was hard to tell as the wound was smeared in some sort of substance, but it looked angry and puckered.

'You'll need more than a few burns if you want to get rid of me,' Kate announced, and Leo laughed, a light, joyful sound that warmed her heart.

'You see?' the nurse told Leo. 'Hollywood might not beckon you to join pretty heart-throbs like Cary Grant or Errol Flynn in the films, but were you planning on going to Hollywood anyway? You've got a sensible girl here, and that's more important than looking perfect in a mirror, so it is.' She shook her head, wonderingly. 'And they say that women are the vainer sex!'

'Sister, you're a treasure, even if you do bully me,' Leo said.

'Bully you? Only because you're after behaving like

a naughty schoolboy. Now, remember. Not a word to Doctor.'

She picked up her tray. 'Pull a chair over, seeing as you're not running away screaming,' she told Kate, and with that she hastened off again.

There was a chair a few feet away. Kate brought it closer and sat down, and Leo reached for her hand again. 'You're sure you're not revolted?' he asked. 'Because I'd understand if—'

Kate sighed and rolled her eyes. 'How many times? I'm quite sure, thank you.' She paused before adding, 'Would you be revolted if I were burned?'

'No!' Leo said, as though she'd suggested something absurd. 'But—'

'But nothing. Now, enough of your appearance. Tell me how you *feel*.'

'A lot better for seeing you, though I know I've been lucky in other ways too. I managed to beat out the flames and land my plane on Allied territory, so I was given help quickly. My eyes are fine and the ear beneath these dressings is mostly intact, even if it's likely to be scarred, so any impairment to my hearing will be negligible. My hand isn't so very bad either, so I should get the use of it back. In fact, I should return to being almost normal again, except for the scarring and some fragility in parts of my skin.'

'You're not thinking of going back into the fighting?'

'There's a war on, sweetheart. We haven't won it yet. Seriously, though, I'm not sure I can fly a Spitfire in combat again. It depends on how the skin on my neck heals and whether I get the full range of movement back. The doctors are hopeful, but come what may, I'll be able to do something. Train other pilots . . . something like that.'

Leo had done his bit as far as Kate was concerned, but she wasn't going to argue about it now.

'Let's not talk only about me,' he said then. 'How are you, my darling?'

'Glad to be with you again.'

'That's good to hear, but keep going. Tell me about the farm.'

She told him about the crops, the wildlife she'd seen, the early morning frosts that were scattering the world with sparkling white crystals . . .

'Your family? The land girls?'

'As busy as ever.' Kate guessed he was working his way up to asking particularly after Fred.

Sure enough, he raised an eyebrow. 'How is your injured brother?'

'Difficult,' Kate admitted. 'But I suspect he's met his match in Pearl. She stands up to him and I think she might do him some good.'

Leo nodded. 'You wrote that he'd suffered leg injuries but you didn't mention details.'

Not wanting to depress Leo, Kate hadn't dwelt on the awfulness of Fred's condition.

'I want to know what's happening in your life,' Leo insisted now. 'I'm a grown man and you've no need to protect me from the realities of war. I already know of men who've received truly terrible wounds. I've often witnessed them, too.'

He was right. Leo must have seen far more dreadful sights than her. She told him the full extent of Fred's injuries.

'Losing one's legs would be a blow to any man, but particularly to a farmer who depended on his physique to earn his living and knows no other way of life,' Leo conceded. 'But Fred still has the use of his arms and his brain, so he'll find a new way forward eventually. Things are still very raw for him. Once he's had time to adjust, he might do better.'

'I hope so.'

'It might be useful to put him in touch with other men who've lost their legs. Not just in war but due to other reasons, too. If he can see how they're getting on with their lives, it might help him to see that the future isn't all bleakness.'

'That's an excellent idea. I'll speak to the matron at Stratton House. She may be able to put me in touch with the right people.'

'Tell me about Churchwood,' Leo said next. 'How are your friends?'

She'd told him about Alice's sad situation in a letter. About Naomi's, too. Now she told him about the plane crash and the death of John Gregson.

'And I thought Churchwood was a quiet sort of place!' Leo said.

'How do *you* feel about John Gregson being a deserter?' Kate asked him.

'I never knew the man and I know nothing of his experiences so I won't condemn him, and I'm proud of you for standing up for his widow and children.' Leo raised Kate's hand and kissed it. 'Whatever John Gregson did or didn't do, those children aren't to blame, and I doubt that his wife bears any responsibility either.'

What a fair-minded man he was! If he felt proud of Kate, she was doubly proud of him.

Two hours passed in the blink of an eye. 'I think I'm expected to leave now,' Kate said reluctantly. 'I can look in on you in the morning before I catch my train, if you'd like that? It'll need to be early, though.'

'Oh, I'd like it,' Leo assured her. 'I imagine only chaste kisses are allowed on the ward, but I'm in the mood for breaking rules today. I apologize in advance if my kissing technique leaves something to be desired, given that half my face is covered in bandages and the rest is tight and sore. But I'm going to give it my best effort.'

He drew her to him for a kiss that was awkward but wonderful all the same.

'Goodbye, then,' Kate said, blushing because other patients must have seen the kiss.

'I'll count the hours until tomorrow,' Leo told her.

She walked down the ward feeling so much lighter than when she'd entered. At the door she paused to exchange waves with Leo and blow him a secret kiss, and as she moved down the corridor, the taps of her shoes no longer sounded echoing but jaunty.

'I can see you had a good visit,' Bessie Bruff said, when Kate returned to the guest house.

'I did.'

'Did you make up your mind about dinner?'

'I . . . er . . .'

'You didn't give it a thought, did you? Too busy floating in happiness, I'll wager.'

'I can go out for something,' Kate suggested.

'No need for that. As I said before, I've plenty of stew and plenty of potatoes to serve with it. Apples and custard to follow. But first, how about a nice cup of tea?'

'Tea would be lovely.'

It felt strange to lie in the little guestroom bed that night. The sounds were different from the ones at home. City sounds – the swish of passing traffic, the voices of people walking by, the clang of an ambulance siren, the distant chugging of trains . . . The bed felt different, too – much firmer than her bed at home with its ancient mattress that sagged in the middle. The sheets were starchier, too, and the pillow wasn't flattened by years of use. Kate slept despite the strangeness, tension oozing out of her pores. The road ahead for Leo and their romance was still strewn with the rocks and potholes of challenges, but they'd walk it together.

Bessie Bruff was apologetic in the morning. 'I've no bacon for your breakfast, I'm afraid, but I have porridge with preserved blackberries to sweeten it. And I have an egg I could boil or fry for you.'

'The porridge sounds lovely. I don't need anything else, thanks.'

'Right you are, dear. I've a tin of corned beef open. How about I slip some between two slices of bread for your journey home?'

'You're wonderful, Mrs Bruff.'

'Just doing the decent thing.' But Bessie was pleased.

A short time later Kate arrived at the hospital to find Leo looking out for her. Eyes bright, he greeted her with a kiss. 'How was your night at Mrs Bruff's?' he asked.

They chatted for a while then Leo said, 'I want to talk about something important.'

'Oh?' Kate grew wary.

'I hope it won't offend you, darling, but I want to talk about money. It must have cost you dear to visit me and I'd hate the expense to be a barrier to you visiting again. Will you let me arrange for you to receive some money from me?'

Kate had been concerned about the costs mounting up and draining her meagre savings, but she also had her pride. 'I'd like to try to manage on my own money first.'

'All right. But the moment expense starts becoming a problem, please tell me. I know you also have commitments to the farm and your family, but I'm selfish enough to want to see you as often as possible. Not that I intend to be stuck in here for long. I've every incentive to get well quickly now I know the sight of me isn't frightening you away.'

What a considerate man he was. Kate's early life had been hard. She'd felt unloved and unappreciated. Desperately lonely, too. But her luck had changed. First Alice had arrived in Churchwood and befriended her, introducing her to more friends along the way, and now Kate had Leo in her life. The joy of it lightened her feet and her entire being, and not even a long delay on the train home – some sort of engine problem – could puncture her happiness.

She was late returning to Churchwood, just managing to catch the last bus because the service had been reduced as a result of the petrol shortage. She bounced along on the walk from the bus stop and, seeing Naomi and Adam ahead of her, rushed to catch them up.

'Kate!' Naomi said. 'You look happy. I take it your visit to Leo went well?'

'It did.'

'He wasn't as badly hurt as you feared?'

'He's hurt badly enough, and he'll always bear some scars.'

'But that doesn't matter as long as you're together?' Adam guessed.

'Exactly.' But she saw that both Naomi and Adam were looking far from happy, though it was clear that both of them were trying to rise above it.

'What's been happening here?' Kate asked. 'Are feelings a little calmer?'

'No such luck,' Naomi told her. 'In fact, feelings have worsened. Someone threw a brick through the Gregsons' window.'

'No! How cruel, especially when there are children living in the house! Do you know who did it?'

'No one saw it,' Adam said. 'Or perhaps it's a case of no one being willing to admit to seeing it.'

'Maybe a child did it,' Kate suggested.

'It's possible, but any such child would have been stirred up by what they've heard adults saying.'

'I'm sure you've both done your best to calm things down.'

'We have. But our best isn't proving good enough. As for Evelyn, she won't let anyone into the house apart from Bert, and she only allowed him in so he could cover her broken window with boards. He's going to replace the boards with glass just as soon as he can, but it must be like a dark cave inside in the meantime.'

'Unfortunately, the timing of Mr Gregson's death couldn't be worse,' Adam ventured.

Kate didn't understand. Surely, it would have been a terrible thing at any time?

'What I mean is that it's all tied up in some people's minds with the loss of the Sunday School Hall and the bookshop. It's as though the Gregsons brought bad luck to the village.'

'That's ridiculous!' Kate declared.

'Superstition is a curious thing,' Adam told her. 'People don't believe it with their heads, but their hearts can operate on more primitive lines and make associations that are . . . Well, you said it, Kate. Ridiculous.'

'The German plane had nothing to do with the Gregsons.'

'We know that. Other people know it too, but they're

upset and full of resentment. Losing the Hall is a blow. So many people have come to rely on the bookshop to bring the community together. I keep hearing how much they were looking forward to a bookshop Christmas with the party, the nativity play and everything else.'

'You were looking forward to it as much as anyone,' Kate told Adam. 'Your first Christmas here was supposed to be special.'

'We're lucky that our church wasn't damaged,' Adam pointed out. 'We'll salvage something from our Christmas plans.'

He was smiling but it was forced and brittle, and Kate could see that his disappointment ran deep. 'I'm sorry,' she said. 'What a mess for everyone!'

'At least you brought good news,' Naomi said kindly, and a moment later they parted, Adam to visit a parishioner, Naomi to pass through the Foxfield gateposts and Kate to walk up Brimbles Lane to the farm.

But once again she paused to look up at The Linnets and, once again, she crossed the road to knock on the door.

'I'd like to see Alice,' she said, when Dr Lovell answered.

He opened his mouth as though to tell her that Alice still wasn't ready for visitors, but then he stared at Kate thoughtfully. 'Perhaps it's time,' he said, and he opened the door wider to let her in.

CHAPTER FORTY-SEVEN

Alice

'Visitor,' Alice's father announced, and she turned in surprise.

What was her father thinking? She'd told him she didn't wish to see anyone, and he was normally so sensitive.

Alice was out in the garden, wrapped in the coat she wore for gardening and a long woollen scarf belonging to her father. Not that she'd been gardening today – she'd been staring into space – but ever since she'd lost the baby she'd been forcing herself to carry out some daily tasks. Getting up, dressing, looking after the chickens, doing sporadic bits of housework and even cooking food she didn't want to eat. Life had to go on. But the miscarriage had enclosed her in a cloud of misery that was hers and Daniel's alone, and she wasn't nearly ready to emerge from it. Not when just the thought of seeing people again filled her with panic and brought her to the edge of tears.

'You need to start getting out of the house,' her father had said several times now, but to force a visitor upon her when she was still so low . . .

'Hello, Alice.'

The visitor was Kate, a dear friend indeed, but her presence still brought a wave of distress to Alice. Breathing became difficult – her chest was too tight – and tears stung her eyes. Unable to speak, she attempted a smile, but it was a sorry, lopsided ghost of a smile.

'Oh, Alice!' Kate moved towards her, and the tears spilled over.

'I'll leave you girls to chat,' Alice's father said, retreating into the cottage.

'I'm sorry,' Alice said, finding it impossible to stem the flood of tears.

'Don't be silly.' Kate led her back inside, and they sat at the kitchen table.

Alice sobbed for a while then slowly got a grip on her emotions. Kate passed her a handkerchief. 'It's a bit grubby with farm mud, but hopefully you can find a clean patch.'

Alice nodded her thanks, wiped her eyes and blew her nose.

'About the baby,' Kate said then. 'I can't tell you how sad I am for you. For Daniel, too.'

'Miscarriages are common. I know that.'

'Maybe so, but I'm not sure it's of any comfort when it's your baby that's lost – the baby you've cherished for weeks and imagined holding in your arms. It can't help when the father of that baby is miles away and may not be home on leave for months.'

Alice was touched by Kate's insight. 'I just need time to come to terms with it.'

'Of course you do. But we miss you. And we need you, too.'

'My father told me about the plane crash. Actually, I heard the explosion and smelled the smoke even here. I heard about the man who died, too. I'm sorry for it.'

'Unfortunately, not all of Churchwood feels the same.'

'There's bound to be a mix of opinions in a community.'

'Yes, but Mrs Gregson and her boys are practically housebound thanks to the weight of opinion against them. And it's getting worse. Last night someone threw a brick at her window and smashed it.'

'That's terrible!'

'It is terrible, isn't it? Someone needs to calm things down.'

'I'm sure Adam would—'

'He's tried. So have Naomi and Bert. Even I've tried, though you know I'm no good at these things. We need *you*, Alice.'

'Me? Oh, no. I can't do anything that can't be done by someone else. I'm sure you'll all make people see sense, even if it takes a while.'

'Alice, do you want Evelyn and her little boys to have more windows broken? Do you want them too scared to leave the house?'

'You know I don't. But you're being unfair, making demands on me at a time like this.' When even the simplest task, like making a cup of tea, needed all Alice's discipline to get her through it, the idea of venturing out and wading into village tensions was impossible. 'I need more time.'

Kate looked disappointed but chastened. Even a little ashamed. 'Sorry. It was wrong of me to put pressure on you, despite—'

She broke off, shaking her head, though Alice guessed she'd been about to say, *Despite the fact that Churchwood really does need you.* For once, Churchwood was going to have to get by in Alice's absence. She was too exhausted. Too raw.

But she didn't want to think only of herself. 'How are you?' she asked.

Kate roused herself. 'All the better for seeing Leo.'

'You saw him? That's wonderful!'

'I'm just on my way home from Manchester, actually.'

'You found him well, I hope? You look happy!'

'I'm happy because I persuaded him that I don't care about his scars. I wouldn't stop loving him if they'd changed his appearance completely, but they haven't. He'll always have some scars but only on one side of his face and his neck. His left hand has some burns, too, but they shouldn't interfere with his daily life much once they've healed.'

'That's good to hear. How is Naomi and everyone else?'

'I've just seen Naomi. She's got a lot on her mind with her divorce. And she's upset about all the ill feeling towards the Gregsons. Adam is upset too – about the Gregsons and the way his Christmas plans came crashing down with that plane. Not that he's complaining, but he's obviously disappointed.'

'I feel for him,' Alice said. 'But I'm sure he'll do his best to make Christmas as good as it can be in the circumstances. I'm having the quietest Christmas possible this year.'

Kate nodded her understanding, though it wasn't hard to guess that she'd hoped Alice might somehow wave a magic wand over Churchwood's difficulties. 'I'd better be getting home,' Kate announced. 'Look after yourself, Alice. You're missed.'

Touched, Alice hugged her friend. Then she walked her to the door and waved her off.

Back at the kitchen table, Alice sighed. Kate meant well but, always glowing with health and vigour, it was difficult for her to understand how low and drained Alice felt. What had happened to the Gregsons was appalling, but Alice just didn't have it in her to go into battle on their behalf. Not yet, anyway. As for Adam and Christmas, everything about the festive season was going to remind her of how joyful she'd expected it to be this year. By next year she'd have rallied, but just now her emotions were much too tender.

She realized she was crying again. Would she ever be empty of tears? One day, she supposed, because that was the way of things with grief. But she needed time to come to terms with her loss. *Their* loss, rather, as Daniel must be grieving too – or would be once her letter arrived. He wouldn't have the luxury of sitting in a kitchen alone and indulging the grief, though. On active service, he *had* to go about his duties. The thought made Alice uncomfortable, but facing people before she was ready still felt like a challenge too far.

Even so, her thoughts as she lay in bed that night weren't limited to Daniel and their lost child, but also stretched to Evelyn and her children. How scared they must have been to have their window smashed into a thousand lacerating shards of hate. It was a pity Adam's big plans for the village had fallen flat, too. He was a lovely man who deserved better.

CHAPTER FORTY-EIGHT

Naomi

'I'm sorry to have to say this, but I think we need to accept that the bookshop in anything like its original form is dead and buried for the time being,' Adam said, having gathered Naomi, Bert, Janet and May together in Foxfield's sitting room.

Naomi made no mention of her hopes for Joe Simpson's house, not wanting to disappoint her friends if they came to nothing. She glanced across at Bert, trusting that he'd make no mention of them either and wanting simply to exchange a smile with him. But Bert was sitting in his usual pose with his arms crossed above his substantial middle and she couldn't catch his eye.

'The Hall was definitely insured and the Diocese wants it to be rebuilt, but it won't happen soon, given the shortages of labour and material, as well as other priorities,' Adam continued. 'The church is too cold for social gatherings at this time of year, and with part of the school damaged, there isn't room for us to gather there, even if we could get permission – something I understand is unlikely anyway due to some odd covenant that was inserted into the deeds when land for the school was donated to the authorities back in the mists of time. The revival of the bookshop is an ambition for the future, not now.'

'It's such a shame,' May said.

Janet nodded. 'Everybody's saying that. The bookshop was the heartbeat of village life and it's going to be sorely missed. Mrs Lloyd told me she's feeling terribly flat now the bookshop is closed. She only has one son, and he lives in Scotland so she rarely gets to see him. The bookshop meant she had regular company, and she loved all the craft sessions.'

'Miss Gibb told me that winter is going to be dreary this year as she's nothing to look forward to any more,' May said.

'It's the same for the men,' Bert said. 'According to Humphrey Guscott, it'll be no fun trying to make wooden toys by himself with no one laughing at his efforts. And Jonah Kerrigan told me he's going to miss playing dominoes and card games.'

'I saw Matron at the hospital the other day,' Adam told them. 'She was upset about the bookshop, too, because it acted on patients like a tonic. All the patients I saw said much the same thing and they'd been so looking forward to the party. I'll keep visiting them to try to cheer them up, of course, and once Alice is feeling better, I imagine she'll resume visiting too.'

He paused as though hoping someone would have encouraging news of Alice's recovery, but when no one spoke he continued with, 'As for our village residents, we can try to bring people together through small tea parties in our houses. It won't be the same, but better than nothing.'

'You're right there, vicar,' Bert approved, 'but inviting folk to our homes is only half of what we need to do. We also need to knock on their doors to check that they're still all right, seeing as we won't have their absence from the bookshop to warn us that something might be amiss. I happened to call on Bill Stopes yesterday and heard that he'd fallen on ice when he tried to go out to the shops. Luckily, no bones were broken, and he managed to get himself back inside, but he didn't get to the shops, so he had hardly any food in the house. No tea for a hot drink either. His cottage is at the end of Pepper Lane, so he couldn't ask for help as no one passes by. He isn't on the telephone so he couldn't ring anyone either.'

'Few of our residents are on the telephone,' Adam agreed. 'It means they're isolated if they can't get out and that's especially worrisome if they're ill or if – like Bill – they're hurt.'

'We'll all have to keep an eye on folk and suggest others do the same,' Bert said. 'We don't want to go back to the days of last summer when the bookshop had to close because of that nitwit vicar.'

Nitwit was a kind word for describing the Reverend Julian Forsyth. He'd been arrogant and intolerant, and so had his wife. Due to their disapproval, the bookshop had dwindled to an end. Not only had this spoiled the fun of village residents, but it had also taken a toll on the strength of the community. Without the bookshop to bring everyone together, people had begun to slip through the net of care. Loneliness had set in for some. Others had fallen ill and, with no one else knowing about it, they'd gone without food, hot drinks and even medicines.

Luckily, the Forsyths had moved on swiftly, and Churchwood had breathed a sigh of relief as Adam had stepped into the role.

'Bert is right. We must all be alert to anyone who might be slipping through the cracks,' Adam said now.

Naomi tried to give Bert an approving smile but, once

again, he was looking elsewhere. A small prickle of unease stirred inside her as she realized that he'd barely looked at her since his arrival.

'Thanks for letting us meet here, Naomi,' he'd said when she'd opened the door to him, but his gaze had merely skittered over her as he'd passed by on his way to join the others in the sitting room, greeting them with a much more cheerful-sounding, 'Morning, all.'

She'd assumed that, as the last to arrive, he'd been keen to avoid holding up the meeting, but now it was beginning to feel odd. Even when she'd passed him a cup of tea and he'd said, 'Thanks very much,' his gaze had been a fleeting, distant thing that communicated nothing to Naomi and stopped her from communicating any-thing to him.

Was something troubling him? Something to do with his market garden, perhaps? No one else appeared to have noticed anything wrong but maybe she was simply more attuned to his moods because their friendship ran deeper. Or – awful thought – had she offended him in some way? After all, he'd had no trouble looking anyone else in the eye when they spoke. The change in him seemed to relate only to her.

Now she came to think of it, she remembered that he'd driven straight past her the previous day, waving an arm but not stopping to chat as he normally would have done. He'd also been in a hurry to leave church.

She racked her brain for an explanation of how she might have offended him and came up with only one possibility. She thought she'd thanked him for accompany-ing her to London last week – certainly, she'd intended to thank him, as she'd been truly grateful – but, caught up in the shock of what they'd discovered and in deciding what to do about it, perhaps she'd simply forgotten. If that was the case, she'd put it right at the first opportunity.

'We need to talk about Christmas now,' Adam said. 'Clearly, it isn't going to be the sort of Christmas I had in mind. We can't do anything about the cancelled party, but I'd still like to put on the Christmas Eve nativity play and carols. The way I see it, a nativity play without costumes is better than no nativity play at all.'

'I suppose it's worth trying,' Janet said, 'though I suspect the children may take some persuading. They'll be terribly disappointed that they can't dress up.'

'Angels without sparkly wings and halos . . .' May put in.

'And wise men without cloaks and crowns . . .' Janet added. 'It's Judy Bowen's turn to play Mary this year, and Cathy Hoskins's turn to be Angel Gabriel. I heard Judy telling her mum that she couldn't wait to wear the long blue dress we made for Mary, and I know Cathy was desperate to wear the wings we made for Angel Gabriel. They were the best wings we've ever had.'

'I heard two boys talking about which of the new crowns they wanted to wear as wise men,' May said. 'But yes, Adam, you're right. Doing something is better than doing nothing.'

'Will Rosa, Samuel and Zofia take part, May?' Janet asked.

'We'll be celebrating Hanukkah, the Jewish Festival of Light, but we'll certainly be along to watch the nativity.'

'I suggest we ask the kids to use their imaginations and pretend they're wearing costumes,' Bert said.

Naomi sent another approving smile in his direction, but he hadn't even glanced her way.

'Good idea,' Adam agreed. 'I think we need to do everything in our power to keep things going. Our community seems to have lost its way a little, and I'd like to try to restore it.'

'I hope you're not thinking of the Gregsons,' May said. 'I'm all for community spirit but I'd prefer not to talk about that particular family. Obviously, it was inexcusable to break their window, but I'm afraid some of us have loved ones in the forces and our loyalty lies with them rather than with men who desert their comrades and country. My loyalty lies with my Marek.'

'And mine lies with my Charlie,' Janet said.

May looked at Janet with fellow feeling then turned back to Adam. 'Please don't preach to us about forgiveness. If men like Marek and Charlie deserted, jackbooted Nazis would be stamping all over Europe and maybe even across the world doing untold harm to so many people, not least my Rosa, Samuel and Zofia. Heaven knows what those Nazis have done to the children's parents and grandparents.'

'I understand,' Adam said. 'German aggression needs to be stopped. But it wasn't Evelyn who deserted. It wasn't those two boys.'

May folded her arms defiantly and Janet looked out of the window as though closing her ears to whatever the vicar might say next.

Adam looked at Naomi and then at Bert. Both shrugged, at a complete loss.

'Perhaps we could ask people to nominate their favourite carol so we can choose which ones to sing at the service,' Naomi suggested, to move the meeting on to safer ground. 'We could ask people to write their preferred carols on slips of paper and either hand them to us or post them through the vicarage door.'

'Another good idea,' Adam confirmed.

A few minutes later, the meeting broke up. 'Could I have a word, Bert?' Naomi asked, hoping to clear the air of any ill feeling, or to help if Bert was worried about something unconnected to her.

He stood aside to let everyone else out through the door and then, before she had a chance to speak, he said, 'I've a lot to do, so could you keep this brief?'

Naomi felt rebuffed. 'Of course. It's just that I'm not sure if I thanked you for all your help in London and—'

'You did thank me.'

'I did? Well, that's a relief.' So what was the problem? Was he offended that she hadn't shared her plans with him after he'd been so helpful? She shared them now.

'Wise and satisfying,' he said, but she hadn't closed the distance between them at all. 'Now, if that's all . . .'

He stepped outside so quickly that her next words, 'Bert, is anything troubling you?' were lost in the chilly December air.

'Thanks again for the hospitality,' he called over his shoulder.

Getting into his truck, he sketched a brief wave and drove away.

There had been times when Bert had infuriated Naomi. He'd mocked her and teased her out of her snobbishness and he'd steered her into situations that had made her ill at ease. But he'd done it for her own good and had helped to transform her life. How much she'd love to be teased by him now!

Despite a heavy feeling in her stomach, Naomi tried to keep an open mind about what might be troubling Bert. He could simply be tired. Market gardening was a physical job, after all, and Bert was well into his fifties now. He might be dispirited over Joe Simpson's death, as the men had been friends. Dispirited, too, about the bookshop.

She realized she was standing with the door open, letting in the cold from outside.

Closing the door, she returned to her sitting room but felt too restless to sit. After a while, she lost patience with herself. Bert's spirits couldn't always be bouncy. No one's could. He might be back to his old self the next time she saw him.

On that hopeful thought, she turned her mind to Evelyn but could think of no way to help except to be kind to the woman and trust to time to take the sting out of the village's anger. As a solution to Evelyn's woes, it was hardly satisfactory, but it was the best Naomi could do for the moment.

She was trusting to time to help Alice out of her grief, too, not just for Alice's own sake, but also because she was loved and needed in the village. *She'd* know what to do about the Gregsons.

There *was* something Naomi could do about her own situation, though. She picked up the telephone to make a call. Moments later she was speaking to Alexander's crisply efficient secretary, Miss Seymour, and moments after that Alexander himself came on the line. 'Hello?' He sounded cautious. Uncertain.

'I wonder if we might meet?' she asked. 'I feel there are things we should discuss before we travel too far down the line of costly legal proceedings.'

'I see,' he said, and the change in his voice was instant. The arrogance was back. He thought she was having second thoughts. How typical of him.

'Could you manage lunch tomorrow?'

'I'm about to go away on business but I think I could

298

accommodate you next week,' he said, as though granting an act of charity for which he deserved to be congratulated.

They settled on a time and place. Naomi was looking forward to it.

CHAPTER FORTY-NINE

Alice

Waking that Tuesday morning, Alice felt the familiar wave of grief wash over her. Several days had passed since she'd written to Daniel to tell him the baby was no more. Was it too soon to expect him to have received her letter? Possibly. How desperately sad he would be when it finally reached his hands, and how desperately awful it was that the war was making it impossible for them to comfort each other.

Tears came into her eyes but today Alice blinked to clear the shimmers away. Doubtless, she'd shed more tears for her lost child in the future, but now was the time gently to ease her grief aside so she could at least try to be useful to some other children and their mother: the Gregsons.

Pushing the bedcovers back, she got up with the intention of calling at their house. She might have to brace herself for the possibility – perhaps even the probability – of being told to go away in savage terms, but she'd make the effort anyway.

It felt natural to take flowers to a person in distress and, even in her grief, Alice had been touched by the posies and other small tokens of concern that she'd received over the past three weeks. But there was little in the cottage garden at this time of year apart from some pretty greenery, and that might remind Evelyn too acutely of the posies her husband had left when he'd taken milk from doorsteps.

Abandoning the idea of flowers, Alice fetched her shopping basket and put in a few items from the cottage store cupboards – two tins of soup, a jar of meat paste and three eggs. Fastening on her coat, hat and scarf, she told her father she was walking into the village and set out.

The first person she saw was Ralph Atkinson. 'It's good to see you out and about,' he said.

Alice had given her father permission to tell her friends about the miscarriage and word must have rippled around the village.

'Thank you. It's good to be out, though I hear there's been some appalling behaviour towards poor Mrs Gregson and her children.'

'Well, I . . .'

Not for a moment did she think he was to blame, but her attitude clearly flustered him. He'd been a soldier himself many years ago in the Boer War and the experience must have given him a strong sense of duty.

'Smashing windows puts me in mind of the Nazis,' Alice said. 'What did they call that night when mobs of paramilitaries and ordinary civilians rampaged through Germany destroying the homes, businesses and even the synagogues of Jewish people? *Kristallnacht*. That was it. The Night of Broken Glass.'

'I hardly think the situation compares,' Mr Atkinson argued.

'What happened here is hardly on the same scale, and the Gregsons aren't Jewish, as far as I know,' Alice admitted. 'But it was still about revenge, spite and intimidation, not justice. That sort of thing hurts the innocent.

Unless we're blaming young children for the acts of their parents now?'

Mr Atkinson's mouth opened but he couldn't seem to find the words he needed to formulate a reply.

Leaving him to think about what she'd said, Alice bade him goodbye and walked on.

She encountered Mrs Hutchings next and received another kind comment about how nice it was that she was out and about. But, again, Alice made a disapproving reference to what had happened.

'Well, Alice, I can't say as I approve of smashing windows either, but I lost two cousins in the 1914 war – brothers, they were – and I understand why people feel so strongly about a man who left others to fight while he shirked his duty.'

'But the window belonged to his wife and children. He wasn't even alive when it was smashed.'

'But *she* sheltered him some nights. Must have done. Don't you remember Marjorie saying she saw him in the Gregsons' garden? He must have been going in for a meal, a bath and a sleep. No, Alice, *he* might have been the deserter, but his wife helped him to stay free.'

'Yes, but—'

'I'm sorry, Alice, but I need to get home. My Albert will be wanting the tobacco I just bought.'

Alice walked on to the shops, thinking that the Gregsons probably needed some basic food supplies – meat, butter, sugar, tea, cheese, margarine . . . But all those things were rationed now and she didn't have the Gregsons' ration books. She managed to buy bread, vegetables, a tin of rice pudding and a copy of the *Beano* comic to add to the supplies in her basket. In each shop she visited, she brought up her disappointment at the way the Gregsons had been treated but, while other customers agreed that they couldn't condone violence, it was soon apparent that the Gregsons had no friends in Churchwood.

Janet was in the baker's and walked out with Alice. 'What do you think of all of this?' Alice asked.

'I understand the anger. I share it. John Gregson was a grown man. My Charlie isn't much more than a boy but he's sticking it out. Deserters like Gregson make us less likely to bring an end to the war quickly, and the longer it goes on, the more my Charlie is in danger. May's husband, too. And your Daniel, of course.'

Alice knew there was sense in what Janet was saying. Even so . . .

'Look, I'm not suggesting that smashing windows is right,' Janet continued. 'Especially not with two innocent children in the house. But I think people are entitled to be angry with Evelyn Gregson. She must have come to Churchwood on purpose to hide her husband. She must have known he was stealing milk.'

'May feels the same, I suppose?'

'It isn't for me to speak for May, but I believe she's of the same mind. She has every reason to be, after all. More reason even than you and me. We've got loved ones in the forces, but May has her refugee children too. Just as deserters make it harder for us to win the war, they also make it easier for Germany to win, and who knows what the Germans are doing to the family of those poor children. May hasn't heard from Poland in a long time now.'

It was a difficult situation all round.

Janet nodded at Alice's basket. 'Is that food for the Gregsons?'

'It is. They may be too frightened to leave the house to buy supplies.'

'You're a kind girl, Alice. I'm not surprised to see you helping the Gregsons even when you've got troubles of your own.'

A fresh wave of grief passed through Alice, but she resisted it. 'Churchwood is a kind place.'

'But you don't think it's being kind just now,' Janet guessed.

'I think people have been quick to judge,' Alice said, but she spoke gently, not wanting to antagonize Janet.

'Bert thinks the same. I believe he's gone to the Gregsons' this morning.'

'It'll be good to see him there.'

'I'll let you get on, then. And I'll think about what you've said.'

Janet patted Alice's arm and walked away. Continuing to the Gregsons', Alice saw Bert fitting glass into the broken window.

'I'm surprised you could find new glass so quickly,' she said.

'I was lucky to get it from a builder's yard in Barton. It wasn't the right size, but I've managed to trim it to fit.'

He pushed some putty on to the frame, shaking his head as he did so. 'Bad business, this.'

'How are Evelyn and the boys?'

'Grieving for their husband and father, and under siege against the village.'

'Do you think Evelyn will let me inside?'

'She took some persuading to let me help, but I'll see what I can do.'

He knocked on the front door and called through the letter box. 'It's me, Mrs Gregson. Bert Makepiece. I've young Alice here wanting a word with you. I can promise she means you no harm. In fact, she's brought a basket of food for you and your boys.'

Nothing happened for a moment or two, then the door opened just a fraction and a narrow section of Evelyn Gregson's face appeared in the shadows behind the gap.

'Bert's right. I mean you no harm,' Alice said. 'I want to help.'

'Why?' Evelyn asked suspiciously.

'Because it's the decent thing to do. And because your husband helped me.'

'My John helped you?' Evelyn couldn't have heard the story.

'Would you like me to tell you about it?'

Evelyn hesitated. Then she opened the door a little wider and beckoned Alice inside, furtively, as though afraid another rock would be thrown if the door stayed open a second longer than necessary.

'First things first,' Alice said as she stood in the hall. 'Where shall I put this food? There isn't much, but hopefully what I've brought will help tide you over. If you trust me with your ration books, I can get more supplies another day. Oh, and this is for the boys.' She took the comic from the basket.

Evelyn looked at the *Beano* and, for a moment, Alice wondered if she might cry. 'They'll like this,' Evelyn said, swallowing hard.

She opened a door into a dining room at the back of the house. The boys had been standing by the window that overlooked the small garden, but as the door opened, they turned and moved closer together in a protective movement that tugged at Alice's heart. Their eyes were solemn and full of fear. 'Boys, Mrs Irvine brought this for you.' Evelyn held out the comic. 'Come on. Take it and say thank you.'

They moved forward cautiously, still nervous but with pleasure lightening their expressions when they saw what was being offered. The elder boy took it and ventured a smile at Alice. 'Thank you.'

'I hope you enjoy it.'

Evelyn led the way into the kitchen, where Alice unpacked her shopping basket on to the table. Once again, she thought Evelyn was close to tears as she picked up each item, studied it and put it away. 'I'm grateful,' Evelyn said, then she bustled to the stove and lit the gas under the kettle. 'You'll stay for a cup of tea?'

'I'd like that.'

Evelyn made the tea efficiently but with trembling fingers. Three cups, Alice saw. 'Is one of those for Bert?' she asked. 'Shall I take it to him?'

She was concerned that Evelyn might not wish to be seen outside or even at her door. Sure enough, she hesitated, as though she hated to appear weak, but then nodded.

'I'm just finishing up,' Bert said as Alice handed the cup to him. 'I'll leave the cup on the doorstep. Will you tell Mrs Gregson I'll call round tomorrow? Just to see how she is.'

'She'll be glad to know you're looking out for her.'

Alice went back inside and gave Evelyn what she hoped was a reassuring smile. 'Bert has fixed the window. He'll come again tomorrow to see how you're doing.'

Evelyn nodded. 'It's very kind of him.' She mused for a moment then said, 'So you met my John.'

Alice gestured to one of the chairs that stood around the table. 'Shall I . . . ?'

'Yes, do.' Evelyn looked flustered, as though good manners were beyond her capabilities just now.

Alice sat and after a moment Evelyn sat too, though she was coiled up with obvious tension.

'Not long ago I had a miscarriage,' Alice said, fighting against the lance of pain that pierced her heart. 'It started when I was walking home from Stratton House along a lonely stretch of Brimbles Lane. The daylight was fading fast, and I might not have been found for hours if your husband hadn't carried me home. He must have known that someone might see him and pursue him, but he did it anyway.'

'He was a good man,' Evelyn insisted. 'Sensitive, though. He liked quietness and nature. Music, poetry, art . . . Not that he was highly educated. He was the son of a miner. Terrible man, John's father. You might know the type. A big, loud bully who thought his boy should be a big, loud bully like him. My gentle husband was a bitter disappointment to him, and he mocked poor John mercilessly for being what he saw as a weak sissy.'

'Was John's mother kinder?'

'In her way. But she never defended him against his father.'

'Perhaps she was afraid of her husband.'

'I suppose she was. Luckily, John had a teacher at his elementary school who encouraged his interests and helped him to win a place at a grammar school, even paying for the uniform. Not that John's success impressed his father. Most fathers would be proud of having a son at grammar school, but not Stanley Gregson. He only mocked John all the more.'

'Were they never reconciled? Not even after John married you and produced two lovely boys?'

'Never. But John and I were happy in our own little family. Until war broke out. John loathed violence but

307

he was keen to do his duty. After all, he was a father and wanted his sons to live in a world where the likes of Adolf Hitler and his cruel thugs had no place. John hoped he'd find a niche in the army as a medical orderly or in some other role that meant he could contribute.'

'That didn't happen.'

'No, it didn't!' Evelyn spoke forcefully. 'He was put in an infantry unit with officers who were just like his father. They called my poor John all sorts of names and played tricks on him, too. They said they were just trying to make a man out of him, but they were cruel and a lot of his fellow soldiers joined in. Currying favour with the officers, I suppose, or just mean-spirited.'

'What sort of tricks?' Alice asked.

'A slug in his bed one time. Letters from home set on fire before John could read them. Orders to deliver fake messages to other officers, which had everyone laughing when he passed them on.'

Spiteful and unkind indeed.

'His private notebook was taken and his poetry was read out to hoots and catcalls,' Evelyn continued. 'They named him the Spineless Poet after that, and then they shortened it to simply Spineless. Oh, so many things – buttons cut from his uniform just before an inspection, food snatched from his plate, tea spilled into his boots . . .'

'It sounds terrible.'

'It was. And far from making a man of him, as they saw it, the bullying began to break him. One of our boys – Alan – fell ill with diphtheria, and John was refused leave to come home and see him. He explained that I was on my own with the boys and that he wanted to help me look after them – just for a little while – but they called him Florence Nightingale and the Nursemaid after that.

Again, those names became shortened to just Florence and the Spineless Maid.'

'Did he never complain? Officially, I mean?'

'Of course, but no one would stand up for him and tell the truth about what was going on, so John was told simply to stiffen his upper lip and learn to accept a joke. He was even told that it was important for chaps to feel relaxed enough to tease each other now and then, as though John was the misery of the regiment. He requested a transfer, too, but that went nowhere, and eventually . . . It became too much for him, do you see?'

Alice did see. 'So he deserted.'

'He didn't want to desert.' Evelyn's tone was defensive. 'He hated the suffocating noise and lack of privacy of army life, but he'd have stuck it out if those bullies had given him a moment's peace. They didn't, though, and he needed to get away before they broke him completely. Already he was in tears every night and dreading every new day. His hands shook all the time, and he knew he couldn't survive with his sanity intact.'

'So one day . . . ?'

'He walked out of the base and kept walking. He had no particular plan in mind. He was just at the end of his tether. For the first couple of miles he expected to be challenged and dragged back to the base. It only dawned on him gradually that he might get away, so he started taking steps to avoid being seen. Keeping an eye open for people, listening out for approaching vehicles . . . that sort of thing.'

Evelyn paused and seemed to be looking inwards at her memories. 'It took him a long time to get back to England. He managed to get aboard a ship returning injured troops, and no one appeared to notice he shouldn't be there.

Some of the time he was on board he hid away. At other times he wore an orderly's outfit he'd got hold of and helped to tend the sick and injured. Don't think he put them in danger. Before the war John was a volunteer for the St John Ambulance Brigade, so he was well qualified to give basic care. That was the kind of man he was – one who wanted to help others. When the ship docked, he drifted away again. He knew the boys and I were moving to Churchwood because Alan's asthma wasn't good in the London smog, so he made his way here by walking and begging for lifts on carts and in vehicles. Once here, he camped out in the woods and waited for us.'

'It must have been hard for him, living rough. Especially as the nights grew colder.'

'It was terrible. He came into the house sometimes, sneaking round the back way, but even that grew risky after that gossipy woman caught a glimpse of him. She's a menace with her gossiping, that woman, especially as half of what she says isn't true. Making my John out to be a giant? He was smaller than many men.'

'Marjorie doesn't mean to be malicious.'

'She should mind her own business. I used to see her, peering out of her windows at all times. John longed for a bath and a shave but, after that woman saw him, he couldn't take the chance of being seen. Occasionally, he'd have a hot drink or some food and nod off in front of the fire, but we were terrified that he'd be caught.'

'It must have been hard to feed him with no ration book for him.'

'The boys and I didn't begrudge sharing our food. We used to hide food in the woods for him, too. It was pitiful to see how hungry he was. But we had to keep his presence a secret.'

'Did you have a plan for getting him to a safer, more comfortable place?' Alice asked.

Evelyn shook her head. 'We couldn't think of one. My mother is still alive, but she lives in a tiny flat and would never have coped with the knowledge that John had deserted. She'd have been all nerves and it would have made her ill. We had no other family or friends to fall back on. We just hoped the war would end soon, and that, once tempers had cooled, John might receive a sympathetic hearing if he gave himself up. I know that sounds hopelessly unrealistic but, until we could think of a better way forward, we felt he had no option but to keep hiding here.'

'Is that why you educated the boys at home? So they couldn't let anything slip about their father?'

'Of course. I really was a teacher before I married, so their education didn't suffer. They missed out socially, but it was a price that had to be paid to keep John safe.' She paused, then added, 'Not that it worked.' And with that her face crumpled.

Alice reached a tentative hand to Evelyn's arm. When Evelyn didn't shrug her away, Alice moved closer and wrapped an arm around the bereaved woman's shoulders.

As though it came as a huge relief to abandon the yoke of self-control at last, Evelyn sobbed and sobbed. Minutes passed before the sobs subsided and she pushed herself upright, digging in her pocket for a handkerchief and using it to wipe her eyes and blow her nose. 'Sorry about that.'

'You've nothing to apologize for.'

'You're practically a stranger.'

'I won't be a stranger if you welcome my friendship.'

'Befriending me might mean you'll lose all your other friends. Churchwood hates me.'

'Churchwood is jumping to conclusions without understanding all the circumstances. I'm willing to risk its disapproval by befriending you.'

Evelyn's eyes filled with tears again, but she blinked them away. 'You've very kind. Kinder than I deserve after I was so sharp with you.'

'Never mind that. You had your reasons.'

'I haven't even said I'm sorry about your miscarriage, but I *am* sorry. I lost a baby in between the boys so I know how devastating it can be.'

Alice's breathing faltered, but she inhaled deeply and forced a smile. 'It *is* devastating, but I've moped at home long enough. Now, I'm going to ask an awkward question, but I hope I can be forgiven as a friend. How are you managing for money?'

Evelyn blinked in surprise. 'That really is an awkward question, but I know you mean well by it. The truth of the matter is that money is tight. My army wife's allowance was stopped when John went AWOL. I can't imagine I'll be entitled to a pension now John is . . . now he's no longer here. Whether I'm entitled to one or not, I need a job and I'm unlikely to find one here. I've a better chance of finding work in London, but the smog was so bad for Alan's asthma that I dread the thought of returning. I'll have to think about what's best to be done.'

'In the meantime . . .?'

'I have a little money put by and my mother sends me what she can spare.'

'I'm pleased to hear it. But don't let pride get in the way if you find you need some more help.'

'I don't deserve your friendship, Alice Irvine.'

'Nonsense.'

Alice was thoughtful as she left Evelyn's house,

promising to return the next day. This visit might have enabled Alice to forge a bond with the young widow, but Evelyn still couldn't face the hatred of the village. More needed to be done to help her, but what?

CHAPTER FIFTY

Kate

'Right,' Ernie said, pushing his empty cup away and casting a sour look around the breakfast table. 'Time to get to work.'

Did he need to be so surly about it? Of course not, but Kate found the roughness bouncing off her today. Seeing Leo again and getting things straight between them had wrapped her in a protective warmth that even Ernie had no power to spoil.

There was a general shuffling and scraping of chairs as they all got up. Except for Fred, of course. 'Throw me that ball of twine, would you, Fred?' Pearl asked.

The ball of twine was at his end of the table, and Pearl was at the other end. Fred had been wary of Pearl since the day she'd wheeled him, protesting, into the sitting room and left him there until Kate had liberated him some time later. But a week had passed since then.

'Fetch it yourself,' he said.

Pearl looked at him as though he were a sulky five-year-old instead of a grown man. 'I didn't realize there was something wrong with your arms.'

'There isn't.'

'Then why won't you throw the twine?'

'Because I can't be bothered,' Fred told her, with the sort of self-satisfied malice that would have done Vinnie proud once upon a time.

'In a mood again, are you?' Pearl made him sound tiresome.

She moved around the table to fetch the twine herself, and Fred smirked with satisfaction – until she suddenly sprang at him and said, 'Boo!'

Startled, Fred jumped and then grasped the edge of the table, presumably to stop her from wheeling him into the other room again.

Pearl simply picked up the twine and walked away.

Fred appeared to take it as a sign that he'd won a battle between them. 'I want a fresh cup of tea,' he announced, looking straight at her.

'Make it yourself,' she told him.

'I can't. In case you haven't noticed, I'm an invalid.'

If he was hoping to make her feel guilty, he failed. 'You just said there's nothing wrong with your arms,' Pearl pointed out. 'Wheel yourself to the stove if you want to boil the kettle.'

'You should do it.'

'Nah,' Pearl said. Face smug, she threw his own words back at him. 'I can't be bothered.'

Grinning, she went out to work, leaving Fred fuming behind her.

'Did you hear that?' he demanded of everyone else. 'That girl refused to make me a cup of tea. You should sack her, Ernie. She's a disgrace.'

But no one was listening, and Fred was left to mutter boorish complaints to himself.

Kate and Ruby carried a basket of washing outside to put it through the mangle and hang it on the line to dry. It took an age for washing to dry at this time of year. Afterwards, Ruby went to clean out the chicken run and Kate headed for the kitchen garden to dig up some parsnips and turnips for the evening's supper.

'That Pearl should be sacked,' Fred repeated, when Kate returned indoors.

'She's a good worker.'

'She's wicked.'

Kate sighed and thought again that maybe Pearl was on to something with the way she was treating Fred. He might be angry, but he also looked more alive. More upright in his wheelchair, even. 'If you don't stop moaning, I'll ask Pearl to take you for your therapy today. She already knows how to drive, so the truck won't be a problem for her.'

'Don't you dare! I'll refuse to go. I'll—'

'If you stop complaining, Fred, I'll take you myself.'

'You don't understand! None of you understand!'

'Pearl or me?' Kate demanded, and Fred shut up.

She was working in the field next to the orchard later when she saw someone walking along Brimbles Lane. 'Alice!' She galloped over to hug her. 'It's good to see you out and about again.'

'You wanted to stir me into action, and you've succeeded.'

'I'm sorry if I was brutal.'

'You did what was necessary. I didn't mean to wallow, but—'

'You were *grieving*!' Kate protested, wanting her friend to be kind to herself.

'I *was* grieving and I still am.' Alice looked woebegone for a moment. 'But you were right to nudge me back into the stream of life.'

'I'm not sure I nudged, exactly. I suspect I stamped on your sensitivities in my work boots.'

'The fact is that you helped.'

'Just don't overdo things before you've got your strength back.'

Alice smiled. 'On Saturday, you wanted me to sail

into the village and right the wrongs being done to the Gregsons.'

'I let myself get carried away, because if anyone can help the Gregsons, it's you. But I was unfair. You need time to—'

Alice brushed Kate's words aside. 'I need to do what I can for them *now*. I've already visited Evelyn.'

'She let you inside the house?'

'Mmm.'

'That proves you're the right woman for the job.'

'I'm not sure how much I'll be able to do, but I want to try. Somehow. I've no ideas as yet.'

'They'll come to you.'

'Let's hope so. In the meantime . . . any word from Leo?'

'A letter came this morning.' Already Kate knew it by heart.

Darling Kate,

I'm happy to report that the docs are pleased with me. Thrilled, in fact. I'm making excellent progress in my recovery and it's all thanks to you, because I can't wait to leave this hospital behind and be with you, my gorgeous sweetheart . . .

'Hopefully it won't be too long before you see him again,' Alice said. 'Do you think you'll be able to get away from the farm?'

'I'm going to insist on it. If Ernie doesn't like it . . .' Kate shrugged.

'Good for you. The family managed to care for Fred before, so I'm sure they'll manage again.'

Kate smiled. 'Actually, Fred's grumbling has come up against some resistance in the form of Pearl.' She told Alice what had happened between them.

317

'It sounds as though Pearl may be just what Fred needs, the same way you were just what I needed to bring me out of the house.'

'Let's hope so.'

'When will you be visiting Leo?'

'Before Christmas, I hope.'

The mention of Christmas had Alice looking woe-begone again, but she managed another smile. 'It'll be lovely for both of you. I'd like to give you the train fare as a gift. The bed and breakfast cost, too.'

How sweet of her, especially considering Alice was far from rich. But Kate smiled and said, 'No need.'

'I hope you're not turning the offer down out of pride?'

'I'm turning it down because I have enough money put by to get me through the next visit at least. But I'm grateful. Just as I'm grateful to Naomi, Bert, Ruby and Pearl for making the same offer. Not to mention Leo. He wants to pay for my visit too.'

'Goodness,' Alice said. 'You're positively inundated with offers.'

'You're all so kind.'

'We all care about you, Kate.'

Knowing it was true, Kate felt blessed.

Naomi had made the first offer. 'I hope we're good enough friends that you won't take offence at what I'm about to say, but travelling and staying overnight in places isn't cheap. I'd like to make you a present of at least one visit to Leo.'

Kate had assured her that she had enough money in her Post Office savings account to be going on with. Besides, with her divorce looming, Naomi was probably keeping a careful eye on what she spent.

Then Bert had taken her aside in the village. 'Don't

be getting on your high horse with pride,' he'd said. 'I've been thinking about a Christmas gift for you, and I've hit on the very thing – the cost of a trip to Manchester to see Leo.'

Again, she'd assured him that she could manage for the time being.

She'd been touched by the joint offer from Ruby and Pearl too, particularly bearing in mind that Ruby had a child to keep and neither land girl earned much money.

'You're both wonderful,' Kate had said, 'but I can afford my next visit. After that, I might ask Ernie for a pay rise. Actually, no, I won't. I'll *demand* a pay rise.'

'He'll grumble, but I'm sure he'll say yes,' Ruby had predicted. 'He's scared of losing you now he knows you're seeing a chap.'

'Precisely,' Kate had said with a wicked smile.

Now she folded Alice into her arms. 'Good luck with your plan for the Gregsons. It deserves to succeed.'

'I'll keep you posted,' Alice promised.

Fred was in an obvious snit over dinner that day, pointedly ignoring Pearl, though if she noticed she gave no sign of it. No one else paid him much attention either, though it was obvious that he wanted to be fussed over. When Ruby served him a bowl of stew, he folded his arms and ignored it.

Kate guessed that he was expecting someone to urge him to eat, but for once she sat and ate her own stew, smiling at something Timmy said about his day at school.

'Aren't you eating that?' Pearl finally asked.

Fred merely sneered as though the stew disgusted him.

'If you don't want it, I'll have it,' she said. 'I worked especially hard today and I'm starving.'

'You can't—' Fred began, but she'd already reached out and swiped his bowl from under his nose.

'Oi!' he protested, but Pearl went ahead and used his spoon to lift some of his food into her mouth. 'Mmm, it's good!'

'You can't eat my food!' Fred yelled.

'Why not?' Pearl swallowed and helped herself to another mouthful. 'You don't want it and food shouldn't be wasted, especially not in wartime.'

'Give it back *now*!'

Fred took hold of the bowl and pulled it back in front of him. 'Fetch me a clean spoon.'

'I didn't hear that,' Pearl told him.

'Yes, you did! I said *fetch me a clean spoon.*'

'One of your words is missing.'

'Eh? You know exactly what I—' The penny dropped. 'You want me to say please?' He sounded incredulous.

'You don't need legs to have good manners.'

Kate held her breath and guessed the others were holding their breath too, wondering if Fred would explode in fury. Instead, he shook his head as though he couldn't believe what was happening. 'You're nuts,' he finally told Pearl.

'Maybe I am. But I'm still waiting.'

Fred looked around the table but received no support from anyone else, and his stew was getting cold. 'All right! *Please*,' he said. 'There. Are you happy now?'

Pearl grinned. 'That didn't hurt, did it?'

She fetched a clean spoon. Fred glowered and muttered under his breath, then began to eat. He noticed Kate watching and demanded, 'What?'

'Nothing,' she answered blandly, and got up to set the kettle to boil. A few minutes later, the tea had been drunk and it was time to return to work.

After eating, everyone headed outside, except for Kate,

who stayed behind to wash the dishes, and for Fred, who continued to sit at the table, brooding over what he doubtless considered to be Pearl's unfair treatment of him. But all of a sudden, he slapped the tabletop and burst out laughing.

Well, well, well. It was the first time Kate had heard him laugh since he'd been injured. Hopefully, it meant his mood was turning at last.

Kate finished the dishes and stepped out into the cold December afternoon, breathing in its frosty crispness. The sky was pale above her, the clouds gleaming like pearls as the sun descended behind them. She watched as birds flew across in a formation that put her in mind of an arrow pointing the way forward.

Leo, Alice, Fred and not least herself . . . Kate felt the tide of life had begun to turn in their favour. Clearly, there were still challenges to be faced, but they all had futures that were worth striving for.

With luck, Naomi would soon emerge from her divorce with peace of mind and Alice would think of something to help the Gregson family by calming the ill feeling in the village. As for the bookshop, Kate had to cling to the belief that they'd find a way to revive it somehow. It was too important to lose.

CHAPTER FIFTY-ONE

Alice

'How kind,' Mr Parkinson said, as Alice offered him a sandwich. 'I hope I haven't timed this visit badly? It's only a social visit, after all. Nothing important.'

'We're delighted to see you,' her father assured him. 'We would have got in touch if it had been inconvenient. I'm only sorry you had to go to the trouble of letting us know you were coming by letter. Having been summoned by telephone at all times of the day and night when I was a practising doctor, the last thing I wanted was one of those infernal machines in the house once I'd retired. But I'm coming round to thinking that a telephone would be useful, and I know Alice would welcome one too. Perhaps I should investigate having one installed.'

'It's good to be back in Churchwood,' Mr Parkinson said, 'though I read in the newspaper that you've had your dramas, and I saw the gaping hole in the row of buildings as I walked from the bus stop.'

They told him about the plane crash.

'It sounds as though the pilot did his best to avoid harming civilians, so I'm glad he survived,' Mr Parkinson said, 'but it's a tragedy that another man lost his life.'

'A tragedy for him and a tragedy for his family,' Alice said. 'The man was a deserter, and the village has turned against his wife and children for helping him.'

'You don't share the village sentiment?'

'We don't,' Alice confirmed. 'John Gregson went through a terrible time in the army and only deserted when he reached desperation point.'

Her father nodded. 'I understand it isn't helping that Mrs Gregson was considered a cold, stand-offish sort of woman even before the plane crash.'

Alice agreed. 'She isn't cold and stand-offish by nature. She was just afraid that if she let anyone get close, they'd find out her husband was hiding nearby. She kept her distance from the village and made her children keep their distance too.'

'Well, if anyone can talk the village round, it's you, Alice.'

'I'm not having much luck so far,' she admitted.

'You'll find a way. As I've said before, you've such a persuasive way with words. You could be—'

'Speech-writer to Winston Churchill?' her father quipped again.

'Why not?' Mr Parkinson asked. 'Not that Mr Churchill is doing a bad job of writing his own speeches. Quite a rousing orator, our prime minister. I remember what he said about fighting the enemy on the beaches and elsewhere.'

'And never surrendering,' her father added.

Stirring stuff, but, unfortunately, Alice wasn't Winston Churchill. Yet, as she poured more tea, an idea burrowed into her mind, and when Mr Parkinson got up to catch the bus home, she stood too. 'I'll walk you to the bus stop.'

She did so, kissing his cheek in parting and waving him off as the bus trundled into the distance. Turning, she saw Adam Potts outside the church and went to join him. 'The very person I wanted to see,' she told him.

'It's always a pleasure to see you, Alice. Now you're out and about, I wonder if we might have a word about Christmas and how we might—'

'I'm afraid I need a very quiet Christmas this year.'

For a moment he looked surprised, but his expression gradually settled into one of understanding, even if it was tempered with regret. Alice was sorry to disappoint him, but Adam had a whole village full of people to help him with Christmas.

'Of course,' he said. 'Then, how may I help?' He gave her a long, assessing look. 'You have a fiery light in your eyes, Alice. Should I brace myself for what you want to tell me?'

'I'm here to ask a favour,' she admitted, and explained what she had in mind.

Early in the evening two days later, the people of Churchwood made their way across the village green to the church and settled in the pews. Snatches of conversation reached Alice's ears.

'Do you know what this is about?'

'No idea, but I hope it finishes soon. My toes are cold already.'

'Mine too . . .'

'Maybe we're going to be asked to fundraise for a new hall.'

'I'll be happy to fundraise if it brings our bookshop back . . .'

'I hope we're not here about you-know-who.'

'The deserter's wife? I wouldn't have bothered coming if I thought we were here to talk about her.'

'Me neither.'

Oh dear. Adam gave Alice a comforting smile and said, 'Here I go. Fingers crossed.'

Alice smiled back and watched him walk to the front of the central aisle to address the audience. 'Thank you all for coming. I appreciate it, especially as it's cold here in the church.'

People were huddled in their coats, their breath emerging in clouds of white mist.

'You won't keep us long, I hope,' Mrs Lloyd called. 'It's perishing in here.'

'I'll try to keep the meeting short, but I hope you'll all stay until the end. It's important.'

'Is it about them traitors in our midst?' a voice called from the back.

'I'm not sure it's fair to call two young boys traitors. Or their mother, either. Not when she acted out of love. As for John Gregson, none of us ever met him, apart from Alice Lovell. Alice Irvine, I should say. We'll be hearing from Alice a little later, but first I ask you to listen to what her father has to say.' Adam turned to him. 'Dr Lovell?'

Alice's father got up and came to the front of the church. She'd coached him in the approach she wanted him to take. 'Good evening, everyone. Like all of you, I never met John Gregson, but I'll always be grateful to him for helping my daughter when she was overcome with a medical emergency. He scooped her up and brought her home, even though it put him at risk of discovery and arrest. My daughter's welfare meant more to him than his own interests, and for that I'd like to shake his hand and tell him how grateful I am.'

He let that sink in with his audience, then – ignoring the murmur of disapproval – he continued. 'I think you're all aware that I was a doctor before I came to Churchwood. Just a simple doctor with a small practice of my own. Nothing fancy. But during the 1914 war I tended to the troops over in France. It's those men I'd like to talk about now.'

The murmur quietened, though Alice felt it was replaced only by brooding suspicion. At least no one had walked out. Not yet, anyway.

'I don't know how many men I treated over there,' her father said. 'Thousands, certainly. Some were scarcely out of short trousers – or so it seemed to me. Others were older – husbands and fathers amongst them. They came from all over Britain and the dominions – Canada, India, Australia . . . They came from many walks of life, too. They were clerks, shop assistants, farmers, foundry workers, postmen, drivers, dock workers, solicitors, waiters, builders, railway porters . . . Oh, and I once tended a man who'd been a magician in civilian life.'

That recollection raised a few faint smiles.

'Shame he couldn't have magicked the war to an earlier finish,' someone called.

'I couldn't agree more,' Alice's father replied, before picking up the threads of what he was here to say. 'I saw thousands of men with a huge variety of interests, experiences and backgrounds. But every last one of them suffered from fear. Fear of death. Of pain and injury. Of receiving wounds that might leave them horribly disfigured or unable to earn a living after the war. Of getting into a blue funk and letting down their comrades . . . Fear in all its shapes and sizes.'

He paused again. 'Only a fool wouldn't have been scared. *I* was scared and I wasn't even facing combat. Danger was constant – from shells, from gunfire, from aircraft, from gas attacks and from torpedoes, if crossing the sea. For much of the time the noise of battle was relentless. The screaming and crashing of shells could go

on all day and all night without a break. I was some distance from the front, but it still gave me no peace. I pitied
the men who were in the thick of it. Four days on the
front line, a few days in reserve and a few days at rest –
that was how it was supposed to be. But men could be
in the trenches for a week at a time, shivering, and with
their toes literally rotting from the chilly water in which
they were forced to stand. It was called Trench Foot. I'm
sure you've heard of it. Rubbing whale oil into the feet
was supposed to help, but that involved removing boots
and sodden socks and exposing bare feet to the elements.
There was nowhere to sleep, nowhere to wash or change
clothes, and sometimes no hot food either. Just cold stew
from a tin and biscuits so hard they could break teeth.'

The audience had grown rapt.

'Some of you will have lost family members or friends
to that conflict. Others amongst you were luckier and had
family members or friends who survived. But, even if they
weren't injured, can you honestly say they were ever quite
the same again?'

No one spoke.

'I saw many a grown man weep in misery. One of
those chaps was a man who shot two toes off his own
foot in the hope that he'd be allowed home. His little
daughter was dying of a blood disease, and he wanted
to hold her in his arms one last time. Instead, he was
arrested, and I never knew what became of him. I did
learn the fate of another young lad who came into my
care because he was a shaking, gibbering wreck from all
the shelling. Neurasthenia, they called it. Shell shock – or
nervous breakdown. The lad's mother wrote to me some
weeks later to tell me her son had spoken kindly of me,
and she wanted me to know that he was dead – shot for

cowardice when he was just a boy who couldn't cope. He was her only child.'

Alice's father swallowed hard, and she knew the memory of it still appalled him. But he raised his chin and went on. 'We all like to have fine ideas about ourselves. We like to think we'd be brave and steadfast in wartime, serving king and country and becoming the pride of our families. Some of you may already have proved yourselves to be exactly that. But what about the rest of us? I don't know all of you very well, but I know enough to be aware that there are flaws in the people of this village, as there are in most of us. *All* of us, I venture to say. Impatience, pettiness, bad temper, gluttony, laziness, meanness, spitefulness, selfishness, a taste for melodrama, gossip or both. And I could go on. It's the same in every village, every town and every city in the country. Across the world, even. To be human is to be imperfect, yet how many of us readily admit to our faults? I suspect most of us play them down or blame others for provoking us – if we admit to having faults at all. If we can't be honest with ourselves about our everyday weaknesses, how can we be honest with ourselves about how we might cope in the armed forces, let alone in battle?'

'We can't,' Adam suggested.

Alice's father nodded. 'I agree. I've met men who've thrived in the kind of life that comes from being in the forces, and other men who've been completely broken down by it. I'm not talking about battle here but day-to-day life. I imagine we all like to think of our services being run with discipline, fairness and professionalism, just as we like to think that there's always comradeship between the men. Alas, there are rotten apples and weak links there, just as there are in general life. Bullies who

328

enjoy power . . . Cruel men who enjoy the suffering of others . . . Weak men who haven't the courage to stand up to such behaviours and even join in so they don't become victims themselves . . . If we're unhappy in civilian life, we can gain some respite when we go home at the end of the day. We have families and friends to comfort us and champion our best interests. We also have the freedom to go elsewhere − another school or another workplace. In the forces there are no such luxuries − no respite and no freedom. Of course, there are occasions when men band together to try to bring about change. Some of you may remember the mutinies at Étaples in 1917.'

A few heads nodded.

'I believe the troops rose up then because they resented the harsh way they were treated in training,' Alice's father said. 'That harshness was especially resented because those in charge − officers and non-commissioned officers − had little, if any, experience of actual combat. In a mutiny, we might think there's safety in numbers, but what if we were the sole victim of bullying? Everyone else's whipping boy? And what if no one else had the courage to stand up for us? How would we cope then? Again, I suggest we can't know. Therefore . . .' He paused as though to give emphasis to the words that would follow. 'Therefore, perhaps we shouldn't judge.'

He let the silence stretch, then said, 'Thank you for listening. My daughter would like to say a few words now. As you probably know, she's the apple of my eye, so I hope you'll extend her the courtesy of listening, just as you've extended that courtesy to me.'

Alice exchanged encouraging smiles with him as they switched positions. Standing in front of the crowd, she tried to gauge the mood. It was sombre, but whether that was because people were annoyed or reconsidering their views was hard to assess.

'Thank you for listening to me,' she began. 'I'll try not to take up too much of your time. My father has spoken about his experiences of tending the sick and injured in wartime. I'd like to talk about John and Evelyn Gregson and their young boys, Alan and Roger. I've spent a lot of time with Evelyn over the past few days and I have her permission to tell her family's story today. She isn't asking for your pity.'

'That's good, as she isn't going to get it,' a voice called.

Alice pressed on regardless. 'She isn't asking for anything, but *I'm* asking for your honesty and your understanding. Before the war, the Gregsons were an ordinary family, a small unit bound together by love and going about their business doing no harm to anyone. Doing good, in fact. John Gregson was a St John Ambulance volunteer, giving time and first aid without receiving a penny in return. Evelyn Gregson taught young children in one of the poorer parts of London, helping them towards better futures than they might otherwise have achieved. Alan and Roger are polite, caring and fun. Without the war, the Gregsons would have continued moving forward in their happy lives and you'd all have been proud to know them. But the war came and sucked the family into its vortex. Now, John Gregson was an honourable man.'

More murmurs of scepticism.

'He didn't wait to be conscripted. He volunteered because he was appalled at what Nazi Germany was doing and he wanted to put a stop to it. As an experienced first aider, he hoped to be a medical orderly, but found himself in a fighting unit instead. There, he was bullied with neither break nor mercy by both officers and so-called comrades. He was sensitive and gentle, and that seemed to act on his tormentors like a red rag to a bull.'

Alice detailed some of the cruel punishments and tricks meted out to him, from being made to clean latrines with a toothbrush time and again, to finding urine in his boots.

'He did his best to stick it out. He also tried to get the bullying stopped, but his appeals went nowhere. If anything, they made his situation worse. Finally, he broke and by some miracle managed to find his way back to England.'

'That's all very well, but men who desert leave other men to face danger. It isn't right. It isn't fair.' The speaker was Mrs Hutchings. 'Your young man is involved in the fighting, Alice. He's sticking it out.'

'Yes, he is. And so far he's coping,' Alice agreed. 'But he's been luckier in his senior officers and his comrades. That may change, so please think on this: if Daniel reached the end of his tether – if he genuinely broke down – and found his way back to England, I can't imagine I'd report his presence to the authorities and cast him off. I think I'd help him as best I could. I'm sorry if that shocks you, but I know my Daniel and I know he wouldn't desert unless he'd tried every way possible to cope.'

She turned to her friend May. 'What would you do, May, if your Marek was in John Gregson's situation?'

'Well, I . . . Oh, heavens.' May looked flustered. But then she drew herself up straighter. 'Actually, I too know my husband and I trust him. No one could be more committed to defeating the tyranny of Adolf Hitler and his kind than Marek. But if he reached the end of his tether, I'd know for a fact that selfishness and cowardice had nothing to do with it, and I'd do all that I could to help him.'

Alice nodded. 'What about you, Janet? What would

you do if your Charlie genuinely felt he couldn't cope in the army a moment longer?'

'He's my son – my youngest baby boy – and I love him,' Janet said. 'I hope he'd never be in that position, but if he was . . . Well, yes. I'd protect him and help him all I could.'

Again, Alice nodded, then addressed the crowd. 'Is there even one amongst you who wouldn't help a loved one in desperate need?'

A few people exchanged looks but no one replied.

'Don't worry. I'm not asking you to stand up and declare yourselves,' Alice assured them. 'I'm simply asking you to be honest with yourselves and think carefully before you judge Evelyn and her boys. That's all I have to say on the subject. I suggest we all go home to our firesides and warm ourselves with cups of tea.'

Bert pushed his bear-like body to his feet to address the audience. 'I'm not asking you lot to join in with me, but I'd like to thank young Alice and her father for talking to us tonight. I'm already trying to help young Evelyn and her boys and, after what I've just heard, I'll be trying all the harder.'

Naomi got up too. 'So will I,' she declared.

'Me too,' May announced, leaping up.

'And me.' Janet also stood up to be counted.

Then Betty Oldroyd heaved herself out of her chair. 'I don't have any family serving in the forces, but Janet's boy Charlie is like my own son, and I could no more turn my back on him than I could fly to the moon.'

'Thank you, Betty,' Adam said, then he addressed the audience as a whole. 'As Alice and Bert just said, we're not asking you to make public declarations of how you feel about the Gregsons, but we do ask that you give careful thought to your attitudes. Thank you all for coming.'

The audience shuffled to its feet and began to file out. There were plenty of murmurs and whispers, but it was hard to hear what anyone was saying.

'Do you think we've made a difference?' Alice asked Adam, and he shrugged.

'We can only hope so.'

CHAPTER FIFTY-TWO

Alice

Alice called on Evelyn Gregson the following morning. 'I haven't come too early?'

'Not at all. You're not the earliest visitor, anyway.'

'Oh?' Alice hoped there hadn't been more trouble.

'Janet Collins and her friend Betty brought me some bread and an apple cake.'

'That was kind of them.'

'It was. A Miss Gibb called with a posy of winter-flowering jasmine, and someone left a potted cyclamen plant outside the door. May Janicki called round, too, and took the boys to her house to play with her Polish children. Whatever you said at your gathering last night seems to have worked with at least some of Churchwood's residents.'

'I'm glad.' Alice thought for a moment then said, 'I wonder . . . if you're feeling brave, would you walk to the shops with me? I won't leave you for a moment. Not on this first trip out. But you can't stay hiding in the house for ever, and perhaps facing people sooner rather than later is preferable to having the prospect of your first venture outside hanging over you.'

Evelyn's face turned even paler. Her eyes widened then appeared to retreat into their sockets as though trying to hide.

'Think of Alan and Roger,' Alice suggested. 'They need some appearance of normality in their lives. I won't pretend to be confident that everyone in the village will be welcoming, but I suspect there'll be enough friendly people to shield you from any unpleasantness.'

Evelyn breathed in deeply as though testing her courage. 'All right. I'll try it.'

'Hold on to my arm,' Alice suggested as they set out, and Evelyn held it tightly, stiffening even more when Edna Hall approached.

'Good morning,' Edna said, nodding to them both. 'I was just on my way to see you, Mrs Gregson. I lost my husband almost two years ago, so I know what it's like to be bereaved. It feels like the world has lost its colour and all that lies ahead of us is bleakness. I didn't cope well at first. I shut myself away and might not be standing here now if Alice and her friend Kate hadn't looked after me through the worst time. I want you to know I'm willing to help you in my turn – if you think I might be of some support? You won't need to pretend to be brave with me. You can weep and wail like a wild thing. Get the emotions out instead of trying to stifle them.'

Evelyn blinked away tears. 'You're very kind, Mrs . . . ?'

'Hall. But call me Edna.'

'Thank you, Edna. I'm Evelyn. If it isn't too much trouble, you could call for a cup of tea later.'

'It's no trouble at all. I'll bring some of my rhubarb cake. People tell me they're partial to my rhubarb cake.'

'It's delicious,' Alice confirmed.

She walked on with Evelyn. Outside the post office, Marjorie Plym was chatting to Mrs Hayes and Mrs Hutchings. She must have heard their approach because she glanced up, saw them and turned red.

'It's that gossipy woman,' Evelyn whispered.

'She has her faults, but don't we all?' Alice said.

'Like my John, you mean. Like me, too. You think I should search for the good in her.'

'And she in you. Marjorie will see it, eventually. She isn't a bad person underneath the tittle-tattle.'

Evelyn sucked in another deep breath as they drew closer to the group.

'Good morning,' Alice said.

'Nice to see you out after your sad loss, Mrs Gregson,' Mrs Hutchings ventured.

'It is,' Mrs Hayes agreed.

Marjorie was flustered. 'I hope you don't think I've been spreading gossip, Mrs Gregson. I take an interest in my neighbours, but I wouldn't like to think of myself as a gossip.'

Alice sensed that Evelyn had been rendered speechless by Marjorie's lack of self-awareness. An anxious look passed over Marjorie's face, and Evelyn rallied to say, 'I hope we'll become friends, Miss Plym.'

Marjorie preened with relief and pleasure. 'If we're to be friends, you must call me Marjorie, and I should call you Evelyn.'

'Of course,' Evelyn said.

Continuing into the shop, they found several villagers inside. Most greeted Evelyn with tentative smiles, but Humphrey Guscott only glared. 'I lost my boy, Percy, in 1916 on the Somme. He didn't let his country down. He gave his life for it.'

With that, he barrelled his way out of the shop.

'I hope you won't take offence at old Humphrey, Mrs Gregson,' the postmaster said. 'He's never got over losing his boy, and age is only making him more bitter.'

Evelyn looked upset – understandably – but managed a nod. 'I'll try not to judge him or anyone else,' she said.

After buying stamps, they moved on to the grocer's and then the greengrocer's. A couple of people looked unsure about what to say to Evelyn, but no one was rude and several people treated her with warmth and understanding.

Heading for home, Evelyn offered Alice tea.

'I'll make it,' Alice said. 'You sit down and rest.'

Evelyn sat in the sitting room, a strained and fragile figure. Alice left her and moved quietly around the kitchen. When she returned, Evelyn was sleeping. Alice fetched a blanket to put over her and then headed back to the kitchen to prepare a stew for the family to eat for their dinner that evening.

Two hours passed before Evelyn appeared at the kitchen door looking dishevelled but calmer than before. 'Sorry. It was rude of me to fall asleep,' she said.

'You needed the rest, and it looks as though it's done you good.'

'I think it has.'

'I hope you don't mind me making free with your kitchen, but I thought it might help if I made a stew.'

'It's very welcome. I haven't had much heart for cooking and eating, but the boys need feeding properly.'

'So do you,' Alice said.

'True. The boys are depending on me more than ever now they've lost their dad, and I won't be a good mum if I'm fainting and weak.'

Alice made more tea, finished the stew and then prepared to leave. 'I'll look in on you tomorrow, if I may?'

'I'd like that.'

A knock sounded on the front door. The caller was

337

Naomi with a plate of sandwiches. 'I'll bet you've hardly eaten in days,' she told Evelyn.

'I haven't, but those sandwiches look delicious.'

Alice left them to it and set off for home. Seeing Adam entering the church, she crossed the green and followed him inside. 'Am I disturbing you?'

'Not at all.'

She told him about her expedition with Evelyn.

'I'm pleased,' Adam said.

'Churchwood disappointed me when it took against the Gregsons, but now the village seems to have returned to its generous and kind ways. Most of the village, anyway.'

'It's a kind place,' Adam agreed. 'That's one of the reasons I was so keen to be your vicar. I love the way people rally round to help each other, even if they do lose sight of what matters from time to time.'

'I'm sorry your first weeks here have been so difficult,' Alice told him. 'I know you had high hopes for Christmas.'

'I'm determined to make the best of things.' He smiled, but his disappointment was visible anyway.

Was Alice making the best of things? Was hiding herself away for the festive season being kind?

'You know, Alice, Christmas is all about hope for a better future,' Adam said, as though he'd guessed the direction of her thoughts.

He was right. Alice understood that now.

CHAPTER FIFTY-THREE

Naomi

The day of John Gregson's funeral was dry but also cold. The sky was a steely grey, the earth hard and the wind cutting. Leaves that had yet to fall shivered on trees like fragile birds. The ravaged stalks of ground plants stood forlornly like old soldiers. And rotting bracken was turning rust-coloured on its way to becoming pulp.

Even so, the people of Churchwood wrapped themselves in coats, scarves, hats and gloves, stuffed their feet into boots and turned out to support the Gregsons in giving John a fitting farewell. Evelyn and the boys were pale and tearful, but Evelyn managed some wan smiles and thanked people for their presence as best she could.

Adam Potts took the service and spoke movingly of the man John Gregson had been before his nerves broke down. Hymns were sung and prayers uttered. Then everyone gathered outside in the churchyard, where a grave waited to receive John into the earth.

'We in Churchwood are poorer for not having known him,' Adam finished. 'But he'll live on in the memory of his wife and sons, who are fast becoming members of our community. With no Sunday School Hall available, Naomi has kindly invited us all to Foxfield to drink a toast in gratitude for John's life, while Bert is offering lifts to anyone who can't cope with the walk. Thank you all for coming.'

They began to file out of the churchyard and along Churchwood Way. 'Evelyn and the boys . . . they're going to be all right?' Naomi said to Adam.

'I think so. Not that it's going to be easy for them. Grief is difficult. It ambushes us from time to time no matter how strong we try to be. But they've got each other, and they've got most of Churchwood, too. It's a good start.'

Naomi realized that something outside the post office was causing a stir. 'What's happening?' she asked, but Adam had no idea either.

Walking over, they saw newspapers being handed around. The newspaper delivery had been late today, but whatever they announced was causing ripples of shock in Churchwood.

'What is it? Naomi asked, but then her gaze fell on the headline of the *Hertfordshire Reporter*.

Japan Attacks Britain and USA!

Adam managed to get hold of a copy and they leaned over it together. *Japan at war with Britain and the USA*, she read, then the reasons were made clear. Japan was attacking British territories, Malaya and Hong Kong, while an air attack on an American naval base, Pearl Harbor, had resulted in the loss of numerous ships and many lives.

'Where's Pearl Harbor?' Mrs Hutchings asked.

'Hawaii,' Adam told her. 'That's in the Pacific Ocean.'

'Fancy.'

'What does all this mean?' Naomi wondered out loud.

'It means tragedy for all the poor people who were killed, injured or captured,' Adam said. 'As for the war itself, I'd say the news is mixed, but with America in the fight – and it's hard to imagine they won't enter the war formally now – things might swing in our favour. Not immediately, but eventually.'

Mindful that it was still the Gregsons' day, they walked on to Foxfield, bringing a copy of the newspaper with them. Naomi intended to hide it from the grieving family, but Evelyn was keen to hear of the developments.

'The war cost my husband his life,' she said. 'The end can't come soon enough.'

Naomi wanted to hear Bert's opinion on the news – and also to try again to take the temperature of their friendship. She'd seen him twice in the week since she'd first noticed a change in him. The first time had been outside the post office, when she'd told him about her forthcoming meeting with Alexander, hoping to see the old spark of humour and satisfaction in his eyes. Instead, he simply said, 'It's high time that icicle got what was coming to him. Fingers crossed he'll give in now and do the decent thing.'

'Fingers crossed,' Naomi had agreed, but Bert had already been walking away.

The second time had been yesterday, in church. As soon as the service had ended, she'd hastened over. 'How are you, Bert?' she'd asked. 'It's cold again and I wonder if you'd like a warming glass of sherry at Foxfield.'

'Kind of you,' he'd said, 'but I already have plans.' With that, he'd walked over to old Jonah Kerrigan and the men had left together. Naomi felt sure that the Bert of old would have found a way to talk to her despite having other demands on his time.

Now Naomi made sure all the mourners had food and drink, and then worked her way into the group of people that surrounded him. They'd moved on from the Japanese attacks to talk about the new law, which was to require young, single women to take up work that contributed to the war effort in some way. Little Suki was worried about it. 'I don't want to leave you, madam,' she'd said tearfully, though she was too young for it to affect her quite yet.

Naomi was sure Bert would have something to say about the law, but no sooner had she managed to get close to him than he went off to fetch a brandy for Evelyn. On his return, he fell into conversation with Jonah, and Naomi felt it would be rude to interrupt them.

He wasn't the first to leave the wake, but he wasn't the last either. 'Thank you, Naomi,' he said. 'You've been as hospitable as ever and kind to Evelyn, too.'

'Yes, thank you very much, Naomi,' Adam said, and as Bert left the house, Naomi's chance of speaking to him privately walked out with him.

When Wednesday came, Naomi was the first to arrive at the restaurant Alexander had chosen, and had the satisfaction of seeing him enter looking thoroughly pleased with himself. It was reprehensible to feel spiteful, but Naomi was going to enjoy seeing that smug smile disintegrate.

'I'm glad you called,' he said, sitting down with all the assurance of a man who had no doubt of his welcome. 'I was disappointed when you set your wolf of a lawyer on our marriage. We're adults, Naomi, and we've been married for a long time. I know things didn't turn out quite the way we envisaged, but it doesn't mean we have no regard for each other.'

He smiled as though to show how much regard he had for her, but Naomi had at last learned to recognize a snake when she saw one.

'You think I missed you,' she said, carefully neutral.

'We missed each other, Naomi.' He reached out to touch her hand with his. Luckily, the waiter's return prompted him to lift it again before she needed to shrug it off.

'Naomi?' Alexander gestured for her to order first.

'I'll have the lamb, please.'

Alexander gave the menu a cursory glance. 'Rib of beef for me, please. Cooked rare.' Just as carnivores liked it. 'We'll have a bottle of Saint-Émilion too, I think. *Grand cru*. After all, a special occasion deserves special wine.'

Naomi waited for the waiter to depart then said, 'This is a special occasion?'

'I think a reconciliation can be called special. We can find a new way of being married, can't we? Some of the time we'll live apart and some of the time we'll live together. Just as before. But now there are no secrets between us, we can better appreciate what we have to offer each other.'

'Which is?'

'Friendship and respect, my dear.'

'Going on as before would mean we could keep Foxfield and the London flat,' Naomi said slowly. 'Our reputations would stay unsullied, too.'

'Exactly.' His clients wouldn't have to know about a divorce. He wouldn't need to risk their disgust and the loss of their business.

The waiter approached again, this time with the wine, which Alexander tasted and approved. 'You'll enjoy it, I think,' he said, though Naomi preferred white wine. After more than a quarter of a century of marriage, he probably didn't realize that.

The waiter poured wine into Naomi's glass and she took a sip. It was pleasant enough.

Alexander nodded for the waiter to leave, then smiled and raised his glass. 'To the future.'

'I'll drink to the future,' Naomi said with feeling.

'So you'll call off your solicitor as soon as possible?' Alexander asked. 'There's no need to waste a penny more in fees.'

'I have a question,' Naomi told him.

'What's that, my dear?'

'What did you do on the fifteenth day of May 1927?'

He'd taken a sip of wine. He managed not to spit it out but froze for a moment before swallowing and using his napkin to dab at his mouth. He was stalling for time, Naomi guessed, seeking an escape route from disaster.

'1927?' He put on a show of thinking about it then shook his head. 'I can't remember. I'm sorry if I've forgotten something important.'

'Let me jog your memory. You spent the day at a register office getting married.'

'*Married?* I hardly think so when I married you long before that.' He let out a fake titter. 'I don't know where your information has come from, but—'

'It's the evidence of my own eyes.' Naomi took a marriage certificate from her bag and held it out so he could see it.

He studied it – or pretended to – then pantomimed a dawning of understanding. 'This certificate knocked me off balance for a moment. I couldn't see what had happened. But look, this relates to an Alexander Harington. One letter "r" in the surname. I have two in mine.'

'You're suggesting that this man with the same name as you but a tiny difference in the spelling – the man who happened to marry an Amelia Jane Ashmore – isn't you?'

'It can't be. There's another difference, too. This chap

is described as a financier. I'm a stockbroker.' The complacent smile was back, but Naomi wouldn't let it linger for long.

'Is that how you thought you'd get away with it? By playing around with a spelling and a job title?'

'It isn't playing around, Naomi. Coincidences happen, and one of them has happened here.'

'Full marks for effort, Alexander, but you're wasting your breath. This isn't my only piece of evidence. I've had an investigator looking into your affairs on my behalf. I was reluctant to involve an investigator at first – it felt so sordid! – but as you're a sordid man with a sordid plan to cheat me of my money, I realized that a sordid investigator was entirely apt. You're welcome to see his report. He went to Virginia Water and talked to your lover, though she had no idea who he was. She confirmed that she married you exactly as the certificate shows.'

Alexander was white-faced and furious. But he also looked scared.

'What happened?' she asked. 'Did you tire of your lover nagging you to make her an honest woman and the children respectable? Did you feel safe in going through with a bigamous marriage when you'd already got away with living a secret life for several years? The trouble with you, Alexander, is that you have too high an opinion of yourself.'

'And the trouble with you is—'

'What?' she asked. The words had started to spill from his mouth like venom.

'You think you're clever, don't you?' he sneered.

'No, actually. I was a fool in being taken in for so long, but worms have a habit of turning, and I've well and truly turned.'

'What do you want?'

'Full disclosure of your financial affairs. If I suspect you're hiding even a penny, your clients, your friends and all the world will know about your crime.'

'You're blackmailing me?'

'Looks like it, doesn't it? Play fair and I'll keep your grubby secret. In fact, I'll divorce you so you can marry again legally.'

'You still want to bleed me dry.'

'The way you've been bleeding me dry for years? You're wrong again. I want fairness, that's all, and I don't want your children to suffer. They're innocents in all of this.'

Alexander still looked as though he wanted to murder her. Probably because he *did*.

'Let me be specific,' Naomi said. 'I want Foxfield. And I also want you to return enough money to my trust fund to bring it up to twenty-five thousand pounds.'

'Twenty-five thousand pounds! I don't have that sort of money!'

'Twenty-five thousand pounds,' Naomi repeated. It seemed a reasonable amount after deducting the cost of buying and fitting out Foxfield together with her personal living costs over the length of her marriage. 'I'm leaving now, and I suggest you don't delay in letting me have a revised account of how your finances stand. An open and honest list this time that shows you're perfectly able to meet my financial demands. Fail to cooperate and you know what will happen.' With that, Naomi walked out, leaving Alexander to pick up the bill for lunch.

Surely, he'd agree to her terms now evidence of his wrongdoing was available for all to see? Naomi could envisage no escape for him, but Alexander was wily. Might there be something she'd overlooked? She could only hope she wouldn't have to wait long to find out.

Another thought occurred to her. Would Bert call on her to find out what had happened today? Naomi could only hope for that too.

CHAPTER FIFTY-FOUR

Alice

Alice's father placed the letter beside her, patted her shoulder and retreated to his study, doubtless to give her some privacy. What a thoughtful parent he was!

The letter was from Daniel. Alice breathed in deeply and opened it.

Dearest Alice,

I was so sorry to hear the sad news about our child. I try not to chafe against our separation, as I know it's a price that must be paid in a just war – and I consider defeating tyranny to be a just war – but oh dear! I'm struggling now, because I long to fold you into my arms and comfort you. To feel your arms around me, too.

Losing the baby is a blow, my love. We'll never forget the little boy or girl who might have been. We need to grieve for him or her, but we mustn't let our grief crush us. Instead, we must trust that one day it won't hurt quite so much and we'll be able to see a way forward into a future that's happy.

I'm relieved beyond measure to know that, physically at least, you're well. Long may this continue . . .

Alice shed some tears – how could she not? But she really had turned a corner in her recovery. She was due at the hospital now, but as soon as she returned home she'd

348

write back to assure Daniel that he had no need to worry about her. She'd tell him about what she'd done for the Gregsons, too. Hopefully, it would cheer him, because he'd be delighted for *them* and proud of *her*.

'Still going to the hospital?' her father asked when she looked in on him.

'I am.'

He smiled. He too was proud of her.

She left the house with her spirits boosted.

Alice was hoping to see Kate and was pleased when her friend waved to her from one of the fields then ran over, her braid bouncing behind her.

'On your way to the hospital?' Kate asked.

'I think it's time.'

'The patients will be glad.'

'I rather think they will.'

Alice studied Kate's face, noting the sparkle in her eyes and the glow in her cheeks despite the December chill. Kate really was a beautiful girl and now she shone with happiness. It wasn't hard to guess the reason. 'You're going to see Leo again?'

'Tomorrow. I can't wait!'

'Give him my love.'

'I will, if I can fit it around all *my* declarations of love for him.'

Alice laughed. 'It's wonderful to see you so . . . radiant!'

'Who could have imagined it, the first time we met?'

'You've come a long way since then, Kate. Your feet may still be planted on Brimbles Farm, but inside your spirit is flying and soon your feet will be following suit.'

'We'll see. Leo needs to get well first, but he's recovering faster than anyone dared to hope. So the docs tell him.'

'That's the best sort of Christmas gift.'

'It is!'

'You *will* be back for Christmas?'

'Yes, and I'm determined to enjoy it. Even if I can't be with Leo, I'll be thinking of him and hoping we can be together next year.'

'Christmas is all about hope, isn't it?' Alice said, and Kate gave her a considering look.

'That sounds as though you're looking forward to it after all.'

'I know I said I wanted a quiet Christmas, but that was when I needed to retreat from the world and come to terms with what had happened. I'm feeling stronger now, so yes, I'm looking forward to it. In fact, I've called a meeting of the bookshop team for tomorrow so we can talk about what we can offer the village. I know you won't be able to come, but I'll let you know what we discuss. I won't keep you chatting now, though. Not when you need to prepare for your journey.'

'And not when your patients will be getting *im*patient waiting for you.'

They parted with a hug and Alice walked on to Stratton House.

'Aren't you a sight for sore eyes?' Tom the porter declared when she walked through the entrance doors. 'It's good to see you back, but are you sure you're up to it?'

'I'm up to it.'

'I'm glad. You've been missed.'

Matron, Alice's nursing friends and patients alike all fussed over her when she moved on to the wards. 'Such a shame about the bookshop closing,' many of them said.

Alice simply smiled and made sympathetic murmurings.

But the next day, when she met with her fellow members of the bookshop organizing team, she spoke with determination. 'We all know we can't have the Christmas we'd planned, but I wonder if we might at least try to fight back against circumstance and still make it a good one?'

'What do you have in mind?' Adam asked eagerly.

'It's the fifteenth of December today, so Christmas Eve is little more than a week away. Why don't we use the week to put together some costumes for the nativity play? We may have to be inventive and settle for far less impressive costumes than we had before, but it won't be the first time we've had to make do with things being less than perfect.'

'Costumes would certainly get the children excited again,' May said, and Janet nodded, saying, 'They were ever so disappointed by the thought of having none at all.'

'How do you suggest we go about it?' Adam asked.

'It was only thanks to the generosity of our residents that we were able to make the costumes we lost in the crash. They may not have much left to give, but it can't hurt to ask.'

'I'm willing to give it a go,' Janet said.

'Me too,' Bert announced. 'Not that I can sew, but I dare say I've enough wood at home to knock up another manger and some shepherds' crooks.'

'I'll help with sewing,' May offered.

'I'll do anything you like,' Naomi said.

'Excellent. But that isn't all,' Alice said. 'I wonder if we shouldn't revive the idea of a party?'

'We haven't anywhere to hold it,' Adam pointed out.

'Why can't we hold it in the church itself, straight after the carols and nativity play? I know the church will be cold, but people can wrap up warmly. They can sit in the pews and dance in the space at the back. Food and drink can be the usual bring-and-share picnic. What do you say, Adam? You're the vicar.'

351

'I say yes!' He was grinning broadly. 'Do you intend to invite the hospital patients?'

'Of course. They may have to be swathed in blankets, but I don't think they'll mind that if it means they can come to a party.'

'I say it's a wonderful idea,' Bert said, and everyone else nodded keenly.

'It's Monday today, so let's meet again on Thursday so we can gauge what sort of response we're getting,' Alice said. 'Time is short, so I suggest we don't waste any of it talking now. Let's get to work!'

CHAPTER FIFTY-FIVE

Naomi

It was wonderful to have Alice back in their midst, bursting with ideas and energy. In just twenty-four hours, she'd woken up the village with her enthusiasm. In shops and in the streets, conversations were abuzz with it. Alice might be a slight person in her appearance but she had the sort of natural leadership that made people sit up, take notice and – best of all – join in.

On the other hand, it was torture waiting for Alexander or the Great Man to get in touch. A week had passed since Naomi had met Alexander in the restaurant. Tick tock, tick tock . . . The chances of settling her financial affairs before Christmas were looking smaller and smaller, and no matter how many times she told herself that it wouldn't be the end of the world if those affairs dragged on into 1942, the thought of beginning the new year still in a state of uncertainty depressed her. Naomi was already exhausted.

Besides, the longer her affairs dragged on, the more likely it was that someone else would buy Joe Simpson's house, putting it out of Naomi's reach as a new home for the bookshop or as a new home for herself, if needed. And it was still possible that Alexander would somehow undermine her evidence of his adultery or keep the money he'd hidden from her in spite of it. If the money existed at all, that was. Naomi might have her suspicions about secret accounts, but suspicions didn't make them real. Keeping Foxfield was therefore far from guaranteed, and the need to move to a more modest home remained a distinct possibility.

Whether that home should be in Churchwood or somewhere else was something her tired, muddled brain couldn't decide. But Naomi wanted the option of remaining and another property might not become available for years.

Bert didn't call either, but she saw him in the grocer's and managed to draw him into a quiet corner where she told him what had happened in the restaurant. 'Well done,' he said. 'It sounds as though you handled the icicle perfectly. Hopefully, you'll soon hear that he's given up the fight.'

'Hopefully, I will,' she said.

He listened to her politely. He even looked her in the eye, but it was as though a barrier now existed between them. 'Bert,' she started to say, but he took a step backwards and looked glad to be able to turn to Edna Hall, who was asking for advice on winter vegetables.

A letter from the Great Man finally came on Thursday morning. Naomi tore open the envelope with trembling fingers and, even in her anxiety, the letter she pulled from inside made her smile as she began to read it.

Dear Mrs Harrington,

It would appear that your husband has reviewed his finances and realized that he was mistaken when he listed his assets in previous correspondence . . .

Mistaken about his assets? Ha! Mistaken about Naomi? Certainly. And about time too.

There are a number of investments that were omitted previously, details of which are set out below. Mr Harrington has a settlement to propose, which is that Foxfield is placed into your sole ownership while the London flat is placed into his. With regard to income and other assets, he proposes that you become independent of each other, with Mr Harrington retaining all his future income in return for adding sufficient funds to your trust to bring it back up to the sum of £25,000 . . .

Mr Harrington proposes this, Mr Harrington proposes that . . . The proposals were Naomi's, but Alexander was seeking to save face. Well, let him. Naomi didn't care what he did as long as she gained her freedom on the terms she wanted.

While this is an encouraging development, I must caution you against any agreement that would make it difficult to make a claim against Mr Harrington's income and retirement investments should you need more financial support in the future . . .

The Great Man was doing his job in advising caution, but Naomi wasn't interested. She wanted rid of Alexander for all time, never again to rely on him financially or in any other way. She planned to tend her own money carefully instead. Not that she intended to be selfish with it.

She took the bus to Barton that same morning and went to see Joe Simpson's sister. 'Please tell me if you think it's too soon to talk about his house,' Naomi urged. 'I know you're grieving and I've no wish to be insensitive.'

'Bless you,' Ellen said, 'but I'll need to do something about the house sooner or later, and, to be honest, the money it raises would be very welcome to my daughters and their families as well as to me. If you know anyone who might be interested in buying the house, you could save me some bother.'

The house was still available! Relief seemed to weaken Naomi's knees then lift her up again. 'I'm interested in buying it myself.'

'Does this mean you're leaving Foxfield?' Ellen's expression was sympathetic. Doubtless, she'd heard about the divorce.

Naomi explained her plans to use the house for the bookshop.

'That's a wonderful idea,' Ellen said. 'It'll bring Church-wood together again, and there's a few of us here in Barton who'll get over when we can. I don't mind admitting we're a little envious of your bookshop. We've nothing like it here.'

'It may be a while before my funds are available and the legal paperwork goes through. I wonder if I might rent the house from you in the meantime?'

'I don't see why not. Joe would be delighted to see his house put to such good use.'

Naomi was thrilled and couldn't wait to share the news with the bookshop team later that afternoon. And who knew? Maybe good news was the very thing Bert needed to bring him back to his usual, comfortable self.

'I know we all want to hear about the Christmas plans, but I have something else to say that I imagine you'll all be pleased to hear,' she announced as the meeting began. 'I've settled my affairs with Alexander, so I know where I stand financially.' She'd feel a lot more secure once the settlement was in her possession since Alexander was an untrustworthy man who was probably searching even now for a way to wriggle out of their agreement. But what could he do beside huff and puff when he had a bigamy charge hanging over his head?

'Even if you're as poor as a church mouse, you'll still be our friend,' Alice said.

Calls of 'You certainly will!' echoed around the room, giving Naomi a warm glow inside, though she'd have given anything for a pithy, 'Of course you'll still be a friend, woman,' from Bert.

Instead, he simply murmured, 'Of course you will,' along with everyone else.

'I'm staying here in Churchwood,' she said then.

'That's good to hear, though I'm shocked that you even thought of leaving a place where you have so many friends!' Alice cried.

Again, the others all agreed.

'I'm keeping Foxfield too.'

'That's doubly wonderful,' May said.

'I have even more news,' Naomi told them. 'I'm buying another house, this time as a home for the bookshop.'

'Joe Simpson's house?' Janet guessed.

'It's nowhere near as big as the Sunday School Hall, of course, but we'll have the large room downstairs and three bedrooms upstairs so we can separate into groups, if necessary.'

'It'll be useful to have some smaller rooms,' May said. 'It hasn't always been easy when we've had young children in at the same time as a woodworking session. I've long lived in fear of a child treading on a nail or getting hold of a hammer and bashing another child over the head with it.'

'That's true,' Naomi said. 'I'm also going to buy some

books. Not as many as we had before, but enough to make a start. I may not be able to buy all the chairs, tables and other things we'll need, but I'll do what I can.'

'People may have spares at home,' Alice suggested. 'We can also fundraise.'

'If it brings the bookshop back, people will be glad to donate or fundraise,' Adam said.

'They will indeed,' Bert agreed, but he still wasn't the Bert of old. At least not to Naomi. With everyone else he appeared to be fine.

She pushed through her worry and forced her smile back to life. 'Now, where have we got to with the nativity costumes?' she asked.

Alice gave a mischievous grin. 'Look what I've been given.' She pulled a pile of white sheets out of a bag.

'Where did you get those?' May asked in wonder.

'Strictly between us, Matron at the hospital donated them. They're old and worn, and full of small burns from patients hiding cigarettes underneath their bedcovers. But we could use them to make angel dresses, and we can cover the burns with stars or something.'

'We can cut stars from this.' May held up some silver tinfoil from her kitchen. 'We can also use it to cover angel halos and wings if we can find something to make the basic shapes.'

'I've got wire for that.' Bert took it from his bag.

They'd also collected old clothes, Naomi's contribution being an evening cloak of midnight-blue velvet that she'd last worn years ago and a burgundy quilted satin dressing-gown that Alexander had left behind. 'They might be useful for wise men outfits,' she suggested.

'They're exactly what we need,' Alice said. 'Luckily, we've had quite a few offers of help with the cutting and sewing. Evelyn Gregson is one of our volunteers. It turns out she's more than a little handy with a sewing machine, and she's donated some old brown curtains from her previous house for making shepherd outfits. Alan and Roger Gregson both want to be shepherds. And young Timmy Turner is going to be the innkeeper. Kate says he's been walking around the farm practising saying, "There's no room at the inn."'

'That's good to hear,' Naomi said. 'People are welcome to come here to sew. I know they like to chat as they work and it'll be good for Evelyn to have company.'

The next morning they turned Alexander's study into a sewing room and it amused Naomi to think of him having a fit over his pristine surfaces being cluttered with fabric, cottons, scissors and pins, while children crawled under the desk or pulled faces through the window as they played in the garden.

By the afternoon, she could bear her distance from Bert no longer. She decided to visit him at home and try to get to the bottom of what was troubling him once and for all.

CHAPTER FIFTY-SIX

Naomi

'I'm just out for some fresh air,' Naomi told Bert when she arrived at his market garden.

'It's certainly fresh,' he said.

The winter's day was raw. She waited, shivering, in the hope that he'd invite her inside for a cup of tea.

Several seconds passed before he finally said, 'Would you like to come in?'

Those passing seconds made her feel unwelcome, but Naomi resisted the impulse to scuttle away in humiliation. Instead, she squared her shoulders and said, 'Yes, please.'

Five minutes later they were sitting on opposite sides of the hearth drinking tea, Elizabeth the cat on the rug between them. Naomi took a deep breath. 'I thought you might be interested in seeing the letter I received from the lawyers.' She held it out to him, and Bert took it, reading it through and muttering 'Ha!' at the exact same places she had on first reading it.

Folding it up again, he passed it back to her. 'Congratulations. Now you'll have everything you need to make you happy.'

Not everything.

'Bert, is all well with you?'

'With *me*? Why do you ask?'

'You don't seem quite yourself.'

He shrugged. 'I'm the same Bert I've ever been. There's nothing complicated about me.'

That wasn't true. 'Have I done something to offend you?'

'No, Naomi, you haven't offended me.'

Elizabeth the cat got up and wound herself around his legs in a plea to be picked up. Bert reached down and scooped her on to his lap with one large hand. She settled into a comfortable position, and he stroked her a couple of times before looking back at Naomi.

'The way you fought back against the icicle is admirable, and I'm pleased you got what you wanted. Foxfield, financial independence . . . They *are* what you wanted?'

'Of course.'

'Then I'm truly glad for you. I want you to be happy.'

Naomi believed him. Even so, something had changed in their friendship, and it made her want to weep, especially as he'd made it obvious that he didn't want to talk about it.

She swallowed and, just to break the silence, said, 'The nativity costumes are coming along well, aren't they?'

'Very well.'

'Everyone loved the little manger you made for baby Jesus.'

'We've all done our bit. It should be a good night. For Adam. For all of us.'

'You're still coming to Foxfield on Christmas Day?'

'Yes, and I'm looking forward to it. We should be a jolly little crowd.' Alice was coming along with her father. May was bringing her three children. Adam was coming too and, of course, so was Marjorie. Janet and Kate were spending the day with their own families but Kate would call in later in the afternoon.

A jolly little crowd. Bert would be jolly with them, but he wouldn't be the teasing, mocking Bert of old with Naomi. Despite winning her battle with Alexander, the world felt off-kilter and she was going to have to force her Christmas cheer.

She didn't linger but got up with her teacup still half full. 'I'd better be on my way. I'm not one of Churchwood's finest needlewomen but I've some angel dresses to hem.'

'Right you are.' The alacrity with which Bert got to his feet signalled his relief that she was leaving. Or so it seemed to Naomi.

'Bert, we *are* still friends?' she asked desperately, as he saw her to the door.

'Of course we're still friends,' he said. 'Why wouldn't we be?'

Naomi had no answer, but as she walked home through the icy twilight, a thought occurred to her. Yes, they were still friends, but they weren't *special* friends any more. Where Naomi had seen a special connection between them, Bert had simply seen a woman with problems and, being a kind man, he'd set out to help with them. Now she was through to the other side of those problems, she'd become . . . well, just an ordinary friend to him.

There was nothing wrong with being an ordinary friend like any other. Nothing at all. Except that it hurt.

CHAPTER FIFTY-SEVEN

Alice

Merry Christmas, darling girl, Daniel had written.

I'm writing before receiving your response to my last letter because Christmas is almost upon us and I can't let it go by without sending you my warmest love.

I received your parcel of Christmas gifts, all beautifully wrapped. I haven't cheated by opening them early, but I know you'll have put a lot of thought into them and I'm grateful for that, especially as you've had such a difficult time recently. I'm so glad to hear that, while you still have moments of sadness, you're feeling calmer and more optimistic. It's how I feel too.

Emotion still had the power to ambush her, but Alice really was moving forward. She had faith in the future and she was sure Daniel had too.

I hope you've received my parcel. Not that I sent it from here, but I arranged for it to be sent from London.

Alice had indeed received it, and she hadn't cheated by opening it early either. Daniel had also sent a parcel for her father, though it wasn't difficult to guess that it contained a book.

Next year I hope to have the pleasure of shopping for your gift in person and of wrapping it in person too, though I might not make a neat job of it. Who knows? We may even get to spend next Christmas together.

Wouldn't that be wonderful?

Be happy and let me know all about your festivities. I imagine you'll be involved in decorating the church, for one thing. In helping the children with their nativity play, too. Singing carols, seeing friends . . . I can't wait to hear about it all.

Alice smiled because Daniel had described exactly what she'd be doing this Christmas Eve, beginning with decorating the church.

She arrived to find Bert unloading his truck of the greenery he'd gathered from in and around his market garden, while Kate unloaded her cart of more greenery from in and around Brimbles Farm.

Adam was holding his arms out, ready to carry some into the church. 'Goodness, what a lot!' he was saying excitedly. 'How lucky we are.'

Alice helped to carry some inside too. Naomi, Janet and May arrived and soon the greenery was on display on window ledges and in small posies that hung from the ends of pews. Fir cones gave the arrangements texture, and candles would add light later when it was dark. St Luke's was going to look beautiful.

There was a rehearsal of the nativity play in the afternoon. It didn't go entirely smoothly. Two little angels squabbled about whose halo was the prettiest. The fluffy sheep went missing – until Adam found them in the churchyard hidden behind the grave of Hildegarde Lamb, spinster of this parish. Then the boy playing Joseph trod on the dress of the girl playing Mary and, when she protested, declared that he'd rather marry a toad than marry her. But peace was negotiated and all went well in the end.

'I think we're as ready as we'll ever be,' Adam finally declared.

The children were sent home to have something to eat and drink before the evening's performance. 'Be back by six,' Adam instructed. 'And remember to wrap up warmly. You'll need vests under your costumes or you'll turn into snowmen.' The church was perishing.

'Is it going to snow?' a girl asked.

'We'll have to wait and see,' Adam said.

Snow wasn't forecast but the sky had been looking still and heavy all day. The children ran off and Bert left too, as he'd be driving to the hospital a little later to pick up some of the patients. Alice, Naomi and Janet set up a couple of trestle tables that had been borrowed for the evening and carried over the tins and other containers of food that had been left as contributions to the night's refreshments.

'It looks as though Churchwood has done us proud again,' Janet said, opening one of the tins. 'These tarts smell like apple and cinnamon.'

Alice opened another tin. 'These are mince pies according to the label, though I imagine they're a variation on the usual recipe, given the shortages.'

'War makes inventors of us all,' Adam said.

'Let's hope people remember that they need to bring their own glasses, cups and plates,' Alice said.

'We've reminded them often enough,' Janet assured her.

It was time for the rest of them to go home.

Naomi walked with Alice. 'How are you feeling?' she asked.

365

'Better,' Alice said.

Naomi looked uncertain, so Alice added, 'I really think I've turned a corner. I'll always carry sadness inside me for the baby I lost. Not just sadness, actually. *Grief*. But I'm still looking forward to the future and I want it to be a happy one.'

She was happy now and it felt good. On that thought, a memory jumped into her mind. A few weeks ago, she'd written a story only to put it away, feeling it was lacking in some way she couldn't quite define. Now she realized what it was. The story had been pleasant enough, but it had lacked the passion she'd put into her speech about Evelyn and into all her village campaigns, from championing the need for the bookshop to fighting against the vicar who'd wanted to close it down. The story wouldn't have made anyone care about those it featured.

Maybe she should try writing stories again and this time put her heart and soul into them. Alice Irvine, author? It wasn't a bad ambition for 1942.

She turned to Naomi. 'I hope you're feeling hopeful, too?'

CHAPTER FIFTY-EIGHT

Naomi

'Of course I'm feeling hopeful,' Naomi told Alice, striving to make her voice sound hearty.

'That's good to hear, but you still need to take care of yourself. I hope you won't mind me saying it, but you're looking a little tired.'

'It's been a challenging year, but I'll soon perk up now I've resolved matters with Alexander.' The church clock struck five. 'We'd better get home or we'll be late back for the play.'

They parted company and Naomi walked on to Foxfield. She wanted a little time alone, as keeping up an appearance of jollity was proving a strain. She also needed to check that all was well with Suki and Cook. Both had volunteered to work on Christmas Day, though Naomi was insisting that they should take a few days off afterwards. 'I can fend for myself perfectly well,' she'd told them. Her appetite for food had dwindled and a few days of solitude might give her a chance to get on top of this annoying low mood.

Letting herself into the house, she reassured Cook that she was confident the Christmas lunch she'd prepare tomorrow would be wonderful, even if Naomi hadn't been able to come by a turkey. Not in an honest transaction, anyway. She wouldn't take advantage of the black market on principle. They'd be having chicken instead and all the guests were contributing something for the feast – sausages, stuffing, potatoes, fresh vegetables . . . May had managed a pudding, to be served with brandy sauce, while Alice was bringing a cake and Bert was bringing home-made wine.

Naomi had already given her cleaning lady, Beryl, a gift of bath salts and scented soaps – precious now there was talk of soap being rationed. She placed the other gifts she'd bought under her Christmas tree. For Cook there was a string of amber beads, which Naomi was confident would be appreciated. For Suki there was a silver bracelet and, again, Naomi was in no doubt that her little maid would love it. There was jewellery for Kate, too – a silver locket. After a lifetime deprived of pretty things, Kate deserved to have something lovely, and she'd be able to carry a photograph of Leo inside it.

Marjorie could rarely afford to treat herself to new things either, so Naomi had bought her soaps too, together with a scarf. For everyone else she'd bought books, know-ing her guests would enjoy hours of pleasure with them and that the books would give more pleasure still as they worked their way into the bookshop store. In the same spirit, Naomi expected to be given books in return.

Seizing the chance to lie down for ten minutes, Naomi allowed her mask of good cheer to slip. Keeping it going had drained her, but the new year was around the corner and surely then she'd begin to feel stronger. After all, she might have been mistaken in thinking that Bert was a particularly close friend, but she had other blessings to count – her financial security, the new bookshop, her various friendships . . . She just needed to be patient with herself.

When the ten minutes had passed, she forced herself to get ready for the evening. A hushed stillness met her when she set out for the church. It was as though Churchwood was waiting expectantly for something. For snow? Certainly, it wasn't hard to imagine white flakes floating down in silent beauty as the evening progressed. Not a flake fell as she walked through the quiet village, though, and the only evidence of life inside the cottages she passed was the smoke curling up from the chimneys and the occasional gleam of light escaping from behind curtains.

It was different when she arrived at St Luke's. Here, there was bustle as children changed into their nativity costumes and the choir practised carols. More children arrived and brought minor crises with them. Pam Cooper's girl was in tears because her brother had sat on her angel wings and bent them out of shape. Alice got to work with more of Bert's wire and some tinfoil. Billy Piper's mother was in a tizzy because she'd spilled soup at home and accidentally reached for the tea towel Billy was supposed to be wearing as his shepherd's headdress. 'I told him he shouldn't leave it on the table like that,' Mrs Piper complained. 'I grabbed it without looking properly and I haven't any other tea towels that are suitable.'

Fortunately, Naomi had a couple of spares on hand for just such an eventuality.

Soon the church pews were filling with people from the village, and from the hospital. Naomi saw Alice waving to her nursing friends, Babs Carter and Pauline Evans. It was good to see Alice smiling with genuine joy again. Meanwhile, Matron fussed over her patients and wrapped them in blankets.

The Brimbles Farm contingent soon followed. Kate looked wonderfully happy, too. She came with Ruby, an excited Timmy and, looking awed, as though they'd never seen the inside of a church before, Kenny and Vinnie. Pearl brought up the rear, pushing Fred in his wheelchair. 'Don't you dare put me somewhere I don't want to be,' Fred was grouching.

'You should practise wheeling yourself. Then you'll be able to go where you like,' Pearl argued back.

'I practise all the time, so you'd better watch out. Soon I'll be able to run over your toes every time you're mean to me.'

'I'm never mean. I just treat you how you deserve.'

'I'll treat you how *you* deserve – by running over your toes.'

Naomi caught Kate's eye and raised an eyebrow. Kate came over. 'It's bicker, bicker, bicker between those two,' she explained, 'but do you know, I think it's good for both of them? In fact, sometimes I wonder if there might be a romantic spark beneath all the abuse.'

Naomi watched as Fred wheeled himself after Kenny and Ruby but paused to look over his shoulder as though to check that Pearl was following. 'Oi, you!' he shouted. 'It doesn't take much for you to abandon a man in need, does it?'

'A man in need?' Pearl scoffed. 'Here's hoping for snow, because what you need is to be tipped into a deep, cold snowdrift until you learn to be more polite.'

Perhaps Kate was right. There was certainly a spark of something between them and romance came in all shapes and sizes. As Naomi watched, Vinnie leered in the direction of Elspeth Walker, a pretty girl, but she only looked horrified and hastened away. There'd be no romance for

Vinnie just yet. Naomi turned back to Kate and smiled. 'I hear you visited Leo again.'

'I did, and it was wonderful. He really is doing well.'

How she was glowing! Naomi was delighted for her, as she was delighted for all her friends who were in happy relationships. She might always feel a pang because she herself was alone, but it didn't stop her from being sincerely glad that her friends were faring better.

When all were settled, Adam appeared in his robes and, with the modest charm that came so naturally to him, he welcomed everyone and announced that the performance was about to begin.

It was a lovely occasion. The angels looked sweet, and there was only a little pushing and shoving as they jostled for the best positions so they could wave at their families. The shepherds raised a laugh by making sheep noises – the Gregson boys included – and Timmy Turner kept the laughter going when he declared, 'There's no room at the inn,' and then – as though compelled by good manners – added an unscripted, 'Sorry. You should have booked earlier.'

One wise man almost dropped the frankincense, but otherwise they behaved as regally as the most magnificent of kings.

In between the scenes, the sound of carol singing rose to the rafters. From 'O Little Town Of Bethlehem' and 'Silent Night' to 'Away In A Manger' and 'O Come All Ye Faithful', the voices rang out to stir what Naomi imagined was a range of emotions – private tears for loved ones who couldn't be present, thanks for another year survived, and hope for the future.

Afterwards, the party began. Kettles of boiling water were brought over from the vicarage for those who wanted tea, while bottles of beer, sherry and home-made wine were opened for those who preferred a tipple. Plates and cutlery appeared and soon people were tucking into food.

Meanwhile, a different sort of music reached to the rafters – Glenn Miller, George Gershwin, Benny Goodman . . . The back of the church became a dance floor and coats were thrown off as Churchwood's residents threw themselves into the fun. At one point, Adam pulled Naomi on to the dance floor, but Bert came nowhere near her, though she could hear his laughter as he talked and joked with others. It made her feel as though her heart were bleeding just a little, though she was pleased to see her friends dancing and looking happy. Evelyn was one of them. She looked shy when Adam led her on to the dance floor. Then Bert took over as her partner and soon she was smiling and looking relaxed. The village had taken her into its arms and made her its own. Her boys, too. Naomi could see them in a corner, swapping marbles with some of the other village children.

Even Pearl wheeled Fred on to the dance floor and mocked him when he sat in horror as people twirled around him, Pearl included. 'Stop being so pathetic,' she chided. 'Dance!'

'You mean imitate a clumsy carthorse like you?' he said.

'You're just jealous because I'm having fun and you're a miserable grouch,' she told him.

Fred glowered at her but soon he was waving his arms about. 'At least I can move in time to the music,' he told her.

'That's what you think.'

Romance in all shapes and sizes indeed.

Moving away from the dance floor, Naomi went to the

trestle tables to serve drinks and take food to those who were too unsteady on their legs to help themselves. It was better to be busy. Time passed, though it couldn't pass quickly enough for Naomi. Her face felt stiff from all the forced smiling, and she was desperate for the solace of her quiet bedroom at home.

Then some children burst back in after venturing outside to cool down. 'It's snowing!' they yelled, starry-eyed with excitement.

It was the signal for the party to wind down at last, as some people hastened outside to see the snow and the hospital party decided they'd better leave in case it made their journey home difficult. Naomi considered pleading a headache and departing too but knew it would be unfair to leave the clearing up to others.

With cries of 'Merry Christmas!' ringing out, she waved people off then joined Alice, Dr Lovell, Janet, Adam and his housekeeper in packing up, sweeping up and washing up in the vicarage. 'I'll finish up here,' Naomi told Alice after a while. 'You and your father get off home.'

'My father wants to see you home safely too,' Alice pointed out.

'It's kind of him but completely unnecessary. I've walked through the village by myself hundreds of times, even in the dark. Not that it'll be fully dark now there's snow on the ground.'

Alice finally gave in and a few minutes later Naomi set out too, glad to have this time alone. Only a few snow-flakes were falling now, and she hadn't gone far before the clouds parted to reveal the sparkle of stars against a navy satin sky. With snow frosting the roofs and trees as well as the ground, the scene was as beautiful as a picture on a Christmas card.

The snow deadened the sound of her footsteps and made her progress almost silent. Naomi felt as though she were walking in a frozen land in which time stood still. But time would waken soon enough and give itself a little shake before moving on. As she must move on too.

She might struggle to lift her spirits over Christmas – though she'd strive to be the perfect hostess tomorrow – but afterwards she'd force herself to rally, come what may. After all, her life was blessed in many, many ways.

Crossing Brimbles Lane to the Foxfield gateposts, she heard a distant rumble stealing up on the silence. Bert's truck was returning from the hospital.

Naomi quickened her pace, still in the mood to be alone, but, to her surprise, Bert steered the truck on to the drive and brought it to a halt beside her. He wound down the window and looked out.

'Have you brought the wine for lunch?' she said, forcing heartiness into her voice. 'What a good idea. It'll save you the job of carrying it tomorrow.'

For a moment Bert didn't answer but continued only to stare at her, his thoughtful expression illuminated by the light reflecting from the snow. 'Do you fancy a night-cap?' he finally said.

Naomi was surprised. And suddenly nervous. 'You're welcome to come inside for a sherry. Or tea, if you'd prefer it?' She gestured towards the front door.

'Come back to my house,' he said instead, but there was no jolliness in the invitation.

Heavens, was he going to tell her that she'd offended him, after all? If so, the timing was terrible. She'd be certain to get upset, and lunch tomorrow would become even harder, with the hostess wishing she could retreat to her room to cry.

Bert might have an entirely different problem to confide, though, and she owed it to him to help as best she could. 'Well, I . . .'

Her words trailed off as Bert swung his large body out of the driver's seat and walked around the truck to open the passenger door for her.

As always, Naomi was horribly conscious of the size of her hips as she scrambled up but was relieved when she managed it without needing a boost from Bert's shoulder.

'The snow is pretty, isn't it?' she said, feeling compelled to fill the strange atmosphere with commonplaces as he returned to the driver's seat.

'It is.'

'The children will enjoy making snowmen tomorrow. If it doesn't melt away overnight.' She realized she was babbling and shut up.

Walking into Bert's kitchen was like entering a cocoon of warmth. A fire burned brightly in the hearth and shadows in the far corners wrapped the room in cosiness.

Bert gestured her to an armchair then fetched glasses and a bottle of sherry. He poured a glass for each of them then sat down opposite her.

Elizabeth the cat raised her head just enough to glance at the visitor, but she quickly curled back up again into the snugness of the rug.

Naomi realized her lips were dry. She took a sip of sherry and then, as Bert seemed to be in no hurry to begin the conversation, she said, 'You've been a good friend to me this year, Bert.'

'I've certainly tried to be.'

'You gave me the confidence and strength to fight Alexander. Now I'm financially secure and I don't need to leave Churchwood. I owe you a lot.'

'You wouldn't have needed to leave Churchwood whatever happened with Alexander.'

'I could have afforded Joe Simpson's house, perhaps, but it might have been . . . I don't know. Awkward.'

Bert grimaced. Did he think she was being foolish or was there another reason for the grimace? 'Bert, I asked you once if I'd offended you and you denied it. I'm not sure I believe you, though. You're . . . different from before. At least, you're different in your behaviour to me.'

'You didn't offend me, Naomi. I told you the truth there. But you . . . hurt me.'

'*I* hurt *you*? But how? When? If I've done something unkind without realizing it, I'd like to put it right.'

'And go back to our old ways?'

'Yes!'

'Maybe our old ways aren't what I want.'

The words hit her like a slap. 'There must be *something* I can do. What did I actually say that hurt you?'

'It was when we were coming home from Somerset House. You said it looked likely that you could keep Foxfield now. I asked if that's what you wanted – to live in that big house all by yourself. You said you did. You even said you couldn't imagine living anywhere else.'

Naomi shook her head, not understanding what had been wrong with her answer.

'Do you think I'm being selfish, living in a house that's larger than my needs? I know some of the bedrooms go unused, but the rest of the house – and the gardens, too – are often used by people from the village.'

Bert waved an impatient hand. 'I know that, woman. It's the fact that it didn't seem to cross your mind that you had other options that hurt. And I'm not talking about Joe Simpson's house. I'm talking about mine.'

Surprise rendered her near speechless. Sudden thoughts clamoured for attention at the back of her mind, but Naomi fought them back. What they were suggesting . . . It wasn't possible. 'I don't—'

'Understand what I mean? Don't be dense, Naomi. You know exactly what I mean.'

'But you *couldn't.*'

'Couldn't love you? Couldn't want to marry you?'

'Both.' Naomi was bewildered. 'I'm not . . .' Oh, how could she explain? 'I'm not that sort of woman.'

'Loveable, you mean?'

Anguish burst out of her. 'Look at me, Bert. I've never turned a man's head in my life, and no one ever wanted to marry me except for my money.' She was too plain. Too dumpy. Too much like a bulldog around the jowls.

'Look at *me*,' he said, patting his sizeable girth. 'I'm hardly a Hollywood film star like that James Stewart or Clark Gable or whoever else has their mug lighting up the cinema screen these days. But I can assure you that my heart beats with emotion just as powerfully as the hearts of more handsome men. You may not be a Greta Garbo or Ginger Rogers either, but you've got just as much heart in you. Besides, can you picture Ginger Rogers sitting in this unbeautiful kitchen or pottering around my market garden?'

Naomi laughed despite her confusion. But she still couldn't believe what he was saying. Bert in love with her? It wasn't possible.

'I can see I'm going to have to do this the proper way, though I was hoping to spare my creaky knees,' he said. 'Be warned. You may have to help me up again, but here goes . . .' He got down on one of those knees. 'Naomi Tuggs – I'm not calling you Harrington, as I think you need to move on from the sorry episode of your marriage to the icicle – will you do me the honour of marrying me?'

'Bert, I can't!'

'Because you're not yet free from the icicle? Don't worry. I'm not asking you to commit bigamy. We'll leave that to him. I'm talking about marrying me *after* you're free.'

'You haven't thought this through, Bert.'

'I can assure you that I've thought of little else. After what you said on the way home from Somerset House, I decided I had no chance with you, but since then you've been looking peakier and peakier instead of happier and happier. It got me wondering if maybe you wanted something more than your big house and trust fund, after all.'

'But you need a useful sort of wife. I may not be Greta Garbo or Ginger Rogers, but I'd be just as hopeless in your market garden and just as hopeless in this house. I've never even boiled an egg.'

'Luckily, I have. And I can teach you all you need to know. Besides, I wouldn't kick up a fuss if you wanted your little girl, Suki, to come and help out. Until she gets called up for war work, that is.

'As for your Cook, I've heard she isn't far off retirement and looking forward to it. Anyway, there's a chance a new person at Foxfield might want to keep her on, along with your cleaning woman and old Sykes.'

'A new person at Foxfield?'

'Only if you want to sell it or let it to a tenant. Your decision, of course. You might prefer to keep it as a bolthole you can flee to when I get on your nerves. Or I could live there with you, though it wouldn't be quite as convenient for my market garden. All of that stuff . . . It's just detail we can sort out later. Now, I hate to spoil the romantic

378

atmosphere, but my knees are killing me, so I need to press you for an answer. The way I see it, the only reason to turn me down is if you don't love me.'

Did she love him? The answer came roaring back at her. Yes, she did. In fact, it was obvious to her, now she was allowing herself to admit it. But Alexander had dented her confidence so badly that it had never crossed her mind that another man might be interested in her.

'Have mercy, woman,' Bert pleaded. 'If you keep me down here for much longer, I'll need more than *your* help to get me up again. I'll need an ambulance. Now, what's your answer?'

'My answer is . . . I'd love to marry you, Bert!'

'Thank the Lord for that! Now give me your arm and let's try to get me back on my feet.'

Giggling, Naomi helped him up. But then she stood back.

'Not getting cold feet already?' he asked.

'No, but—'

'You're thinking about practical things again. How you'll cope.'

'I don't want to disappoint you.'

'There's no fear o' that. Sit down, woman.' He steered her back to her chair then pulled his own chair closer so he could hold both of her hands. 'What I want is to wake up in the morning and feel gladdened because you're there beside me. To look up of an evening and see your smile. And to share the hours in between with everything that's important to us, not least Churchwood and the bookshop. Of course, you'll be sliding down the social scale a number of notches by marrying me.'

'I don't care about that sort of thing. Not any more.'

'That's what I thought. So, we'll bumble along together,

379

making mistakes but laughing at them. Learning a better future together.'

It sounded wonderful.

'If you're wondering about a ring, I don't have one, but I'll get one as soon as you like. Maybe we could choose it together as that's how we're going to live our lives – together.'

'I'd like that. It needn't be an expensive ring.'

'Don't think I've any intention of competing with the icicle when it comes to grandness. I'll buy a ring that we like. Not one we think will impress anyone else. But I'm not a poor man, Naomi. You might think I'm poor to look at me.' He glanced down at his trousers, which had patches on the knees, and at his sweater, which had seen better days long ago. 'I'm just not a flashy sort of chap.'

'I know you're not. And I couldn't care a jot.'

'That's settled, then. Tomorrow we'll tell our friends, yes?'

'They'll be delighted.'

'I reckon they will. Now kick your shoes off, wife-to-be. I know they're pinching you. And don't think you have to bother with a girdle when you're with me. It's you I love, and if your waist isn't trim . . . Well, neither is mine. First things first, though.'

Naomi frowned, not understanding again.

'We've made a bargain to spend the rest of our lives together. We should seal that bargain with a kiss.'

'Oh!' Naomi felt herself blush. The truth was that she didn't really know *how* to kiss. She might have been married for more than a quarter of a century, but Alexander's rare kisses had been cold things that had left her feeling only awkward.

He drew her closer and for a moment she resisted,

telling herself he was going too fast, but then his mouth touched hers and she discovered that a kiss could be delightful.

'That's how a man who loves you kisses,' he said afterwards, and he winked.

Oh, heavens!

Acknowledgements

I had the great privilege of having two fabulous teams in my corner as I wrote this book. The team at Transworld is one of them and includes editor extraordinaire, Alice Rodgers; eagle-eyed copy editor, Eleanor Updegraff; Production Editor, Vivien Thompson, and all involved in proofreading, artwork, sales and marketing. Thank you!

The second team is the Kate Nash Literary Agency, especially super-agent, Kate. Thanks to you, too!

Warmest thanks are also due to my lovely readers. Your kind support and generous reviews never cease to humble and inspire me.

Then there are family and friends. My daughters, Olivia and Isobel, have unwavering faith in me, while the encouragement of my friends is immense. Thanks! You know who you are.

About the Author

Lesley Eames is an author of historical sagas, her preferred writing place being the kitchen due to its proximity to the kettle. Lesley loves tea, as do many of her characters. Having previously written sagas set around the time of the First World War and into the Roaring Twenties, she has ventured into the Second World War period with *The Wartime Bookshop* series.

Originally from the northwest of England (Manchester), Lesley's home is now Hertfordshire where *The Wartime Bookshop*'s fictional village of Churchwood is set. Along her journey as a writer, Lesley has been thrilled to have had ninety short stories published and to have enjoyed success in competitions in genres as varied as crime writing and writing for children. She is particularly honoured to have won the Festival of Romance New Talent Award, the Romantic Novelists' Association's Elizabeth Goudge Cup and to have been twice shortlisted in the UK Romantic Novel Awards (RONAs).

Learn more by visiting her website:
www.lesleyeames.com
Or follow her on Facebook:
www.facebook.com/LesleyEamesWriter

Don't miss the start of *The Wartime Bookshop* series . . .

The Wartime Bookshop
Book 1 in *The Wartime Bookshop* series

Alice is nursing an injured hand and a broken heart when
she moves to the village of Churchwood at the start of WWII.
She is desperate to be independent but worries that her
injuries will make that impossible.

Kate lives with her family on Brimbles Farm, where
her father and brothers treat her no better than a servant. With
no mother or sisters, and shunned by the locals,
Kate longs for a friend of her own.

Naomi is looked up to for owning the best house
in the village. But privately, she carries the hurts of
childlessness, a husband who has little time for her
and some deep-rooted insecurities.

**With war raging overseas, and difficulties to overcome at
home, friendship is needed now more than ever. Can the war
effort and a shared love of books bring these women – and
the community of Churchwood – together?**

AVAILABLE NOW

Land Girls at the Wartime Bookshop
Book 2 in *The Wartime Bookshop* series

The residents of Churchwood have never needed their bookshop, or its community, more. But when the bookshop comes under threat at the worst possible time, can Alice, Kate and Naomi pull together to keep spirits high?

Kate has always found life on Brimbles Farm difficult, but now she is struggling more than ever to find time for the things that matter to her – particularly helping to save the village bookshop and seeing handsome pilot Leo Kinsella. Can two Land Girls help? Or will they be more trouble than they're worth?

Naomi has found new friends and purpose through the bookshop and is devastated when its future is threatened. But when she begins to suspect her husband of being unfaithful, she finds her attention divided. With old insecurities rearing up, she needs to uncover the truth.

Alice has a lot on her plate. Can she fight to save the bookshop while also looking for a job and worrying about her fiancé Daniel away fighting in the war?

AVAILABLE NOW

And pre-order the next book:

Evacuees at the Wartime Bookshop
Book 4 in _The Wartime Bookshop_ series

Catch up with Alice, Kate and Naomi as the war
intensifies and relationships are challenged in the
brand-new instalment of _The Wartime Bookshop_ series.

AVAILABLE FOR PRE-ORDER NOW

SIGN UP TO OUR SAGA NEWSLETTER

Penny Street

The home of heart-warming reads

Welcome to **Penny Street**, your **number one stop for emotional and heartfelt historical reads**. Meet casts of characters you'll never forget, memories you'll treasure as your own, and places that will forever stay with you long after the last page.

Join our online **community** bringing you the latest book deals, competitions and new saga series releases.

You can also find extra content, talk to your favourite authors and share your discoveries with other saga fans on Facebook.

Join today by visiting
www.penguin.co.uk/pennystreet

Follow us on Facebook
www.facebook.com/welcometopennystreet